To love & to cherish

BOOK ONE IN THE PASTOR MAGGIE SERIES

Dear May,
Cherish the ones
you love ♡

Barb Edema

ISBN: 978-1-68313-138-0
Library of Congress Number: 2017960523

Pen-L Publishing
www.Pen-L.com
First Edition
Printed and bound in the USA

Cover and interior design by Kelsey Rice.

To Love & To Cherish

BOOK ONE IN THE PASTOR MAGGIE SERIES

BARBARA EDEMA

Pen-L Publishing
Fayetteville, Arkansas
Pen-L.com

Books by Barbara Edema:

THE PASTOR MAGGIE SERIES

To Love and To Cherish

To Have and To Hold

For Richer, For Poorer

To Doug,
the one I love and cherish

And in memory of
Dr. James I. Cook
Professor, mentor, friend

And...
Mr. Howard Baker
You knocked my socks off

List of Characters

RESIDENTS OF CHERISH, MICHIGAN

Pastor Maggie Elzinga – Pastor of Loving the Lord Community Church

Hank Arthur – Administrative Assistant at LTLCC, married to Pamela Arthur, hospital volunteer

Doris Walters – Custodian at LTLCC, married to Chester Walters

Irena Dalca – Organist at LTLCC, fan of miniskirts and vodka

Marla Wiggins – Sunday school superintendent, married to Tom Wiggins, owner of The Cherish Hardware Store; mother of Jason and Addie

Verna Abernathy – Zinnia loving church crank and know-it-all

Chief Charlotte Tuggle – Cherish Chief of Police, married to gravel pit owner Fred Tuggle; mother of twins, Brock and Mason, and daughter, Liz

Officer Bernie Bumble – Charlotte's inexperienced deputy

Martha – Nosy police dispatcher

Cate Carlson – Maggie worshiper and a student at the University of Michigan

Cole Porter – Owner and proprietor of The Porter Funeral Home; husband of Lynn Porter, and father of Penny and Molly (with one on the way)

Harold Brinkmeyer – Successful young lawyer

Dr. Jack Elliot – Family practice doctor on the staff of Heal Thyself Community Hospital

Ellen Bright – Nurse at Heal Thyself; good friend of Pastor Maggie

Bill Baxter – Builder and handyman to all in Cherish

Sylvia Smits – Owner of The Garden Shop

Mrs. Polly Popkin – Owner and proprietress of The Sugarplum Bakery

Cassandra Moffet – Distracted mother of Carrie and Carl, her two small children

Jennifer and Beth Becker – Sisters and owners of The Page Turner Book Shop

Fitch Dervish – Building inspector in Cherish

Redford Johnson – Financial planner and slimy character

Max Solomon – Always sits in the last pew

SHUT-INS IN CHERISH

Katharine Smits – Sylvia Baxter's mother

Marvin Green – Hates women ministers

Howard Baker – Only a partial shut-in and a big flirt

Mr. Thompson

Mrs. Landry

Various other old darlings

RESIDENTS OF ZEELAND, MICHIGAN

Dirk and Mimi Elzinga – Maggie's parents

Bryan Elzinga – Maggie's younger brother

RESIDENTS OF HOLLAND, MICHIGAN

Dr. Edward James – Beloved seminary professor, married to Joanna James

Nora Drew – Maggie's best friend from seminary

Dan Wellman – Another good seminary friend

Kristy – Hospital patient, married to Mike

Reverend Dill – Inept hospital chaplain

**If you are interested in knowing more about
the fictional organization Africa Hope,
please visit the website of the real organization
MAMAHOPE.ORG**

Prologue

One warm day in a faraway land, God whispered in her ear. Being only twenty-two, she didn't exactly hear the first whisper; she just felt a tickle. She pulled her hair up into a messy bun, believing flyaway hair was the culprit, and kept walking the rough terrain. So God laughed and kept whispering. After six months of being far away from all she knew as normal life, Maggie was quiet one day and heard the ticklish words: "Tell the story."

After the fifteen-hour flight home, she finally landed in Grand Rapids, Michigan. Her parents, brother, and even Ed and Jo, were there to meet her. Her mother quietly surveyed Maggie to see if she had lost too much weight, but Maggie looked healthy enough—tan and lean and full of stories. The family and friends began unpacking six months of life. But one story mattered the most to Maggie. That ticklish whisper, that gentle command.

She sat down with Ed at her backyard picnic table. They each had a plate of all-American food: hamburgers, potato salad, baked beans, watermelon, and of course, apple pie made by Jo. Secretly, Maggie just wanted a falafel.

Ed watched Maggie pick at her food for a few minutes, then leaned his gray head closer to her blonde one.

"What happened, Maggie? Something has changed." Then his blue eyes smiled into hers.

"I think I know what I need to do with my life," she said dreamily. "I tried not to listen, but God doesn't shut up." Her voice became less dreamy and more focused. "I think I'll be joining you this fall. I don't want to do anything else with my life but tell the story."

Next came four years of theological training under Ed's mentorship, friendship, and good care. Then Maggie graduated. At the age of twenty-six, she packed up her diploma and her idealism, along with a little naiveté and a whole suitcase full of optimism. She loaded these things, along with her cat, Marmalade, into her Dodge Caliber and drove across the state of Michigan.

Reverend Maggie Elzinga was ready to tell the story.

Whether or not people wanted to listen was a completely different matter.

PART 1

To Cherish
SUMMER 2014

1

Maggie, wearing her black lace funeral dress, stomped up the front steps of the parsonage. She opened the door and controlled herself just barely enough to keep from slamming it once inside. She picked up one of the pillows on the once-white-now-gray couch, put it over her face, and screamed as loudly as she could. She screamed one more time for good measure. When she put the pillow back on the couch, she looked up to see Marmalade looking directly at her from his perch on the blue chintz chair. His eyes were unblinking as he seemed to ask, "Now what happened today to cause such dramatics? I'm in the middle of my eight-hour nap here."

Maggie looked at her orange tomcat with his bright golden eyes and smiled.

"Marms, I don't know why we are here. I thought we came here for me to take care of people, preach remarkable and uplifting sermons, visit the sick and the shut-ins, and be a good shepherdess for these people over all. Why is it I want to strangle so many of the people I profess to love?"

Marmalade blinked.

Maggie went on. "I'm pretty sure my first funeral was a disaster. How do you eulogize a man who apparently despised his family, was a mean neighbor, and left his children in debt due to his careless and selfish way of living? You know how he died? Guess!"

Marmalade blinked twice.

"He sat down and ate a whole chicken. Yep. He ate a whole, entire chicken, bones and all. It was the bones that got him. Do you know which one?"

Marmalade yawned.

"The wishbone! Ha! Can you believe it? Unfortunately, too many people made jokes about that, especially his three children. 'Wishes do come true.' I had no idea where to start with this one. And it's my first! What nice things can you possibly say about such a mean person unless you tell lies? Well, I wasn't going to do that. At least not blatantly. So, I read Psalm 23. But when I got to the part about 'You prepare a table before me in the presence of my enemies,' I could hardly finish the reading. All I could imagine was how large that table would have to be, and how many roasted chickens would have to be on it to accommodate all the enemies Rupert Solomon made throughout his lifetime."

Marmalade decided this would be a good time to wash his face since a nap seemed out of the question.

Maggie thought back to how the day had begun. She awoke at five a.m. and pulled on her shorts, T-shirt, and running shoes. She drank one cup of coffee as she put Marmalade's breakfast in his food dish. With caffeine on board, she took off out the front door of the parsonage and turned left down Middle Street. She ran down Middle to the cemetery and ran past the gravestones until she got to Freer Road. She turned right, ran down Freer, sprinted up the hill, and before she got to the high school, turned left on a dirt road called Meadowview. This was her favorite part of the run. She felt as if she could run faster, breathe the cool dawn air more deeply, and catch glimpses of the many deer and other creatures living in the woods. She enjoyed the sound of the dirt under her running shoes and watched the sun peek at her through the trees. She made a U-turn after two miles on the dirt road, then made her way home. This is how Maggie began each day, five miles of running solitude.

She cleaned up when she got back and had two more cups of coffee and her favorite oatmeal with sliced banana and pure maple syrup drizzled on top. After spending some time looking over her funeral notes and the eulogy, she put on her black funeral dress for the very first time and got chills. *My first funeral.* She realized she had never had an actual class at seminary about funerals. Weddings either, for that matter. A few details about how to officiate a marriage or a death were tucked into a practical theology class. There wasn't a lot of time devoted to either of these ceremonies, yet they were so significant in the life of a pastor and congregation. She had a small jolt of panic. Maybe she was more nervous than she thought.

She had been to funerals but had never buried anyone before. What if she messed it up? She should have called Ed about this. He would have encouraged her, given her some practical advice, and then cracked a joke to make her laugh. Why hadn't she called him? Did she have to prove she could do this ministry thing all on her own? She looked in the mirror.

"You little idiot!"

Marmalade was curled up like a big orange cinnamon roll on her pillow. She removed her black nylons from under his girth, shook off the cat hair, and shimmied into them. She jumped when the phone rang. She reached for it and tried to get her breathing under control.

"Good morning, Pastor Maggie speaking."

"Pastor Maggie, Hank here. It seems we have a little ruckus going on, and I wonder if you could come over and straighten things out."

Hank was Maggie's assistant. He was tall, with a medium build, and at fifty-five years old, he'd just begun to gray at the temples. He had a little paunch around his middle due to daily runs across the street to The Sugarplum Bakery. Hank loved his sweets and what his wife, Pamela, didn't know (although, how could she not?) didn't hurt her (apparently).

"What is it, Hank? We have Mr. Solomon's funeral in two hours. We don't have time for a ruckus."

"I agree, Pastor Maggie, yessireebob I do. But Mr. Porter is here from the funeral home, and Mrs. Abernathy is here from wherever it is she comes from, and there is a catfight to beat the band going on over the flower arrangements. I thought you should get here before members of the Solomon family arrive."

"Thanks, Hank. I'll be right there."

She hung up the phone, ran into the closet to get her shoes, grabbed her lipstick from the bathroom counter and dashed it across her lips, then was out the door.

Marmalade tucked his orange head under one white paw, thankful for peace and quiet at last.

Maggie was in the narthex of the church within seconds of Hank's call, one of the perks of living in the parsonage right next door. She immediately assessed the situation.

Mrs. Abernathy, the resident know-it-all, bossy boots, and self-appointed Queen of the World, was clutching five large vases filled with various colored zinnias. She was trying to place them on the stands that the funeral director, Cole Porter (yes, that's his real name), was using for other flowers sent by family and friends. As one arrangement was set down by Cole, it was immediately taken up by Mrs. Abernathy and replaced with her zinnias. Round and round they went. Hank was standing in the doorway to the church office, shaking his head. This was not in his job description.

Maggie thought back to the day she had interviewed Hank. It was her first day at Loving the Lord Community Church. She had enthusiastically skipped from the parsonage to the church and then subdued herself just enough to sedately walk through the sanctuary doors. Several people had gathered to greet her on her first day as "Pastor Maggie." She had done her best to dress herself for this momentous occasion. But Maggie was challenged in this area. Although her mother was absolute elegance and class, the genetics of style had completely bypassed Maggie. If she had any kind of style at all, it could be called something like "Bohemian Flower Child." She liked long flowing skirts and pastel peasant blouses. Ballet slippers did nothing to elevate her five-foot-three-inch frame. Her long blonde hair fell down past her shoulders, and that's where she left it. All she needed was a wreath of daisies in her hair and she would be the ultimate poster child for the 1960s free love campaign. The truth was, Maggie looked like a walking ragbag.

Her mother had gently tried to reform Maggie's dressing debacles without much success. The only thing she demanded was that Maggie own a proper black dress for funerals and a well-tailored, cream-colored suit to officiate weddings. Maggie reluctantly agreed. Her mother also bought her two different pairs of three-inch sandals and two pairs of pumps: one taupe and one black. Then she sat back and prayed that Maggie would actually wear them.

Maggie had been informed the week before she arrived at Loving the Lord that the part-time volunteer secretary was "retiring" to help take care of her grandchildren. The church had decided it was time to hire the first paid secretary in its history. It was all very exciting. Maggie had four interviews set up the first afternoon in her new church office. Hank was the last of the four.

He entered Maggie's office precisely at the prearranged time. He wore pressed khaki slacks, brown leather loafers, and a bright-blue button-down shirt. This was a nice change from the first three interviews.

"You must be Hank Arthur," Maggie said with a smile.

"Yessireebob, Reverend . . . uhh . . . I'm sorry, how do you pronounce your last name? El*zing*a?" Hank looked embarrassed.

Maggie laughed. "It's *Elzinga*, with the emphasis on the first syllable. It's Dutch, and no one has ever been able to pronounce it, so no worries. Besides, I would much prefer it if you would call me Maggie. Why don't you have a seat?"

Hank smiled. "Well, I'm here to apply for the secretarial position, although I would prefer being called 'assistant' if I get the job."

"Hank, I'm curious as to why you want this job? I've never known of a male secretary . . . uhh . . . *assistant* in a church before. What made you apply?"

"Pastor Maggie, I have worked all my life in the hand lotion business. I have bought, sold, marketed, photographed, and even tested on my very own skin the Skin-So-Tight lotion line. Have you ever tried it?"

Maggie shook her head, "I'm sorry, I haven't."

"Pity." Hank continued, "When they asked me last year if I would like to take an early retirement due to cutbacks, it didn't take me long to say, 'Yessireebob!' I packed up my desk and said bye-bye to Skin-So-Tight. I thought retirement was what I had been waiting for my whole life, and it was. For about two and a half weeks. Then I realized I was bored silly. My wife, Pamela, seemed to be a little on edge too, if you know what I mean."

Maggie thought she did.

"Anyway, one day she said to me, 'Hank, either you have to get another job, or I'm moving to Australia. Alone.' Just like that! So, I saw your ad in the *Cherish Life and Times*, and here I am. You will find me more than adequate on the computer. I can organize, file, answer the phone, run any office machinery, and I make a great cup of coffee."

Maggie said, "You understand it's only a part-time job, don't you? Is that enough time away to . . . hmm . . . keep your wife from moving to Australia?"

Hank quickly replied, "It will be just the thing. She's taking a macramé class in the afternoons, and she volunteers at the hospital regularly, so I won't see her until dinnertime."

Maggie hesitated. "Working in a church usually means no two days are ever alike. Confidentiality is key. What you see and hear within these walls can never be repeated."

Not that Maggie had an inkling of what would be seen or heard within "these walls." She was trying hard to sound like a pastor, but she felt like a little girl playing dress-up.

She continued, "Crises come up, people show up unannounced, and there are still the regular weekly things that have to get done. I guess what I'm saying is that you will have to be discreet, flexible, and polite under sometimes strenuous circumstances. Does that make sense?"

Hank seemed to bounce slightly. "Yessireebob, Pastor Maggie! I am the soul of discretion. Nothing that happens in this sacred place will ever leave my lips." He made a cross over his mouth. "Would you like me to promise on the Bible?"

Maggie giggled. "No, that won't be necessary, Hank. I think you will be just right. Shall we give it a try?"

Hank bounced right out of his chair, quite sprightly for a fifty-five-year-old, and he enthusiastically shook Maggie's hand.

"Thank you, Pastor Maggie. You will not be disappointed!"

And she hadn't been. Hank had turned out to be her confidant, her cheerleader, and her protector from Mrs. Abernathy and others of that ilk. He was prompt, efficient, and he worked forty hours a week for twenty hours of pay. Pamela had stopped all threats of moving to Australia, and they both joined the church, much to Maggie's delight. When she said her prayers, thanking God for Hank was always at the top of her list.

Now, watching Mrs. Abernathy and Cole Porter fight over flowers, Maggie realized that this situation was beyond Hank's control. She moved into the flower fray and said a little too loudly, "Good morning, Cole. Good morning, Mrs. Abernathy. How are we doing this morning?"

Mrs. Abernathy, who always seemed to look as if she had just had a violent encounter with a lemon, pursed her lips and said, "Pastor Margaret, first of all, it is not a 'good' morning. We are preparing to bury the dead. Second, *we* are not doing well at all. I have worked painstakingly to have these zinnias arranged in order to bring the most comfort to the family of . . . of . . . the deceased . . . man. Mr. Porter is disrupting the setup for this sad, sad occasion."

Cole Porter and his beautiful wife, Lynn, ran the local funeral home. Cole had heard every joke under the sun about being named after the famous jazz composer. Lynn was expecting their third child. She secretly hoped for a little boy to join their two girls. The Porter Funeral Home had been in the Porter family for three generations.

Cole and Lynn seemed to have one of those marriages other couples envy. They didn't waste time arguing or picking at each other. Instead, they shared kindnesses that often wore out after fifteen years of marriage. They supported each other in their mutual work of burying the dead and caring for the grieving families who came through their door. That didn't mean every funeral was easy or that every family was a delight to work with. Cole had discovered at a young age that funerals brought out the best and the worst in a family. He had learned how to handle both. This was the first funeral he and Maggie would do together, but he and Lynn were both impressed with her pastoring skills so far, even though she dressed a little strangely.

Maggie rolled her eyes, not that Mrs. Abernathy noticed. She was too busy glaring at Cole in Christian love. Ever since Maggie had arrived in Cherish two months earlier, she'd had regular entanglements with Mrs. Abernathy. Mrs. Abernathy was called "Mrs. Abernathy" by everyone in the town of Cherish. No one really remembered anymore what her first name was (it was Verna). She was a widow of ten years. She was a tall, thin woman with thick gray hair, which she strong-armed into a large bun on the back of her head. Jesus, Loving the Lord Community Church, and her garden were her three passions. When at church for worship services, Mrs. Abernathy wore *polyester* flower print dresses belted at the waist (she considered these proper church clothes) and practical rubber-wedged, beige shoes. The rest of the week she could be seen in *cotton* flower print dresses belted at the waist (her work clothes) and Wellington boots, with a kerchief tented over her gray bun.

Zinnias were Mrs. Abernathy's favorite flower because they were sturdy, practical, and suitable for any and every situation of life, death, and all days in between. Or so Mrs. Abernathy thought. But there was another reason she loved zinnias, a very private reason.

Mrs. Abernathy was the chairperson of the search committee that had interviewed Maggie in March. Mrs. Abernathy asked the questions, checked Maggie's references, and arranged a neutral pulpit so the search committee could hear Maggie preach without letting the rest of the congregation know what they were up to. Due to the lack of viable candidates, Mrs. Abernathy agreed with the rest of the committee that Maggie preached the best sermon and gave the strongest interview. But her mind was changing as the weeks went on. It unnerved her to see a "little girl" in the pulpit each Sunday. Where were the good, sturdy men?

Mrs. Abernathy had assigned herself Flower Coordinator for Sunday services and other church events. No one had the energy to stop her.

Maggie had the energy.

"Mrs. Abernathy, I realize this is our first funeral together. Thank you for your promptness and your help. But I do believe that Mr. Porter has some flower arrangements from the friends and family of Mr. Solomon, and they must be displayed." (Cole nodded emphatically.) "It's courtesy to the bereaved, Mrs. Abernathy." (Cole looked like a bobblehead.) "So how about we put your lovely (first lie of the day) zinnias on the dining tables in the basement. They will bring cheer (second lie) to those who share in the luncheon following the service. Then Mr. Porter can display the purchased arrangements on these stands for the mourners to see and be comforted by."

Maggie felt as if she had handled this beautifully. She looked over at Hank, still in the doorway. He had his hand against his forehead and his eyes closed. He knew what was coming.

Mrs. Abernathy's mouth was so puckered, Maggie could only marvel at the amount of wrinkles gathered around her lips. Would she actually be able to speak? Oh, yes, she would. Lack of verbiage was never a problem for Mrs. Abernathy.

2

Maggie remembered her first moments as Pastor Maggie. At six p.m. on the first Sunday of June, 2014, Maggie pulled into the driveway of exactly where God wanted her to be. She had arrived at the parsonage located right next door to Loving the Lord Community Church and was on the verge of unlocking the door to her future. As dramatic as that sounds, she literally was. She had a shiny brass key in her hand meant for the front door of the parsonage. She had another brass key for the front doors of the church, which she would use the next morning.

She experienced one of those moments when hope, excitement, and the fear of the unknown spectacularly collide—crazy fireworks in the soul. But her hope and excitement overrode her fear. At the age of twenty-six, with her seminary diploma barely dry, she was the new pastor of her first church. What was there to be afraid of?

She grabbed Marmalade's cat carrier and noticed the freshly plant-ed border of begonias, impatiens, and geraniums down the walkway and around the porch. Someone had taken a great deal of time and care to plant the annuals along the walkway and encircle the perennial bushes with this lovely array of pinks, whites, and reds. The begonias and impatiens were in just enough shade to keep them from frying. The only things that looked a little out of place were the bright rust-colored zinnias exploding out of several terra cotta pots on the porch.

Maggie wrinkled her nose. She wasn't a fan of either the color rust or zinnias. But all in all, it was obvious someone put a lot of work into making her new home and parsonage lovely.

As she opened the front door, she smelled a mix of lavender-scented Pine-Sol, Lemon Pledge, Clorox bleach, and new paint. The carpet was freshly vacuumed. Maggie was sure she knew who had cleaned the parsonage so beautifully, if not ferociously. Doris Walters was the janitor at Loving the Lord. Maggie had met her during the interview process. Doris was a hard worker and truly believed that "cleanliness is next to godliness, and maybe slightly above it."

Maggie walked down the hallway of the parsonage, past the living room, and into the kitchen. The walls in the large kitchen were pale yellow, the countertops white Formica. All the rest of the walls in the house were creamy beige. Completely unremarkable.

The rest of the downstairs held a formal living room with a once-white-now-gray velvet couch and a matching loveseat that looked as if they had been sat on for the last hundred years. Next to the loveseat was a blue chintz chair, also dulled in color due to age and usage. There was a coffee table, and between the chair and loveseat sat one end table with a blue porcelain lamp in the center.

She moved through a doorway into a large dining room. It held a solid oak table and chairs for twenty, some stored in the basement, if needed. A family room was across the hall from the kitchen. It had overstuffed, nonmatching furniture and several beanbag chairs tossed around. It looked like youth group Sunday school space. She had toured the home after she received her call to LTLCC, and now she let it sink in that this was her home. Her really huge home. She was aware that the parsonage was used for council meetings, certain committee meetings, and all youth events. That was fine with her. She just hoped no one was allergic to felines.

In the very back of the house was a study with a small maple desk and matching hard-backed chair, two red-and-white checked wing-backed chairs, and three bookshelves. A half-bath was attached to the study. *Convenient*, Maggie thought. There was also a floor-to-ceiling window that looked out on three pine trees and lush green grass. Under the largest pine tree was a red wagon used as a planter. It was overflowing with marigolds and purple petunias. It made Maggie laugh. It looked so haphazard and joyful. She took this as a happy omen for her new life in Cherish.

There were four bedrooms upstairs with two full bathrooms. Each bedroom had a set of bunk beds except for the master bedroom, which had a queen-sized bed. Parsonages were created for pastors with large families. Way back in the olden days, churches offered homes for their pastors and even paid them in kind with food and farm animals.

Maggie had no intention of having a family, at least not this year. She didn't even have a boyfriend, much to her father's dismay. She actually had no personal familial intentions at all. Her church would be her family. Unless, of course, Bradley Cooper came waltzing into church one Sunday morning and, on bended knee, professed his love and proposed holy matrimony. Then . . . yes, definitely, yes. She would marry him. He could usher and read Scripture in church on Sundays.

Maggie looked around. She'd have to think of something to do with all the extra space. She became lost in thought as to all the families who had lived in that big, beautiful house. She thought of the babies who had been born there, the marriages and deaths and celebrations and all the mundane happenings of life that had filled up the years in that house. That *home*. What memories would she make there?

Decades after the earlier generation of clergy, many pastors realized that, as convenient as it was to have a home ready and waiting when they arrived at their new place of ministry, by the time they retired, they had no place to go and no means to purchase their own homes. Maggie wasn't worried about that yet and was happy to live in the provided home next door to the church. What could be better than walking twenty feet to work and back?

Indignant howls rose from the cat carrier in the living room and burst into Maggie's dreamland. She ran downstairs and opened the latch. Out walked the proud owner of a jaunty orange-and-white ringed tail, which he immediately flourished in the midst of his new-found freedom.

Marmalade was a two-month-old kitten when Maggie first laid eyes on him three months ago. He was found hanging on the window screen of Maggie's room in seminary housing. It was in the middle of a violent spring thunderstorm that Maggie first heard his cries. She went outside to peel him off the screen just as another lightning bolt and crash of thunder boomed through the sky. Every bone was sticking out of his little carcass, and he was so wet she could have wrung him out. She brought him inside, toweled him off, and opened a pouch of her favorite tuna fish. He ate like nobody's business and then crawled into her lap to wash his face. True love. The greatest coup was that she and her roommate, Nora, kept him a secret from the seminary administration for three months. For his part, Marmalade ate copious amounts of kitten chow and was growing into a beautiful orange boy with a pristine coat, ringed tail, and long white whiskers. Now he was the Cat of the Manse in Cherish. Maggie unloaded the rest of her car while Marmalade sniffed his way through the parsonage. Scents of people and pets gone by filled his small nose.

She had four boxes for the kitchen: dishes, pots and pans, baking tins and sheets, and utensils. She had done most of the cooking for herself and Nora during seminary, and where she lacked in being able to dress herself, she was very accomplished in the kitchen. Baking pies was one thing in which she was exceptional. She had learned from her Grandma Elzinga, and the lessons were so fun, she had mastered the art of crusts and fillings. She could bake any kind of pie, savory or sweet. They delighted everyone who tasted them. Baking pie not only calmed Maggie, she felt as though she created a piece of art with each one. It was also a great bribe when she needed help with homework at seminary. It didn't matter to Maggie that it disappeared in a fraction of the time that it took to create.

She put her kitchen items in appropriate cupboards and drawers. The parsonage had its own set of dishes, china from a long gone era. Maggie was careful not to move the pieces around much. She noticed there was a large closet pantry next to the refrigerator. It was empty but had five shelves on the back wall and another five on one side wall. There was plenty of room for her kitcheny-type things. She also noticed the appliances were new, not the ones she had seen on her first walk-through the month before. She wondered how that had happened. She knew the financial limitations of the church. Someone had paid some very pretty pennies for the lovely brushed-aluminum appliances.

Maggie brought six boxes of books into the study at the back of the parsonage, set them near the bookshelves, and began to unpack them. She had kept every book from every class she took in seminary. Each semester she browsed the bookstore and purchased books that her professors recommended for a pastor's library. Her parents had given her an entire set of commentaries for graduation. She placed each book on her new shelves, organizing them by class and topic. She knew she would love studying, reading, and writing in this beautiful room. She plugged in her computer, put out the framed photographs of her parents, her brother Bryan, and a graduation picture of her with her arms around Nora, their graduation caps askew. They looked happy and slightly ridiculous. There was one other important graduation picture of her with Ed. She gave it a place of honor on her desk.

When she brought her clothes up to the bedroom with the queen-sized bed, Marmalade was already curled up on the pillow. He had claimed his territory. Maggie gave him a pet and was rewarded with a brief purr. *Ahhh, bliss.* What could be better than a woman pastor in her new parsonage with an independent, self-absorbed cat?

Maggie went down to the kitchen and realized she hadn't had any dinner. She knew she would not go out to find a grocery store in the dark. She should have paid more attention to the town when she interviewed two months earlier, but she only had eyes for the little church on Middle Street (and perhaps The Sugarplum Bakery directly across the street).

She was starving. She had half a bag of trail mix in her car and a warm Diet Coke. *Oh yummy.*

She jumped when the doorbell rang. It sounded like Westminster chimes.

She opened the door and saw the familiar faces of the search committee: Harold Brinkmeyer, Attorney at Law; Marla Wiggins, Sunday school superintendent; Bill Baxter, builder, town handyman, and plumber; Sylvia Smits, sweet and faithful parishioner, also a little emotional; Howard Baker, a delightful, eighty-year-old flirt; and Mrs. Abernathy. Each person was holding two bags of groceries, except for Sylvia, who had a bag of garden vegetables, and Marla, who was holding two pizza boxes and a bottle of Diet Coke.

"We have been waiting and watching for you, Pastor Maggie!" Sylvia nearly shouted. Sylvia's nose crinkled as she sniffled loudly, and her eyes misted over. "We're so glad you're finally here," she said as she wiped her nose on her sleeve, almost dropping her bag of vegetables.

Maggie stepped in to help as everyone talked over each other and pushed into the parsonage with their Magi-worthy gifts for their new pastor.

Groceries were deposited in the kitchen, and Maggie watched as everyone had an opinion on where the food should go. She let them organize her pantry, listened to their cheerful banter, and felt tears fill her own eyes. She was looking at her family.

Everyone held hands. Maggie prayed with a full heart. Paper plates and cups were set out on the big oak table in the dining room. It was the finest pizza supper any of them had had in a very long time.

Dear Maggie,

If you are reading this, you are in your new office with "Reverend Margaret Elzinga" on the door. No one will be able to pronounce your last name, but that's okay. You have arrived at your new home. Congratulations! You are where you are meant to be. You listened to

God's call on your life, followed His leading, studied hard, and grew in your spirit and faith. That last word is the one that counts so much. You have been faithful to the God who will always be, and has always been, faithful to you.

You came to seminary with a huge heart and an open, inquisitive mind. Both have grown in beautiful ways. Now you will use both every single day. You won't always have a week to study for your next test. You will think on your feet. You will also have trouble controlling your emotions, something lovely about you, which also may get you into a little trouble. Be sure to stay self-aware and share your deep-down feelings with someone you trust. Think before you leap into words or action! Yes, I know you.

Preach the good news every week. Your congregation will choose to come to church over staying home and reading the paper with a second cup of coffee. They will come because they need to hear what is good and right and true. Some will need hope. Some will need to have their fears relieved. Some will need to sing their favorite hymn. All need to meet God in your sanctuary. Be the conduit.

I remember when you told me what you learned that day in your chaplaincy when you cared for a patient on the maternity ward. "Listen, listen, listen." People will talk a lot. They are often saying so many things without using words. Hear what they say through their silence and their noise.

The truth is, most people love to talk about themselves; conversely, most people dislike listening to other people talk about themselves. Often, some just wait for the opportunity to interrupt and begin to talk about themselves again. There will be days when this makes you tired. But they need to be heard. You will minister through your ears.

Keep running. Take your vitamins. Pet your Marmalade— although you know I personally have an aversion to cats. Pray every day—often. Caring for yourself will help you care for your new flock. God's good hands will care for you all.

Maggie, I am so proud of you. Jo and I will be there for your first sermon. God bless, bless, bless YOU.

With much love,
Ed

3

Mrs. Abernathy's lips looked like the end of a roll of crepe paper. Maggie desperately wanted to put a thumb on each side of Mrs. Abernathy's mouth and stretch as hard as she could. Just pull and stretch and pull and stretch . . .

Oh dear! What is happening? How could she think such a mean thing? She was meant to love this woman. This sour, dour, bossy, condescending, angry, zinnia-loving woman. She had only known Mrs. Abernathy for two months, a little longer if you count the search process they went through together. But during that time of visits and interviews Maggie had been focused on the questions of the committee and her very certain belief that she was meant to be at LTLCC. She was aware that Mrs. Abernathy was running the meetings, but that was because she was the chairperson of the search committee. She was efficient and no-nonsense, and Maggie appreciated that.

But as the weeks went on, Maggie realized that Mrs. Abernathy was not only no-nonsense, she was also no-fun, no-smiling, and no-kindness. And she was angry. Maggie's default when confronted with angry people was to run and hide.

"Hank! Tell her I'm in a meeting!" she would hiss while stealthily closing her church office door when she heard Mrs. Abernathy's voice. But she knew that was wrong.

Maggie and Ed had many conversations in his cluttered seminary office about her tendency to avoid confrontation.

"Maggie," Ed said carefully, "as a pastor you give up the right to pick and choose whom you will love and especially whom you will like. There certainly will be those folks who will show up in your office and you'll want to jump out your window. But remember, no matter what they say or how they say it, they need to be heard. If you listen closely, you will hear what they're really saying behind their words. Anger is the jagged and ragged mask for pain. Discover the pain, and there is a chance for healing."

She'd always nodded her head gravely whenever Ed spoke like this. He knew everything worth knowing. He never exaggerated but always spoke the truth plainly. He was kind. In her mind, he was the fount of all wisdom, and if he told her to fling herself off the side of a mountain, she would cheerfully do so.

Maggie was fortunate in that she had known Ed since she was a little girl. She was raised in the church where Ed and his wife Jo attended. Ed had even been her Sunday school teacher in high school. He was the first person who saw gifts of ministry in Maggie—and told her so. She adored him. Eventually, she began to believe his words and knew seminary would be her pathway to ministry.

Ed, or Dr. James, as he was first introduced to the new class of seminary students on that first day of orientation, was the professor of New Testament studies. He would guide them through learning Greek and then interpreting most of the New Testament from the ancient language. He was thorough, and he was tough. The rumor was no one could get an A out of him. Maggie never did. He also loved to teach, loved his students, and loved God most of all. Maggie had never met anyone who lived the words "Man of God" so completely. She spent much of her first year in Greek sobbing in Ed's office, certain that seminary was the worst idea ever and that Greek was the most difficult and ridiculous language in the history of the world. (Maggie tended to be dramatic.) Ed would silently hand over the box of tissues (was he a professor or a therapist?) and let her finish her teary tirade.

Ed and his lovely wife, Joanna, regularly had groups of students in their home for family-style dinners. Jo was an excellent cook and was as enthusiastic about the seminary students as her husband. Their home was a sanctuary for many. As a couple, they couldn't be more perfectly matched. Ed was five foot eight and slim due to regular games of table tennis (not ping-pong!). Joanna was five foot five and was slim from gardening in the summer and shoveling snow in the winter. They both had short gray hair, although Ed's was thinner and wispier than his wife's. When they spoke to each other, their words were always gentle, sometimes teasing, and always complimentary. Maggie was in love with them both. She relied heavily on Ed during her interview process but came to realize she needed his guidance more than ever now that she had the "call of her dreams."

Remembering Ed's guidance on the subject, she knew she had to be kind but hold firm for the sake of Cole Porter and the family arriving any moment for a funeral.

"Mrs. Abernathy, I must insist that you bring the zinnias to the dining room so that Mr. Porter can finish placing his flowers here in the narthex. We don't have time to argue. The family will be here to pay their last respects any minute." Maggie used her most grown-up voice.

Mrs. Abernathy was on the verge of another assault when a flash of purple caught her eye. Maggie also turned to look. As she did so, Hank moved deftly into the narthex and relieved Mrs. Abernathy of three of her vases.

"Let me help you with these, Mrs. Abernathy." He began to herd her toward the stairs.

Maggie smiled thankfully at him before she turned again to see what was gliding by.

Irena Dalca came racing past with her arms full of sheet music and three hymnals. She marched through the gathering area on her way to the organ.

Irena made Maggie feel tall. Irena was five feet tall, *if* she had on four-inch heels, which she always did, probably even when she slept. Irena maybe weighed eighty pounds. She had been the organist at Loving the Lord for the past eight years. It was hard to guess her age. The only telltale signs were silver-gray roots in her hair when she waited too long to dye it.

Irena's hair.

Irena's hair was, well, astonishing. She favored dark shades of red and purple, mainly. She did her own hair coloring over her kitchen sink. Sometimes it worked. The dark-purple flash that caught Maggie's eye was something that *hadn't* worked in Irena's kitchen. Her hair looked like an eggplant.

Having been at LTLCC for eight years had given the congregation time to get used to Irena's quirks, and there were many. She was hired because she was a brilliant (if somewhat enthusiastic) musician. She had been born in Romania and brought out of that country by her mother, who had been a piano instructor. Irena and her mother had settled in Detroit, where Irena learned English badly but excelled at every instrument she could get her hands on. She and her mother had lived in two small rooms in the back of the music studio. Irena learned enough English and math skills to speak to her mother's students and also to keep the financial books.

She was as harsh and explosive as a lightning bolt wrapped in a firework.

Irena's four-inch heels were filled with feet connected to legs tightly ensconced in black fishnet stockings. She wore short, tight skirts and sheer blouses that were cut a little too low. This made it easier to see her brightly colored push-up bras. Her makeup looked as though she had taken a course at clown school. The clashes of bright colors—red lips, orange cheeks, green eye shadow—on such a small face was astounding. At a glance, Irena looked like a streetwalker working the circus circuit. But she was brilliant on the organ and piano and playing the violin, among other instruments. Her outward appearance caused second and third glances from visitors, but the rest of the church had grown to love her as their own. Or at least they were sufficiently afraid of her so as to never complain.

In the past two months, Maggie and Irena had circled each other warily, like two rival lionesses. Maggie tried to stake her claim as pastor of the church, Irena as ruler of the universe. As soon as Irena realized that Maggie was not going to try to make any musical decisions whatsoever, she allowed life to continue as usual. Maggie learned that Irena was all prickles and thorns but that she played music from the angels in heaven every Sunday morning. Loud angels, that is. Irena could regularly bring Maggie to tears when she touched a musical instrument.

"Irena, I'm so glad you're here!" After the tussle with Mrs. Abernathy, Maggie felt like Irena was her lifelong best friend. For one brief second.

"Ov coourse you are," Irena stated as she set up her hymnals and shuffled through her sheet music. "Dees funral ees unconveeniant for my day, but must be done."

I'm sure it's "unconveeniant" for Mr. Solomon as well, thought Maggie. She smiled with her mouth but not her eyes and turned and headed for her church office before she screamed or threw a hymnal at Irena's head. She passed Cole, who was finally able to set up the flower arrangements before the family showed up. As Maggie moved across the gathering area, she walked right into the coffin, which was tucked behind a glass display case. She gasped and made an involuntary choking sound as she halted in her tracks. She looked down—right into Rupert Solomon's pasty, dead face. She gasped again.

Cole looked over and said, "Pastor Maggie, are you all right?"

"Yes, Cole, thank you. I'm fine. I didn't realize Mr. Solomon was, umm, resting here."

Maggie felt a little dizzy and leaned forward to steady herself, putting her hands on the coffin. The coffin began rolling into Hank's office. Maggie stumbled as Cole quickly made his way to her and grabbed the end of the coffin. He moved it back into place and took her elbow.

"Let's get you a glass of water, Pastor Maggie." His eyes were a gentle hazel and seemed to be very concerned as Maggie looked up at him. "This is your first funeral, right?"

They could hear Irena on the organ blaring "Great Is Thy Faithfulness" as if it were a warm-up exercise for an aerobics class.

"Yes," Maggie replied. "I've looked over the service, and I practiced the eulogy in front of Marmalade last night. He slept through most of it. But yes, this is my first funeral, the first time I've touched a coffin, and I have no idea what I'm doing." She was on the verge of tears.

Cole walked her to her office, brought her a glass of water, and said, "Maggie, you will do great today. Your job is to remember the dead man, remind his family and all the rest of us of God's promise that death has been overcome by Jesus Christ. You pray. We all sing. And Irena will play a little too loudly until everyone is downstairs for the luncheon."

He chuckled, and Maggie laughed, slightly hysterically.

"Thank you, Cole. I needed that. I don't know how you do what you do, but I'm glad that you do . . . do it . . . if you know what I mean."

"I do. Now, fifteen minutes before the service, I'll bring the family in here. You can speak with them and say a prayer. Then you bring them out into the gathering area, and you will all follow the coffin down the center aisle. I will seat the family, and you will begin. When you finish with the last prayer, I will make the announcement about luncheon in the dining room. How does that sound?"

"I think you should do it," Maggie said.

"Make the announcement? I will."

"No. The whole funeral." Maggie looked at him and giggled.

He grinned and stood up to leave.

"You are feeling better, I can tell. I will pray for you today."

Cole left her office, and Maggie thought she really might cry. In the last two months, she had prayed and prayed for everyone, but no one had ever said the words "I will pray for you." The comfort of those words was like someone wrapping a warm blanket around her.

The funeral was one Maggie would never forget. Not only was it her first, but the family members showed up twenty minutes late. Irena became more and more cranky with the delay and proceeded to blast every funeral hymn in the hymnal, decibels rising with each one until Cole asked her to tone it down. Finally, Maggie and the tardy family followed the coffin down the aisle. The service began and then mercifully, after thirty minutes, came to an end.

". . . and so," Maggie finished, "even though we don't know why Rupert Solomon ate a whole chicken, with the bones, which caused his tragic death, we do know that God knows all these things and that Rupert is enjoying paradise at this very moment. Let us pray."

After the prayer, Maggie took a deep breath. Had she actually held her breath through the whole funeral? Her lungs thought so.

Cole made his announcement about the lunch, and everyone began to file out to Irena's peppy rendition of "The Old Rugged Cross." Maggie was collecting her notes from the pulpit when she was interrupted by Harold Brinkmeyer. Harold was in his late thirties. He had sandy blond hair, straight white teeth—which worked themselves into a dazzling smile—and was an attorney in the local law office of Cherish. Harold was single and hadn't thought much about his single status until Maggie showed up two months earlier. He was the chairperson of the church council, which meant he and Maggie planned meeting agendas together. Maggie thought Harold was bright and pragmatic. He was able to bring some normalcy to the ab-normalcy of church life.

"Maggie, you did an excellent job with that. You were able to make sense out of something that was, well, quite odd," Harold said, using all his dazzling teeth.

"Thanks, Harold. It *was* odd. I had only met Rupert twice, and I had never met his family before. I'm guessing they're in your hands now as they unravel Rupert's estate." Maggie was feeling such an immense rush of relief to be done with the funeral, she was practically gushing.

"Yes, let the unraveling begin! You really did a great job. I'll stop by later this week to go over the agenda for the council meeting. I was also wondering about something else, but this isn't the place." Harold's eyes slid to the floor.

"Sure, Harold. Give me a call, or we can talk later." She wondered why he was staring at the floor.

As she looked over his shoulder, she saw several more parishioners milling around, waiting to speak to her. Cole was in the back of the sanctuary, and when he caught her eye, he gave her two thumbs-up and a big grin. She grinned back.

Harold looked up to see her smiling, and his teeth responded in turn.

"Well, I better let you go. We'll definitely talk later." Harold's eyes lingered, but Maggie didn't notice.

Marla Wiggins was next in line. Marla was Loving the Lord's Sunday school superintendent. Marla was in her early fifties with short, dark hair and small brown eyes. Marla loved children. Marla's husband, Tom, owned the hardware store in town, and he was known for his honesty and generosity.

It hadn't taken Maggie long to figure out that it was Tom who had replaced all the appliances in the parsonage. When she had thanked him for his incredible generosity, he had shuffled his feet and said, "Pastor Maggie, we couldn't have you using a stove with only two working burners and a refrigerator that howls. Maybe you could give the oven a whirl with one of your famous pies."

She had done so and brought a beautiful triple berry pie straight to Tom as a thank you. Tom and Marla had a son, Jason, in the ninth grade, and a daughter, Addie, in the eleventh grade. The family never missed a Sunday in church, although Jason and Addie rarely made it to Sunday school. Because of his store, Tom was the head of the Building and Grounds Committee—free hardware supplies for the church. He and Bill Baxter, the local builder, handyman, and plumber, kept the church and parsonage in good shape. Maggie enjoyed working with Marla.

"Marla, it's so good to see you here."

Marla smiled and gave Maggie a huge hug. "You did a wonderful job with the funeral. We are so blessed to have you here!"

"No, Marla, I'm the one who's blessed."

("Maggie, you need to learn how to take compliments," Ed gently hammered into her psyche. He hadn't hammered hard enough, as of yet.)

Marla and Maggie continued their mutual admiration society every time they were together, always talking in exclamation points. It was a little nauseating.

"Pastor Maggie, I thought I should research some curriculum on death. The funeral reminded me that we have nothing in our library for the children of our church regarding death. They are all going to lose someone someday, and we might as well help them get ready for it, don't you think? Whether it's a pet or a grandparent, we must teach them that Jesus cares and has a place prepared."

The fact that there were only four children under the age of ten didn't matter. Marla gave them the best Christian education in all of Southeast Michigan.

"That's a great idea, Marla. Maybe we could teach a class together."

("Maggie, don't take on too much. Let the people of the church do the work of the church. You'll burn yourself out if you try to do it all." When Ed spoke like this, all Maggie heard was the voice of an adult in a Charlie Brown cartoon.)

Maggie saw Marla stare at the floor, then she heard someone blowing their nose and turned to see Sylvia Smits.

"Oh dear, Sylvia, whatever is the matter?"

Maggie patted Marla's arm as a goodbye and then gave Sylvia a quick hug.

With a large tissue box tucked beneath her arm, and between her sniffs and snorts, Sylvia was able to say, "Oh, Pastor Maggie, this is all so terribly sad. Poor, poor Mr. Solomon. I just can't imagine choking to death on chicken bones. And there was no one there to help him. And . . . he died on the very same day I brought you fresh produce from my garden. Don't you find that uncanny?"

Sylvia regularly brought Maggie copious amounts of vegetables from her garden. There were some mornings when the top of Maggie's desk was completely covered with zucchini, peppers, carrots, tomatoes, onions, and other vegetables. Sylvia brought Maggie vegetables the way a cat brings dead field creatures as loving gifts to its owner. At first, Maggie didn't know what to do with so much fresh produce. She ate as much as she could, pawned off bags to Hank at the end of the day, and had even brought baskets to her parents and Ed and Jo on her last trip to the west side of the state. But there was still too much, so some had to go—under cover of darkness, hidden in several paper bags—straight into the trash.

Maggie's office smelled like a produce stand. Even when she burned her "biblical spices" scented candles, she couldn't get rid of the smell.

Maggie did not see the uncanniness of Sylvia's produce deposit and Rupert Solomon's death, but she smiled and nodded anyway. She also noticed Sylvia's eyes drifting down to the floor. What in the world was everyone looking at down there? They acted like shy first-day-of-school children.

Sylvia moved away, blowing her nose while she contemplated the tragedies of life.

Another tragedy arose as Maggie heard the disturbing sound of a vacuum cleaner. *What in the world?* Maggie looked to her left and saw Doris, draped in her yellow apron, vacuuming the side aisle of the sanctuary. Maggie practically tripped down the steps of the altar and sprinted toward her.

Doris wheeled her cleaning cart and large trash can through the church on a daily basis. Her large yellow apron had five pockets sewn on the front. One pocket held a feather duster. The other pockets held a can of air freshener, Windex, a roll of paper towels, and attachments for the vacuum. She looked like a big, lumpy, yellow snowman as she sprayed, wiped, dusted, and vacuumed her way around the church. She had no patience for people leaving coffee cups and bulletins lying around on Sunday mornings, and she had no problem saying so. Doris was married to Chester, and the two of them were in "their" pew every Sunday morning. Maggie suspected Doris was only a member of the church so she could keep an eye on things.

Maggie planted one foot on the vacuum.

"Doris! Doris! DORIS!" Maggie shouted.

Doris turned off the vacuum.

"Doris, do you think you could wait until the guests are out of the sanctuary before you start cleaning?"

Doris stared blankly. "Why?"

"Well, don't you think it's rude to run the vacuum when family members of the deceased are still in the sanctuary?" This was unbelievable.

"Why?"

"Just wait until everyone is downstairs!" Maggie scream-whispered.

"Fine," said Doris. "By the way, did you know that you . . . ?"

But Maggie had turned and walked back to the pulpit.

Maggie smiled when she saw Ellen Bright standing on the altar. Ellen looked exactly as her name sounded: bright. She was in her mid-thirties, with dark-brown hair and luminous (and compassionate) brown eyes. Her smile filled her entire face and was contagious. Ellen was a nurse at Heal Thyself Community Hospital. Heal Thyself was on the southeast side of town, nestled in a beautiful wooded area where patients could see deer and other wildlife as they were recovering. Ellen was one of Maggie's favorite people, and they were beginning to strike up a comfortable friendship. Ellen was one of those rare people who only saw the best in others. Just being around her made Maggie feel like a better person. Maggie *wanted* to be a better person when she was around Ellen. Maggie had also noticed that Ellen and Dr. Jack Elliot, a physician at Heal Thyself, were spending time together. *Hmmm . . .*

"Pastor Maggie, I just wanted to share a little memory with you. I remember the time Mr. Solomon was driving out to his farm when he saw a dog in the middle of the road. Someone had hit the poor thing and left it right there, dying. Mr. Solomon stopped and picked up the little beast, expecting it to die on the front seat of his truck. But it didn't. He brought it to Dr. Dana Drake, the vet, and after a surgery for internal bleeding and casts on two broken legs, Mr. Solomon paid the entire bill and brought Charlie home. That dog lived for another fifteen years. Those two were inseparable. Mr. Solomon cried and cried when Charlie finally died. It broke his heart. I thought you might like to know that story."

"Thank you for telling me, Ellen." Maggie was glad to hear the story but felt guilty because her only memory of Mr. Solomon was that he was a cranky old man who smelled like whiskey at ten a.m.

Ellen gave Maggie's hand a squeeze and moved toward the basement.

"You're good for my soul, Ellen," Maggie said.

Behind Ellen was (secretly) one of Maggie's least favorite parishioners: Redford Johnson. Redford was one of those men who was just a little too arrogant for his own good. His job as a financial planner in Cherish kept him on the hunt for new clientele. He had a reputation of risky investments that sometimes paid off—and sometimes did not. But, somehow, he always got paid his share. "Slimy" was a good word to describe him. He was in his late thirties, tall, with black hair and a petulant face. No one was as in love with Redford as Redford. He was sure women were completely charmed by his, well, charm. Most women had too much self-esteem and good sense to pay any attention to him. The bottom line was, Redford looked at women the way he would look at a dog: they were utilitarian. He came to church when there was nothing better to do. His reason for being at the funeral became readily apparent.

"Great funeral, Madge. That was a tricky one."

"Maggie," Maggie replied.

"What?"

"My name is Maggie, not Madge. You may call me Pastor Maggie. How are you, Redford?" Maggie spoke in a formal, staccato voice, sounding very much like Mrs. Hughes from *Downton Abbey*.

"Me? I'm great, as usual. Hey, did this guy have a widow or kids or anything? Anyone I could get a little business from?"

He ran his fingers through his hair and looked meaningfully into Maggie's eyes. She wanted to punch him. She stood as tall as she possibly could and straightened her shoulders.

"Wow, I don't think I have ever heard anything so inappropriate at a funeral before. So, I'm going to pretend that you didn't just say that." Maggie was sure she had put him in his place. No doubt about it.

Redford didn't hear her. He stared at the floor. Finally, she looked down just as he spoke.

"Hey, Madge. Nice shoes! Is that special just for funerals?" He laughed as he walked away.

Maggie looked down at her shoes.

She was horrified. In her rush to get over to the "flower wars" earlier, she had grabbed one taupe pump and one black pump. She had done the entire funeral wearing two different shoes.

Then Maggie heard a loud metallic snap. She looked toward the bell tower of the sanctuary and couldn't believe her eyes. Fitch Dervish came through the door as he rewound his measuring tape. He walked toward Maggie down the side aisle of the church. He tried to put his measuring tape away, didn't see Doris and her vacuum, and tripped over the cord. Fitch caught himself by grabbing Doris's head.

"Let go of me, you big moose!" Doris shouted.

Maggie cringed.

"Sorry, Mrs. Walters," Fitch said as he righted himself.

Doris glared.

Fitch was the building inspector in Cherish and regularly annoyed the people trying to build or renovate anything. Most building inspectors came at the start and the finish of a building project. Fitch felt it was his absolute duty to visit sites on a daily basis. And because not a lot of building happened at one time *ever* in Cherish, he was able to oversee (micromanage) most projects. He was a builder's nightmare.

Fitch was a tall man, always dressed in a white button-down shirt, khaki pants, and large white tennis shoes. He cinched his pants with a brown leather belt, which caused wrinkles and puckers around the waistband. A mysterious man-bag slung over his shoulder completed his uniform. Fitch had an unbelievably large rear end, unbalanced by slim shoulders and skinny arms. His glasses were the type that changed from dark to light, depending on the level of light indoors and out, and he tightly clenched a large clipboard at all times.

Fitch took his job very seriously. Not one square inch was out of place on any building project being undertaken in Cherish. He had an uncanny way of finding hidden or secretive ventures, and he slapped fines on the delinquents trying to get away with sneaky construction. It was lucky for him he had no idea how much he was disliked in the community.

Maggie had been warned early on when she arrived in Cherish that the handicapped ramp in front of the church was not up to code. The church had decided to hire Bill Baxter to replace the ramp. Fitch was keeping the shy and fully capable builder frustrated.

On more than one occasion, Maggie had walked from the parsonage to church only to hear Fitch comment condescendingly to Bill regarding the ramp, the small brick wall in front of the ramp, and the black iron railing encircling the bell tower. Fitch was the expert, at least in his own mind. After all, he had taken the on-line course, paid his six-hundred-dollar fee, and passed the exam on his third try (although ninety percent of the people who did this passed on their first).

Bill Baxter, on the other hand, had been raised on his father's construction sites. Being the owner of Baxter's Construction, Bill's father was well known in Southeast Michigan. Bill had been a keen learner since the age of ten, when he went to the various jobs with his dad and picked up nails and scraps of drywall while the builders did their jobs. Bill had learned to pour concrete, frame a house or business building, install the plumbing and electricity, drywall, paint, and do the intricate finish work. The codes for buildings and zones were in his head.

Fitch had to regularly pull his manual out of his man-bag to refresh himself on certain codes. Then he spoke as if he was the only person who had ever learned the complexities of building laws.

With funeral guests still milling about, Maggie quickly made her way to Fitch. She desperately wished she could fling off her mismatched shoes, but soldiered on in her attempt to protect Rupert Solomon's family once again.

"Fitch, what are you doing in here?"

Fitch looked down at Maggie with such scorn, she felt like a child.

"Pastor Maggie, you know exactly what I'm doing here, now don't you? We are trying to get this old church up to snuff, aren't we?"

Maggie wanted to push and shove him right out the sanctuary doors and down the front steps.

"Fitch, please don't talk to me as if I were in elementary school. I have just officiated a funeral. Look, there's the coffin."

Maggie pointed to the gathering area where Cole directed the pall bearers.

Fitch looked over at Cole. Maggie watched as Fitch's shoulders slumped slightly and his face turned white.

"Fitch, are you okay?" Maggie asked. "Didn't you see the hearse parked out front?"

Fitch began to back up, but his large, rubber-soled tennis shoe caught on the bottom of the pew behind him. His tall frame jolted to the side as he fell backward then sideways into the pew. His arms flailed, and hymnals, a Bible, and prayer request cards went flying. He landed with a thump, which caused the funeral guests to turn and stare.

Maggie reacted quickly and smiled kindly at the bereaved. Then she grabbed Fitch by the arm and helped him sit up.

"Are you all right? Would you like some water?" Maggie sounded like a mother with a badly behaved child.

"No, no. Thank you. I just need to get out of here," Fitch mumbled. "I don't like dead people." Using the pew in front of him, he pulled himself up and stood for a few seconds. "I'll be back for more inspection later this week."

He turned and walked back to the bell tower door.

Maggie sighed as she cleaned up the mess he had made and then walked in the other direction. She grabbed her Bible and notes from the pulpit. She wanted to make a quick getaway so she could wallow in her embarrassment of shoes and Fitch. As she turned, Irena came up beside her, arms loaded down with music.

"Vell, dat's done! Funrals are so annoying. I vould prefer more notice so I can prractice, you know?"

"Irena, you did a wonderful job." Maggie tried to pull herself together. She also tried to pretend there was a tiny shred of camaraderie between the two of them.

"Yesss. I know. I am brrilliant musician. Vat's wrong vit yoor shoos?"

Maggie could feel her face getting hot. "I dressed in a hurry this morning. I need to change them."

Irena looked piercingly into Maggie's eyes. "Yesss, you do. You look stuupid. I am going now. Goodbye."

Her high heels began to *click-clack* down the hallway. *Trip, trap, trip, trap.* She sounded like the littlest Billy Goat Gruff.

Goodbye, thought Maggie, *and good riddance.*

She placed her Bible and notes back on the pulpit. As she stalked out the front doors of the church and stomped up the steps of the parsonage all she could think was, *Sometimes there just aren't enough chicken bones to go around!*

Dear Ed,

I am writing you this letter but have no intention of mailing it. I must tell you of the horrors of my first funeral and then let you know, in no uncertain terms, that parish ministry is the last place on earth I should be. God has made a huge mistake.

I buried a man today who was nice to his dog, but that's about it. His children disliked him, as did most of the town. How do you eulogize someone like that?

I was called to church early to break up a flower brawl between Cole Porter and Mrs. Abernathy. I think I might go and mow down every one of her stiff, stinky zinnias tonight.

I bumped into the casket and nearly fainted. I guess I'm not used to dead bodies yet. When does that happen??

Irena dyed her hair purple by mistake.

The family showed up twenty minutes late.

I almost laughed out loud when reading the 23rd Psalm, wondering how God would arrange a large enough table to accommodate all of Rupert Solomon's enemies.

I had to put up with Redford. Again.

Doris began vacuuming before the family was even out of the sanctuary.

The insanely annoying building inspector of Cherish showed up and almost fainted when he saw the casket.

I wore two completely different shoes throughout the entire service!!!!

After the little revelation about my shoes, I marched home and screamed into one of my pillows. Twice.

Then I put on matching shoes and went back to church. I ate three cookies while I ever so pleasantly chatted with family and guests.

Rupert had been loaded up in the hearse, and we all went the two blocks east, where the graveside service took place. Rupert has been laid to rest, but it was a bumpy ride getting him to the end of the day.

I finally got home for good and cried and cried and cried. I'm so embarrassed about my first funeral. Will God and Rupert ever forgive me?

Also, I know we were told in seminary not to make close friends with parishioners. We can't have favorites, blah, blah, blah. But I like Ellen Bright. She is a kindred spirit, and she's good for my soul. AND I'M KEEPING HER!!

Hi to Jo.

Love,
Maggie

Maggie addressed the envelope, even though she wasn't going to. Then she put a stamp on it. She washed her face. She walked across the street, down the alley behind The Sugarplum Bakery, straight to the post box, and slipped the letter down the chute.

Then she went home and baked a chocolate coconut cream pie.

4

The morning after the funeral, Maggie awoke with a start. Marmalade was happily bashing his little orange head against her ear and purring loudly. She opened her eyes and smiled at her companion. It only took about two seconds for her to remember the embarrassment of the prior day. *Aagghh!* She rolled over and hid her head under her pillow. That did not deter Marmalade, who followed her under the pillow and continued his wake-up call.

As Maggie emerged from her pillow, she had a tiny flash of insight. She felt she hadn't done a good job with Rupert's funeral. It wasn't just her shoe mix-up. She didn't think she had brought the comfort Cole had talked about before the funeral. But people had told her she did a nice job. In the midst of her crazy amount of idealistic, sunshiny optimism was a dark cloud of insecurity she hadn't noticed before. Where had that cloud come from? She didn't like it.

Maggie got out of bed, pondered her new insight, and dazedly pulled on her shorts, T-shirt, and running shoes. She slurped down her coffee and burned her mouth as she did so. Then forgot to put breakfast in Marmalade's bowl. She grabbed the chocolate coconut cream pie she'd made the night before out of the refrigerator and walked out the front door and down the block and a half to the Porter's home. Cole answered the door, and Maggie put the pie in his hands.

"Good morning, Cole. This is for you. It's a Thank You Pie for being so kind and helpful yesterday."

Cole looked surprised and pleased at the same time. "Maggie, this looks delicious. I won't tell you that you don't need to thank me. That would be insulting, and then you would argue and be annoying. But I do want you to know that you did a beautiful job with your first funeral. You brought comfort, hope, and promise to all of us."

Maggie grimaced. "Thanks, Cole. It's a new day, right? I'll be over the humiliation of yesterday in a month or so."

Lynn came to the door and saw the pie. "Ooh, Pastor Maggie! That looks amazing. May we plan on a pie following every funeral?" She laughed.

"Only when I officiate in two different shoes." Maggie waved and stepped away. "I'm off to run. I'll say hi to Rupert as I go through the cemetery."

Maggie ran. As she did so, the burden of the day before began to blow away. Maggie usually spent her runs praying, thinking of sermon ideas, and basically communing with God. There was never an interruption when she ran, besides having to retie an errant shoelace. She had five miles of pure God time. That morning as she ran, she relived the funeral. The farther she ran, the more her embarrassment and feelings of pastor inferiority began to dissipate. She was learning. Seminary wasn't the end of knowledge. She had brand-new lessons to learn. When she got back to the parsonage, she felt relieved. She gave Marmalade a sweaty hug, which he didn't seem to appreciate. He immediately threw himself into a self-cleaning frenzy while Maggie grabbed a shower and got ready for the day.

After her oatmeal and Marmalade's breakfast (finally!), she crossed the street to The Sugarplum Bakery. As she opened the door, the lovely sound of fairy bells met her ears. The bells, along with the scent of butter cream frosting, chocolate and vanilla cupcakes, ginger scones, and freshly fried donuts almost put Maggie into a sugar coma. She just knew this was what heaven would smell like for all eternity.

"Well, hokey tooters!" Mrs. Popkin exclaimed. "Good morning, Pastor Maggie!"

Polly Popkin had owned and operated The Sugarplum Bakery for the past twenty years. She employed local girls to work with her, and they were as loyal as puppies. Mrs. Popkin was sturdy, five feet tall, and had the figure of one who never deprived herself of a cupcake. She wore a white baker's coat and a large white baker's hat that didn't quite cover the riot of dark-brown curls escaping from below the band around her head. She had merry brown eyes and was the most jovial person Maggie had ever met. That morning she had a smudge of pink frosting on her cheek.

"Good morning, Mrs. Popkin." Maggie couldn't help but catch the happy spirit in the bakery. "It's like Disneyland for the nose in here!"

Mrs. Popkin's laugh was loud and long.

Maggie looked into the display case and touched her finger to her lips as she tried to decide what to buy.

"I'll take a dozen donuts—mixed, but four chocolate cake for sure." Maggie was beginning to salivate.

"Hokey tooters, I'll box those up right away." Mrs. Popkin began to package up the donuts. "Pastor Maggie, I heard you did a real fine funeral for Mr. Solomon. People talked about it yesterday afternoon, and I heard only good things. We're so glad you came to Cherish."

Maggie was surprised but said, "Thank you, Mrs. Popkin. I'm glad to be in Cherish." Maybe yesterday wasn't as bad as she thought.

Mrs. Popkin continued. "He was a cantankerous old goat, but everyone oughta be buried with a little dignity. That's what you did, or so I hear." She handed Maggie a blueberry scone. "On the house!" she exclaimed.

Maggie couldn't wait, so she took a huge bite right there. "Mishush Popkin, thish ish angelsh food."

Mrs. Popkin beamed and thought to herself, *Then you're the perfect person to be eating it!*

Maggie walked across the street and arrived at the church office just moments after Hank. She set the donuts down on top of the copy machine.

"Good morning, Hank. It's a beautiful day full of possibilities!"

Hank sat behind his desk, which was covered with funeral bulletins, paper cups, a half-eaten ham-on-bun sandwich, and a glob of green Jell-O that had slid off someone's plate. Hank glared.

"Do you people think my desk looks like a trash can? Do you know how many mornings I come in here, after leaving my desk spotless the night before, and sit down to a pile of refuse? I need to put out a sign: *I don't dump my trash in your pew, please don't dump trash on my desk!* I've had about enough!"

Just then the phone rang. Hank's voice changed from whiny to professional in a nanosecond. "Good morning. Loving the Lord Community Church. May I help you?"

Maggie began to clean up the bulletins, paper cups, and disgusting bits of food.

Hank said, "Yes, she is. May I ask who is calling? Just a moment please, Mrs. Abernathy." He looked at Maggie, who winced but walked into her office to take the call.

Since the office door was open, Maggie heard Doris walk into the office with her large rolling trash can through Mrs. Abernathy's daily rant. Doris had been skeptical about having a male secretary. She refused to call him an "assistant." She was certain that a man would make more work for her because men were slobs. She took in the sight of his desk and shook her head in disgust.

"Just like a man!" she exhaled.

"THIS IS NOT MY MESS!"

Maggie cringed. Doris knew how to get under Hank's skin.

Doris spied the donut box on the copy machine and picked it up to throw in her rolling trash can.

"Stop right there!" Hank stood up and grabbed one end of the box. "Pastor Maggie just brought that in. Put it down, Doris!"

Doris lifted a corner of the lid and peeked in. The smell of fresh donuts wafted up. Doris looked at Hank and let him take the box.

"Do you think those are for all of us?" she asked, her voice suddenly softened.

"I'm sure I don't know, but Pastor Maggie placed them on the copy machine, so I don't think she intends to eat them all herself hidden away in her office. When she gets off the phone, maybe we will find out."

Maggie stretched the phone cord as far as possible and waved and smiled at Hank and Doris. She mouthed the words, "Eat the donuts. They're for you."

"Yes, Mrs. Abernathy . . . I think that's a great . . . Gladiolas? Yes, I like . . . No, I haven't seen Sylvia's gladiolas but . . . Well, it seems like a variety would be nice . . . Zinnias, ahh . . . If you think so, Mrs. Abernathy . . . Mrs. Abernathy? I know I can leave Sunday's flowers in your more than capable hands. After all, you have been doing the flowers for . . . Perhaps Sylvia just wants to help . . . Remember, we are all part of the church family. If Sylvia wants to contribute . . . Certainly you can arrange them with the zinnias, but zinnias? Really, Mrs. Abernathy?"

Hank and Doris looked up when they heard the *click-clack* of Irena's high heels. Doris and Hank were united in one thing: they were both terrified of Irena. Her shoes were coming closer and closer. Then she appeared in Hank's office, half hidden behind a stack of music. Unfortunately, her purple hair and startling makeup were not hidden. She looked as if she'd had a toddler spray paint her face—everything too bright and outside the lines.

"Goood moorning, Hunk. Goood moorning, Dooriss. Vere is Pastooorr Maggie?"

Hank looked with horrified fascination at Irena's face and hair.

"She is indisposed at this time, Irena. May I help you?"

Irena could hear Maggie talking in her office and was headed in that direction when she spied the donut box. Maggie waved, but Irena had been completely detoured. Maggie watched Irena as Mrs. Abernathy continued her diatribe.

"Vat's in dat box?" Irena had her eyes glued to the donut box.

"Donuts," Hank replied.

"Who day fooor?" Irena moved around the desk.

"I'm not sure. Pastor Maggie brought them in."

"Den day fooor us!"

Irena snatched the lid off the box and grabbed two donuts with her free hand.

She sat down in the one extra chair in the office and began eating the donuts, making loud smacking noises. With her mouth full she said, "I vait foor Pastoor. Giff me a napkin."

Doris picked up a used napkin from Hank's desk and handed it over. Irena took it and wiped her mouth. Hank and Doris stared. Finally, Doris took Hank's trash can and emptied it into her larger one. She began to clear the trash off his desk, but she kept one eye on Irena at all times.

Irena stared back and said, "Vat? You tink I bite you?"

"Yes," said Doris. "I do."

She took a donut out of the box, turned, and wheeled her trash can out of the office.

Hank and Irena heard Maggie say, "Mrs. Abernathy, I need to go now, but I know the flowers will be exquisite on Sunday . . . Thank you for calling . . . Goodbye."

Irena stood up and walked into Maggie's office.

Maggie had her head in her hands and sighed. "Oh dear me." She hadn't seen Irena enter.

Maggie jumped as Irena said, "Vat 'oh dear me'? Pastooorr Maggie, you have headache? Take aspirin tablets. Now . . ." Irena moved two onions, three tomatoes, and a zucchini to the edge of Maggie's desk with her pointy elbow, then forcefully put down her stack of music. "Ve must speeak museek." Irena licked chocolate frosting off her small fingers, then wiped her hands on one of the curtains hanging in the window. "I tink, Christmas cantata. I tink, Handel's *Messiah*. I tink . . ." Irena was getting a little dreamy now, staring off into space, into the fantasy land of musicians. "Violinns, cellos, trrumpets, drrums . . . de orchestrra—yes!"

Maggie marveled at the idiocy of this scheme. "Irena, wow. It's only August and you're already thinking of Christmas. You are a planner, aren't you? I think Handel's *Messiah* is one of the most beautiful and significant pieces of music ever composed, but you lost me a little with the orchestra idea. And quite frankly, would our choir of five be able to pull it off?"

Irena began to tremble with excitement. "Vere dere's a vill, dere's a vay!! I can seee itt. I can heear itt. Can you heeear itt?! You alvays say, 'God vill prrovide!'"

"Yes, Irena, I do say that, and I also believe it. Handel's *Messiah* it is. I leave it in your more than capable hands to get it done." Maggie had learned from Ed the importance of letting others take responsibility in the life of the church. (I leave this in your capable hands was an Ed-ism she used regularly.) "Now, shall we look at hymns for Sunday?"

Just then, Maggie heard Sylvia Smits come into the church office. She looked out her door and saw Sylvia with a bunch of brightly colored gladiolas and two grocery bags of fresh garden vegetables. Sylvia owned and ran The Garden Shop in town.

"Howdy doody, Hank! What a glorious day!" She kept right on moving toward Maggie's office. "Is Pastor Maggie in?"

"I'm sorry, Sylvia, but she's with someone right now." Hank's mouth was full of donut. "You'll have to wait."

Hank got up from his desk, wiping his sticky fingers on his pants, but was too late to stop her. Sylvia walked into Maggie's office. Irena turned on her, her face contorting. Sylvia didn't notice.

Smiling, with a little giggle, she said, "Good morning, Pastor Maggie! Good morning, Irena! These were all picked fresh from my vegetable garden behind the shop just this very morning. I seem to live in the Garden of Eden." Sylvia chortled with glee. "And I brought you some gladiolas too. Aren't they gorgeous? I was hoping we could have some on the altar for Sunday, but you-know-who won't hear of it. Oh well, you can enjoy."

"GET OUT! GET OUT! GET OUT!!!" Irena screamed, irate at the interruption.

Maggie thought Irena's head might actually explode.

"Irena, please stop." She turned to Sylvia, who was now on the verge of tears. "Thank you, Sylvia. The gladiolas are lovely. And thank you for the vegetables. But you do know that I live alone, don't you? I just can't eat all these by myself, but I appreciate your generosity. Are there others who—?"

Irena picked up her music and her glare shot daggers at both Maggie and Sylvia.

"Intolerrable! I vill not be treated in dis fashion. No cantata! No Handel! No Irena! I qvit!!"

She turned to leave. As she got to the door, one of her high heels got stuck in a wayward zucchini. She kept walking, spraying zucchini mush with each step.

Sylvia said, "Oh, I'm so sorry. I . . . I didn't mean to cause such a . . ." But the tears were flowing now.

Maggie moved some green peppers from the top of her Kleenex box and handed it over to Sylvia.

"Sylvia, have a seat. We'll have a cup of coffee together. I'll be right back."

Maggie walked into Hank's office just in time to see him stuff half a donut in his mouth.

"Hank, would you mind making some of that fantastic coffee of yours and then bringing two cups into my office?"

Still chewing he said, "I'm on it, Pastor Maggie. Yessireebob, I am."

Maggie walked around to the sanctuary. It was empty. She sat in one of the back pews and said a quick prayer: "God, help. Irena . . . Sylvia . . . you know. Amen."

She made her way back to her office and sat with Sylvia, handing her tissue after tissue, until she calmed down. Maggie cheerfully accepted all the vegetables and the gladiolas. The two women sipped their coffee, and Maggie heard all about the flowers and vegetables that consumed Sylvia's life. Sylvia seemed lonely. No, Sylvia was lonely. It wasn't surprising when her entire focus was tending to plant life. She reminded Maggie of Prince Charles, who apparently regularly chatted away to his garden plants.

When Sylvia finally left, Maggie called Irena and apologized for the interruption to their meeting earlier. Maggie had learned in the past two months that Irena's feathers ruffled quickly, but she only needed some overstated praise to unruffle them again. Maggie gave the overstated praise. *More lies.* Irena ranted on for good measure but was talking about Sunday's hymns by the end of the conversation. Another deep sigh for Maggie. *How often do I stop breathing during the day?*

Maggie was getting ready to go back to the parsonage so she could begin her sermon for Sunday when Hank led Max Solomon into her office. Max was the youngest son of the dead Rupert Solomon.

"Well, hi, Max," Maggie said, surprised. "How are you doing today?"

"Pastor Maggie," Max began, "I don't want to take up too much of your time. But I wanted to thank you again for the service you did for my dad yesterday. He didn't always have the best reputation, and he wasn't always the greatest dad, but he tried. He raised all three of us boys after our mother died. I was only four years old at the time. I'll just say that he got some things right once in a while. My brothers don't have a lot of good to say about him. But I remember the good, and I'm trying to forget the bad. I'm not a church-going man, but yesterday I think I met God for the first time. And I liked him. Pastor Maggie, you were the one who introduced me to him. So, thank you, and I'll see you Sunday."

Max stood up and held out his hand. Maggie stood and shook his hand. She looked him in the eye and said quietly, "I can hardly wait. Bless you, Max."

"I have been." He made his way toward the door and then turned. "You must really like vegetables."

5

Maggie's best friend in seminary was Nora Drew. Maggie and Nora also shared a huge crush on Bradley Cooper. Maggie was in love with his eyes, Nora with his teeth. Until the day Nora saw Dan Wellman. The first day of Hebrew class, Dan walked purposefully into the classroom—a lanky six foot four, with brown hair and green eyes and a smile that put Bradley's to shame, according to Nora. For the first time in her life she wished she wasn't wearing sweats and that she had at least attempted to get a brush through her curly hair.

Dan didn't seem to mind. That Friday night they shared a chicken pesto pizza and talked baseball. Dan became a regular guest at Maggie and Nora's apartment. The three friends studied, ate, and dreamt of the future. Secretly, Maggie was glad to have Bradley all to herself.

During seminary, each student spent one year in a local ministry internship. Many students completed their internships in a church. Some students worked as chaplain assistants in nursing homes and funeral homes. Maggie did her seminary internship at the local hospital, working in the chaplain's office. Dan and Nora worked at Jesus Lives and So Do We! megachurch. They taught middle school students and ran the youth group. Nora loved their energy, curiosity, and willingness to try new things, and she welcomed the chance to encourage them through the bumpy years of adolescence.

During their final year of seminary, Nora and Dan remained at Jesus Lives and So Do We! part-time. No one was surprised when they got the call to full-time youth ministry. Nora chose to stay with the middle school youth. Dan took charge of the high school kids. Maggie patiently waited for some engagement news from her two best friends. Their romance was evident, exciting, and a little nauseating.

Maggie's experience in the chaplain's office had been less fun than the work with youth. In her young eyes, Maggie saw Reverend Dill, the hospital chaplain, as too methodical and trite. He entered each patient's room with Maggie in tow. He had three questions he asked each patient:

"How are you doing today?"

"What are you here for?"

"May I pray with you?"

These weren't terrible questions. What was terrible was when he repeated them to the exact same patient the following day. His pat remark, "God heals our every ill," along with his memorized word-for-word prayer, made Maggie cringe.

One day she asked, "Reverend Dill, is there something I can do here at the hospital to help you with the visits? It might be a good learning experience for me."

Reverend Dill didn't make eye contact. "Now, Maggie, a hospital isn't a place to make mistakes with pastoral care. It's important for you to watch and learn. I've done this for forty years. You haven't even graduated from seminary yet." He chuckled. It wasn't a pleasant chuckle. He was annoyed. Why had the seminary sent a female? "I'm afraid some of the cases you will see might make you a little too emotional."

He walked down the hall away from her. Maggie fumed at his condescension and self-righteousness.

"Reverend Dill?" He turned. "Don't you think that maybe the women patients would be more comfortable talking with a woman?"

"I don't think that's the case. I think all patients want someone experienced. A man of God." He didn't even hear himself. "How old are you, Margaret?"

"Twenty-five."

"Then I doubt you could connect with a woman in her seventies dealing with cancer."

"I don't think connecting with other people is dependent on age, do you?"

"I do. Now this conversation is over. Let's get to room five fifty-four." That was the end of that.

Maggie realized she could learn as much about how to do ministry well by watching someone do it poorly. She made mental notes about what *not* to do when visiting the sick.

Maggie obeyed Reverend Dill and did as she was told. Except on one occasion.

One Friday afternoon, Maggie trotted after Reverend Dill to the maternity ward. They were on their way to visit a young mother who had just lost her baby to stillbirth. Of course, she and her husband were inconsolable. Reverend Dill asked his three questions and recited his prayer. Maggie desperately wanted to disappear or crack him over the head with a chair, but she remained silent.

But the next morning, Maggie drove back to the hospital. She bypassed the chaplain's office, even though she knew Reverend Dill wouldn't be there on the weekend, and made her way to the maternity ward. The mother (who was no longer a mother) was sleeping. Maggie spotted on the outside of the door that the woman's name was Kristy. She awoke when Maggie sat down. When she saw Maggie, she overflowed with tears as she remembered her lost little baby. Maggie sat and held her hand. Maggie felt her eyes fill with tears and then felt the tears slide down her cheeks. They cried together until they had no more tears for the time being.

As they both blew their noses, Kristy asked Maggie, "Is my baby in heaven? I need to know that she isn't just dead, that she isn't just nothing out there."

Maggie thought she understood. She looked into Kristy's swollen eyes and tried to swallow the large lump in her own throat.

"What was your baby's name?"

"Anna Lee."

Maggie cleared her throat. "Kristy, Anna Lee is in heaven. I believe that completely. It's not right because she should be here in your arms.

You should be getting ready to take her home and be her mom. And I am so sorry that you cannot do that." Maggie's eyes began to leak again, but she pulled herself together enough to say, "Anna Lee's death doesn't make sense. It's not the way it should be. You can be as angry and as heartbroken as you want. You have that right. You can scream and yell and blame God. You can even hate God for as long as you need to. He can take it. Only remember, Anna Lee isn't 'just nothing out there.' She is safe, and she is loved."

Maggie stopped. She knew more words wouldn't help, and this mother (who was no longer a mother) was going to have to make the long journey into and through the worst kind of grief—the loss of a child.

Maggie stayed until Kristy's husband, Mike, came to take her home. Maggie didn't pray with them. They didn't want her to. God had seemed to betray them. Talking to God in front of them would only be painful. So she hugged them both as they left the room, Kristy in a wheelchair with a pink diaper bag on her lap.

Then Maggie sat down on Kristy's bed and prayed *for* them. She prayed and questioned and hoped. She wondered how much pain a human being could survive. She wondered what God had to say for himself on a day like this.

She drove home and poured out the whole story to Nora, who had tears to shed for Kristy, Mike, Anna Lee, and her best friend. They cried and talked and finally decided to watch *Mary Poppins* as a way of escape.

Maggie owned every Walt Disney movie ever made. She collected them throughout high school. Over the years, she added every season of *The Vicar of Dibley*, Agatha Christie's *Miss Marple*, and *Midsomer Murders*. She pulled out the bin after a big exam or a particularly hard day in Greek.

Maggie and Nora agreed that even *Mary Poppins* couldn't relieve the pain of the day on the maternity ward. Maggie didn't sleep that night.

The day Maggie sat with Kristy was the day she learned two important lessons about ministry: listen for the need of the person you are with (whether or not they can tell you with words), and sometimes people just need you there to help them cry. There aren't always answers. After Maggie told Ed about these two discoveries, he never ceased to set her own words before her.

It was August, and Maggie had been in full-time ministry at Loving the Lord for two months. It had been six months since Anna Lee had died. She had never seen Kristy again. She didn't even know her last name. But Maggie still prayed for Kristy and Mike. They would pop into her head at different times, and she would immediately send out a prayer for their broken hearts.

That morning, Maggie was out early for her run and it was already hot. August in Michigan was only two things: hot and miserable. Maggie began to sweat just tying her running shoes. She loved the parsonage; however, the lack of air conditioning made the days and nights uncomfortable at best. The church had provided fans, and Maggie made good use of them. There were promises of an air conditioning system to be installed, but that hadn't happened yet. Maggie put ice cubes in Marmalade's water bowl to help keep him cool. He was wearing a fur coat, after all.

As she ran down Freer Road on her way to Meadow View, she saw a sign in the front yard of what had become a familiar house because of the large tire swing hanging from an oak tree in the front. The sign said, *FREE KITTENS. MOTHER KILLED. NEED GOOD HOMES.*

Maggie stopped in her sweaty tracks. Her heart sank as she reread the sign. It was pretty straightforward. She walked up to the front door and knocked, completely forgetting it was six thirty a.m. A little girl who looked to be five years old opened the door. She was blonde with a pixie haircut and dressed in a fairy costume, waving a long, pink feather. Maggie could hear a television in the background.

"Hi there," Maggie said as she bent down. "Is your mommy home?"

"I'm going to cast a spell on you!" The little pixie giggled and flourished her feather wand.

"Oh, no! What will happen to me?" Maggie played along.

"You will be an ugly witch until a frog kisses you!" The pixie was giggling so hard she began to drool.

Maggie was enchanted. Just then, the pixie's mother came to the door.

"Carrie, what are you doing?" She didn't sound angry, just a little frazzled. Behind her, a little boy hung on her leg. Definitely the pixie's little brother. They were flanked by two huge black Labrador Retrievers, and Maggie got a glimpse of a large Siamese cat on the kitchen counter.

Maggie smiled and said, "I believe I'm going to be turned into an ugly witch any second now. I may be in need of a frog."

The pixie's brother looked up at her with solemn eyes. "I'm a fwog."

"Oh! Well, that's a huge relief." Maggie wanted to squeeze him.

She stood up and looked at the mother. "Hi, I'm Maggie Elzinga. I'm the new pastor at Loving the Lord Community Church. I run past your house every day, and I just saw your sign. I'm wondering about your poor kittens."

"Come on in. We're just starting our day, aren't we, kids? You have already met Carrie, and this is Carl. I'm Cassandra Moffet."

"It's nice to meet all three of you," Maggie said.

Cassandra continued, "We found these three kittens in one of our front bushes. They were howling like their lives depended on it, which come to find out, they did. The poor mama cat had been hit by a car right out front. We had a little funeral for her, didn't we, kids?"

Carrie became very serious. "I said the words at the funeral. We buried her in Mommy's shoe box."

Maggie thought Carrie probably did a better job with the cat than Maggie had done with Rupert Solomon. Maybe Carrie could give her some advice.

"Well, Carrie, that was very nice of you. What will you do with the babies now?"

Carl piped up. "They need new mommies."

Maggie could hear Ed's voice in the back of her head. *Maggie, don't be so impetuous. You make a lot of emotional decisions. Take the time to think things through. You already have a cat. That's one too many.*

Maggie waved Ed out of her brain and asked, "May I see them?"

When Maggie first saw the little creatures, she could hardly believe they would survive without a feline mother. They were the tiniest kittens she had ever seen. Their eyes were barely open, which Cassandra explained meant they were, at the most, three weeks old. They would need milk.

"I've been using an eyedropper every four hours to feed them. But if you had a little bit of milk in a small bowl near one, I think they drink on their own. You would need to keep them in a confined place for a bit to stay safe until they could be on their own and were steady on their paws."

Maggie looked at the two little calicos and the one little tabby. One of the calicos opened her mouth and let out a squeak. Maggie picked her up and held her close.

"Would you like to come home with me?"

After more chatting, with much direction-giving by Cassandra—she had no idea how many kittens Maggie had raised with an eyedropper, but Maggie just let her talk—Maggie made an invitation to the little family to come to church the following Sunday morning.

The calico kitten was carried home with her new human.

"I think I'll call you Cheerio," Maggie whispered.

Marmalade had a *cat*astrophic fit. It was an absolute *cat*astrophe. Maggie quickly realized that bringing a baby kitten home to her "only child" meant no sleep for her and terror for the kitten. Marmalade sniffed around his cat carrier (*his* cat carrier!) where the little infidel was ensconced.

Maggie put her sweatshirt in the carrier because it was the softest thing she owned. She had put in a tiny teabag holder full of milk and a shoebox lid with some kitty litter. Surprisingly, the wobbly little kitten could toddle into the lid and take care of her private business. Her little pink tongue lapped up the milk. It was another outrage for Marmalade, who never got milk.

On day two, Maggie let Cheerio out of the carrier. Marmalade circled the enemy and hissed. Cheerio began to follow Marmalade around, perhaps hoping for a cuddle. Marmalade sniffed, hissed, sniffed, and growled. Maggie lifted Cheerio to the kitchen tabletop. Cheerio walked around the perimeter of the table on unsteady legs but with her tiny tail held high. Then she crawled into Maggie's empty teacup and looked up pathetically.

"Mew."

On day three, Cheerio walked out of the carrier and straight up to Marmalade and sniffed. Cheerio chirped. Maggie waited for Marmalade's hiss and growl, but he didn't do either. Instead, miracle of miracles, he began to lick the little kitten's face. He gave her a head-to-toe bath and then curled up next to her on the kitchen rug. They took a very long nap.

And that was that. Marmalade was raising a kitten. He was a very thorough mother.

Maggie picked up her phone and dialed.

"Hello, Maggie," said her mother.

"Hi ya, Mom. How's it going over there?"

"It's hot. How is life in lovely little Cherish?"

"It's lovely and hot. I just wanted to tell you that I adopted a new family member this week. She's very tiny but she lost her mother. So I gave her to Marmalade."

Maggie's mother was the guilty party when it came to Maggie's love of cats. Both her mom and dad loved animals and weren't above rescuing a stray here and there. Maggie grew up with cats and dogs, laboratory rats (her mother was a psychologist and spent time in the lab), hamsters, and birds. Maggie and her brother, Bryan, were crazy about animals. Her mother, who was always educating her children, would buy books about each new pet so that Maggie and Bryan could learn about habits and habitat. Maggie knew calling her mother and telling her about Cheerio would give her the affirmation she needed for her impulsive action.

"What did the church council say?" her mother asked pragmatically. "Didn't you tell me the church has a 'no pets' policy, but they were being nice about Marmalade?"

Silence.

"Maggie?"

"Mmmm?"

"The church council?"

"They don't know quite yet. But I don't think it will be a problem. She fits in a teacup, and she knows what litter is for. She's very brilliant. Plus, you're supposed to say, 'Oh, how sweet! Oh, how cute! Maggie, you're wonderful!'"

"I don't talk like that."

"Well, I just wanted you to know. I'll tell the council at the meeting this Thursday." Maggie felt a little deflated.

"I do think it's wonderful that you saved the kitten, Maggie. You have a good heart. Have a pleasant sleep."

"Thanks, Mumsy, you too."

"Hi, Nora. I rescued a motherless kitten three days ago. Marmalade hated her for two days and now is madly in love. He's a good mama. Her name is Cheerio. She fits in a teacup."

"What did the church council say?"

"You sound like my mother."

6

Maggie made the trek from the parsonage to the church, having left Marmalade in charge for the morning. He and Cheerio were curled up on Maggie's robe on the floor because Cheerio was still unable to jump up or jump down from anything as skyscraper-ish as a bed or a couch.

As she got closer to the sanctuary, she saw Bill Baxter's red hair and Fitch Dervish's large rear end. *Oh, good grief!* She almost retraced her steps to the parsonage, but Bill had seen her and Fitch turned to see what Bill was looking at.

"Good morning, Pastor Maggie," Bill said miserably.

"Good morning, Bill," Maggie said brightly. "Fitch," she said, less brightly.

"Good morning there, Pastor Maggie," Fitch responded. "We're just making sure this new ramp is legal and up to code, unlike the other one that must have been built in the dark ages. It was a death trap." Fitch clenched his clipboard a little tighter.

"I'm guessing Bill knows what he's doing. He's been building things practically since the day he was born," Maggie said, smiling at Bill.

Fitch let out a long, deep sigh. "Well, that's where you might be wrong, miss. Just about anyone can build. It's all about the codes. You'd be surprised at some of the 'building' that goes on in this town without a permit." He tried to make air quotes when he said "building," but his clipboard got in the way. "Last week, I discovered a deck going up on the back of a house without a permit. It was being built with spit and a prayer, I tell you what. We can't have those kind of shenanigans going on now, can we?"

Maggie looked at Bill, who rolled his eyes then looked at the ground.

"I wondered if I might steal Bill away from you for a bit," Maggie said, looking at Fitch. His glasses were going from dark to light as clouds slowly rolled through the sky. "It's just that I have something in my office that needs fixing. Nothing big, but I need Bill's expertise."

"Well, maybe we should both take a look."

Fitch slung his man-bag over his shoulder and began to head into church.

"Bill can handle it. Why don't you just check your codes out here?" Then Maggie had a very naughty thought. "Oh, and by the way, when I was running this morning, I think I noticed a shed being built behind a house out on Dancer Road. I'm sorry, I don't remember the house number. But I'm sure you already know about it, Fitch." Maggie had never run to Dancer Road. It was five miles from the parsonage.

Fitch stood at attention like a hunting dog. "Can you give me an approximate location?"

"Wait, it might have been Lima Center. Gosh, Fitch, I wish I could remember which one it was. I'm so sorry."

"Don't you worry a bit. I have a nose for these things. I'll go take a look around. Bill, I'll meet you back here later."

Fitch walked to his truck, his rear end wobbling as he walked at breakneck speed.

Bill looked at Maggie with a shy smile. Then he actually laughed. Maggie had never heard him laugh before. She had barely ever heard him speak.

"I don't have anything for you to look at, Bill. But this might buy you some time to work on the ramp in peace."

"Thanks, Pastor Maggie. Do you tell lies a lot? It's just that I didn't think you were supposed to do that."

Maggie thought for a moment. "Only occasionally, for the good of a parishioner who may be in danger of being annoyed to death."

Bill's warm laugh escaped again. Maggie liked the sound.

"I'll see you later, Bill." Maggie skipped up the steps to the sanctuary.

Hank was busy typing Sunday's bulletin, and Maggie could hear Doris vacuuming somewhere in the depths of the church.

"Good morning, Hank."

"Good morning, Pastor Maggie." Hank didn't lift his eyes from his work. "I need a sermon title for Sunday when you get a chance, and Marla is waiting for you in your office."

"Thank you." She headed toward her office door.

"I hear you have a new cat." Hank continued typing.

"What? How did you know that, Hank?" Maggie was slightly horrified.

"Does the church council know?" he asked, typing away.

"No, Hank, they don't."

"Well, you better tell them. Word's getting around."

"How in the world is the word getting around, Hank?"

"Cassandra Moffet was in The Sugarplum yesterday and told everyone that the nice pastor from Loving the Lord had adopted one of her orphaned kittens. I believe that nice pastor is you."

"Well, good grief." Maggie didn't know what to think. She felt as if she had been caught robbing a bank. "The council meeting is tonight. They can all meet her then." Maggie tried to lift her chin but couldn't quite maneuver it.

She went into her office to see Marla's happy face. Marla was stacking vegetables on top of Maggie's small bookshelf, trying to clear a space on the desk.

"Good morning, Pastor Maggie. I was just organizing your vegetables. Won't it be nice when gardening season is over?" She giggled.

"Yes indeedy!" Maggie said with gusto. "I'm preparing myself for autumn squash and root vegetables from Sylvia throughout the fall, but then a nice little reprieve come November. How are you? It's so good to see your friendly face." Maggie was still stinging inside from Cheerio's unplanned public premiere.

"I hear you have a delicious new kitten at the parsonage."

55

Marla threw a rotten tomato into the trash can.

"Yes. I have a delicious new kitten at the parsonage. Is that a problem?" Maggie was getting a little nervous.

"Oh, not for me," said Marla, looking up. "Mrs. Abernathy is the one. She is being quite a silly-billy about this, I must say." Sometimes Marla spoke in her "children and worship" voice without knowing it.

"Well, I can't handle her right now. I'll deal with her later. Tonight's meeting should be quite interesting. What can I do for you this morning?"

"Ah! I am so excited! I did my research and I found some children's books on death, so you and I can begin planning our 'Death for Children' class."

"We might want to reconsider that title," said Maggie carefully. "What are the books?"

Marla laid them out on Maggie's desk:

No, Johnny, Grandpa Isn't Asleep

You Can Be an Angel Too Someday!

Heaven Really Isn't as Boring as It Sounds

Maggie was speechless. Not in a good way.

"Wow, Marla, you have put a lot of work into this." She was thinking fast now. "How about one last piece of research? What if you do a survey of the parents and see how many of them would like this class for their children? Then we might have a better idea of what the needs are. Could you type up a survey and have it ready by Sunday?"

Marla was awestruck once again by Pastor Maggie's sheer brilliance. "Of course! That is a great idea, Pastor Maggie. I will have a survey configured for your perusal on Sunday. I won't report on this at the council meeting tonight. You and I will discuss my findings sometime next week. I love working with you."

Maggie and Marla's mutual admiration society fed both their needs to be appreciated and to have an ally in the midst of any church war. Their dramatics were lost on both of them.

"Marla, you are a dream. Thanks for everything you do. Oh, I'm not sure if we'll see them, but I invited Cassandra, Carrie, and Carl to come to church on Sunday. It would be nice to have them here."

Marla packed up her books and said, "Yes, it would. Those children need a good dose of Jesus, and the sooner the better!" She walked toward the door. "See you tonight, Pastor Maggie. And don't worry too much about Mrs. Abernathy. She's not happy unless she's upset about something. Have a good day."

"And you." Maggie took a deep breath. *I can handle this. I am the pastor, not a little girl to be chastised.*

Maggie could hear raised voices in Hank's office. Apparently, Doris had come in to clean and not only cleaned all the furniture but also attacked Hank's head with her feather duster.

"Doris! I don't need to be dusted! Thank you very much!"

Doris ignored his rant and made her way into Maggie's office.

"Good morning, Pastor Maggie," she said and grabbed the trash can. "What's this? Why is there a rotten tomato in this trash can?" she asked accusingly, eyebrows racing toward one another.

"Good morning, Doris. Because Marla was going through the vegetables and found it, and she didn't want it dripping down my bookcase."

"Well, now I have to wash out this trash can. We can't have tomato mush in the trash. Do you know how unsanitary that is?"

All of sudden, Doris dropped the trash, grabbed a can of Raid from her cleaning cart, and sprayed long and hard at a spot on Maggie's wall.

"Doris! What are you doing?!"

"Killing a fly."

"Please, could you come back later to clean? I'm going back to the parsonage in a bit to work on my sermon, and then the office is all yours, okay?"

"I hear you have a new cat."

Maggie ignored her, got up, and went into Hank's office.

"Do you have the council agendas?"

He silently handed them to her.

"Thank you. Sermon title: 'No One Walks on Water but Jesus.' I'll be in the parsonage for the rest of the day."

Maggie noticed she was getting unnaturally good at stomping.

Doris came out of Maggie's office and looked at Hank. "What's her problem?"

Maggie entered the parsonage, went straight to the kitchen, and put the tea kettle on. She looked at her tea cup. It was the one Cheerio had been sitting in four days ago. *A kitten in a teacup. A tempest in a teacup.* Maybe living in the parsonage hadn't been the best idea.

At first, she had loved when parishioners dropped by to say hello. Everyone wanted to see how she was settling in. Some people came by to see how she decorated. Some dropped off plates of cookies and loaves of homemade bread. It was a good way to get to know people fast. But there was that day last month when she wanted to get a little sun. She was lying on a towel in her bathing suit in the backyard when not only "slimy" Redford stopped by but also Harold Brinkmeyer and then, worst of all, Mrs. Abernathy. Maggie was quickly aware that her bikini was not "suitable" attire for a pastor.

Now, as she made her Lady Grey tea, she felt overwhelmed. She had a sermon to write and a council meeting in the dining room that night. She had the high school Sunday school lesson to prepare. There were only six high school students, and rarely did they all show up at the same time on any given Sunday. Maggie had grown frustrated as she spoke to the parents about the importance of church for the youth. She wanted to strangle the ones who looked at her helplessly and said, "But I can't *make* him go to church." She wanted to say, "How is it they show up at school, then? Don't they have a choice about that too?"

In the middle of July, after her first six weeks, she had called Ed.

"I think we're supposed to be in the 'honeymoon' stage, but it doesn't feel like it. Hank is great, but people take advantage of him, and he hates it when they dump trash on his desk. Irena is just scary. You know what she told me yesterday when we argued about the choir picnic? 'Pastoor Maggie, you know vat it means, my last name, *Dalca*?' I said, 'No, Irena. I don't.' She glared at me out of her bright-green shadowed eyes and said, 'Lightning!' I actually jumped! Doris thinks cleaning takes priority over everything else. I also think I could be on the verge of death-by-vegetables. And Mrs. Abernathy and her horrid zinnias are a constant bane of my existence. Seminary taught me Greek and church history but not a whole lot about how to deal with so many personalities. If it weren't for the people, work would be great."

"Maggie, the church is people," Ed replied. "People are work. You are good at your work. Like any family, we all get on each other's nerves from time to time. You are loved, Maggie, and you know how to love. Every one of your parishioners is carrying around their own load. You may never know what that is, but just remember they have their own invisible baggage."

"You're right. I'll try to do better with that. It's just that some days seem so unmanageable. How do I manage them?"

"Maybe you're not supposed to. Just be sure they don't manage you." Maggie came back to the present and sipped her tea. This day would not manage her. She sat in her lovely parsonage study and stared out at the three pine trees and the red wagon full of dancing flowers. She slowly closed her eyes, and instead of whining, she began to thank God for vegetables, for Raid and feather dusters, for the enthusiasm of Marla, and she tried to add Mrs. Abernathy to the mix but had significantly less conviction.

She opened her eyes. She had work to do. She walked back to the kitchen and took out the flour, sugar, butter, and eggs. She would bake a pie for the council meeting tonight. Then she would write her sermon. Cheerio tiptoed into the room and meowed. Maggie picked her up and was immediately struck with an idea.

It was six forty-five p.m., and the Westminster chimes rang in the parsonage. Maggie answered the door and welcomed Harold Brinkmeyer into the dining room. Harold's teeth were on full display. He came early to discuss the agenda for the meeting.

It was only the second council meeting for Maggie. In June, she had met with the council for the first time, and it was basically a love-fest to welcome her. It included an ice cream social with the whole congregation. At that time, Maggie had only been in residence for three weeks. The church never met in July due to people being away on vacations, and just to have a break in the summertime. Now it was the first Thursday of August, and that night would be Maggie's first "real" council meeting. Beginning in September, the council meetings would go back to the third Thursday of the month. But after going without a meeting in July, Harold and Maggie thought it a good idea to have August's meeting earlier.

"Hi, Pastor Maggie," Harold grinned. "Hank sent me the agenda, and it all looks in order. The meeting should be short and sweet."

He couldn't help thinking that's exactly how he would describe Maggie. He looked at the dining room table set with small china plates, coffee cups, and saucers from the church's collection. In the middle of the table was a beautiful lemon custard pie topped with clouds of meringue. Harold could smell the lemony sweetness and swallowed hard.

"What have you made for us tonight? That pie looks delicious!" Harold was very effusive with his praise and teeth.

"I hope you all enjoy it, Harold," Maggie said as she set the forks and napkins around the table. "Everyone should be here tonight. I will be adding one more item to the agenda."

Just then Marmalade walked into the room followed by his hero-worshiping kitten. Harold looked down and smiled. He had heard about the kerfuffle regarding the new kitten and had decided immediately to back Maggie in keeping the little orphan.

"Would that happen to be the agenda item?" he asked, pointing at Cheerio.

"As a matter of fact, yes." Maggie picked up the kitten, much to Marmalade's distress. He began to paw at her leg, staring beseechingly at his kitten. "I'm going to feed them to get them out of the way. Excuse us."

She hoisted Marmalade underneath her arm and carried the felines into the kitchen.

Harold was besotted.

When Maggie returned, Redford, Jack, and Ellen had arrived. Maggie observed with secret delight that Jack and Ellen were seated next to each other. What if they were her first wedding? Redford stood a little too close to her and said, "Hey, Marge! How's it going?"

"Maggie."

"What?"

"Redford, my name is Maggie. Not Madge or Marge or Margie or Meg. Just Maggie. Pastor Maggie."

"You're so funny," Redford said in a monotone voice, adding an unattractive sneer.

"Thank you."

She turned to greet Charlotte Tuggle, who had just entered the dining room. Charlotte was the police chief of Cherish. Charlotte was fifty-six years old, stood six foot two, and weighed about two hundred fifty pounds. She wasn't to be messed with. She had twin boys, Mason and Brock, who were juniors in high school, and a daughter, Liz, who was a sophomore. Her husband, Fred, owned the gravel pit just north of town. Charlotte was no-nonsense and no-drama. She ran her police station and the entire town of Cherish with efficiency. She never overlooked the law.

Maggie had received several parking tickets during her first weeks in Cherish. First, the church had decided it was time to repave the driveway of the parsonage. For five nights, she had to park on the street, which was prohibited at night. Charlotte left a ticket on her car each night. When Maggie tried to dispute this, having no other place to park, she was met with a recitation of the exact law that prohibited parking on the streets of Cherish from one a.m. to five a.m. Maggie was livid. Charlotte remained calm. Second, Maggie had parked on the street in front of the Friendly Elder Care building to visit shut-ins. She had stayed longer than the allotted three hours. Visiting shut-ins was no reason to break the law, according to Charlotte. Maggie still hadn't paid her parking tickets. It was a point of contention between the two women.

"Good evening, Charlotte."

"Good evening, Pastor Maggie. We seem to have a little issue that hasn't yet been resolved."

"Charlotte, I am not paying those tickets. The church kindly kicked me out of my driveway to repave it, and I was visiting shut-ins, which is my job. I can't leave a parishioner in the middle of a conversation just to move my car, can I? I am the pastor of the church, taking care of the people of the church. I'm not a criminal. And so, I repeat: I am not paying those tickets. It's the principle of the matter." Maggie gave a sharp nod and quickly sat down, but her heart was racing. Charlotte was intimidating.

The rest of the council arrived—Sylvia with the inevitable bag of vegetables and Mrs. Abernathy carrying a vase of zinnias. She glanced suspiciously about the parsonage for the illegal alien. Everyone was finally seated around the dining room table. Harold passed out the agendas and began the meeting.

Agenda for Council Meeting
August 7, 2014

Pastor Maggie opens with prayer
Harold Brinkmeyer – Chairperson
Dr. Jack Elliot – Vice Chairperson
Charlotte Tuggle - Clerk
Report: Tom Wiggins – Building and Grounds
Report: Marla Wiggins – Education
Report: Redford Johnson – Finance
Report: Ellen Bright – Worship
Report: Mrs. Abernathy – Member Care
Report: Sylvia Smits – Fellowship
Any other business
Pastor Maggie closes with prayer

The meeting went well except for one little tussle between Mrs. Abernathy, Marla, and Sylvia regarding the Sunday school picnic. Mrs. Abernathy wanted to do a traditional Vacation Bible School program, similar to what she did in the 1970s. Marla wanted to rent a blow up bouncy castle to remind the children they were all part of God's royalty. Sylvia added to the castle idea by saying she would make crowns from the vines and gladiola flowers in her garden. Maggie could hardly believe the time being spent on this topic, but she was learning that every voice needed to be heard.

Maggie suggested the children, parents, and teachers go to the lake for a Saturday afternoon. They could roast hotdogs, make s'mores, swim, and play. Marla and Sylvia agreed that this was the best idea they had ever heard. Sylvia still offered to make crowns, and finally the discussion came to an end. Mrs. Abernathy was not pleased. Her mouth was drawn so tightly, her eyes bulged. Everyone ignored her.

They got to the end of the agenda, having heartily enjoyed the lemon custard pie and coffee, when Harold asked if there was any other business. Tiny Cheerio entered, as if on cue. Mrs. Abernathy, still stinging from the picnic disagreement, saw the kitten. The agenda in her hand began to shake. At her throat, a blotchy redness began to crawl up her face.

Maggie quickly picked up the kitten and said, "Yes. There is one more piece of business. This is it. Her name is Cheerio. I have heard throughout the day that some parishioners are upset that I've adopted a kitten. In retrospect, I should have brought this to the council first." At this point, Maggie put Cheerio on the table.

Cheerio looked at all the faces. Her little tail went up in the air, and she began a wobbly walk around the circumference of the table. Everyone, except Mrs. Abernathy, was charmed. The kitten was so tiny, so delicate, and so helpless. Maggie watched as Cheerio silently made her own case to stay in the parsonage. She walked in front of Jack and Ellen, and Ellen reached out to pet the tiny head. Again, on cue, Cheerio began to purr. Everyone, except for Mrs. Abernathy, began to *ooh* and *ahh* as Cheerio curled herself around Ellen's hand.

Then there was a startling howl. An orange blur flew onto the table. Marmalade was having none of this little parade. He looked like an angry, orange powder puff.

Maggie cried, "Marmalade! No! Stop!" She frantically reached for him.

Sylvia screamed.

Charlotte stood up, as if to break up a disorderly conduct situation, and then realized it was a cat.

Everyone watched in fascinated horror.

Marmalade, slipping on the smooth oak table, lost his purchase and unceremoniously slid into the empty pie plate, china dessert plates, cups, and saucers and sent them crashing into a million sticky pieces against the wall and onto the floor. Maggie watched as if it was happening in slow motion while the dishes flew off the table. Dishes that belonged to the parsonage! Marmalade was a cat in a china shop. Cheerio huddled under Ellen's hand, but Marmalade grabbed his kitten by the scruff of her neck and jumped down from the table, growling. He ran out of the dining room and up the stairs with the kitten in his mouth. Everyone was silent. Maggie put her head in her hands and groaned.

Just as Mrs. Abernathy gasped, ready to begin her lambast, Jack Elliot began to laugh. He sat back in his chair and laughed so hard that the others couldn't help but join in. The laughing continued as Maggie and Sylvia quickly picked up the worst of the mess and threw away the broken dishes. Maggie waved her off, saying she would get the rest of it later.

"Pastor Maggie," Jack said as they sat back down again, "I don't think Cheerio can go anywhere. What would happen to Marmalade if you took her away? That was the most hilarious thing I've seen in a long time. Too bad no one was recording it, or we could put it on YouTube. I'm sorry about the dishes, however."

"You think this is a joke, Dr. Elliot?" Mrs. Abernathy sputtered.

"No, Mrs. Abernathy, I don't," Jack said calmly. "I also don't think it's a tragedy, or even a problem."

Maggie smiled with relief. She didn't look at Mrs. Abernathy's end of the table as she said, "I had an idea today. I planned on Cheerio as my intro tonight, but that didn't work the way I thought it would. My idea is this: I would like to have an animal blessing service. It would be something we would do this fall. It is traditionally a Catholic and Episcopalian service, but why can't we have one? I know many of you have pets, along with other parishioners. What if we take a Sunday afternoon and thank God for them?"

The council members were smiling and nodding now.

"You can't possibly mean let animals into the sanctuary!" Mrs. Abernathy gasped.

"Yes. I mean precisely that. They are God's creatures, and we are meant to care for them. I want to bless them." Maggie gained courage by the second. "And furthermore, there are still two orphaned kittens at Cassandra's house in need of good homes. What do you say? Are any of you interested in adopting?"

Mrs. Abernathy ferociously gathered up her papers and notebook. Her cheeks were bright red now, and her eyes protruded right out of her face.

"First, you put a filthy animal on the dining room table where we eat. Then we endure animals breaking the lovely antique dishes belonging *to the church*! Do you realize the damage cats can do to this parsonage? We have provided this house with carpeting and furniture, but they are not *yours*. Animals are not meant to be in this parsonage. Now you want to bring animals into our sanctuary. You think this is some kind of joke. I vote against you keeping the kitten, and against your ridiculous animal service. I want that on record, Charlotte!"

Mrs. Abernathy looked around the table and back at Maggie. Her voice became low and too controlled.

"I don't think you understand something. We are here to *train* you. This is your first church, and you are very young. It is our job as a council and a church to teach you how to be a pastor. We are here to show you what is right and what is wrong. You need guidance. There will be no animal blessing."

Maggie felt the air leave her lungs and the blood drain from her face. It felt as if she had been slapped. Tears began to sting her eyes, but she fought them back with all her strength. Mrs. Abernathy would not have the satisfaction of making her cry in front of the council.

A cacophony of voices erupted. Mrs. Abernathy was on the receiving end of the council's mutual anger and frustration. She sat in her chair in shocked silence. Finally, Maggie spoke.

"Please, everyone, just a moment, please."

She knew her face was flushed with embarrassment. She sat up as straight as she could, although she felt more like a Raggedy Ann doll. Everyone quieted down.

"Mrs. Abernathy," Maggie swallowed hard, "what you just said was not only hurtful to me, it was also insulting and disrespectful to everyone sitting here. It's true that I am young. It's true that this is my first call to a church. But I *have* been called by God. I'm sure I will make mistakes. I already have." Maggie took a shaky breath. "I love learning about church life by experiencing it every day here at Loving the Lord. But, Mrs. Abernathy," Maggie could feel her anger spurring her on, "I am not a child to be raised or trained by you. I am your pastor. I am a servant of this church, and I am also the leader. I have been called by *God*. If you don't like it, that's who you should take it up with. I will keep the kitten. The animal blessing will be the first Sunday of October. If there is no more business, I will close in prayer."

But before Maggie could begin to pray, Mrs. Abernathy had gathered her papers and stalked out into the night.

Dear Ed,

Mrs. Abernathy and I have each thrown down a gauntlet. I have no idea how this will turn out.

I already know what you will say about the kitten, so there is no need for you to say anything. However, I do need your wisdom regarding Mrs. Abernathy. I have never met such an angry woman. She patronizes me and is rude to everyone else. I know her anger is masking something, her invisible baggage. The thing is, she won't let me get close enough to find out.

I need your advice. Does this happen to all first-time pastors? I had no idea how hard this was going to be. We were all safe at seminary. We were encouraged to try new worship styles. We were expected to question, to argue, and to form our belief systems. But trying to change the way "things have always been" doesn't seem to work out here in the real church.

Give my love to Jo.
Maggie

Maggie turned out the light on her desk. After Mrs. Abernathy left, the others had done their best to lighten the evening. Harold, Ellen, Marla, and Sylvia stayed after everyone else left. They helped her clean up the rest of the mess of the dishes and the spatters of lemon custard on the floor and wall. They cooed over Cheerio. But by the time they had left, Maggie wasn't sure what being a pastor meant at all. She was only two months into ministry, and she felt like a failure.

Maggie made her way upstairs. All she wanted to do now was read the latest G. M. Malliet novel and disappear into the English countryside with Max Tudor and a wonderful murder mystery. That would definitely cheer her.

When she got to her room, she saw Marmalade and Cheerio. Cheerio was curled up in Maggie's fuzzy pink slipper, and Marmalade had wrapped himself around slipper and kitten. He was snoring blissfully. Maggie smiled, got ready for bed, and in her nightly prayers thanked God for cats.

∞

Mrs. Abernathy looked at her bedside clock. Three thirty-seven a.m. Only four minutes had elapsed since the last time she checked. As much as she told herself she would fall back to sleep, she knew she wouldn't. She had been awake since she got into bed at eleven p.m. She read two chapters from the Bible, as she did every night, but she was in Second Kings right now. It was as dry as crackers. Besides, she was distracted by other things.

She reached her hand around to the middle of her back. The bandage was bulky and larger than she had expected it to be. The doctor had told her to keep it bandaged for three days and then remove it, clean the wound, and rebandage it. The anesthetic had worn off from the afternoon, and the wound was causing her quite a bit of pain. She contemplated taking one of the prescribed pain pills.

Mrs. Abernathy had her yearly physical earlier in the month, and her doctor had noticed a suspicious lesion on her back. He had sent her to a dermatologist for more testing. When the dermatologist had scheduled a biopsy of the area, Mrs. Abernathy could sense his concern. For once in her adult life, she had been silent. Today had been the day, and she had driven herself into Ann Arbor. She would never have her doctoring done in Cherish. Too many busy-bodies spreading gossip. Plus, she wanted real professionals, thank you very much. The University of Michigan Health System, that's where any level-headed person would want to have treatment. And so, she went and had a quarter-sized piece of flesh removed from the middle of her back. She had requested a morning appointment so as not to miss the council meeting that evening. It would be Monday before she had the results of the biopsy. Mrs. Abernathy couldn't remember ever feeling so afraid.

Well, maybe . . .

She took a pain pill and after about twenty minutes fell into a fitful sleep.

7

Maggie awoke on Friday morning to an orange furry face and guttural purring. Marmalade was certain it was time for breakfast. Maggie looked and saw Cheerio still curled up in her slipper. Maggie got out of bed, pulled on her running clothes, and carried the two beasts downstairs. After leaving them breakfast, she was out the door. Her run and her prayer time were fraught with memories of the previous night's council meeting. She prayed for guidance (which she definitely needed), and she prayed for patience (which she needed more). Five miles later, she was back and cleaning up for the day. She had decided the council meeting could have been worse (maybe), and she needed to focus on that coming Sunday instead of thinking about the humiliation of Mrs. Abernathy.

She was excited because her parents, brother, Ed, and Jo were all making the drive over for the church service and staying for lunch afterward. Maggie was looking forward to the visit. She loved looking out into the congregation and seeing their faces. Her parents and Bryan had come once in June and again in July. The congregation fell all over them, welcomed them to worship, and surrounded them during coffee time.

Maggie's father, Dirk Elzinga, was an architect. He owned an architectural firm in Holland, Michigan, and his designs could be seen in many of the buildings of downtown Grand Rapids, Lansing, and even

Detroit. He was a mild man with a balding gray head, gentle blue eyes, and a subtle sense of humor. He loved his family and was proud of Maggie and her call into ministry.

When he'd heard rumbles in their local church in Zeeland about Maggie going into ministry, he went straight to the council and said he would like to be in on the conversation. He sat patiently, waiting for someone to speak. The pastor stumbled through some Scripture quotations about women not teaching men, but his voice trailed off when he looked at Dirk. Another council member, who looked as if his tie was strangling him due to the girth of his neck, said, "Now, now, why can't Maggie just teach Sunday school or sing in the choir? Those are the places for women."

Dirk had pulled out his own Bible and opened it. He read, "Galatians 3:27–28: 'As many of you as were baptized into Christ have clothed yourselves with Christ. There is no longer Jew or Greek, there is no longer slave or free, there is no longer male or female; for all of you are one in Christ Jesus.'" He looked at the entire council and said, "If you won't ordain women, then you better stop baptizing them as infants. You can't pick and choose how much of the covenant women receive. They are full members. It seems to me the apostle Paul says we're all one in Christ Jesus. Maggie's a daughter of this church. God has called her to ministry. There's nothing anyone can do about that. She needs love, support, and encouragement right now." He closed his Bible, stood, and left the room.

Maggie's mother, Mimi (Bootsma), was also from Dutch heritage. She was small, smaller than Maggie, had frosted blonde hair cut short and sparkling brown eyes. She had worked for years with mentally impaired patients at the local state hospitals. Now, she ran the psychology department at the college Maggie and her brother had graduated from in Holland. She was no-nonsense and spoke directly and honestly. She dressed professionally, always. She had a reputation as being one of the toughest professors at the college but was also very beloved. Students learned a great deal in her classroom and discovered the workload was actually worth it. Maggie idolized her mother.

Mimi never would have wasted her time going to a council meeting to defend Maggie. Not that she wouldn't defend Maggie to the death. She certainly would. But she wouldn't sit in a room of overstuffed men who had little, if any, cultural, biblical, or theological understanding. Even their pastor came woefully short on these issues. Being the daughter of a pastor, she had a shrewd eye for other pastors and people in a congregation. She encouraged Maggie to keep moving straight ahead and keep on God's path without being deterred by those infected with the disease of "perceived power" and prejudice. She knew all too well Maggie's tendency to take everything personally and then trip and fall into self-doubt.

Although the church council had originally voted not to support Maggie in her ministry aspirations, after Dirk's brief visit, they had another discussion and ended up voting seven to five to be her sponsoring church throughout her time at seminary. These were the guidelines of the seminary, but it was noted that she would not be allowed to preach in their pulpit. Ever. No one really knew what happened in that meeting, but it wasn't beyond the realm of possibility that the amount of money Dirk and Mimi tithed each year was a factor.

Bryan was Maggie's joy. He was three years younger than Maggie, and since his birth, she had made it clear to her mother that he was Maggie's baby. She helped bathe him and dress him, she gave him an occasional bottle, and she sang songs to him all day long. As he grew older, they were often mistaken for twins, their looks were so similar.

They became best friends and staunch allies, with the occasional rollicking fight thrown in for good measure. Mimi's lack of patience for these shenanigans often landed Bryan and Maggie in their respective rooms. They would have to draw an "apology picture" for each other. When they became older, they had to write an apology note, which was then read out loud. It was a brilliant tactic that taught personal responsibility and remorse for unkindness. Maggie and Bryan became better people and were never heard to say, "It wasn't my fault!"

Bryan went into college not knowing exactly what he wanted to do. But after spending a month in Uganda with a group from college, he was on fire for the plight of the poor and in love with the continent of Africa. He earned his international studies and political science degrees. Once he graduated, he searched for a non-profit job working directly with the countries of Africa.

He found one.

That coming Sunday would be the last time Maggie would see her brother for a long time. The following week he would fly to San Francisco to begin working with the Africa Hope organization. The whole family was excited for Bryan. They were all devastated for themselves. He was a true light in their lives.

Ed and Joanna were present for Maggie's first sermon and now would make their second visit. Ed wouldn't dissect her sermon immediately afterward. He had the wisdom to know it would be too raw and emotional. He would help Maggie dissect it later in the week. Maggie could sit with it for a while first, but he would have already received her letter regarding the council meeting. They would have a chance to discuss that little fiasco.

Jo would hug and kiss her and point out, very specifically, each statement of the sermon she thought Maggie so brilliantly made.

Who wouldn't love these people sitting in the pews?

But today was Friday. Maggie needed to start memorizing her sermon and put her Sunday school lesson together. She would need to go to the Cherish Market and pick up a roast and the ingredients for Bryan's favorite strawberry rhubarb pie. Her parents, along with Ed and Jo, would be bringing salads and bread to round out the meal.

Maggie was startled out of her thoughts when the Westminster chimes rang. She opened the front door and was surprised to see Dr. Jack Elliot standing there.

"Hi, Dr. Jack."

"Good morning, Pastor Maggie. I hope this isn't too early."

"No, of course not. Come on into the kitchen. May I get you some tea or coffee?"

"Coffee would be great."

He sat down on one of the chairs and then noticed Marmalade and Cheerio curled up on Maggie's bathrobe, which had become a fixture on the kitchen floor.

"How are you doing after the fireworks of last night?" he asked.

"Surprisingly well." She brewed him a cup of coffee from her Keurig. She hoped he liked hazelnut crème. "Normally, I would have hidden under my pillow for as long as possible, then gone for a run with a mask over my face, and then avoided the office and the entire town of Cherish for the day. Maybe I'm just getting used to being hated by Mrs. Abernathy." She laughed as she brewed herself a cup.

"She is a hard woman to like. I don't know her well, but she's clearly unhappy. Anyway, I'm glad you are fine. I really stopped by to let you know that Mrs. Becker isn't doing very well at Friendly Elder Care. She had a massive heart attack last night. We have called in hospice, and they are being careful not to say how much time she has left. But I can't imagine her lasting longer than a day or two."

Maggie sat up. "I need to get over there. Is she in a lot of pain, Jack?"

"No. She's on morphine now and is comfortable. I'm not just saying that. I know it sounds like something from a doctor TV show."

Maggie smiled. "I know you wouldn't just say that. I'll head over and see the family. I really appreciate you letting me know this."

They quickly finished their coffee and left the parsonage.

Maggie hopped in her car and drove down Middle Street to Friendly Elder Care. She found Mrs. Becker resting, just as Jack had said. Her two daughters, Beth and Jennifer, were with her. Maggie hadn't gotten to know Mrs. Becker well in the past two months but had visited a few times. She had met her daughters on separate occasions during those visits. They were long-time members of Loving the Lord, and both sisters were in their early fifties. She sat down on a folding chair and received the latest update.

"Mother had a heart attack last night," Beth explained slowly. "She was rushed to the hospital, but the damage had been extreme. Dr. Elliot sat with us for several hours as we made the decision to put Mother in hospice care."

"Dr. Elliot stayed with us through the night," Jennifer said. "He knew we were having a hard time deciding what to do. He was there for us and helped us with our decision. I'll never forget it." Jennifer sniffed, and Beth quickly joined her. "We finally decided to bring her back here from the hospital."

The three women settled in as they watched Mrs. Becker's chest slowly rise and fall.

Maggie couldn't help but wonder how this would go. She had never sat at the bedside of a dying person before. Her mind wandered to her sermon preparation and her lack of a Sunday school lesson. She had a pie to bake. *Good grief, Maggie. Stop it! This woman is dying!* Jack had said it wouldn't be long. She could do this. She hoped. She remembered Ed's wise words, *People won't remember your sermons, Maggie, but they will remember you being with them at the most significant times of their lives. Always show up.*

The hospice nurses regularly came in and checked on their patient. They brought coffee and cookies for Beth, Jennifer, and Maggie from the dining room. Maggie heard story after story about Mrs. Becker as her daughters comforted themselves with these memories. It seemed Mrs. Becker was a remarkable woman.

Beth and Jennifer laughed when they told Maggie about the day their mother said she was going on strike because no one picked up their things, like clothes and books, around the house. For an entire day, there was no cooking, no lunches made for school, and no washing. She didn't pick up one single thing from anyone's floor. By that evening, the girls and their father realized the tragic future that awaited them if they didn't put their things in the proper places.

"Mother never had to go on strike again!" Jennifer smiled.

Then they cried as they remembered how, every Saturday night, their mother would package up a chicken casserole, a loaf of homemade bread, green vegetables, and a pie or cake. She put it all in a large cardboard box. Then she would drive it over to a young widow with four children who lived by the train depot.

"Mother never missed a Saturday night, and when we were old enough, she brought us along and told us to remember how to always take care of our neighbors, even if we didn't know their names."

Beth wiped at the tears sliding down her cheeks. They told stories about how their mother loved to dance. Their father disliked dancing, but he couldn't resist his wife's pleadings.

"They even took professional dancing lessons for a time," Jennifer said.

The stories continued late into the night. The two older women, and one younger, sat crying and laughing together around Mrs. Becker's bedside.

Maggie startled awake. She couldn't figure out where she was at first, then she felt someone's hand on her shoulder. It was Jack.

"Pastor Maggie, Mrs. Becker is leaving us."

Maggie witnessed Beth and Jennifer's grief as they said goodbye. They were on each side of their mother, holding her hands and kissing her forehead.

Maggie sat up quickly. "What time is it, Jack?"

"It's ten a.m. on Saturday. You've been here over twenty-four hours."

Maggie put her hand on Mrs. Becker's leg. "Jennifer, Beth, I'm so sorry I fell asleep."

"We all did, Pastor Maggie. A slumber party at the old people's home." Beth smiled.

"May I pray?"

They nodded, and Maggie prayed. She thanked God for all the goodness he had packed into Mrs. Becker's soul. She thanked God for the two lovely daughters, who reflected their mother's love so beautifully. She thanked God for heaven and for preparing a place for Mrs. Becker and for everyone. She held Beth and Jennifer's hands, and the three of them kept a sacred circle for another hour until Mrs. Becker took her last breath.

Jack had stood back and observed. In his professional opinion, Pastor Maggie didn't need to be "trained" in anything.

Soon after, Cole Porter had come to Mrs. Becker's room. Maggie, Beth, and Jennifer had made some preliminary plans for the funeral with him. Then Maggie went down to retrieve her car and head home. On the window was one of Officer Tuggle's dreaded parking tickets. Maggie took the ticket and dropped it down the storm sewer next to her car.

She drove home feeling as if she desperately needed to scour her teeth with some steel wool and iron out all the kinks in her back. When she arrived at the parsonage, she was surprised to find the cat food bowl full of cat chow. There was a note on the table.

Dear Pastor Maggie,

Just stopped by to check on the feline inmates of the parsonage. Gave them breakfast. Jack said you were with Mrs. Becker's family. God bless you!

Love,
Ellen

Maggie smiled at the note and hugged the inmates. She was tired. She was sad for Beth and Jennifer. She was happy for Mrs. Becker.

Mrs. Becker, who was dancing in heaven today.

Verna Abernathy decided to remove the bandage and clean the wound Saturday morning. She could have waited until Sunday, but Sunday would be such a busy day. She couldn't be bothered with bandages and antiseptic cream. She quickly ripped the bandage off and almost cried out loud. She needed to slow down. When she finally had the courage to use her hand mirror and look at the wound, she thought she might be sick. The long line of black stitches reminded her of Frankenstein's monster. She sat down on the toilet lid and tried to breathe normally.

The clean bandage was ready on the counter. She squeezed out a dab of antiseptic cream, reached around to her back, quite awkwardly, and placed the bandage over her wound. The self-adhesive edges seemed to stick. Done.

She slipped a cotton camisole over her head and felt her stitches pull uncomfortably. She couldn't wear her bra due to the incision site. Fortunately, her breasts were of no consequence when it came to wearing a bra. She only did so as a matter of principle.

She finished dressing and went downstairs for a bowl of bran flakes with sliced banana and a glass of orange juice. It was time to figure out what to do about those cats at the parsonage. And the pastor.

8

All Maggie wanted to do was sleep. Her night at Friendly Elder Care with Mrs. Becker, Beth, and Jennifer had taken both a physical and emotional toll. But she had to get to the Cherish Market and buy the groceries for tomorrow's lunch. She hadn't even begun to memorize her sermon, and she had no idea what she was doing for Sunday school. It was one o'clock in the afternoon. She felt as if she were walking through molasses.

She put her grocery list together, grabbed her bag, and headed back to her car. Officer Bernie Bumble, Charlotte's deputy, so to speak, was walking down the street with his long chalk holder, marking tires. He would make his circular walk around town, and if the cars had been parked longer than the allotted three hours, he would get out his ticket pad. Maggie liked Bernie, except when he was in his police uniform. He was her age, twenty-six, but seemed to wield superhuman powers with his chalk and tickets.

"Good morning, Bernie," Maggie said as she walked around to the driver's side of her car.

"I think you mean 'good afternoon' don't you, Pastor Maggie?" Bernie said, looking at his watch.

"Oh, yes. Right. I forgot what time it was."

She opened her door, and Bernie said, "Pastor Maggie, I'm sorry I had to leave a . . . uhh . . . a ticket on your windshield last night. But you know you aren't allowed to park on the streets after one a.m."

"Yes. I know, Bernie. I was with Mrs. Becker and her daughters at the Friendly Elder Care."

"Well, I'm sorry to hear that, but laws are laws," Bernie said just a tad defensively. He sounded like an insecure Charlotte. Bernie had left several tickets on Maggie's windshield in the past weeks.

"Mrs. Becker died this morning," Maggie said, not above using a little Dutch guilt.

Bernie was stumped. How did laws work when dead people were involved? He was going to have to speak to Officer Tuggle about this one.

"Goodbye, Bernie. See you in church tomorrow?" Maggie asked.

"Yes, ma'am. I'll be there, Pastor Maggie."

He walked away, still puzzled over parking tickets and the dead. He walked halfway down the block without marking the cars with his diabolical chalk stick, lost in thought.

Maggie hopped in her car and drove over to the market. She made her purchases for Sunday dinner. Then she returned to the parsonage and simultaneously made a pie crust while memorizing her sermon. It didn't really work. She chopped rhubarb and sliced strawberries and mixed up the filling. As the pie baked, she kept trying to cram her sermon into her brain. When she was in her preaching class, she had been told, in no uncertain terms, to *never, never, never* bring a manuscript into the pulpit. She had a good head for memorizing, but this week had certainly gotten away from her. The timer rang and jolted Maggie awake from what had been an accidental snooze in her chair. She hoped this wasn't going to be the outcome for her parishioners when they heard whatever it was she was going to preach. It always unnerved her to see someone sleeping in the pew.

The pie cooled, and the parsonage smelled wonderful. Maggie thought it would be a good idea to go for a little walk around the block and blow the sleep out of her brain. It was still warm, and the smells of freshly cut grass and summer flowers filled the air. She waved to Lynn Porter, who was taking laundry down from the clothesline in her backyard.

She returned to the parsonage feeling invigorated. She was also surprised to see Harold Brinkmeyer standing on the porch holding a reusable grocery bag.

"Hi, Harold."

"Hi, Pastor Maggie. I hope you don't mind me stopping by. I was going to talk to you after the council meeting on Thursday, but with all the *cat*robatics," he chuckled to himself, "I thought it would be better to wait. Then last night I stopped by, but you were gone. I ran into Ellen, and she said you were with Mrs. Becker. So, I thought tonight might be 'third time's the charm.'" He was talking too fast, and his teeth were desperately trying to keep up with his lips.

Maggie smiled and opened the parsonage door.

"Come on in, Harold."

She didn't know his real reason for stopping by, but he seemed uptight. She was ready to listen. Maybe there was a ruckus in the law office or—just maybe—he was upset by the council meeting and this insane cat issue. She got a little chill. Was he going to tell her that Cheerio had to go? Did the others send him to deliver the bad news? What would she do? She loved Cheerio! And what about Marmalade? Maggie was working herself into an emotional category four tornado frenzy.

As they entered the kitchen, she turned and blurted out, "Harold, is this about Cheerio?"

He looked at her, confused. "Is what about Cheerio?"

"This visit."

"What? Cheerio? No, no. Maggie, this has nothing to do with Cheerio." He smiled handsomely and set his grocery bag on the kitchen table. "It smells wonderful in here. What have you been baking today?"

Maggie felt such a waterfall of relief that Cheerio would not be evicted, her voice raised an octave and her smile matched Harold's tooth for tooth.

"Oh, just a strawberry rhubarb pie. It's my brother Bryan's favorite. He and my parents are coming for church tomorrow and staying for Sunday dinner. He leaves for San Francisco next week for a new job, so I thought I'd send him off with his favorite. But that's not important. What can I help you with, Harold?"

Harold decided he may as well bite the bullet. "Well, Maggie, I know you have been here just over two months now, and I wanted to bring you a housewarming gift and see if you might be interested in . . ." His voice trailed off. He looked at the grocery bag. "I found these things on the international aisle at the market." He pulled out a round package of Dutch rusks and set it on the table. He reached back in and pulled out Double Salted Drop (black licorice). He then took out a wedge of Gouda cheese, a tin of Wilhelmina Peppermints, and a boxed mix for oliebollen. Last but not least, a small bunch of tulips in a vase. Harold looked quite pleased with himself.

Maggie smiled and said, "Harold, how did you know to even look for these Dutch treats? I don't think Brinkmeyer is a Dutch name."

"No," Harold replied, "Brinkmeyer is all German."

Maggie was so happily surprised with the treats that she didn't notice Harold moving a little closer to her.

"Maggie?"

He was so close now Maggie could smell his breath. It smelled like he had stolen one of the Wilhelmina Peppermints before he came into the house.

"Yes, Harold?"

The Westminster chimes sounded. Maggie and Harold both jumped. Maggie walked to the door, and Harold cursed whomever it was on the other side of it.

It was Ellen.

"Hi, Ellen." Maggie was happy to see her friend. Also relieved. She was beginning to get an inkling of what Harold might be interested in. And it wasn't just peppermints and oliebollen.

"Hi, Maggie. I just wanted to stop by and see how you were doing. What a long night you had last night. I also wanted to give Cheerio a little cuddle. Gosh, it smells good in here. What have you been baking?" Ellen followed Maggie into the kitchen and saw Harold and the array of snacks. "Oh, hi, Harold. I didn't know you were here. I'm sorry to interrupt." She looked quizzically at Maggie.

"You didn't interrupt anything," Maggie said quickly. "Harold just stopped by and brought me tastes from my motherland."

Harold smiled heroically and said, "Yes, I hope you enjoy them. Perhaps your family will also enjoy them tomorrow. Well, I should be going." His teeth were beginning to give him away as his smile faltered.

"No," Maggie said. "Why don't you and Ellen stay for a bit. We'll open these goodies and try some of the licorice first. I can't wait to see both your faces when you taste it." Maggie knew the first blast of salt could almost bring tears to the eyes, but the salt gave way to such an intense licorice flavor, a person had to have more. It was addictive.

Harold and Ellen settled in, and as they unwrapped and tasted the different Dutch foods, Marmalade and Cheerio made their feline presences known in hopes of treats of the cat variety.

Maggie was aware in the depths of her brain that she should be practicing her sermon. She still had nothing prepared for Sunday school. But after her night in the nursing home and planning for her next funeral, she was happy to have company. She watched as Harold and Ellen tried the licorice. Harold almost spit his out, but Ellen forced herself to chew it to the bitter end. Not to be outdone, Harold gagged and ate his piece. Both wanted another. And then a third. Maggie laughed. She had fun telling them about each different food and how she had such happy memories of eating all these things at the tables of both sets of her grandparents. The afternoon flew by.

They were all surprised when they looked at the clock and saw it was eight. Harold and Ellen started to make departure noises when the Westminster chimes rang again. The parsonage was a busy place.

Maggie went to the door and had one of those moments of context confusion. She recognized the faces, but they didn't belong at the parsonage.

Nora and Dan stood on the porch. Maggie stared. Then Nora threw herself into Maggie's arms, screaming with glee. Maggie hugged Nora back and grabbed Dan's arm.

"What are you two doing here?"

Nora held out her left hand, where a lovely round diamond rested on her ring finger.

"We're engaged! We told our families, but then we had to tell our best friend. Especially since she's going to be officiating our wedding."

Nora began to cry and enveloped her small friend again with another bear hug. When she finally let go, she saw that Maggie was laughing and crying and bouncing. Maggie ushered Dan and Nora into the kitchen and found a box of tissues, which were desperately needed. She introduced Harold and Ellen to Dan and Nora, and all five of them sat down at the table.

At first, Harold and Ellen wanted to leave and let Maggie enjoy being with her friends. But it became clear that Maggie, Dan, and Nora were people who believed in "the more, the merrier." Nothing made Maggie happier than combining old friends and new. Maggie added more snacks from her cupboards to the remainder of goodies Harold had brought. The feasting began again in earnest.

Dan and Nora were all happy froth and bubbles over their new, true love. The engagement wasn't a big surprise in one way, but in another it was like when you know a baby is coming but are not exactly sure when. When the baby shows up, it's a big surprise miracle. Dan and Nora were living in the miracle of their brand-new future.

After much pleading on Maggie's part, Dan and Nora told their story. Going back and forth, they explained that yesterday had been a lazy Friday afternoon at the beach on Lake Michigan. They often did this on their afternoon off. Afterward, they would get a pizza and eat it while watching a movie or sporting event on TV. That afternoon had been no different. They enjoyed the beach, watched people, read books, and dozed in the sun. Then Dan reached over and touched Nora's hand.

"What do you think?" Dan had asked.

"About what?" Nora said drowsily.

"Shall we get married?" Dan asked as he tickled her fingers.

"Umm, yes. Yes, I think we should," Nora said and flipped over onto her back. She was having the most delightful nap.

Dan sat up, picked up Nora like a rag doll, and as she began to squeal and tried to wriggle away, he threw her into the lake. She grabbed his leg and pulled him in just in time for a wave to break over them both. They came up sputtering and laughing.

A long walk on the shore followed the attempted double drowning, and they began to dream and hope of their new life together. Later that evening, with a little more romance involved, Dan produced a ring so stunning Nora was speechless. He carefully placed it on her finger and said, "Nora Drew, will you marry me and have a family with me and get wrinkly with me?"

Nora gave him her answer without using any words. He took it as a "yes."

What Nora didn't know was that Dan had made an insert for the bulletin at Jesus Lives and So Do We! megachurch. Tomorrow morning, as everyone prepared for worship and opened their bulletins, they would read:

Wanted: All middle school and high school youth
Meeting: Tonight (Sunday) 6:00 p.m.
Place: Youth room
Purpose: To plan Dan and Nora's wedding
See you tonight!

Maggie, Ellen, and Harold listened with wide eyes, enjoying every detail of the story. Maggie was especially taken with the story since she had been waiting for this proposal to take place for years. Well, maybe only months, but whatever. She knew Dan and Nora were meant for each other.

They all ate, talked, and laughed under the watchful and curious eyes of Marmalade and Cheerio. Finally, Dan and Nora had to get ready for the two-and-a-half-hour drive back to Holland. They, along with their best friend, had church to think about. In the living room, Dan secretly told Maggie about the bulletin insert. Maggie thought it was the most romantic thing she had ever heard. It must be fun to be in love, she decided.

Harold said his goodbyes to everyone and looked wistfully at Maggie. This wasn't exactly the evening he had had in mind, but hearing Dan and Nora's story gave him a little hope for another night. At least to have a proper date with this elusive woman.

Ellen helped Maggie clean up and then watched as Maggie took out the beef roast and a pile of Sylvia's vegetables. She chopped carrots, potatoes, onions, and celery and dumped the whole pile of vegetables into the Crock-Pot. Then she placed the roast on top of the veggies and sprinkled it liberally with salt and pepper. She pressed the twelve-hour start button. *God bless Crock-Pots.* The parsonage would smell delicious when she woke up.

Ellen was cuddling Cheerio when she said, "That was so easy. I've never made a roast before, but I think even I could do what you just did. I'll collect some vegetables from your desk after church tomorrow. I saw there was a new deposit."

"Please, take as many vegetables as you can," Maggie pleaded. "About the roast, my grandma taught me how to make this recipe. She could make anything and make it look easy."

"Dan and Nora are adorable," Ellen said. "I think their joy is going to stick with me all week. They seem to be a great couple."

"They are. I have been crazy about their coupledom for a long time now. I really can't believe they drove all the way here today just to share the news in person."

Maggie went on to tell Ellen about the surprise in the bulletin tomorrow. Ellen laughed at the thought of Nora opening the bulletin and seeing the invitation for the youth group to plan her wedding. Maggie knew Nora would love it.

"So, you have your first wedding to look forward to," said Ellen. "That's a nice change from funerals."

"Well," said Maggie a little hesitantly, "I thought I might have a different first wedding."

Ellen looked surprised and then immediately donned her conspiratorial face. "Who?"

Maggie looked at Ellen to see if she was making fun of her. It didn't look like it. Ellen really didn't have a clue what Maggie was talking about.

"Why, you and Jack, silly! You both seem pretty cozy, and you're both wonderful. Maybe you two will be my second wedding?"

Ellen stared at Maggie and then began to laugh. "Only if you want to break the law."

"What?" Maggie was completely confused.

"Jack and I would never get married. Ever."

"Why not, for heaven's sake?"

"Maggie, we're cousins."

9

Maggie hadn't crawled into bed until almost one a.m. Her alarm blared into action at four thirty, which was normal for Sundays. Maggie liked to be up early to pray, run, prepare, and get her brain focused. She rolled over and groaned. Marmalade took this as an invitation to smash his little head against hers.

"Marmy! Stop it!"

He didn't.

Maggie stumbled out of bed and was determined to be cranky due to lack of sleep. She was pulling on her running clothes when two very important things happened: first, she smelled the beef roast and vegetables filling the parsonage. *Delicious.* Her family was coming today. And second, she remembered the wonderful news of Dan and Nora's engagement. She laughed out loud as she brewed her Keurig cup. She thought about how Nora's face would arrange itself when she opened the bulletin at church that morning. She thought about how the congregation would respond. Nora's youth group would be all giggles and squeals from the girls and confused looks from the boys. What fun they would have tonight "planning the wedding." Maggie loved the way joy never stayed put. It seeped and slopped into the lives of others, with and without permission.

Maggie swallowed her coffee in big gulps, gave the fur balls their breakfast, and was out the door. It was still dark, but she knew her route so well, she took off down Middle Street at a quick pace. She got to the cemetery and said good morning to Rupert as she ran past his grave. Was that sacrilegious? She didn't think so. On Tuesday, Mrs. Becker would join Rupert there in the graveyard. Maggie contemplated the rhythms every life traversed. That morning Dan and Nora would wake deliriously happy. Jennifer and Beth Becker would wake with tears. These thoughts filled her head as she prayed with joy and made her requests known to God. She believed they were all duly noted by the Almighty.

Once back at the parsonage, Maggie got cleaned up and double-checked her suit and shoes to make sure she was appropriately dressed. Then she made her oatmeal, wondering what on earth she was going to do with the high school Sunday school class that morning. Maybe no one would show up. She never got around to planning a lesson yesterday.

And she certainly hadn't studied her sermon long enough. So instead of doing one of those two very important things, she set the table for Sunday dinner. Maggie was a brilliant procrastinator.

When the table was set, she walked across the street to The Sugarplum Bakery. Mrs. Popkin opened the bakery every Sunday morning from eight until ten a.m. Then she closed the door and walked across the street to church, often forgetting to remove her white baker's apron and hat. Maggie knew that the adult Sunday school class met at the bakery each week. She wasn't sure what they did, exactly, except eat donuts and drink gallons of coffee.

"Good morning, Mrs. Popkin. May I have a dozen donuts, please? I don't know if I will have anyone in Sunday school today, but I better be prepared."

"Well, Pastor Maggie, hokey tooters! I've been waiting for you. I have a dozen fresh out of the fryer. They're on the cooling rack. I'll ice them up and have them for you in a jiffy."

Mrs. Popkin was laughing, as usual.

Maggie looked around and saw Marla and Tom Wiggins, Ellen, Jack, Bill Baxter, and Sylvia sitting at a table covered with napkins, donut crumbs, and coffee cups. Maggie was glad to see Bill Baxter. His red hair shown out from the corner of the bakery.

Maggie thought about the interaction with Fitch Dervish earlier in the week. She knew Fitch was making Bill's work on the ramp more difficult than necessary. Bill was kind enough to fix things at church and at the parsonage without charge. He had been on the search committee when Maggie was going through the interview process. In all those weeks, he never said one word. He was a quiet supporter, and she knew it. She wanted to keep Fitch and his list of codes away from Bill, but there was no way to accomplish that until the ramp was finished.

"Hi everyone." Maggie walked over to the Sunday school table and gave Bill's shoulder a little squeeze. "It looks like you are studying hard over here. I'd guess you are discussing which donut Jesus would like, right?"

They all chuckled politely. Pastor Maggie was terrible at making jokes.

"We think he liked bagels," Tom said, straight-faced. Everyone laughed except Marla, who rolled her eyes.

Ellen looked at Maggie and said, "I hope you don't mind, Pastor Maggie, but I told them about your dream that Jack and I might marry."

Maggie looked at Jack as more laughter came from the table. She didn't even bother to blush.

"Don't worry, I have completely scrapped your wedding ceremony. I'll have to find another hapless couple." Maggie noticed Bill glance quickly at Sylvia. *Well now . . .* "Sylvia, I want you to know the parsonage smells like a very large piece of heaven with a beef roast and your delicious vegetables having cooked all night long."

Sylvia smiled. "Pastor Maggie, I have already dropped off another two bags of veggies in your office this morning. Enjoy!"

Maggie had a slight sinking feeling but smiled brightly and said, "Oh, great!"

"Pastor Maggie," Mrs. Popkin boomed, "here are your donuts. I hope you have some attendees this morning."

"I do too," Maggie lied happily. She absolutely didn't want attendees. She could use the time to get her sermon in some sort of order. She took her bakery box and waved goodbye to the small crowd.

Of course, since she was completely unprepared, Maggie did have attendees. All six of her rumpled, grumpy students showed up: Jason and Addie Wiggins; Mason, Brock, and Liz Tuggle; and Cate Carlson, who was really a college freshman but came to high school Sunday school because she liked Maggie, and it was only for the summer anyway. It should be said that Cate was neither rumpled nor grumpy. She was more like a rambunctious sunbeam. The other students cowered in her happiness.

"Hi, Pastor Maggie!" Cate said to the annoyance of the high school crowd.

"Good morning, Cate, and all my favorite church members," Maggie responded, looking at her underwhelmed students.

Cate beamed a huge smile at Maggie.

Maggie silently cursed for not being prepared for Sunday school. She could only blame herself, and she knew it. She plastered a smile on her face and set down the box of donuts.

"Have some donuts, and I'll be right back."

She quickly went to her study and looked on her bookshelf. She grabbed two copies each of *Who's Who in the Old Testament* and *Who's Who in the New Testament*. She had bought these at a used book sale and now took a moment to praise herself for doing so. She stacked two Bibles on top and went back to her students.

Back in the family/Sunday school room, Marmalade and Cheerio had made their entrance to check out the strange voices. Maggie could hear the girls cooing over Cheerio, and the boys seemed to be dazed by her smallness.

"I didn't know cats came that little," Mason said with his mouth full of donut.

"You have to special order them that way," Maggie said as she entered the room with her stack of books. *Why didn't anyone laugh?* Maggie thought that was pretty funny, *special order.*

Cate asked, "Pastor Maggie, where did you get it?"

"I got *her* at Cassandra Moffet's house. There were three kittens without a mother. I took Cheerio home."

That got a reaction. *Ahhhs* and *ohhhs* and "Cheerio, what a cute name!"

By the time the eating, cooing, and shared animal stories had stopped, there were only twenty minutes left in the hour. Maggie began the class, acting as if she had been planning for days.

"I would like each of you to take one of these books. I have decided that we will plan a Youth Sunday for this fall. Cate, I know we would all love it if you are able to come home for the service. We can work it around your college schedule. Now, I would like you to think about the most interesting or confusing character in the Bible. It can be someone who is good or evil or in-between. These books will help you know the characters better."

The kids looked at the books with little interest. This sounded like school, and school wasn't starting for almost another three weeks.

"Just think." Maggie was actually getting a little excited about it, now that she knew what she was up to. Her voice got more dramatic. "You could be King Herod. Or Deborah the judge. David, Ruth, Jonah, Eve, Mary, Elizabeth, Jesus, Paul! Just think about how many cool people there are in the Bible. We'll have costumes and props, and you can act out your characters for the whole church!"

Good grief, she was brilliant. She could see the whole service unfolding with biblical characters bringing the congregation to tears and laughter and finally . . . enlightenment! She would call it: Bible Alive! Sunday.

She looked at her group of actors . . . uhh . . . students. They looked as though they might be sick.

"Pastor Maggie," Mason said, "there's no way we're going to do that. Are you joking? That would be the lamest thing ever."

The others began to join in, mumbling their complaints about pretending to be Bible people.

"It would be so embarrassing."

"What if my friends at school heard about it?"

"No one has ever done anything so weird at church before."

Maggie began to deflate.

"I actually think it would be kind of fun," Cate said. "We can pick anyone we want to be out of the whole Bible. If we're all doing it, then it won't be lame. Are you going to be someone too, Pastor Maggie?"

The other kids looked up. She had no intention of being a character. She was the pastor, after all.

"Of course!" she said with a forced smile. "Maybe I'll be Mrs. Noah." She tried to laugh, but it came out as a snort. This was not in her plan— the plan she came up with just five minutes ago.

"Let's at least look at the possible characters," Cate continued. "Just think, Mason, if you were Jonah, you could do your whole role inside the belly of a whale!"

The others laughed at this, and Maggie marveled at how Cate reeled them in.

"Addie, you could be Hannah, Samuel's mother. Can you imagine dropping your two-year-old off at church and leaving him there forever?"

None of them could imagine having a two-year-old, but they got the gist. They opened the *Who's Who* books and started looking at the many colorful characters. Hopefully, none of the girls would choose Jezebel.

Maggie tried to regain a little control and said, "If you aren't comfortable doing this alone, you can buddy up and do two characters out of the same story." *Now, that was a great idea, Maggie.*

They spent the remaining time looking at characters and laughing at the dorky ways they could portray them, but Maggie knew they were hooked.

She said, "I think this is going to be the best Youth Sunday ever. I need you to make a commitment to be here every Sunday as we work on these stories. I'll help any way I can, but you've got to come to Sunday school. Can we make a deal?"

"Will you double the donuts?" Jason Wiggins asked.

"Absolutely!"

They all agreed, at least for now, to come back every Sunday.

"I want you to have your ideas narrowed down to two or three characters by next Sunday. And you may borrow these books for the week if you'd like."

Cate, Addie, and Liz each grabbed a book.

"Gentlemen?" Maggie asked, looking at the boys, who were looking at something fascinating on the ceiling.

"I'll look at Addie's," said Jason.

"Liz has one for us," said Brock while Mason nodded.

"One last thing," Maggie said. "I'm also planning an animal blessing service on October fifth. Do any of you have pets?" They all nodded. "Good. Then plan on bringing them to be blessed."

"I'll bring Ralph," Mason said, showing a remarkable amount of enthusiasm.

"Is that your dog?" Maggie asked as she cleaned up the donut box.

"No. My ferret," Mason replied.

"Terrific," Maggie said. *Well, even ferrets need to be blessed.*

She said a closing prayer, and the students were out the door.

"Hey, Cate," Maggie called. Cate turned and came back in the room. "Cate, what you just did was great. Thank you for supporting me in this. As soon as you began talking, they began listening."

"Pastor Maggie, high schoolers *have* to think anything an adult says is idiotic. They don't see me as an adult. If I think it's cool, then it must be cool. I'm a college student, so I have a magical aura." Cate laughed. "And I don't mind coming back for the service in the fall. I've already decided I'm going to be Queen Esther or maybe the Witch of Endor." Cate's laugh bubbled up delightfully.

Maggie gave Cate a hug. *This must be what it's like to have a sister,* Maggie mused. They headed over to the church for worship, arm in arm, which was undignified but delightful.

As they entered the sanctuary, Maggie felt someone grab her elbow. It was Harold. Cate disappeared into the crowd.

"Pastor Maggie," Harold began, "I'm sorry to bother you right now before worship, but I thought I better let you know, Mrs. Abernathy called me this morning and said she wanted an emergency council meeting this afternoon."

"What?" Maggie was completely caught off guard. She was still pre-occupied with the brilliance of her Youth Sunday scheme. "We can't meet this afternoon. I have my family here for the day. What's her agenda?"

"She wants to discuss 'care of the parsonage,' which means 'how to get rid of the cats.'"

Maggie felt the heat rise in her face. Why did this issue make her feel like a naughty little girl? She wanted to say a really bad word.

Just then, Irena unceremoniously interrupted Maggie and Harold. "Pastooor Maggie, I make change to hymns for dis moorning." She thrust a piece of paper with scribbles on it into Maggie's hand. "Heere are changes. You announce before singing." She flounced off, looking like a fluorescent voodoo doll.

As Maggie turned to continue her conversation with Harold, she felt someone lock elbows with her and swing her around.

"Bryan!"

Maggie's brother gave her a bear hug, lifting her completely off the ground, and said, "How's it going, Pastor Maggie?" He laughed because he still wasn't used to her title.

Maggie looked over his shoulder and saw her mother and father.

Her mother said, "Bryan, put your sister down. She must be in the middle of five hundred things right now. Good morning, Maggie." Her mother gave her a kiss on her cheek. "We have food that needs to go in the refrigerator. Is the parsonage open?"

Maggie marveled at her mother. Mimi always could read a situation with remarkable clarity. Maggie's emotions usually muddled up her own vision.

"I'm so glad you're here," Maggie said, looking at her family. "Yes, the parsonage is open. You can put the food in the fridge and get back here before worship begins."

Her dad gave her a quick hug before they went to the parsonage.

Maggie turned to Harold. "What time is the meeting?"

"Mrs. Abernathy wants it this afternoon. I can set the meeting for later tonight, if you'd rather."

Maggie thought quickly. "Let's have it after worship. I think that will keep it from going on and on. What do you think?"

"Great idea. Everyone will be ready to go home and not want to stay to talk about cats. I'll make the announcement."

"Oh, Pastor Maggie! I've been looking for you." Marla was breathless and carrying a manila folder. "I have the surveys completed regarding death education for the children. Shall I pass them out to the parents?"

Maggie was bewildered for a moment and then remembered Marla's newest mission.

"Would it be okay if you and I look at the survey first, maybe tomorrow?"

"Absolutely. I'll be in your office first thing. By the way, Carrie and Carl were in Sunday school this morning. Quite a handful, they are." Marla said this with a tense smile. "But, of course, it's wonderful to have them here. We can start their theological training immediately." She lowered her voice, "And do they need it. Carrie was quite adamant that Jesus was a prince from England, just like Prince William." Marla looked absolutely scandalized.

Maggie wanted to go to the parsonage and crawl back in bed with the infidel cats.

"Marla, we'll solve this later. I should really get ready for worship now."

They could hear Irena ratcheting up the decibels of her prelude to drown out the pleasant chatter of the parishioners. Irena became irate when people did not sit quietly and listen to her preludes.

Maggie headed toward her office to gather Bible, bulletin, and her thoughts. No such luck. Sylvia was organizing vegetables on Maggie's desk.

"Pastor Maggie, do you have a second? I just don't know what to do. I brought gladiolas in for today's flowers on the altar table, but Mrs.

Abernathy set them on Hank's desk and put her awful zinnias on the altar instead." Sylvia began to tear up. "I had my gladiolas there first."

Maggie shoved the Kleenex box into Sylvia's hands.

"Your gladiolas are on Hank's desk?"

Sylvia nodded and snorted into a tissue. Maggie left her office and picked up the vase of gladiolas. She marched through the secret door into the front of the sanctuary. (It wasn't really a "secret" door. It was the pastor's entrance to the pulpit. Maggie called it "secret" because it sounded more mysterious.) She placed the gladiolas next to the zinnias and sat firmly in the chair behind the pulpit, waiting for Irena to finish her prelude.

The service began. Harold got up and stood behind the lectern.

"Good morning. I have two announcements. First, Mrs. Wanda Becker's funeral will be Tuesday. Eleven o'clock a.m., here in the sanctuary. A luncheon will follow. Visitation will be tomorrow from two o'clock to four o'clock p.m. at The Porter Funeral Home. Second, there will be a brief council meeting immediately following worship this morning in Pastor Maggie's office." Harold glanced at Maggie, then sat down in the front pew as she stood up.

"Good morning," Maggie said from behind the pulpit. "This is the day the Lord has made. Let us rejoice and be glad in it. We can be glad because our help is in the name of the Lord, who made heaven and earth." She cleared her throat. "Irena has changed the hymns for this morning." This irritated Maggie. She read the new hymn numbers to her congregation and began the service.

They all limped through the first hymn. No one recognized it. Finally, it was time for the sermon.

Maggie stood behind the pulpit and read Matthew 14:22–33. It was the story of Jesus walking on water and Peter's attempt to join him.

She closed her Bible and looked at the congregation. Her mind went absolutely blank. She couldn't remember one single thing she had meant to say. She looked at the expectant faces in front of her.

There was Sylvia with her Kleenex (sans vegetables), and Bill Baxter the (hopeful?) builder and handyman on one side of her, with Bernie

Bumble in uniform (it must be his Sunday on duty) on the other side. Hank and Pamela were in the third pew on the left, with Doris and Chester right behind them. It looked like Hank was reading the bulletin to make sure he had made no grammatical errors. Doris was shifting her gaze from side to side in the sanctuary, looking for possible mess-makers. Marla, Tom, Jason, and Addie Wiggins were toward the front on the left. Jason and Addie looked ready for a nap after the excitement of Sunday school. Maggie saw Sunday-school-saving Cate Carlson sitting with her parents.

Cole, Lynn, and their little girls, Penny and Molly, were in a back pew in case of a little girl, or pregnant mom, bathroom emergency. Maggie and Cole would have their second funeral together that week.

Dr. Jack and Ellen were sitting in the same pew as Jennifer and Beth Becker. The two sisters looked tear-stained in a sweet, saintly way. The entire Tuggle family was lined up in a row, Charlotte and Fred acting as human bookends for Liz, Mason, and Brock. Maggie remembered her parking tickets when she saw Charlotte, but quickly looked away.

Maggie saw Cassandra Moffet with Carrie and Carl. Carrie was wearing a bright-pink tutu, a leotard covered in feathers, and a tiara. She still had her feather wand and waved it enthusiastically when Maggie spied her. Carl had his thumb in his mouth but waved with his other hand.

Maggie saw her parents and Bryan, along with Ed and Jo. They had made it on time. Maggie felt a lump in her throat that she couldn't seem to swallow. *Bryan is leaving this week. He is leaving this week . . .*

Irena was perched like a parrot on the organ bench and looked cross. Mrs. Popkin wore her baker's hat but smiled with anticipation. Next to her, Mrs. Abernathy looked as pinched and puckered as sour milk. Howard Baker was next to her and gave Maggie a flirty wink. In the last pew, Maggie saw Max Solomon, sitting alone. She wondered how he was doing since his father's funeral.

Maggie swallowed her lump.

"Our passage today is about a rough boat ride, high hopes for a miracle, and a near-drowning. Often this story focuses on Peter's hope to meet Jesus on top of the waves. Jesus walked with no problem. Peter steps out of the boat, takes a couple of steps, but then he starts to sink. There are words from Jesus about faith and the lack of it." Maggie paused. *Now what?* What was she going to say next about Peter and Jesus? Her brain seemed to have completely shut down. She looked at the rows of people in front of her. She had a thought.

"But Jesus and Peter aren't the only two in this story, are they? What about the disciples who are in the boat with their hands on the oars just trying to keep the boat afloat in the storm? That's hard work. It means cooperation and support for one another. It means hanging on when the big waves come. It means bailing out the water that is pouring into the boat. It takes a group of disciples to keep the boat upright and headed to shore. The disciples row, and bail, and hold onto each other." She stopped for a moment and took a breath. "I think that's who we are. We're the disciples in the boat, rowing and making the journey together."

Maggie looked at her parishioners. The lump was back, and she bit her lower lip.

Her parents, who had been watching and listening intently, quietly turned to one another. They knew that look from when Maggie was a little girl. She would bite her little lip right before tears of exhaustion, frustration, anger, or sadness fell. They both turned their attention back to their daughter.

Maggie felt the tears coming. She had to get a grip. She had to finish that terrible casserole of a sermon so Irena could play something loud and obnoxious. She looked directly at Mrs. Abernathy and immediately felt able to keep the emotion at bay. It always helped to look at the "enemy" when one needed a little courage.

Maggie continued, "We are all in the boat together. We may have different ideas about how to row or the best way to follow Jesus. We may get tired and cranky with each other, or we may want to get out and try to make it on our own. But we keep rowing. We allow each other to rest when necessary. We bail water for each other. We keep heading for that beautiful shore where there are no more storms, and in the end, we get there together because that's what disciples do. That's what families do. Jesus leads the way, and we row, row, row like crazy to follow him." Maggie strung a few more words together before she said "Amen."

She was met with silence. Maggie looked back at Irena and was astonished to see her wiping her eyes, making an even more shocking display of smeared black, orange, and green on her face.

Then there was a small a cappella voice: "Row, row, row, your boat gently down the stream. Merrily, merrily, merrily, merrily, life is but a dream!"

It was Carrie. She was standing on her pew, and when she finished her brief performance, she waved her feather wand as a benediction over the congregation. Then she curtsied and sat back down with a rustle of her tutu and a flounce of her feathers.

After all the chuckles, there wasn't a dry eye in the church.

Except for the two eyes glaring out of Mrs. Abernathy's face.

10

After the service, there was a palpable energy among the congregants. Maggie's first move after the last hymn was to get to Irena. Maggie had never seen her cry before.

She got to the organ bench just as Irena began the postlude. Maggie waited. And waited. She shook people's hands as they passed by. She kept waiting. Was Irena playing to avoid her? Finally, the postlude ended, and Irena began to shut the organ down and gather her music.

In a sneak attack, Maggie threw her arms around the unsuspecting organist. Irena became as stiff as a petrified tree.

"Vat you doing?" She gasped and tried to push Maggie away.

"I wanted to tell you the hymn changes were perfect." Maggie slowly unwrapped her arms from Irena's small shoulders.

"Of cooourse. I know already how goood." Irena slammed a hymnal shut.

"I just wanted to thank you for everything you do here. I'm glad we work together, Irena."

"Yes, I know. I'm veery excellent." For a split second, she looked Maggie in the eye. Then she turned away and headed for the music room.

Personally, Maggie was stinging with humiliation over what she thought was a mess of a sermon. Of all the Sundays for Ed to be there. And now Irena was in the midst of an emotional breakdown for some reason. Maggie still had to go to the impromptu council meeting before she could enjoy her family. And worst of all, she might lose her cats. Maggie's insecurity and immaturity were in full force.

After Irena stomped away, Maggie looked around at everyone laughing and enjoying their coffee and cookies. There was a group of people surrounding Maggie's family and Ed and Jo. Maggie couldn't help but notice Cate standing near Bryan, watching his every move. When he finally noticed Cate, they engaged in a conversation about classes and college life. Cate was all smiles and bright eyes. Bryan gave her his full attention.

Maggie wanted to continue watching this little interaction, but her attention was hijacked by Redford, who had collected all the offering plates and was taking them into Hank's office. Alone. The rule for counting the offering was there had to be two people counting together. Redford should have been with someone else from the finance committee. Maggie walked through the gathering area, trying to get to Redford, when she overheard someone say, "Now that was a sermon worth listening to."

She felt a tug on her skirt. She looked down and saw Carrie, with Carl in tow, staring up at her.

"Hi, Pastor Maggie!"

Maggie immediately refocused. She knelt and gathered them both in her arms as she said, "Carrie, your solo today was beautiful. Thank you for singing for us."

Carrie giggled with delight. She pulled away from Maggie's embrace and did a little twirl and a bow, knighting Maggie on the head with her feather wand. Carl watched his sister with pure adoration. Maggie looked up and saw Cassandra.

"Pastor Maggie, I'm sorry if Carrie was a little out of line there in church. She hasn't been here before, and I apologize."

Maggie stood and shook her head. "Cassandra, Carrie was just perfect. There isn't anything to apologize for. I think we should have her sing again."

Carrie's eyes opened wide with delight. Just then, Harold took Maggie's arm.

"May I speak with you, Pastor Maggie?"

Maggie turned to Cassandra and the children. "Excuse us, please."

Harold led Maggie into Hank's office, which was already beginning to look like a trash dump. Maggie instinctively began throwing away paper cups, napkins, and tossing bulletins into the recycle bin. She didn't see Redford anywhere.

"Maggie," Harold said, "I have spoken to most of the council members and told them Mrs. Abernathy's agenda. We all feel terrible that this is happening today after that incredible sermon and the visit from your family and friends. Would you like me to postpone the meeting?"

All Maggie heard was "incredible sermon," and she felt surprised and thrilled at the same time. She smiled.

"Harold, let's get this done and over with. Is everyone ready?"

"Yes. They are all in your office. I put them there because it will be a standing meeting—not enough chairs. It should go faster that way."

They entered Maggie's office. All the council members were there, talking quietly and trying to avoid stepping on the vegetables that had fallen on the floor. Maggie pinned her eyes on Redford, who stood in the corner. There was no evidence of the offering plates.

Harold began the meeting and made it clear there was only one agenda item, then he gave the floor to Mrs. Abernathy.

"This is not really what I had in mind when I called for the meeting this morning. I don't want to rush the discussion or have people miss being with their family and visitors," she said as she looked at Maggie. "But one must soldier on." She took a deep breath before she continued.

"The agenda item," began Mrs. Abernathy, "continues from this past week's meeting. There cannot be animals in the parsonage or in the church. We keep the parsonage in trust for our pastors. If those animals ruin the parsonage now, just imagine what we will have to repair when our next pastor arrives." She looked intensely at each council member, avoiding Maggie, of course.

Oh dear! She is already planning for the next pastor.

It was Jack who spoke. "Mrs. Abernathy, we can take a vote on this if you like. But this is old news that cannot continue to be resurrected as new news. Pets have been in the parsonage before, I know you are aware of that. Pastor Blake had a cocker spaniel. Pastor Elton had a cat and two retrievers. If our pastors find joy in their pets, why would we keep it from them?"

Mrs. Abernathy stiffened, wavered slightly, and reached for the desk to steady herself. Her face went white, as did her knuckles when she grabbed the desk. She looked like death's leftovers.

"Mrs. Abernathy? Are you okay?" Jack asked. He could see the blood draining from her face and suspected she might faint. "Do you need to sit down?"

He reached around to help her and put his hand directly on her bandaged wound. She yelped with the pain and pulled away.

"Let me go, Dr. Elliot. I'm perfectly fine. I thought this was a council that saw sense, but obviously you are all transfixed by this girl and her unconventional ways. Mark my words, when she leaves, we will have a mess on our hands."

She steadied herself and left the office. She had the habit of storming out when things didn't go her way. No one ever followed her.

"Pastor Maggie," Harold said, "I apologize for her rudeness. You are neither a girl nor unconventional. I speak for the council when I say that we are pleased that you are our pastor. We hope you will not leave for a very, very long time. And your cats are welcome in the parsonage, which is your home. I call this meeting adjourned."

Everyone made their way out of the church, sweetening up the bitterness Mrs. Abernathy had left behind with their positive comments about the sermon and Carrie's little solo. Somehow Maggie's impromptu sermon had come across as something she had spent hours and hours on. *Shock.* And everyone was besotted by little Carrie Moffet. *Obviously.*

Jack said to Maggie as they all parted ways on the front steps of the church, "You have brought a new spirit to our church. Thank you."

"Thank you, Jack. And thank you for your words in the meeting. Hopefully, this issue is closed. But I won't count on it."

She walked across the lawn to the parsonage. Harold was still on the church steps as he watched her go.

Before she went into the parsonage, Maggie spotted someone at the back of the church. Redford came out the kitchen door. She saw him walk quickly behind the church toward downtown. He held an envelope tightly in his hand.

Well, that doesn't look suspicious at all, she thought with a grimace.

Finally, Maggie sat at the oak dining room table with her parents, brother, Ed, and Jo. They had all just finished putting the pot roast, vegetables, salads, and breads on the long table. It promised to be a delicious meal.

"I want to know what happened in the council meeting," Bryan said after Maggie prayed. "Are the fur balls in or out?"

Maggie had kept her family in the loop about Mrs. Abernathy's obsession to remove her and the felines.

"In," Maggie said as she passed Sylvia's vegetables to her father.

"And what happened to Irena's face?" Bryan reverted to college behavior, shoving food in his mouth just as some sentence was trying to escape.

"I don't know exactly," Maggie said thoughtfully as she buttered a piece of Jo's homemade French bread.

"We saw you waiting to speak to her," Ed said. "It seemed as if she was going to play the organ as long as it took for you to go away."

Everyone laughed.

"She did her best to wait me out," Maggie agreed, "then completely avoid me. But alas, I wouldn't let her out of my clutches. And by clutches, I mean I gave her a hug. Sunday mornings are always full of surprises."

"That's a bit of an understatement," said Ed. "If I remember correctly, and tell me if I'm not," he said to Jo, "Sunday mornings are the time when all questions, suggestions, criticisms, and random thoughts of parishioners make their presence known. I was always amazed how right before worship, almost every week, a certain woman in our congregation, we'll just say she lost her smile somewhere, would tell me the most dreadful news." Ed shook his head and smiled. He and Jo served a church when he was studying for his Ph.D.

"I remember," said Jo. "Her name was Edith. One Sunday, she stopped Ed as he was getting ready to begin church to tell him of a man who lost both his legs in a skiing accident. It was terribly gruesome. The man was no one she knew. He was from Utah. She always did crazy things like that." Jo, who did not think these pronouncements were funny at the time, laughed now as she helped herself to more vegetables.

"That's how it feels sometimes," Maggie agreed. "So many people just have to tell me so many things, I go into the pulpit with my head spinning." Then she looked at Bryan. "I saw you talking to Cate Carlson this morning, speaking of heads spinning."

"Oh, is that her name?" Bryan looked purposefully at a potato on his plate, refusing to make eye contact with his sister.

Maggie grinned at her mother.

After they had eaten dinner and sliced the pie, to Bryan's delight, Ed and Maggie went into her study. Standing by the floor-to-ceiling windows, they admired the pine trees in the backyard and the little wagon overflowing with flowers.

"This is a beautiful study," Ed said appreciatively. "And the view is inspiring. God has brought you to a good place, Maggie. I'm happy for you."

"I love Cherish and the church and this parsonage." Maggie sighed.

"How did you feel about this morning, Maggie?" Ed asked in his soft, loping voice.

"When I stood up in the pulpit to preach, everything I thought I was going to say went right out of my head. To be perfectly honest,

I didn't prepare the way I should have. This week didn't go quite as I planned. Plus, I still procrastinate, just like in seminary."

"That's ministry," Ed said. "As soon as you think you have a plan, you don't. But you have the right personality for that. You aren't stuck in patterns."

"Well, this morning, without proper preparation, I looked out from the pulpit, and all I could see were people I love, some I tolerate, and some I could punch. But they are all in the boat. How does a church function when people are so different and opinionated? I'm tired of feeling like a child being punished for bringing a homeless kitten into the parsonage, which actually is my home, but not my home. When will I ever feel like a pastor?" Her eyes were stinging again. *Drat!*

Ed sat down in one of the red-and-white wing-backed chairs.

"First of all, this morning's worship was very powerful. I would never recommend winging it on purpose, which you never would, but when weeks are out of your control, do your best and let God use you. Second, the best pastors are the ones who question themselves honestly and often as they go about their ministry day to day. I worry more about the students who walk out of the seminary into a church and immediately seem to have all the answers. Tell me, Maggie, in this past week was there ever a time you felt like you were pastoring well?"

Maggie thought. "When I was with Mrs. Becker and her daughters."

"Any other time?"

"Well, there were some issues in the office this week that I think I handled okay."

"What would you have liked to be different this past week?" Ed continued.

"I wish I would have handled the council meeting better after the Cheerio debacle. And I really wish Mrs. Abernathy would move to Saudi Arabia."

Ed laughed. "There will be other parishioners like Mrs. Abernathy along the way. Everyone has their silent baggage. They either learn to unpack and dispose of it, or they keep carrying it around, allowing it to burden them, body and soul. Unfortunately, the rot of it seeps into other people's lives. Does Mrs. Abernathy have any friends?"

"I'm not sure. I don't know her well enough, personally. She and Irena both keep people at bay. Irena does it through her bombastic outbursts and scary makeup. Mrs. Abernathy does it through her iciness and criticism. They are both older than I am, which doesn't help. Actually, almost everyone is older than I am. But there is a different feeling from Ellen, Harold, Marla, Tom, and Sylvia, to name a few. They seem to show more . . . more . . . I don't know," Maggie stumbled.

"Respect," Ed piped in. "My guess is they all know how to do what they do in life, and they believe wholeheartedly that you do too. They wouldn't want your job for anything and are thankful that you are their pastor. Just a guess." He smiled.

"So, what do I do about the ones who want to instruct me on how to do my job, or even do it for me?" Maggie whined a little.

"Maggie, go to her. Go to Mrs. Abernathy and do what you do so well—listen."

I would rather gnaw off my own hand. "I can't."

"You can. The best way to deal with bullies and cowards—and remember, all bullies are cowards—is to walk right up to them and ask them what's really going on. As her pastor, your job is to care for Mrs. Abernathy." Ed was as serious as Maggie had ever seen him. She knew she was learning a not-taught-in-seminary lesson. He continued, "Set up a time to go to her home. She will feel safer there. Then let her talk. I believe she will, once she figures out you're not there for battle. This is just a suggestion."

Maggie sighed. "So, I take it you don't think she'll move to Saudi Arabia?"

After Maggie and Ed returned to the kitchen, she grabbed Bryan and excused them both. She dragged him out the front door and down

Middle Street toward the cemetery. She locked her elbow through his, the way they used to do as children.

"I'm going to cry now and tell you how much I'm going to miss you while you're in San Francisco, and I suspect that won't be the farthest place you will go." Maggie snuffled. "If I say I'm proud of you, I'll sound like Mom. But I am proud. You could have muddled and partied your way through college and come out with a mediocre job and had a plain old life. But you went out in the world, and in Uganda that changed you." She was really crying now. "And you're going to listen to people as they tell you what they need, then they'll be able to sustain a good life because you believe they can, and now they will too. You blow me away."

"Megs, I watched you. I've always watched you. You do the exact same thing." He patted her on top of her head, his own way of showing affection to his short sister. "I'll be home for Christmas. I'll even come to Cherish and hang out with you and your cats."

"Of course you will, you idiot. I just have one question for you."

"Yes?" Bryan looked at his sister.

"When are you going to shave that fuzz off your face? You look like a bum."

Bryan had been trying to grow a beard all through college. It was woeful. He could grow a patch on his chin, a patch on his left cheek, and a sparse (at best) mustache. Maggie knew that Mimi hated it, but Mimi figured, if this was Bryan's big rebellion in college and beyond, she would keep her mouth shut. Maggie didn't concur. She wanted to see her brother's smooth face again. She also wanted to take him in for a haircut. That was the second part of his rebellion: shaggy, hippy hair. Maggie was more than happy to be the spokeswoman against all this fur.

"I'm not shaving. I look really cool. All my friends say so. And they are highly educated grad students, not just college fraternity brothers." Bryan frowned.

"They all think you look like their fraternity puppy," Maggie said blandly. "They like to walk you around town and watch people pet you."

Bryan laughed. "Well, you dress like a gypsy hippy."

They kept squabbling as they walked down the street. Then things got a little more serious.

"Are you excited to get to San Francisco?" Maggie asked.

"I can't wait. My five new roommates sound pretty great. Three girls and two guys. All five of them work in the city, so I will have help figuring out BART. But I mainly want to get to work. So many things are happening in the countries of Africa, Megs!"

Maggie had rarely seen Bryan that animated.

"Like what?" she asked.

"Like we just finished building a health clinic that will serve twenty-six thousand people, and we're building a school that will educate three hundred children. We're digging several wells to bring fresh water to rural communities. If you don't stop me, I'll keep going."

"Who's 'we'?" Maggie asked.

"You know, Africa Hope. I've been working with them for the last couple of months from home. I can't wait to be there in person." Bryan was almost giddy. He continued with more stories about the people he had met in the villages in Uganda and his hope to manage more projects in several countries.

Maggie realized how wrapped up in Cherish life she had been since she arrived at Loving the Lord. She and Bryan hadn't said more than a few sentences to each other in their sporadic phone calls of the last two months. But it didn't take long for Maggie to be drawn into Bryan's dream. Her imagination began to swirl and bubble and envision what could be for people she had never met but whom she was beginning to love.

"Will you help me get some vegetables out of my office before we go back to the parsonage?" Maggie asked, pulling herself from her own fantasyland.

"Sure. Why do you have vegetables in your office?"

"It's a long, long, long story of an over-generous parishioner." Maggie sighed.

As they walked in through the front doors of the church, Maggie remembered seeing Redford after the council meeting with the envelope. She wondered what to do. Was Redford stealing from the church? Maybe he was taking the money to the bank. She would call Harold. He would be helpful in this situation as chair of the council.

Bryan helped Maggie gather up some bags of vegetables to pawn off on their parents and Ed and Jo. They made their way back to the parsonage laden with their bags. The vegetables were met with no pleasure whatsoever but finally resignation.

The Elzingas and Ed and Jo gathered their belongings. Maggie hugged and kissed everyone as they left. She hugged Bryan last.

"Have a great trip, and call me, please." And then she punched him in the arm as he picked her up and threw her on the once-white-now-gray couch.

Their mother just shook her head as she watched her children behave like wolf puppies. Their father laughed out loud.

"Maggie! Bryan!" Mimi snapped. "Get up. It's time for us to leave."

They got up, and Maggie walked everyone to the front porch, her hair disheveled and her face bright red from laughing. Her mother looked her straight in the eye and said, "Your sermon this morning was the best I've heard in weeks."

And then they were gone.

It was almost seven p.m., and Maggie was tired. But she purposefully walked upstairs to her bedroom, put on her Sunday suit and shoes for the second time that day, brushed her hair, and walked out the front door. She got into her car and drove down Main Street to Summit. She turned right and pulled into the second driveway on the right.

She walked straight up to the front door and rang the bell.

Mrs. Abernathy had left church that morning with angry tears in her eyes. She'd read somewhere that when women cry it is usually caused by anger; when men cry it is usually caused by sadness. Probably a bunch of hogwash. But she was *angry*. The church was going to hell in a hand basket, and no one seemed to notice but her.

What a ridiculous service they endured that morning. A sermon that made no sense. Hymns that weren't in the bulletin. That ridiculous child wearing feathers in church—*feathers in church*! And then the child sang while standing on the pew. Mrs. Abernathy could feel her throat clench as she fought back her anger again and again. Maggie Elzinga had brought frivolity and carelessness to worship. She was just a silly child with a diploma in her hand. She didn't understand the sacred, the holy, or the fear of God. She was turning the church into "Sundays at Disneyland." Even her professor, the one whom Mrs. Abernathy was at first impressed with, seemed to think Maggie was doing the Lord's work. She overheard him at coffee time telling someone how proud he was of Maggie. It made no sense. What kind of professors did they hire at that seminary, anyway?

She made herself a bowl of tomato soup after she checked her bandage. She had been afraid Dr. Elliot pulled the bandage away from her wound when he put his hand on her back. The bandage was intact.

After her lunch, she washed her bowl, spoon, and cup. Then she sat down to read her daily devotional. She was startled awake when her mantle clock struck five o'clock in the evening. She felt dazed. She had slept the entire afternoon. She never wasted an afternoon sleeping. She went upstairs and changed out of her Sunday clothes, put on her cotton dress, and went to the garden to check on her zinnias.

As she watered her flowers, her mind wandered to that place it so often visited—an emotional sinkhole that drew her into the darkest places of her life. She remembered her mother. Her husband. Caroline. Anguish filled her.

She grabbed her trowel and began to dig feverishly. Her tears fell, one by one, into the fresh dirt around her flowers. Her hands used the trowel as a weapon. She stabbed the earth, as if trying to kill her harshest memories. She dug into the ground until the hole was deep. Then she took her trowel in both hands and plunged it into the hole. As she did so, she felt the stitches in her back tear apart. The sound that came out of her was the scream of an animal caught in a trap, but the scream wasn't from the pain in her back. The tears flowed as she shuddered.

Something caught her eye, and she looked up.

Maggie was standing at the back garden gate, her hand on the latch. "Oh, Mrs. Abernathy! Please, may I come in?"

11

Mrs. Verna Abernathy regularly lost track of time when she was in her garden. Her memories and thoughts filled her mind until the setting sun reminded her the day was coming to a close. Her garden was her solace, in one way, a harbinger of the past in another. She couldn't escape the thoughts in her head. They had taken up permanent residence. As she worked with her zinnias, cut her grass, and trimmed the bushes and shrubs, she would ride that same merry-go-round of misery she had been riding since she was a little girl. She had given up long ago thinking her story was unique.

Oh, for many years her martyrdom had been her secret and delicious pleasure. She nurtured it and fed it with each memory of injustice and pain. She stood straighter and walked with purpose as she carried her many burdens on her shoulders and in her soul. She looked upon the world as the enemy—a sneaky, violent enemy, ready to attack. Whenever anyone did attack, whether real or perceived, she cut them off with scalpel quick precision. She never allowed anyone to attack twice.

Except for her mother.

Willa Brown only saw a doctor once in her life: the day she gave birth to her daughter, Verna. If Willa had seen a doctor in any other circumstance than childbirth, she would have been diagnosed with a severe personality disorder. But being in labor hid all other ills from a doctor focused on bringing a baby into the world. There was little that could have been done at that time for Verna's mother even if a doctor had noticed. The disorder worsened after Verna was born. Willa's alcoholism didn't help. One of the side effects of deep depression and personality changes was that other people didn't want to be around such people. Willa's depression manifested itself in aggression and withdrawal. The few people in her life were "invited" to stay away.

Verna had been raised in that isolated and dark world. She had no awareness that her father had left her and her mother when Verna was only three years old. Her father appeared periodically, leaving food and money on the kitchen table. He then disappeared into a happier world of which Verna had no knowledge. He must have come in the middle of the night when he visited because the food, money, and, every once in a while, a coloring book with colored pencils would be waiting in the morning. When she began to understand the gifts her father had left, she would climb on a chair and take as much of the food as she could carry to her closet. She had put sheets and an old pink baby blanket in her closet as well. Sleeping there felt safe. She would eat there, opening boxes of crackers and cereal.

When she got older and stronger, she could open jars of peanut butter and honey. Occasionally, there were apples, which she squirreled away as fast as she could. In the winter, there would be oranges and packages of figs and dates. The money always disappeared, but Verna fed herself without her mother's knowledge or punishment. If she stayed quiet, she and her mother would orbit one another like two isolated planets. But intermittently, a collision would leave Verna so battered she would stay in her closet for days.

One hot summer day when Verna was six years old, there was a knock on the door. Standing on the other side was a woman Verna had never seen before. Verna had seen very few people in her life. The woman was plump, with a round, shiny face, and she asked to speak to Verna's mother. Willa had been drinking again, but she tried to act as if she hadn't been. The woman at the door held out her hand. Willa did not reciprocate.

"Good afternoon," the woman said, lowering her hand, "my name is Mrs. Charles. I am a teacher at the local elementary school. I heard there was a school-aged child here."

She looked past Willa and saw Verna, dirty and wearing something that looked like her mother's old blouse.

Mrs. Charles's heart broke.

"I've come to . . . uh . . . register her for school, which begins in two weeks' time. What's your name, dear?"

She looked at Verna, who remained mute. Willa smiled with too much enthusiasm and stepped out onto the front porch.

"Her name is Verna."

Her words were slightly slurred, and the air between the two women quickly began to smell like a distillery. Mrs. Charles had to hold her breath. She took a step back and pulled some documents from her small case.

"These are the papers you need to sign. Then I will have Verna completely registered with the school and assigned to a classroom."

Mrs. Charles smiled at Verna. Willa scribbled a signature on several different documents that Mrs. Charles handed her. Verna watched and listened without understanding. What was school?

"Now, I just need to see a copy of Verna's immunizations record."

Mrs. Charles briskly put the signed documents back into her case. She looked up when Willa didn't move from the porch.

"She hasn't had any," Willa said with a slushy voice.

"What? No immunizations? But there's not a doctor in town who would let that happen." Mrs. Charles was dumbfounded.

"She's never been to a doctor. She's fine. She's good. No problems." Willa swayed a little.

"Well, she will have to begin the series of shots before school starts. She can catch up over the next year. Would it be helpful if I set up a doctor's appointment for next week?" Mrs. Charles was doing her best to remain friendly, but her anger at this neglectful mother was beginning to burn. Who could treat a child this way? She looked directly at Willa. "Let's plan on that. I will call and make an appointment. I will stop by and let you know the day and time." Now her voice was clipped. She turned and walked down the steps of the porch, then she turned back and smiled at Verna, standing to the side of her mother. "I'll see you soon, Verna! It was so nice to meet you."

Willa's embarrassment at being "caught out" by Mrs. Charles, and the lack of medical care for Verna, manifested itself on Verna's little body. It was a brutal beating. Verna tried to get away when she saw her mother coming, but she was too small. The fist came down on her head. Blow after blow until Verna saw the room spin once and then turn black.

When Mrs. Charles came back an hour later, she didn't see Verna. Willa kept her from coming into the house once again.

"The appointment is set for Monday at nine a.m.," Mrs. Charles said, looking past Willa to find Verna.

No luck. The door was shut in her face.

Mrs. Charles picked up Willa and Verna for the immunization appointment. Verna had never been in a car before. It was so alien and terrifyingly loud. Verna put her fingers in her ears and closed her eyes as tightly as she could. She was wearing an old T-shirt of her mother's and a pair of sandals that were much too big for her little feet.

At the doctor's office, things went from bad to worse. Verna was underweight. She had unexplained bruises. Several of her teeth were rotted out, and she had lice. A nurse whisked her away and began to run a fine-toothed comb through Verna's hair. Then she scrubbed her head so hard with a harsh-smelling liquid that Verna could not control her tears. Another nurse came in with three syringes and, without ceremony or explanation, jabbed them one after another into Verna's thigh. Neither of these nurses were cruel; in fact, like Mrs. Charles, their hearts broke for this pathetic little girl. But their work was to give her medical care, and they did it efficiently. They removed her oversized shirt and sandals and put her in two doctor's gowns, one tying in the front and the other tying in the back. Verna had never been so frightened in her life.

Until she walked back into the doctor's waiting room.

Willa was nowhere to be seen. Verna searched the room with her large eyes, trying to find her mother. Mrs. Charles sat in a plastic chair and looked pitifully at Verna. Even in her startled and confused state, Verna did not like that look of pity. She immediately looked at the floor.

"Verna?" Mrs. Charles spoke softly. "Verna, dear? I would like to bring you home with me today. We will have something to eat, and I will get you some new clothes. Won't that be nice? We'll have a little visit."

"Mother?" Verna asked.

"She's not feeling well, my dear. She is going to get some help from a doctor to feel better. It will take some time for her to get well. Please, don't be frightened, Verna. I will take care of you. I promise."

Of course, Verna didn't have a choice. Does any six-year-old? She followed Mrs. Charles out to her very loud car. She kept her eyes open this time and watched out the window. What she saw was fascinating. She saw streets going in different directions. There were trees on all the streets. She saw houses, and in front of many of them there were beautiful flowers. She thought they only existed in her coloring book, but apparently, they were real.

For the first time in her life, Verna saw other children. They were outside. Some were running. Some were riding on something with two wheels that Verna didn't recognize. Some were just sitting and talking. To each other. Her eyes couldn't take it all in. It was too foreign and too frightening. Her head felt funny and everything looked fuzzy. Mrs. Charles's car roared in Verna's ears. She closed her eyes and quietly fainted on the floor of the front seat.

Mrs. Abernathy saw Maggie at the gate of the backyard, and her rage was fueled. Her embarrassment at being seen and caught in such an emotional state left her unable to rebuild her protective wall of condescension and disdain. Mrs. Abernathy was out of control. She stood shakily and turned toward her back door. She had to escape that wretched girl.

Maggie quickly opened the gate and flew at Mrs. Abernathy like a small bird.

"Mrs. Abernathy. Please, stop. Mrs. Abernathy, I've come to—"

All of a sudden, Maggie saw the blood stain on Mrs. Abernathy's back. The blood was seeping through her dress, and the stain was spreading. Maggie's voice grew low and serious.

"Mrs. Abernathy, you're hurt. You're bleeding. You must let me help you. I don't care how much you hate me right now, I'm not going anywhere."

Mrs. Abernathy instinctively reached a hand around to carefully feel her back. She felt the warm stickiness of the blood but kept walking toward the door. With boots and legs covered in dirt and mud, she went inside and tried to shut Maggie out, but the pain in her back kept her from being able to close the door. Maggie barged into the kitchen and stood there defiantly, also scared to death.

"Tell me how to help you, or I'm calling 911," Maggie said a little dramatically. "Or . . . I'm calling Dr. Elliot!"

Mrs. Abernathy sank into one of the kitchen chairs. Maggie could see her face turning white as she slowly laid her head in her hands on the table. Maggie went to the sink, got a glass from the cupboard, and filled it with water. She brought it to Mrs. Abernathy and sat down next to her.

Mrs. Abernathy had her eyes closed, but Maggie could see the tears streaming out. Soon Mrs. Abernathy's back was convulsing in sobs. The blood began to spread again.

Maggie looked around the room for a box of tissues. None. She went in search and found some in the bathroom. She brought them back and gently pushed a handful of tissues into Mrs. Abernathy's hand. Maggie didn't know what to do next. She wished her mother were there to tell her the next practical thing to do. Should she try to stop the bleeding? Should she get Mrs. Abernathy to bed? Should she go get a neighbor?

She looked back at Mrs. Abernathy's contorted face—her sad, sad face. Quietly Maggie said, "Mrs. Abernathy, I don't know what to do next. I can see you are hurt and your back is bleeding. And I can see that something else is hurting you too. I can't leave. I hope you understand." Then Maggie took a breath and said, "I also won't mention a word of this to anyone. I promise."

Mrs. Abernathy opened her eyes and looked up at Maggie. The look of hatred had been washed away by pure, raw sadness.

"There's no way you could ever understand."

"You're right," Maggie said, relieved Mrs. Abernathy wasn't dead or dying. "But that doesn't mean I can't help you, and it doesn't mean you can't help me to understand. Does it?"

Mrs. Abernathy's eyes filled again, and she pressed the tissues against them. For the first time, she seemed so very human to Maggie. Mrs. Abernathy cleared her throat and looked at Maggie.

"Do you know how to make tea, girl?"

"Yes," said Maggie with a slight lift of her chin, "as a matter of fact, I do."

Six-year-old Verna awoke without any awareness of where she was. She looked around at a strange room and realized she was lying on something soft. She had never been on a bed before. The walls were painted a pale blue. There were pieces of furniture in the room, but she couldn't identify them. She had never seen anything like them. She stayed very still. After a time, she heard the door open with a small squeak. Mrs. Charles came into the room. She sat on the bed near Verna and smiled.

"Verna, I'm glad you are awake. I was very frightened in the car when you fainted. How are you feeling?"

"Where?" Verna whispered.

"Where are you?" Mrs. Charles asked.

Verna nodded.

"You're in my home. You will stay here for a while. Please don't be afraid. Are you hungry?"

Verna just stared. She had no comprehension. Verna's only experience with language was listening to the radio whenever her mother turned it on.

Mrs. Charles led Verna into the kitchen. She had prepared egg salad sandwiches, small sweet pickles, green grapes, and oatmeal cookies. The table was set for two with plates, silverware, cloth napkins, teacups, and glasses of lemonade. A large bouquet of yellow zinnias made the table look cheerful.

Mrs. Charles helped Verna onto a chair and sat down next to her. Then she handed Verna the plate of sandwiches. Verna didn't know what to do. She set the sandwich plate on top of her empty plate. Mrs. Charles showed her how to take a sandwich and put it on her plate and then pass the sandwiches back. She did this with the bowls of pickles and grapes. Verna learned quickly. They ate in silence. Verna imitated Mrs. Charles when she wiped her mouth with the napkin. They each ate two cookies for dessert. Mrs. Charles had made a pot of tea and showed Verna how to pour it into the cups and add sugar and milk.

"Verna," Mrs. Charles said quietly, "I want you to know you are safe now. You will always be safe in this house. I was thinking you might enjoy a bubble bath."

Mrs. Charles was quite certain Verna had never experienced a bubble bath. Verna followed mutely as they went into the bathroom, and she watched the water fill the large, white bathtub with bubbles covering the surface. Mrs. Charles helped Verna out of the two doctor's gowns and lifted her into the bubbles. She hid her shock at the bruises up and down Verna's body. Verna looked at her, at first afraid, then she gave a shy smile. The warm water felt so good on her skin. Mrs. Charles carefully washed the harsh chemicals out of Verna's hair with shampoo. She let Verna sit in the tub and poke at the bubbles. Then she dried her off with a large yellow towel.

While Verna had been asleep, Mrs. Charles had phoned another mother from the school with a daughter Verna's age and asked to borrow some clothes. The mother had brought over several items for Verna to keep. Mrs. Charles helped Verna step into new underpants and a cotton dress covered in orange flowers. Then she put her arms around Verna's thin shoulders and gently gave her a hug. Verna stood absolutely still.

Mrs. Abernathy placed her hands on the table as she slowly rose to stand. Maggie could see the unsteadiness in Mrs. Abernathy's legs. She quickly said, "Mrs. Abernathy, please don't. I'm going to beg you for three things."

Mrs. Abernathy looked at Maggie with all the disdain she could muster, which ended up looking as though she needed to have a bowel movement.

"Three things?" Her voice was raspy.

"Yes," said Maggie, trying not to antagonize. "One, please sit back down. Two, I don't know, or need to know, why your back is bleeding, but you need medical attention. Now, I could drive you into Ann Arbor, and we could sit in the emergency room for a few hours together tonight, or I could call Dr. Elliot. He would be here in minutes, and I know he could care for you. And three, could we call a truce, just for tonight?"

Mrs. Abernathy seemed at a loss as to how to respond to the kindly directness, but she didn't have any more energy left to fight. Maybe by tomorrow.

"You may call Dr. Elliot. But I don't want you in the room when he's here."

"Of course. Thank you." Maggie kept her voice monotone as she reached for her cell phone.

She quickly pulled up Jack's number and was thrilled when he answered on the third ring. She kept her voice steady, knowing Mrs. Abernathy was watching and listening like a hawk.

"Dr. Elliot? This is Maggie." (She purposely didn't say "Pastor Maggie" so as not to rile Mrs. Abernathy.) "I'm at Mrs. Abernathy's house . . . yes . . . yes, really . . . Listen, she needs a little medical care, and I wondered if you could come over . . . as quickly as possible . . . She may need some stitches." At this, she carefully looked at Mrs. Abernathy, who nodded resignedly. "Yes, definitely . . . Thank you. Goodbye."

Maggie looked at Mrs. Abernathy, who had her head in her hands again.

"I have one last question," Maggie said gently. Mrs. Abernathy looked up. "How do you take your tea? With lemon or milk and sugar?"

"Milk and sugar."

Jack arrived within fifteen minutes. He had a real black bag, which Maggie didn't think existed anymore. He was professional, which seemed to put Mrs. Abernathy at ease, and extremely kind, which made her fight back tears.

"I'll just step into the living room," Maggie said when Jack began to open his bag.

"Now Mrs. Abernathy," Jack said calmly, "I'm going to clean the wound, numb the area, and then stitch you back up. This won't take long."

"Get on with it, please." Mrs. Abernathy sighed.

"Do you have any pain pills to help with the pain of the wound?" Jack asked.

"Yes. They are upstairs. I don't like to take them often because they make me groggy."

"May I ask Maggie to get them, please?" Jack asked as he swabbed her back.

She didn't answer, so Jack called out, "Pastor Maggie, could you please get the pain pills upstairs in the . . ." He looked at Mrs. Abernathy.

"My bedroom." The intrusion on her privacy hurt worse than the tear in her back.

"The bedroom," Jack finished.

They heard Maggie make her way up the stairs.

When Jack had taped the bandage into place, Maggie came back into the kitchen and brought the steeping tea to the table with a sugar bowl and creamer of milk.

In the most unlikely of circumstances, Maggie, Jack, and Mrs. Abernathy sat together and drank a pot of tea.

Mrs. Abernathy looked at Maggie. "This is a decent cup of tea. Surprisingly."

Maggie smiled. "I'm a tea expert. It's how I got through seminary. My grandma taught me how to make it."

"Don't you just dunk a teabag in hot water?" Jack asked.

Mrs. Abernathy and Maggie looked at him like he was a sad, silly little boy. But then, he was just a doctor. How could he know anything of the great nuances of tea?

Maggie slipped into thoughts of the sparseness of Mrs. Abernathy's living room, and when Jack asked Maggie to bring Mrs. Abernathy's pain pills from the bedroom, Maggie saw how little Mrs. Abernathy either owned or chose to display. There wasn't one photograph to be seen anywhere. Every room and piece of furniture was spotless. The colors were several varied shades of white. The only true colors were the vases of orange, rust, and yellow zinnias. They were in every room of the house.

Jack checked the prescription on the pill bottle and told Mrs. Abernathy to take the pills as recommended, not as she pleased. He knew she wasn't taking them often enough, which meant she was in pain.

"These will help you sleep. They will also help with pain during the day. There is no reason for you not to take them, Mrs. Abernathy," Jack said in his gravest doctor voice.

"I don't like having a fuzzy head, and that's what they do to me," Mrs. Abernathy replied.

"Take them until your back is healed. When you see your doctor again, she or he may prescribe something different if you still need anything. You may feel well enough without them. Also, no more digging in the garden until after you see your doctor. That's my order." But he said it with a smile.

She smiled back weakly, defeated.

"Mrs. Abernathy," Maggie said, "Dr. Elliot and I will never speak of this evening to anyone. You have our word. I'm sorry if I embarrassed you in any way. I understand the need for privacy. I just want you to know that, if you do need anything, I would be happy to bring it to you or to drive you places. I'm just saying, I would be happy to keep the truce going for a little longer than tonight if you do." She waited for a response and realized she was holding her breath.

"Thank you for your courtesy tonight, both of you," Mrs. Abernathy began. "I believe I will be fine now and able to care for myself. Please don't think this has changed anything regarding the cats in the parsonage or my questions regarding your fitness for ministry." She looked directly at Maggie. "You are a nice girl, but that does not a pastor make."

She was sounding more like herself now. Maggie was almost relieved. Cranky Mrs. Abernathy was easier to handle than the more vulnerable version.

Mrs. Abernathy saw them both to the front door and thanked them again before ushering them out, closing the door, and turning off the porch light.

Maggie and Jack stood in the driveway. Jack spoke first.

"You know you did the right thing, don't you?"

"Yes," Maggie said tiredly. "Thanks for coming so fast. I was afraid she would change her mind, and then I didn't know what I was going to do. I think she was scared when she felt the blood. Is she going to be all right?"

"I don't know. She didn't want to talk about the reason for the stitches. I told her to call her doctor tomorrow and explain everything. I'd guess she had a growth removed for a biopsy. I just broke doctor/patient confidentiality by telling you that." Jack smiled, and in the light of the street lamp his tall, dark, and handsome seemed taller, darker, and handsomer.

Maggie smiled. "I'm keeping secrets tonight. Yours is safe. Hey, I have two pieces of strawberry rhubarb pie left at home. Would you like a piece?"

"Is Cheerio still there?"

"I believe so."

"Then I guess I can force down a piece of pie."

Gosh, he's handsome. How had she not noticed before?

They got in their cars and made their way to the parsonage.

Back inside the house, Mrs. Abernathy surveyed her kitchen and had to grudgingly admit that Maggie had done a proper job of cleaning up the tea things. She slowly turned off the downstairs lights and walked up to her bedroom. Then she carefully got ready for bed. She had taken a pain pill in front of Dr. Elliot because he insisted. He had nerve. She was feeling just the littlest bit woozy, and it felt good to crawl into her bed.

As she was falling asleep, her mind went back to the first night she ever slept in a bed. She had been six years old, and it was a feather bed, so soft. She was covered with a down comforter. She was in Caroline Charles's house. She was clean and smelled like bubble bath. Her tummy was full of something called spaghetti. Caroline had read her a story before bed. Then Caroline had pulled a soft pillow snuggly down to her shoulders, and then she did the most remarkable thing of all— she kissed Verna on the forehead.

Verna lay very still. She felt her eyes getting heavier and finally closing. She was falling . . . falling, falling, falling . . . asleep.

12

When Jack first sat down, Marmalade and Cheerio roused themselves from their latest nap. Cheerio wobbled sleepily over to Jack, her tail straight up and curled at the end like a question mark. Jack picked her up, and she nestled in the crook of his arm. Marmalade watched, then curled up at Jack's feet, keeping one golden eyeball on his kitten.

"I can make some more tea," Maggie said without enthusiasm, "but would you rather have something else?" She put two plates of pie on the table.

"Do you have any milk?" Jack asked.

Maggie laughed. "Yes, Dr. Elliot, I have milk."

She poured him a large glass to go with his pie.

"You make a lot of pie," Jack said, polite enough to swallow first. "It's great."

"I love making pie," Maggie said, stabbing a strawberry. "My grandma taught me when I was little. It's a stress reliever for me, actually. When I bake, I relax. Then I feed people, which fulfills a strange mothering instinct."

"That's great," Jack said, "but I can't call you Mom. Sorry."

"Good. I'm sure you have your own mom." Maggie wrinkled her nose.

Cheerio had gotten a whiff of Jack's milk, jumped on the table, and helped herself to a few tongue laps. Jack gave her a pet and then took a gulp himself. Maggie was immensely impressed that he would drink after a cat. It wouldn't bother her, but it would bother many people. Clearly, not the handsome doctor. Cheerio helped herself to a few more laps and then curled up in Jack's arm again.

"But I can call you Pastor Maggie. What made you want to be a pastor?"

Jack truly seemed interested. Maggie had often been surprised how many people avoided asking her about her call to ministry. She hadn't figured out why.

"I had no intention of being a pastor. I thought I might follow my mom into psychology. I like figuring out how people work. I also loved drama and spent a lot of time in plays and shows all through high school and then college."

Maggie flipped her hair dramatically and flourished her hand around her head.

Jack laughed. "That sounds terrifying."

"It wasn't. It was fun to 'be' other characters and work together with a group to make a performance successful. Anyway, after college I had an opportunity to go to Israel with a drama team to act in two Christian plays. I was so excited to be 'a real actress.' But God was just having a little fun and laughing the whole time."

She got up and got herself a glass of water. Telling the story always got her excited.

"Really? How long were you there?" Jack had stopped eating.

"Six months. Six glorious months. We saw everything but spent most of our time in Jerusalem and Bethlehem." Maggie was getting dreamy.

"So, I take it something happened there to move you from psychology to theology?"

"Yes. God spoke to me."

Jack didn't laugh.

"I was standing on the hills of Bethlehem, trying to herd several little angels around. The children were playing and laughing. It was nighttime, and I looked up at the stars in the sky. They were so bright because there were no city lights to dim them. And God spoke. Or I felt God speaking, somewhere inside. I heard in my head, or my soul, that God wanted me to tell this incredible story. The story of where Jesus was born, where he walked, what he said, how he lived, how he died, and how he blew death away by living again. It seemed so simple. It seemed as if I could just come home, go to seminary, tell the story, and change the world."

Jack, who couldn't imagine living in a foreign country for six months, saw an adventurous depth in Maggie. What was he feeling? Envy?

"I tend to be somewhat idealistic," Maggie continued, petting Marmalade. "But that was the night that changed my life. I realized God had to throw me halfway around the world to get my attention. Then he had to speak very loudly on a Bethlehem hillside to tell me what he expected me to do with my life." Then Maggie felt embarrassed. "I'm doing way too much talking. I want to know about you. Medical school, being a doctor, all of it."

Jack was slightly taken aback. He had been enthralled by her story. "Wait, I want to know what it was like for you to come home after six months of that." His voice was insistent. He hadn't heard enough.

"I had a bit of culture shock, actually. Life here seemed so simplistic compared to how the people lived all over Israel. We heard bombs go off. It was terrifying, but the people there had somehow become immune to hearing the blasts. I walked and lived where Jesus walked and lived. It was electrifying. When I came home, I saw Americans as entitled, elitist, self-indulgent, and too comfortable, especially the Christians. I say that because sometimes I make sweeping, emotional generalizations." She grimaced.

Jack laughed at this, and Cheerio jumped.

"So how did you get your emotional sweepings under control?" Jack was feeling emotionally swept himself.

"It was Ed," she continued, "my professor, Ed James."

"I spoke with him at coffee time this morning," Jack said. "He seems to think you actually do walk on water, in spite of the title of your sermon."

Jack watched her look down at the table. He hadn't wanted to embarrass her. She looked up and gazed into his eyes. She wanted Jack to know the rest of the story.

"Ed let me spew my judgments and question the inequities of life. I had seen many of the poorest residents in the Arab settlements, and couldn't understand the political, historical, and theological history that kept this small country at war with itself. Ed painstakingly educated me through stories, articles, books, and conversation. He also believed I had heard God. Ed figuratively and literally led me to the seminary doors. He explained later that, once God had spoken, there was no way I could get away from my call to ministry. No protest, yelling, kicking, or screaming could stand up to God's plan. So, I blame Ed. And I thank God for him every day. Ed was God-in-the-flesh for me. He was also my seminary jailer. I love that man!" She grinned.

"That's an amazing story. I'm glad God and Ed brought you to Cherish. I hope it wasn't amidst yelling, kicking, and screaming." His brown eyes twinkled.

"Nope. But that's only because I didn't know how awful Mrs. Abernathy would turn out to be. God left that as a little surprise."

Maggie looked at the clock. Ten thirty. Jack followed her gaze and gently put Cheerio on the floor next to Marmalade.

"I should go. It's late, and we've had a busy night forcing Mrs. Abernathy to accept help, and then pie, and the riveting story of your life. Thank you for all the excitement." Jack stood.

Maggie said, "It looks like you're bringing a little bit of Cheerio home with you. Sorry about that." She picked the fluff off his arm.

"I don't mind. I saw a plaque once that read, 'No outfit is complete without cat hair.' She just spiffed me up tonight. You need to know I grew up with litters and litters of barn cats. They were always pets to us. I'm a fan."

Well, good grief! Maggie thought. *He's handsome, and he loves barn cats.*

"When will I get to hear your riveting life story?" Maggie asked, walking him to the front door of the parsonage.

"We will pick a time very soon. I promise."

They said their goodbyes and Maggie went upstairs. She picked up her phone to text Nora.

> Did you have a wonderful day sharing your news??
> I'm so thrilled for you and Dan.

> It was the best day! You should hear some of the ideas the youth group has for our wedding!
> One: On the beach in bathing suits!?!
> How was your day with family and Ed and Jo?

> Great with them! Every other minute crazy. Ended the day with Dr. Jack over here for pie after a Mrs. Abernathy crisis. He likes cats.

> Mmmmmmmmmm......Let's talk soon!

> Sleep tight and so will I.

The next morning, after a serious head bashing from Marmalade, Maggie finally got up and went downstairs for coffee, oatmeal, and cat breakfasts. She decided to be organized and make a to-do list.

- Clean church office—get rid of leftover veggies
- Meet with Jennifer and Beth Becker re: Mrs. Becker's funeral tomorrow
- Double-check funeral arrangements with Cole
- Call Marla re: Sunday school picnic set for September 6
- Begin Sunday sermon prep
- Thank you note to Ed and Jo

That was a good start. She would manage this day. It would not manage her. Yesterday she felt as if she had been on a rollercoaster with no seatbelt—too much emotional whiplash.

She went upstairs and put on a flowing, gauzy skirt and peasant blouse. She brushed her hair and teeth, used a little mascara and lipstick, and then took in her appearance. She looked fabulous. Of course, her mother would shudder and say, "No, Maggie. Not to the church office!" in the same way she used to say, "No, Maggie. You can't wear that to school!"

Maggie slipped her feet into her flip-flops, pet the kitties, and floated over to church like an ethereal swirl of cotton candy.

Bill Baxter was in front of the church, using a nail gun to build the new ramp. The wood from the old ramp was stacked in the back of his pickup truck. Maggie looked around for Fitch Dervish. He wasn't there.

"Good morning, Bill."

Bill looked up, somewhat startled. The nail gun went off, and a nail shot into the flower bed.

"Whoa! Sorry, Pastor Maggie. You surprised me, I guess." Bill's face turned as red as his hair.

"No, I'm sorry. You were working so intently. I didn't mean to scare you." Maggie was amazed, once again, at how incredibly shy Bill was.

"I have about an hour before Fitch gets back from doing an inspection on Kalmbach Road. I wanted to get the ramp built." He looked down at the nail. "By the way, thanks for that little goose-chase you sent him on the other day. He never found your imaginary shed." Bill chuckled.

"My pleasure. I wish you didn't have to work with him breathing down your neck all the time."

"Yep."

"I'll let you get to it."

Maggie walked up the steps and opened the large oak doors to the sanctuary. Something was not quite right. She could hear voices coming from the office. She quickly walked across the gathering area and opened Hank's office.

"PASTOR MAGGIE!" Five voices shouted at once.

She jumped. Hank was standing behind a desk piled high with rubbish from yesterday. Doris was there with her cleaning cart. Her arms were crossed, and she was shaking her head. Irena teetered on her high heels, carrying her usual stack of music. *What did she actually do with all that music?* Beyond those three, Maggie could see Sylvia standing in her office. She held two bags with carrot fronds sticking up. Marla was also there, sorting copies of something on the work table.

"I've had it!" Hank bellowed. "Monday mornings are all the same. I get to work and find my desk buried in refuse. I don't know how else to say it. *My desk is not a trash can!!*"

"Well, don't look at me," Doris scowled back. "Do you think I enjoy finding all the creative places people leave their trash? Under pews, on the windowsills, in the plants, and on the library bookshelves? Why do we even have trash cans?"

Maggie felt the tension begin to build in her shoulders.

"Vat ees yoor complaineeng?" Irena joined the fray from behind her music. "Eef you two shut up and moove trash, dis vould all be cleean by now. Vat surprise, Hunk? Yoour desk ees alvays a mess on Mondays. De end." She began to teeter again, and Maggie reached out to steady her. "Pastoor Maggie, now de museek for de funral tomorrow. Vee talk!"

Maggie realized she hadn't been breathing and took a deep breath.

"Irena, I'm meeting with Jennifer and Beth Becker in one hour. Could you and I meet after that? I'll get some ideas from them of their mother's favorite hymns and music."

"Okay, dat's fine." Irena tottered off without a fuss.

Maggie, Hank, and Doris stood flabbergasted at this normal response coming from abnormal Irena. Maggie turned to Hank.

"Hank, we have to come up with another idea for your desk. The announcements in the bulletin aren't working. Announcements from the pulpit aren't working either. We must think of something more dramatic so that Mondays aren't so traumatic . . . for all of us. And Doris," Maggie swiveled in her direction, "if you could be a little more helpful with Hank's desk, it would be appreciated. I promise we will find a way to teach this congregation to clean up their messes." She walked on through to her own office and greeted Sylvia and Marla. "Hi, you two!"

Marla greeted Maggie the way she always did, with a big hug.

"Oh, Pastor Maggie! Your sermon yesterday was so powerful. All of us in the boat. All of us disciples! How do you do it?" She looked as if she might cry.

Maggie quickly said, "Thanks, Marla. By the way, Jason and Addie were so much fun in Sunday school yesterday. I think we will have a great Youth Sunday in October."

Marla blushed under these compliments of her children, just as Maggie expected, although she was speaking the truth. Marla had completely forgotten about the sermon, as Maggie had hoped.

"And," Maggie continued, "I just wanted to double-check that the Sunday school picnic is still set for September six and is under control."

"Pastor Maggie, it is completely under control. Sylvia and I will handle everything. We have the games planned, and the bouncy castle is ordered." Marla chortled with glee. "We have the picnic sign-up sheets ready for this coming Sunday. Actually, here they are if you would like to take a look. Pastor Maggie, you just come to the picnic and enjoy yourself." Marla sounded as if she were reporting the strategy of the infantry.

Maggie briefly browsed the sheets on the work table. She looked over at Sylvia and saw her place the bags of vegetables on the desk.

"I can't believe how your garden grows, Sylvia," Maggie said. "But I'm just about out of room right now. Can you think of anyone else who could use some?"

Marla stealthily made her way out of the office. She couldn't handle any more vegetables either, being the owner of two children who wouldn't touch them.

"Well," said Sylvia, "I really don't know who else to give them to." She looked stumped.

"How about Bill Baxter? I would think a single guy would enjoy some homegrown veggies. Maybe you could even make him a vegetable casserole. I bet he hasn't had a homemade meal in a long time." Maggie stealthily planted the seed and now hoped to watch it grow. "He's outside right now working on the ramp. You could ask him what his favorite veggies are." *Please.*

That idea seemed to intrigue Sylvia. She retrieved her bags from the desk.

"Pastor Maggie, that is a fantastic idea. I think I'll make him a summer squash and carrot soufflé. But first, I'll put one of these bags in his truck. Then he'll have veggies for the week."

Maggie silently apologized to Bill Baxter.

Sylvia left, and Maggie helped Hank clean off his desk. As her "to-do" list was getting done, her mind wandered to the night before. She kept thinking she could smell Jack's aftershave, but they hadn't even shaken hands when he left. She replayed their conversation over and over and almost threw Hank's lunch in the trash before he brought her back to reality with a little bark.

"Pastor Maggie! That's my lunch. Put it down and go back to your office."

Maggie burst into laughter. Hank thought maybe Pastor Maggie needed to go for a walk around the block.

When Jennifer and Beth Becker arrived, Hank ushered them into Maggie's office. The stories Jennifer and Beth had told Maggie when they were together at the Friendly Elder Care had given Maggie a good start for her eulogy. They told her their mother's favorite Bible verses and her favorite hymns. Maggie made notes of everything to share with Irena.

This funeral would be different from Rupert Solomon's. But then, every funeral would be different because every person and every family would be different. She told herself that she had to make sure to remember the life of the one who died and to never use the same service over again. She heard that some pastors did that. *Lazy.* Death was the last chance to let someone be their true, unique self, whether for good or for ill. Mrs. Becker was truly good.

Maggie was surprised to see it was already eleven thirty. The morning was flying by. Jennifer and Beth thanked her for her time then quietly left. She would see them at The Porter Funeral Home later for the visitation.

Maggie found Irena in the sanctuary, practicing loudly on the organ. Maggie caught her breath as she took in Irena's appearance, which had been hidden behind the stack of music she carried into Hank's office. Irena had found a new green eye shadow embedded with gold glitter. Maggie thought staring at her eyelids could possibly cause seizures. Besides her fantastical eyes, her breasts were definitely spilling out of her push-up bra. Every time she leaned over the organ, her flesh inched out a little farther. Maggie averted her eyes in embarrassment.

"Irena!" Maggie said.

Nothing.

"IRENA!!"

Irena turned abruptly, jerking her hands away from the organ keys. "Vy you screeaming at me like dat? You tink I'm deff?"

"Sorry," Maggie said, not rolling her eyes but really wanting to. "I have the hymns for Mrs. Becker's funeral. They're all familiar, and I know you will do a wonderful job, as usual."

Maggie handed the list of hymns to Irena, who pointed to the organ bench. Maggie set them down.

"Ov coourse." Irena turned back to her music, and Maggie turned to leave when Irena said, "All in de boat, yes?"

Maggie turned back. "What?"

"All in de boat. All row. Ve row." Irena turned her glittered eyes on Maggie.

"Yes," said Maggie, "we're all in the boat, and we're rowing together. And I'm glad you're in the boat, Irena."

"Ov coourse you are." Irena sniffed, quickly turned her head, and raised her hands above the keys. "Juust remember, I am de driver."

Her hands went down, and the sanctuary was filled with the sound of the pipe organ.

"I think Jesus is the driver," Maggie said as she walked away, her eyes rolling like marbles.

As she walked into Hank's office, Maggie was surprised to see Harold sitting in her office. Hank looked at her and whispered, "He just got here. Were you expecting him?"

"I don't think so. But who knows? I really should keep a calendar," Maggie whispered back.

She walked into her office and saw Harold's sandy-colored head and many perfect teeth. He was dressed in a pale-gray silk suit with a royal-blue shirt and a gray-and-blue paisley tie. His bright-blue eyes almost glowed. Harold actually could give Bradley Cooper a run for his money. But for some reason, all Maggie could think of was Jack.

"Hi, Harold. Did we have a meeting that I've forgotten? My mother has told me to keep a calendar for years. I think it's time I do what she says," Maggie said, smiling a little too much.

"No, no, Pastor Maggie. I just stopped by to see if I could take you to lunch. We could . . . umm . . . look at next month's agenda for the council meeting."

He seemed a little awkward to Maggie. Or maybe she was the one feeling awkward. He kept talking.

"I figured you had to eat, and since I do too, I thought we could walk over to O'Leary's Pub for a quick bite. How about it?" He looked tentatively hopeful.

"Well, sure. Thank you," Maggie said a little stiffly. "That sounds great. I haven't been to O'Leary's yet." Then she had another thought. This would be the perfect time to tell Harold about Redford and the envelope she saw him carrying yesterday after church.

As she rose, she heard someone enter Hank's office. Looking through the door, she spotted Cole Porter.

She looked at Harold and said, "Excuse me for just a moment please, Harold."

She walked into Hank's office and greeted Cole.

"You are on my to-do list today, Cole, and here you are. I planned to walk down to the funeral home this afternoon. Jennifer and Beth were just in and gave me some special verses and hymns for the service."

"I thought I'd stop in and give you the final details of Mrs. Becker's funeral. Visitation is this afternoon beginning at two o'clock at the funeral home. I'll bring the flowers here tomorrow morning around nine. Is that okay?"

"Of course. Hank and I will both be here."

She gave a little nod to Hank, who nodded back. His face was very funereal. Maggie almost laughed.

"Good. I'll see you later this afternoon, then?" Cole asked as he turned toward the door.

"I'll be there. Thanks, Cole, for everything."

After Cole left, Hank looked at Maggie and said, "I don't know that flip-flops are the proper thing to wear to a visitation, Pastor Maggie."

Her face flushed as she looked at her feet. "Well, of course they aren't. I was planning on changing, Hank." *Lie. Why do shoes and clothes have to matter so much?* "Harold and I are going to O'Leary's for some lunch, and then I'll be back."

"I'll hold down the fort, yessireebob!" Hank said as he pulled out his rescued brown-bag lunch.

Harold and Maggie walked around the corner and found an empty table in the midst of the lunch crowd at O'Leary's. They saw several people from church at the other tables. Sylvia and Marla were having lunch, no doubt discussing the Sunday school picnic. Ellen and another nurse Maggie didn't recognize were eating and laughing at a table by the door. Redford was at the bar. Maggie seriously hoped he wasn't drinking at this hour. The menu was one of good Irish pub food. Maggie forgot her discomfort with Harold for the moment as she realized how hungry she was. She decided on the fish and chips. She closed her menu and looked up at Harold. He was staring intensely at her.

"Do you know what you're ordering already, Harold?" she asked. "I think I'll have the fish and chips. Have you had them here before?"

"Maggie, thank you for having lunch with me today." Harold completely ignored her question. "I have wanted to talk to you for quite a while." His voice was like honey, soft and gooey.

Maggie's internal warning system went on full alert. She had certainly had boyfriends before and had enjoyed a fun dating life in college. But she had also known some boys who *wanted* to be her boyfriend. They had the same gooey, honey voice. *No, no, no!* She had to shut him up before he said something ridiculous and then felt embarrassed every time he saw her from then on. They had to work together, for heaven's sake.

"Harold," Maggie spoke quickly, "I have something I want to run by you."

Harold nodded, giving her one hundred percent of his attention and teeth.

"Yesterday, after the council meeting, I saw Redford Johnson leaving with a large envelope. I don't want to make false accusations, but it looked like the bank offering envelope."

Harold stopped smiling and looked serious.

"I wondered what the protocol was with the offering. I was taught it is important for the pastor not to be part of the actual week-to-week counting and banking. I've chosen not to know the combination of the safe at church. It's just smart. I understand the budget, but who does the banking? I've been taught that two people must count the weekly offering together." Maggie took a deep breath.

"In our bylaws it is stipulated that the secretary of church, Hank, the chairperson of council, me, the chairperson of finance, Redford, and the clerk of council, Charlotte Tuggle, will all know the combination for the safe. Of course, those people change every few years when the council changes, but then, so does the combination. As for counting and banking, you are right. Two members of the finance committee are supposed to count the money on Sundays after church and then give the total with a tally sheet to the clerk of the council to deposit at the bank on Monday." Harold looked down at his napkin. "But I have to admit, we've become little slack in the last few months. Redford has been doing most of the work alone."

"What have I been doing alone?"

Maggie and Harold physically jumped in their chairs. How long had Redford been standing there? He reeked of whiskey.

"I asked a question, friends."

"Redford." Harold stood up. "Were you eavesdropping on a private conversation?"

"Well, I heard my name. So, what's your problem?"

He bent down and leaned into Maggie's face. She pulled away quickly.

Harold took Redford's shoulder, gently steered him away from Maggie, and said calmly, "Redford, we are in a very public place right now. Your behavior is unacceptable. We will set a council meeting to discuss financial issues and different protocols. It seems things have gotten sloppy. But we won't discuss it here. Please leave our table. Now."

Redford looked as if he would unleash a torrent of foul language for the entire restaurant to feast upon, but something caught his eye at the door of the pub. Instead, he stumbled slightly and moved back toward the bar. He climbed onto a barstool far from the door.

Harold turned, and Maggie looked up to see Charlotte Tuggle and Bernie Bumble—both in their police uniforms—with Hank and Doris right behind them. Charlotte squinted to adjust to the low lighting in the pub. Once she saw Maggie and Harold, she made a beeline to their table. As fast as a two-hundred-fifty-pound bee can move.

"Pastor Margaret Elzinga," Charlotte used her powerful police voice, "you are under arrest for unpaid parking tickets. I have to ask you to come with me."

Maggie was stunned. Harold's mouth dropped open. The pub became very quiet. The only sound to be heard was the Irish music playing in the background.

"Charlotte, what are you doing?" Maggie hissed. "You can't arrest me for unpaid parking tickets. That's ridiculous!"

"Actually, it isn't. Now will you come along calmly or not?" Charlotte stood ramrod straight and prepared to reach for her handcuffs.

Maggie noticed Bernie staring at the floor and shaking his head. She couldn't remember ever feeling this kind of embarrassment before.

Everyone stared at her, her parishioners and strangers alike. The owner of the pub was walking over to the table. Redford smiled from the bar.

Maggie was certain she was in a *Twilight Zone* nightmare.

"Of course I'll come calmly." Maggie turned to Harold. "I apologize, Harold, for not being able to stay for lunch. Apparently, you almost ate with a hardened criminal."

Maggie stood as tall as her five-foot-three-inch frame would allow her to stand. *Drat! Why did I put on flip-flops, today of all days?* She flip-flopped out of the pub in between Charlotte and Bernie. As she passed Hank, she whispered, "My purse is hanging on the back of my study door at home. Would you bring it to me?"

Hank looked as though he might cry. "Of course, Pastor Maggie. Yessireebob, I'll bring it right to you."

He trotted off in the direction of the church and parsonage. Doris and Irena stared as Maggie walked by. Maggie did not return either gaze. They followed anyway, as did Ellen, Marla, and Sylvia.

Redford remained at the bar, chuckling into his whiskey. *It's just what she deserves. She's nothing but trouble, and now she's in it big*, he thought. But then he had another thought. He paid his bill quickly and high-tailed it to his office, albeit somewhat wobbly.

There was no need for a police car to chauffeur Maggie, due to the close proximity of the pub and police station, which was on Main and Summit. They walked the three blocks down Main Street, Maggie and her many escorts. When they came to the door of the station, Maggie turned to look down Summit Street.

As it happened, Mrs. Abernathy's front yard came out just far enough to see the front door of the police station. Mrs. Abernathy was standing in her yard, watching the whole police parade, and then saw Officer Tuggle take Maggie by the arm and lead her into the station.

Mrs. Abernathy wasn't alone. Jack was there making a quick visit to his patient of the previous night. They both watched as Maggie disappeared through the police station doors.

13

Mrs. Abernathy had woken up on Monday morning in a daze. She had been sleeping on her side, but as soon as she rolled onto her back, she winced and slowly sat up. Her back ached where she had been restitched. She had a rush of memories from last evening. Her face suffused in heat from embarrassment but quickly gave way to her emotion of choice: anger. Maggie and Dr. Elliot had infiltrated and interfered with her very personal life. It was often the volcanic heat of humiliation that washed over her when she had been too open with her life in a moment of vulnerability. Mrs. Abernathy had learned at a young age to avoid giving anyone too much personal information. It could ricochet back in a harsh comment or a secret let loose by an uncaring listener. She had shared too much last night.

She slowly got up, made the bed meticulously, then carefully dressed for the day. She would see her doctor in Ann Arbor at nine that morning. She had not told Dr. Elliot that last night, but it was none of his business. She would find out that morning both her diagnosis and prognosis. She went through her silent house, down the stairs, and into the kitchen. She steeped a cup of tea and begrudgingly admitted to herself that Maggie did indeed know how to make a perfect pot. She measured her half cup of bran flakes and four ounces of orange juice. Breakfast was quickly dispatched and dishes washed and replaced in the cupboard. Eating was a utilitarian endeavor for Mrs. Abernathy. She had to eat to remain alive. It was rarely enjoyable.

She completed her morning ministrations, read her devotions, and did a check of her garden, where she saw the spade wedged in the dirt. She quickly pulled it out and put it with her gardening tools in the garage. Then she got in her car for the drive to Ann Arbor.

When Jack had arrived at Mrs. Abernathy's house at noon (he was using his lunch break to make a house call), he was greeted almost charitably by Mrs. Abernathy, who was in her garden enjoying her own, along with God's, handiwork. She welcomed him through the same gate Maggie had stood behind the night before.

"How are you doing today, Mrs. Abernathy?" Jack asked kindly.

Mrs. Abernathy couldn't help it. She smiled. "Dr. Elliot, thank you for coming by. And I must thank you again for your help last night. I saw my own doctor this morning and received good news."

"Excellent." Jack smiled. He wanted to know exactly what the good news was but waited for her timing.

"My doctor also said that you did a very good job stitching up my wound. Do you know Dr. Crisp?"

"Yes, he was a few years ahead of me in medical school. He is a respected oncologist. Were you expecting at a diagnosis of skin cancer?" Jack asked carefully.

"Yes. He removed a basal cell carcinoma. You saw how much was removed from my back. He told me today that the margins were clear and he believes he removed all the cancer. I will go back in six months for another checkup." Mrs. Abernathy's face was so animated, she appeared almost pretty.

"Mrs. Abernathy, I am happy for you. I really mean that. I would guess that you have been worried about this for some time. I'm sorry you went through it alone. If I can ever be of any assistance, please let me know."

Jack was thankful when anyone had a good outcome from a medical scare. His favorite words for a patient were, "Oh, this isn't serious. We can take care of this in no time!"

Mrs. Abernathy reached out her hand to his. "Thank you, Dr. Elliot. I am grateful for your help. I apologize for misjudging you these past two months." She didn't go on with any explanation. They both knew she meant her behavior since Pastor Maggie arrived. She walked him to the front yard.

Jack said, "I know Pastor Maggie would be relieved to know you are well. She was very worried about you last night."

"I will phone her later and thank her for her concern," Mrs. Abernathy said a little stiffly.

Just then, she and Jack looked down the street toward the police station. They were both astonished to see Maggie being led into the station by Officers Tuggle and Bumble, with several parishioners in tow.

They walked quickly toward the station.

With the distraction of Maggie's arrest, Redford left O'Leary's and headed down South Street to his small financial services office. A little unsteady on his feet from his lunch of whiskeys, he fumbled with the lock on the door and wobbled slightly to his desk. From the locked bottom drawer, he pulled out the church's offering bank envelope. He tucked it into the inside pocket of his sport coat, relocked the drawer and office door, then walked unsteadily to church. He slithered through the back alley behind the Cherish Café, drunkenly thinking he wouldn't be seen that way.

Once at church, Redford went straight into Hank's office and opened the back closet door. There was the safe. It took him a few tries since he couldn't quite see straight, but it eventually opened. Before he put the envelope in the safe, he opened it and slid out several bills. He shoved them in his pocket, threw the envelope in with a blank counting sheet tucked inside, then locked the safe.

When he came out of the closet, he found himself face to face with Hank.

Hank was standing in the doorway with Maggie's purse slung over his shoulder. From Maggie's parsonage study window, he had seen Redford going into the church.

"What are you doing here?" Hank asked.

"Not's that ish any of your busineshh," Redford slurred.

"It is my business. But I have to get this purse to Pastor Maggie. I'll let her know you were here. In the safe," Hank said with disdain.

"Listen, I was jusht getting the bank envelope to bring to Charlotte. She makesh the deposits on Mondays." Redford tried to sound normal, which just made him sound drunker.

"Then why did you put the envelope *in* the safe instead of taking it *out*?" Hank growled.

He pushed Redford aside, opened the safe, and grabbed the blank counting sheet and the envelope. Then he quickly locked the safe and walked out of the office.

The police station really wasn't meant for crowds of people. Maggie had never been in it before and therefore had no idea how small it was. It smelled like old wood, ancient food smells from an old microwave, and printer ink. The printer was spitting out several sheets of a document with a regular shushing sound. The tiny reception area had five plastic chairs up against the side wall of the station. A pale-green linoleum countertop ran along the length of the room behind which Martha Babcock, the dispatcher, sat with two different police radios and stacks of files. At the end of the countertop was a small swinging half door to let the officers in and out.

To the right of the small door was a poor impersonation of a jail cell. It was four feet by four feet with a bench bolted to the wall. Maggie thought the wood looked so old and worn that if anyone actually sat on it they would end up with a bottom full of splinters. She did not want to be put in that cell. The cell was not meant to keep anyone confined for long. Cherish police didn't often deal with what most people interpreted as "crime."

Maggie looked around and thought with great condescension that it looked like *The Andy Griffith Show*. She knew all about that show because it was one of her father's favorites. Her frustration and humiliation began to burn again.

Doris, Irena, Ellen, Sylvia, and Marla, along with Tom, Bill, and Fitch, who had seen and joined the procession in passing, all crowded into the small reception area. Martha Babcock, the dispatcher, who had been eating her lunch and playing Candy Crush on her iPhone, jumped to attention as though caught committing a crime herself.

"Officer Tuggle, ma'am," Martha said with a mouthful of sandwich, "what do we have here?"

"I have brought Pastor Maggie in to finally pay her parking tickets. She'll pay or she'll stay," Charlotte said with great authority.

Martha took a sideways glance at the pitiful jail cell.

"But we can only keep someone in the cell for two hours, maximum, until the state police come to make a pick-up." Martha swallowed.

Charlotte was not going to be sidetracked by this fact. Pastor Maggie was going to have to learn that crime didn't pay. She would learn this lesson by paying for her crime.

The door to the station opened, and Jack entered, along with Mrs. Abernathy. Maggie hung her head. For two very different reasons, Maggie's humiliation began to manifest itself in her tear ducts. Before she could speak or even get a quick wipe at her eyes, the door opened again. There didn't seem to be any more room, but in came Harold, carrying a Styrofoam carry-out box. Right behind him was Hank, holding Maggie's purse.

"Pastor Maggie," Harold said breathlessly, "I brought you your lunch." The smell of fish and chips began wafting into the air.

"Pastor Maggie!" Hank was practically yelling. "I've got your purse right here, yessireebob!"

Hank pushed his way through the crowd. He discreetly placed the bank envelope on the counter next to Charlotte and then handed Maggie her purse. Maggie smiled up at him, and as she looked into his kindhearted and concerned eyes, she gave way to the jumble of emotions washing over her: anger, humiliation, dread, and thanksgiving for someone as kind as Hank for running down Main Street carrying her purse. As the tears fell onto her red cheeks, voices rose so that none could be heard clearly. Finally, one rose above the rest.

"This is the most ridiculous thing I have ever heard of or seen with my own eyes. Charlotte, what do you think you are doing with our pastor? *Your* pastor?"

It was Mrs. Abernathy.

Suddenly the only noise anyone could hear was the chatter on the police radios.

Charlotte had stepped behind the counter through the swinging door, as if for protection. Then she reached down. When she lifted her hand again, she had a three-inch stack of parking tickets. Granted, they were all in triplicate on thick paper, so it looked worse than it was.

"Pastor Maggie owes two hundred dollars for these twenty tickets. She has refused to pay, but she will pay today. I'm sorry, Pastor Maggie," she said a little softer, "but you can't keep parking anywhere you want anytime you want. That's the law."

"I believe several of those tickets were written when Maggie was forced out of her driveway so that the church could repave it." Mrs. Abernathy sounded just like herself.

"And," Bernie chimed in, "I wrote her a ticket, not knowing that she was with Mrs. Becker, who was dying and is now completely dead."

Maggie listened as more voices chimed in with support.

"Officer Tuggle, have you thought this through?" Sylvia asked. "Pastor Maggie is preparing for the funeral tomorrow. There's a visitation shortly. She can't be in jail."

"Stuuupid! Stuuupid! Stuuupid! Idiocy! Stuuupid!!" Irena added her two cents' worth.

Harold chimed in as the fish and chips continued to waft through the station.

"Charlotte, I'm prepared to fight this in court. You will not win. Pastor Maggie is clergy." This obvious and emotional statement was mainly ignored.

Ellen moved closer to Maggie and grabbed her hand.

"Officer Tuggle." It was Jack speaking now. "What can we do to give Pastor Maggie a special parking permit? Her job takes her out at all times of the day and night. She doesn't always know how long she might be at the hospital or the Elder Care. She doesn't abuse parking around town. She's just working."

"Charlotte, this is a waste of your time and Pastor Maggie's." Mrs. Abernathy put the exclamation point on Jack's good sense.

Heads nodded in agreement. It made the most sense of anything being said. Charlotte was trying to keep her composure, but when she saw Bernie chiming in again with everyone else, she knew she could do nothing but release Maggie. She had thought she was taking a stand, but she could see the tide had turned against her.

She didn't really want to put Maggie in jail. Charlotte really liked Maggie. Her kids did too. But she had to uphold the law and just wanted Maggie to pay the tickets. Maybe Jack's idea about a special parking permit could work. Now Charlotte just had to find a way to back out of the situation with grace and authority.

She looked at Maggie and said, "Pastor Maggie, I'm willing to rethink this. I certainly didn't want to distress you, and perhaps I have made a mountain out of a molehill, so to speak. We will figure out how to issue you a parking pass that you can use for work-related parking issues. But don't you be abusing that by shopping or taking too long to eat in a restaurant!" Charlotte was desperately trying to sound as if she were in charge, which she definitely was not. "You are free to go. And so are the rest of you."

Maggie heard Charlotte speaking, but she couldn't take her eyes off Mrs. Abernathy, who had fought so staunchly on her behalf.

The truce was holding.

Ed,

What had started out as something so embarrassing turned out to be something completely affirming! Charlotte finally took the stack of tickets and tore them in half right in front of everyone. She put them in the trash, and as she did so, everyone clapped and whistled. I wish I could control my emotions better, but I just stood there crying like a baby. I wonder when I'll ever stop embarrassing myself this way.

Of course, the biggest surprise was Mrs. Abernathy. This could have been more explosive fuel for the pyre she has planned for my live burning, but she stood up for me. I think it was her voice that made Charlotte back down. Who would have thought?

Once we all left the police station, Harold wanted to go back to O'Leary's for a proper lunch. The fish and chips really began to stink up the station, but all I wanted to do was bake. So I begged off and went straight home. First for some cat therapy, and then I baked the most decadent banana rum cream pie.

I have Mrs. Becker's funeral tomorrow. It should be quite different from Rupert Solomon's.

Love to Jo, and so much love and appreciation to you, my dear friend, mentor, and the one who got me into this ministry life! I could do none of this without you. And God, of course.

Maggie

P.S. Another black mark on seminary education—no classes on what to do when you are arrested in front of your congregation and then have to preach a funeral the following day.

Maggie brought the banana rum cream pie to Mrs. Abernathy's later that afternoon. Earlier, while the pie had been cooling, Maggie looked over the eulogy for Mrs. Becker, changed her clothes—she would never, ever, ever wear flip-flops to church again—and walked down the block to Porter's Funeral Home for the Becker visitation. She saw both Jennifer and Beth and was chagrined when they, and Cole, all referred to her "arrest." She walked back to the parsonage, picked up the pie, and drove to Mrs. Abernathy's.

Maggie hadn't expected warm fuzzies and butterflies, so she wasn't surprised when Mrs. Abernathy greeted her grim-faced and stiff in stature.

"Well, what's this?" Mrs. Abernathy's voice was its usual staccato.

"It's a banana cream pie," Maggie said, leaving out the word *rum*. "It's a thank you pie for your support today at the police station. You didn't have to defend me. Actually, I don't know why you did. But I wanted to bake you a thank you, and here it is. May I ask how your back is doing?" Maggie hadn't meant to ask that question. It seemed too personal. But today she hadn't felt in control of her feelings, actions, or words. Everything just tumbled out of her mouth as if orchestrated from somewhere or someone else.

"You may ask. I have received good news today regarding a procedure that could have been very bad news. My stitches have to heal, but I should be fine after that." Mrs. Abernathy's voice softened almost imperceptibly. "Pastor Maggie, thank you for what you did last night. I appreciate you calling Dr. Elliot. Your maturity and wisdom surprised me."

Ouch.

"Uhh . . . thank you. I'm glad we both could help. And again, I'm thankful for your help today. I hope this will all settle down now. Enjoy the pie!"

Maggie turned to go when Mrs. Abernathy said, "There's no way I can eat this whole pie by myself."

"You could invite some of your friends over," Maggie said hesitantly, convinced Mrs. Abernathy had not one single friend on all the earth.

"I would appreciate your company. And I will make the tea, although you certainly know your way around a teapot."

Maggie just wanted to go home, make some popcorn, grab the kitties, and watch anything Disney.

"Sure. I'd love to stay." Maggie smiled as she wondered what God was up to. It felt like another joke on her.

But it wasn't. It was a piece of pie and a cup of tea with an adversary-turned-less-adversarial. The conversation didn't go too deep. Mainly they talked of Cherish, flowers, church life, and surprisingly, at the end, Mrs. Abernathy said, "I hope your new kitten is settling in. That was kind of you to take in something unwanted and without much of a future. I will not say anything against it anymore."

Maggie thought she might choke on her pie and quickly washed it down with a gulp of tea.

"Then I owe you another thank you." Maggie coughed. "I will make sure the cats don't ruin the beauty of the parsonage. It just broke my heart when I saw the sign in Cassandra's yard. Such little creatures without a mother."

"Your heart is very interesting," Mrs. Abernathy remarked. "I don't recognize it or how it functions. It seems to get you into trouble now and then."

"My mother would agree with you. She has been trying to help me control it all my life. But that's what mothers do, right?" Maggie was almost giggling. Thinking of her mother made her smile.

Mrs. Abernathy stood abruptly and began to clear the dishes and tea things from the table. Maggie watched her.

"Maybe someday you will tell me what changed your mind. About the cat," Maggie said.

"I thank you for the pie and your company."

Mrs. Abernathy's body language was lifting Maggie from her chair and pushing her through the living room and toward the front door. Without word or touch, she was able to move Maggie as if she had an invisible hand. Maggie nodded her head as she said goodbye and left the house. She didn't hear Mrs. Abernathy whisper, "Maybe, someday, I will tell you."

When Maggie arrived back at the parsonage, she changed into her sweats as the popcorn popper did its job of filling itself with light, fluffy kernels. Maggie grabbed the popcorn, a Diet Coke, and *Beauty and the Beast*. She, Marmalade, and Cheerio ate their popcorn while Belle and the Beast found their way to true love. Then the three movie watchers went upstairs and curled up to sleep.

It was three a.m. when Maggie sat straight up in bed. She had an inspiration. Did she dare? Yes. She did. But not now. Tomorrow would hold tomorrow's work. She lay back down and slept the rest of the night.

Her dreams were full of cream pies filling the church and litters of kittens walking through all of them and then jumping on the pews with their creamy, sticky paws. She dreamt of parking tickets stacked in piles fifteen feet high on her driveway so she couldn't get her car out, even though she had to get to the hospital for an emergency. She dreamt she was precisely chopping vegetables in the pulpit while delivering Mrs. Becker's eulogy. She dreamt of Mrs. Abernathy's bloody back and the healing power of tea as Maggie gently poured it over the wound.

14

It was one p.m. on Tuesday, August 12. Mrs. Becker's funeral had been at eleven a.m., followed by a luncheon in the church dining room. The funeral had gone beautifully, with everything that had gone wrong in Rupert Solomon's funeral going right in this one. There had been no fighting over flowers. Mrs. Abernathy had arrived at ten and saw that Cole had already placed the flowers from the funeral home on the altar. She brought her zinnias to the dining room and put small vases on each table. Maggie had been in the dining room at the time, stealing a cookie from one of the luncheon trays, when she saw Mrs. Abernathy.

"Good morning, Mrs. Abernathy," Maggie said with a mouthful of cookie.

"Good morning, Pastor Maggie. Stealing cookies, I see." Mrs. Abernathy said this without looking up, but her voice was light and held no malice.

"Yes," replied Maggie. "I love Mrs. Popkin's cookies. I could eat this whole tray, but that would be rude. My mother would be aghast."

Maggie took a breath and said, "Mrs. Abernathy, may I stop by later this afternoon for a little visit?"

"You won't be bringing another pie, will you? I'll never be able to finish the one you brought yesterday." Mrs. Abernathy sounded more familiar now.

"I promise I won't bring a pie. How about two o'clock?" Maggie kept her tone flat because her nerves were rolling through her body like a mini tsunami.

"That would be fine. I'll have the tea ready." Mrs. Abernathy turned and walked up the stairs.

Maggie took a deep breath and grabbed another cookie to steady her nerves. Her nerves were not due to the funeral.

As Maggie made her way to her office, she heard Hank and Doris talking and heard the snap of plastic. What was going on now? As she walked into Hank's office, her mouth dropped open as she saw Hank and Doris each holding the ends of a large blue tarpaulin. They pulled as they draped it over Hank's desk and secured it with hymnals on the floor.

"So, whatcha guys doing?" Maggie asked, trying not to giggle.

Doris looked up and asked, "What's it look like? We're keeping the enemy at bay."

"You know you're talking about your fellow church members?"

"Pastor Maggie," Hank said plaintively, "they may well be, but they are rude and thoughtless on every Sabbath and at funerals. We'll have to see how they behave at weddings. We haven't had one of those yet."

"Well," Maggie said as she walked through to her office, "I think this might just get your message across. Are you planning on putting tarpaulins over the pews and the plants too?"

Hank sighed. Sometimes Pastor Maggie just didn't get it. "No, there is a funeral this morning."

"Ahhh . . . you're right." Maggie laughed.

Doris and Hank did not laugh with her.

"We have a plan," Doris said. "After the funeral, I will be staying in the sanctuary, watching for the infidels who leave trash in the pews. Hank here will maneuver around the gathering area to protect the plants."

Maggie turned and looked at them both, rearranging her face to look grave. "That's an excellent plan. I expect a full report tomorrow."

She saluted them both, went into her office, and shut the door.

∞

Soon it was finished—the funeral and the luncheon and the guarding of all things sacred from trash and debris. Jennifer and Beth were both tearfully grateful for how their mother was remembered. Irena had toned down her usual big-top-style music after Cole had asked her three times. At the end of it all, Hank and Doris had a secret toast with funeral punch to celebrate the thwarting of the usual trash-mongers.

Maggie had gone back to the parsonage and changed into her usual gauzy skirt and top, but she had strapped on sandals instead of sliding into flip-flops. She got into her car and headed to the store first, and then her secret destination. After taking care of business, she made her way to Summit Street with much trepidation. She was second-guessing herself—a common problem for impetuous people. Mrs. Abernathy had been so wonderful in the police station yesterday and almost friendly that morning. *Will I be sabotaging the little bit of progress that has been made?* It was too late to worry now. She was in Mrs. Abernathy's driveway. She grabbed her grocery bag and her other item and walked up to the front door.

Mrs. Abernathy answered with a pleasant face, until she saw what was in Maggie's arm. Cheerio's sister stared out of round green eyes and mewed piteously.

Maggie quickly said, "Mrs. Abernathy, please don't shut the door. Just hear me out, and then I'll do whatever you want."

Mrs. Abernathy shook her head but stepped aside, probably in horror, as Maggie slowly moved through the door with her little charge. She walked into the living room and set down her grocery bag.

"May I sit here?" Maggie asked, pointing to a couch that looked older and more worn than the one in the parsonage. Maggie sat without waiting for a reply. She figured she would just keep plowing forward as long as she could, which wasn't very long.

"Why have you brought that creature into my house?" Mrs. Abernathy was visibly shaking.

"Because she needs you," Maggie said simply.

That caught Mrs. Abernathy off guard. She sank down into an antiquated chair, utterly speechless.

Maggie continued, "I was hoping you would be willing to give her a little trial period. Let her stay for, let's say, three days. If it isn't working out, I'll take her back to Cassandra's and beg your forgiveness." Maggie took a quick breath. "She doesn't have a mother or a home. I know she's just a cat, but still, can you imagine how awful it must be for any little creature?" As if on cue, the kitten looked up and gave a pathetic squeak. Maggie tried to think of her next tactic. "I . . . I . . . have everything she needs in this grocery bag. Kittens are easy to care for. They don't need a lot of maintenance, not like a puppy." Now Maggie was rambling.

The kitten crawled out of Maggie's arm and wobbled down her leg. She sat on Maggie's knee and stared at her surroundings. Then she began to carefully wash her face.

"And cats are very clean," Maggie added lamely.

Mrs. Abernathy watched the kitten. She was a tiny calico, decorated almost exactly like Cheerio, but this one had a black patch over her left eye, which made her look particularly pathetic. Maggie gave her a little pet, and the faintest rumbling sound could be heard. The kitten was purring.

"So?" Maggie said, feeling quite secure in the fact that she would be bringing this kitten back to Cassandra's within the next few minutes. "What do you think, Mrs. Abernathy?"

Mrs. Abernathy had her eyes glued on the kitten. "Three days?"

"Yes. It's a good biblical number, don't you think?"

Mrs. Abernathy looked at Maggie. "I don't know how you do it, but you seem to be able to pull people toward your way of thinking. It's as if you cast some kind of spell."

"Well, now, that makes me sound like a witch, which I am not," said Maggie, getting her sense of humor back. *Could this scheme possibly work?*

"What is in your bag?"

"I have some kitten chow, a food bowl, a water bowl, a litter box, some litter, and a cat toy."

In the end, after asking for Mrs. Abernathy's preference, Maggie set up the litter box on the back porch. She put the filled food and water bowls in a corner of the kitchen and handed Mrs. Abernathy the kitten, along with her one toy.

"Now she will need to be petted so that she doesn't feel alone," Maggie directed. "She will find secluded places to sleep, like under the furniture, so don't worry if you don't see her right away."

Finally, Maggie left, saying a little prayer for the next three days as she walked to her car. She had told Mrs. Abernathy that she would come back for the final answer on Friday morning.

It wasn't until she was driving that she realized she hadn't stayed for a cup of tea.

Maggie went back to the parsonage to begin work on Sunday's sermon. She settled in her study and picked up one of Barbara Brown Taylor's books, *An Altar in the World,* to get herself in the right frame of mind. Maggie and Nora counted Barbara Brown Taylor as the one person they would crawl on their hands and knees to meet. Sometimes they were a little dramatic.

As often happened, Maggie became immersed in the book and was startled when the doorbell rang. She looked at her watch and saw that it was six p.m. That's when she also realized she was starving.

Maggie was delighted to see Cate Carlson at the door. Cate had a slight smudge of pink on the side of her nose, and she smelled like a walking sugar cookie.

"Hi, Pastor Maggie!" Cate said enthusiastically. "I just finished my shift at The Sugarplum and thought I'd see what you were up to tonight."

Maggie's delight continued. Cate was getting ready to head off to the University of Michigan in a week. She had been one of Mrs. Popkin's "girls" all through high school and, like most of the girls, loved working at The Sugarplum. Cate was the youngest of four sisters, but her parents had never spoiled or coddled her for being the baby, so she grew up to be a kind and thoughtful young woman. Maggie had never met anyone that young with so much poise. She would miss Cate when she left for school.

"Cate! You have frosting on your nose, and you smell delicious. Come on in." Maggie stepped aside as Cate wafted sugar and vanilla through the air. "Are you hungry? I just realized how late it is, and I'm starving."

"I had my share of day-old cookies, but I haven't had dinner." Cate smiled.

Maggie called It's Not Your Mama's Pizza pizza parlor and ordered a large supreme to be delivered to the parsonage. She was told that it would be an hour, so she asked Cate if they could go for a quick walk. Like just about everyone in the world, Maggie loved summer evenings. Cate and Maggie walked down Middle Street toward the cemetery. As they walked and talked and looked at the gravestones, Maggie noticed Mrs. Becker's fresh grave and the flowers left by her daughters that morning. Maggie had only been in Cherish for two and a half months, but she felt as if she had been a resident for years.

"Are you excited to get to the U?" Maggie asked Cate.

"I am! I've heard rumors that the first semester of freshman year is meant to weed out the 'less-than' students. I'm determined to stay. My mom and dad will take me next week to move into my dorm."

Maggie noticed Cate chewing on her index fingernail. She had never noticed this habit before. Cate must be more nervous about school than she let on. All of Cate's nails were so short—gnawing on them must be a regular habit. Maggie was glad Mrs. Popkin made all the girls wear gloves at The Sugarplum. Poor Cate. And lucky Cate.

"You will do great. The professors will beg you to take all their classes." Maggie thought again how much she would miss Cate in the pew on Sundays. "What classes are you taking?"

Cate went through her schedule and told Maggie about her roommate, whom she had only met online so far.

As they walked around the edge of the cemetery, Maggie picked several stems of Queen Anne's Lace. August always brought forth this lovely flower (Maggie refused to believe it was really a weed), and she had vases of it around the parsonage. She and Cate walked back down Middle Street but had to run the last two blocks because the pizza was delivered earlier than expected. Maggie paid for the pizza, and the two girls sat down to feast.

"I'll miss you this fall," Maggie said.

"I'll miss you too. But remember that I will be back for Youth Sunday with my monologue ready. I'll try to come back a couple of times before then too."

Cate was serious, but Maggie knew how much fun Cate would be having in school by the time October rolled around.

"So, it sounds like your brother is moving to San Francisco," Cate said, taking a bite of pizza and not looking Maggie in the eye.

"Yes, he is. I would complain and say that's too far away, but he'll head to Uganda, Kenya, Ghana, and other African countries for his new job. So I just have to shut up and be thankful for Skype and cell phones." Maggie smiled as she watched Cate. "But he'll be back at Christmas. I'm sure he'll be here for part of your break."

"Really?" Cate was completely unable to control her delight.

Maggie did what Maggie did best. She made a snap decision and grabbed her computer. After tapping the necessary keys, she heard the familiar beeps for a Skype call. Bryan's fuzzy face filled the computer screen. He looked as though he hadn't showered in a week, and he didn't have a shirt on.

"Hey, Megs!"

"Hi, Bry! Are you busy?"

"Not really. I'm just trying to pack, but I don't know exactly what to bring."

"Well, stop for a second. Here, say hi to a friend. Cate's here."

Maggie turned the computer toward Cate's face. The girl's index fingernail immediately went into her mouth, and she began to gnaw. Maggie gently pulled Cate's hand down.

"Hey, Cate! What are you doing at that boring old parsonage?" Bryan asked, trying to sound cool but looking around frantically for a shirt. He found a t-shirt and pulled it on inside out. Without realizing it, he began to run his fingers through his greasy hair.

"Hey, Bryan!" Cate giggled. "I just stopped over after work, and then Pastor Maggie and I ate a whole pizza together."

Maggie turned the computer back to herself. "You look like crap. Don't you bathe anymore?"

Bryan turned beet red and decided he would absolutely roll Maggie into a snowball when he came home for Christmas.

"I just got back from a work out," Bryan lied. "I was just going to hop in the shower. Don't pay attention to my idiotic sister, Cate. A little warning might have been nice, sister dear."

Both Maggie and Cate laughed. Ah, the joys of Skype and Face-Time.

Finally, they all said goodbye with promises of more Skype sessions.

"As long as we set them up in advance," Bryan reiterated.

He really did look like a bum. But, somehow, Cate didn't notice.

"Your brother is pretty awesome. It will be fun to see him at Christmas."

Cate immediately began chewing on the first finger she could get to her mouth.

"Quit it," Maggie said. "You're too old to chew on yourself. So, Bryan is a fuzzy goofball. I wouldn't call him awesome. I could almost smell him through the computer. But thanks for talking with him. I'm sure he has a few nerves about his trip."

"Oh, sure!" Cate couldn't smile any wider. "Skype is so easy, isn't it? I've tried to train my parents, but they don't get it."

"Well, next time you're here, we'll Skype Bryan again, with warning, just to see how he's doing out west," Maggie said, watching Cate's reaction, which was predictable.

"Okaaay!" This was said in many octaves and notes.

Their evening ended at nine o'clock when Cate, with effusive thanks for dinner and Skype conversation, took her leave.

Maggie looked at Marmalade and Cheerio, who had received an overabundance of affection from Cate.

"Well, you two, it's been quite a day, and it ended so nicely. Cheerio, we'll see what happens with your sister this week. I hope she has found a home."

Cheerio squeaked, which was Marmalade's cue to give her a bath.

Mrs. Abernathy had followed the kitten around all afternoon. No one would have known if it was fear or fascination which made her do so. She had never had a pet. In her mind, all animals belonged outside and far away from her. What if this kitten had a disease or fleas? And what did Maggie mean when she said the kitten "needed" her? Sometimes Maggie seemed as if she lived day to day in a fairy tale. The kitten wobbled into the kitchen. Her nose seemed to tell her where the food was.

As Mrs. Abernathy watched the kitten discover her new home, her thoughts were drawn back to those first weeks at Caroline Charles's house. As a little girl, she learned quickly what to do and not do in that new world. On her first night, she dragged the blankets off the bed and made a nest in the closet. Caroline had come in to tuck her into bed and had found her curled up in the closet.

"Oh, Verna, dear, you can't sleep in the closet. You must sleep in the bed."

She lifted Verna gently out of the closet and then remade the bed. Then she tucked Verna under the down comforter. Verna stared into Caroline's face. Caroline smiled at her.

Each day she learned something new. Caroline taught her how to pour bowls of cereal for breakfast, how to put her dirty clothes in the hamper in her room, how to paint with watercolors, and always how to make the tea, which was served at every meal.

Caroline's husband, Walter, was a kind man who looked at Verna with pity and wonder. Verna didn't like being pitied, but each day with Caroline was an adventure. Caroline was like a continuous live radio program. She explained everything she was doing throughout the day so that Verna would hear all the words and hopefully make connections with things and actions.

Verna did.

"Now, Verna, today we will do the laundry. First, we take all the laundry and separate it into piles. I would like you to put all the white things in a pile. Can you do that for me?"

Caroline laughed. Caroline was patient. Caroline was kind. Caroline was love.

Language began to make sense, and Verna enjoyed trying her new words in her new world. Without realizing it, Verna wasn't afraid anymore.

Every day the two of them would go out into Caroline's garden. Caroline taught Verna the names of all the flowers and blooming shrubs. She taught Verna how to pull weeds and how to water the plants if there hadn't been enough rain. Caroline took Verna to a local farm where they still had some flowers for sale.

"Verna, I would like you to look at all these lovely flowers. When you are ready, you may choose your favorites, and then we will go home and make your own special garden."

Verna chose several colors of a flower that caught her eye. They were called zinnias. She and Caroline brought them home and made a small garden with the flowers and some stones. Something about the earth and the loveliness of the flowers comforted Verna. Not that she was able to understand or express that emotion, but she had her own garden. Her very own.

One day, Caroline told Verna that they would drive to the school. School would begin the following week, but Caroline wanted Verna to see it before it was filled with all the children. Verna was learning to ride in the car without fainting and enjoyed having the window down and feeling the warm August air on her face. When they arrived at school, Caroline began her commentary on each classroom, the office of the principal, and the play yard. Verna took it all in. Caroline showed Verna where her classroom was and told her about her new teacher.

Caroline could never have imagined how terrified Verna was to go to school. Verna wanted to stay in Caroline's house or tend her small garden plot. She wanted to drink tea and eat cookies. She wanted the days of her new life to continue. Caroline's home was a healing balm for the little girl. The thought of school overwhelmed her.

Verna could vividly recall that feeling of terror as she watch the kitten venture around the house. She seemed to tiptoe around the downstairs. Every so often, she would let out a tiny wail. Mrs. Abernathy watched mutely as this small creature seemed to fill up each room. Finally, the kitten crawled under the small footstool in the living room and curled herself into a ball. She slept for three hours.

While she was sleeping, Mrs. Abernathy slid her hand under the footstool and rested it on the furry ball. She immediately felt and heard the little rumble of a purr.

Maggie called Ed on Wednesday morning to tell him about Mrs. Becker's funeral.

"I keep wondering what a normal week will feel like," Maggie said. "The funeral was so much fun. Is it okay for me to say that?"

"Of course it is," Ed replied. "I would guess you mean 'fun' because it was meaningful, is that right?"

"Yes. The stories Jennifer and Beth had told me were beautiful to share. Don't we all want to have good stories said about us at our funerals?" Maggie asked.

"I think the highest praise any of us can receive at our funerals is that we lived a life that mattered—we made a difference in the world beyond ourselves. It sounds like Mrs. Becker did that, and you had the honor of sharing that with your congregation. Now, you also mentioned a tarpaulin and jail? I can't figure out how those words fit into your story."

Ed sat back in his office chair. He knew this would be good.

And it was. Ed laughed hysterically over these adventures. He could hardly wait to tell Jo. Maggie momentarily debated whether or not she should tell Ed about the kitten. But, as usual, she dove right in.

"I'm going back on Friday to get Mrs. Abernathy's answer about keeping the kitten, but I hope three days of caring for the pathetic little thing will help her feel needed and, more importantly, connected to another creature. She is the loneliest person I have ever met."

"Maggie, how does it feel to be a pastor?" Ed asked.

"I don't know. I keep doing so many things without my permission. I pastor by being impetuous and reactionary. But so far, I guess, it seems to work. How are things at the seminary?"

"Quiet. The summers are peaceful around here, unless you're teaching or attending summer Greek." Ed knew he was pushing a button.

"Ahhhgggg! Don't remind me," Maggie groaned.

Ed smiled to himself. "We are excited to receive the new fall class. We have the highest enrollment in ten years."

"That is good news. I hope every one of them is able to sit in your classroom and learn at your feet," she said dramatically.

"Thank you, Maggie. I'll tell you all about them when they get here. Now, you better get to that sermon."

"Ed, I'll tell you again, and it won't be the last time, you mean the world to me. Thank you for continually teaching me how to be a pastor."

"Maggie, you are a pastor. Believe it." Ed's voice was serious.

They said their goodbyes, and Maggie thought about Ed's words. *Believe it.* She desperately wanted to believe it. She worked on her sermon the rest of the morning. At noon, she went out to her front yard. She had noticed the flowers that lined her walkway were being choked by weeds, so she pulled weeds as her sermon ideas percolated in her brain. She found that she needed that kind of brainless task to solidify her thoughts. Sometimes it meant going for a walk or baking a batch of cookies. By the time she finished pulling weeds, an hour and a half later, both her yard and her sermon were in good shape.

∞

Friday morning arrived, and Maggie realized she had been more nervous about it than she had admitted. She went for her run, ate her oatmeal, and prepared to go to Mrs. Abernathy's house.

"Cross your paws," she said to Marmalade and Cheerio as she walked out the door.

When she arrived, Mrs. Abernathy invited Maggie into the living room. Maggie looked for the kitten.

"She's in the kitchen," Mrs. Abernathy said calmly.

"Mrs. Abernathy, please just tell me what you're going to do. I can't stand it," Maggie blurted out a little too loudly as she tried to peer into the kitchen.

"I want you to know that what you did on Tuesday was impertinent and rude. People don't just bring stray animals to other people's homes and leave them." Mrs. Abernathy wasn't smiling. "I imagine you have been told before that you are impetuous and emotional. If not, your seminary training was certainly subpar and so were your parents."

Double ouch!

Mrs. Abernathy continued, "Your rudeness has been inconvenient for me. I want you to know that, from now on, whenever I see this kind of behavior in you, I will be pointing it out until you learn to control yourself."

So what's new about that?

Maggie jumped in while Mrs. Abernathy took a breath and gathered steam.

"I'll take her back to Cassandra's house this morning. I apologize for the inconvenience."

Maggie moved toward the kitchen, saw the cat toy, and picked it up on the way. The kitten was by the food dish. Maggie began to collect the paraphernalia.

"What are you doing?" Mrs. Abernathy snapped.

"I'm taking the kitten back."

"Put that down now," Mrs. Abernathy said as Maggie lifted the kitten from the floor.

Maggie stared at Mrs. Abernathy and then sighed. "I don't understand."

Mrs. Abernathy took the kitten from Maggie's hands. "I'm keeping her, of course. You were right. She does need me. I just wanted you to know that your behavior is beyond the pale and you need to control yourself."

Maggie wanted to bite back once bitten, but she had a flash of insight. Mrs. Abernathy wanted the kitten desperately. But she couldn't admit that to Maggie—too much pride damage. Maggie had brought the kitten to Mrs. Abernathy knowing how much Mrs. Abernathy needed something to love and care for. It had worked.

"Well, maybe we should think of a name," Maggie said quietly, making sure to keep her eyes on the kitten and not on Mrs. Abernathy.

"She has a name."

"Oh. Right. What is it?" Maggie asked, feeling a teeny-tiny jolt of excitement.

"Caroline."

15

The warm August days rolled lazily into September. The heat remained, and Maggie's window fans were on night and day in the parsonage. With no air conditioning in the church, Maggie felt perpetually shiny with sweat.

Bill Baxter was supposed to install a new air conditioner/furnace in the parsonage, but Fitch had all but stopped the ramp from being finished. He regularly had a reason Bill had to redo what had already had been done. Maggie suspected Bill would like to use his nail gun on Fitch's head.

She had made two trips over to the west side of the state in the last month. She met with Nora and Dan to talk all things wedding and eat bowls of ice cream. She orchestrated dinners with her parents and Ed and Jo. But the best day was when she and Ed had a whole afternoon at the seminary together. They talked it away as Maggie laid her foibles and accomplishments at Ed's feet. His sense of humor, blended with his thoughtful wisdom, watered her soul.

"I can't believe it is September already!" Maggie exclaimed. "The summer has gone so quickly, and now we are getting ready for the Sunday school picnic, and next month is going to be crazy fun with the animal blessing and Youth Sunday. Does the church year ever slow down?"

"I think the question is, 'Does Pastor Maggie ever slow down?'" Ed said lightly.

Maggie smiled. "Enough about Cherish. How is the new fall class of students?"

"It is a talented group. It's nice to have the classrooms full. I think all the professors would admit that the new students keep us on our toes. As always, there is a wide variety of personalities. Some of them are here to tell us how to teach our classes, some are here to soak up everything like sponges, and then every personality in-between. The weakest students are the ones who are most arrogant and the ones with the lowest self-esteem. Hopefully, their seminary education will help cure those ailments."

"If seminary doesn't quite do it, being in the church will," Maggie remarked. She continued thoughtfully, "It's that mix of being a servant and being a leader, all at the same time. I am constantly surprised at how people react so differently to similar situations.

"Last week, I visited two of our older members, dying in the hospital. I walked into the first room and the man, Mr. Thompson, looked so desperately at me, as if hoping I could perform a miracle. I sat for a long time and listened to him talk of his years of depression and both his fear and hope of dying. I felt helpless. I walked into the next room and the woman, Mrs. Landry, looked at me and said, 'Who are you? The Angel of Death?' That's because I always wear my black lace dress to do hospital visits. Mrs. Landry is dying but has decided to laugh all the way to the grave. I had to rearrange my whole face and attitude."

"That's ministry," Ed commented. "You can never be fully ready for how anyone reacts to life's situations. I remember when I was in the church, many years ago, and I was preparing a funeral for a man who was killed in a tragic car accident. I met with his wife, and we put the service together highlighting his great contributions to his family and the community. I felt I was doing the service just as she requested. The morning of the funeral, a large bouquet of flowers arrived at the church. It was signed, 'I'll love you always. Joan.' When his wife showed up, she saw the flowers and flew into a rage. She took the vase and threw it right out of the front door of the church. It smashed all over the front steps—glass, flowers, and water everywhere. Just then, the guests began to arrive for the funeral. The wife came storming into my office and said we had to cancel the funeral. I sat with my mouth hanging open and my heart beating right out of my chest. I tried to tell her that we couldn't cancel the funeral, but had to go forward. She screamed and cried, and I had no idea what to say or do. I was paralyzed. Finally, I asked her why it had to be cancelled. 'Because his mistress sent a bouquet of flowers on *this* day to *this* place!' she sobbed."

Maggie was dumbfounded. She had absolutely no idea what she would do if this happened to her.

"What in the world did you do?" Maggie asked.

"I got her calm enough to sit with her family in the sanctuary. And then I stood up and read the whole funeral, as I had written it. Every time I said something positive about the dead man, I saw his wife cringe and shake her head. I tried to ad-lib. I've never been able to do that. I was awkward and kept repeating myself. Even Jo said she had no idea what I was talking about. The wife and her five children never set foot in church again. It took a long time for my ego to recover from that one. I've looked back on that over the years and have redone that funeral in my head dozens of times." Ed gave a chuckle. "One thing about ministry, it's never boring, and it keeps pastors humble."

Maggie thought about Ed's story and thought of Rupert Solomon's funeral, her very first one. In ten years, when she looked back on it, how would she redo it in her mind?

"Ed," Maggie said, "thank you for telling me that story."

Ed smiled. "Of course. Our most embarrassing stories usually turn out to be our greatest lessons. I have many. I'm not going to tell you about the time I was baptizing a baby and called her by the wrong name. *Through the entire service!* The parents never said a word, but everyone else in the congregation did for days."

"Ed, you are the pastor and professor of legends. I'm sure about that," Maggie said with stars in her eyes.

"Good. You just keep believing that legend stuff, and I won't tell you any more stories that might endanger your perceptions." Ed laughed and shook his head.

"I do have a more serious question for you," Maggie said, her smile fading.

Ed remained quiet, ready to listen.

"It seems Redford has been stealing some of the offering money. We're not exactly sure, but Hank caught him in the safe acting strangely last month. Redford had begun to collect and count the money on his own, and then gave the bank envelope to Charlotte the next day."

"What did you do when Hank told you the story about the safe?" Ed asked.

"I called for a council meeting without Redford. Harold had the good idea of inviting Fred Tuggle and Hank as well. Fred is on the finance committee and used to do the counting with Redford, but Redford told Fred not to worry about the counting, that he would find someone else to do it. And Fred's so busy at his stone quarry that he agreed."

"It's easy to make patchwork arrangements in a small church. It can be a blessing and a danger," Ed said.

"We all decided to reinforce the bylaws that state two people must count the money each Sunday. Fred and Charlotte will do the counting from now on. Charlotte will keep the envelope until Monday morning, when she normally makes the bank deposit. Redford will remain finance committee chairperson but not have charge of financial documents. I'm sure he will be voted off council at the next election. After this council meeting, Harold and I met with Redford."

"How did that go?" Ed asked. He knew from past scandals that stealing from the church could be too easy for someone with no conscience, or who was desperate. He had witnessed pastors and church members being prosecuted by the denomination and the law for this very thing. It was serious, and he didn't like Maggie having to deal with such a slippery problem. But she was capable.

"As you would expect. He got defensive, foulmouthed. He made some empty threats against Hank, but Harold handled that beautifully. He told Redford, if there were any problems, Harold would take legal measures. We are lucky we never used Redford's finance company for the church's investments." Maggie took a breath. She was getting a crash course in the darker side of human nature and the church, not to mention finance.

"But here's the crazy thing. Since we have taken Redford off the counting responsibilities, our weekly offering has gone up by five hundred dollars per week. We don't have any proof Redford had been stealing, but there hasn't been a surge of new members. And we don't think the present members have become stricken with over-generosity," Maggie said ruefully.

"You're right," Ed said, "you don't have hard proof, but it looks like Redford was taking the cash. People are always better off tithing with checks. It's just good, practical sense."

"Redford hasn't been in church the last few weeks. Not surprising, I guess," Maggie said. "So what do I do with him now? I'm still his pastor."

Ed was thoughtful. This was where her gender did get in her way. Ed hated that truth.

"When you see him, be kind, which you would be naturally. But let the council do their work as well. Harold and Fred can also keep tabs on Redford. I believe Redford has no respect for you, or perhaps any woman, from what you have told me in the past. This is a time when you can let the church be the church, a community that cares for one another and also holds each other accountable. Keep pastoring. It will be interesting to see when he comes back, if ever."

They continued talking through the warm afternoon, soothing away the bad taste of Redford with ice cream cones from Kilwins candy shop downtown. Ed was an unabashed chocoholic. He had two scoops of triple chocolate fudge chunk. Maggie had one scoop of vanilla peanut butter cup. She counted that afternoon as one of her life's treasures.

Not because of the ice cream.

∞

The next day, September 6, was the church picnic. Sylvia had asked Max Solomon if the picnic could be at his house on Cavanaugh Lake. Max had been in church every Sunday since his father died in July and was happy to offer his section of the beach for the picnic. Marla got her way to have a bouncy castle and was as excited as the children.

"I just knew this was going to be a hit!" Marla exclaimed to Sylvia and Maggie. "And Sylvia, the crowns you made are just beautiful. Pastor Maggie, don't you think Sylvia's flowers are just beautiful?"

"I do." Sylvia had brought several bouquets to the parsonage, along with an abundance of vegetables Maggie thought would never end. "Sylvia, I'm just wondering what you do in the wintertime when there are no gardens to be grown?" Maggie asked, dreaming of a season without produce.

"Well, Pastor Maggie, I have my work at The Garden Shop, so I look online for garden decorations and get things ordered. Once mother went into the Friendly Elder Care Center, I became the owner. It's quite a responsibility. I buy seeds and plan for the spring flowers and produce I'll need to grow. In February, I plant in the greenhouses. That's how I'm able to have so much produce at the beginning of the summer instead of halfway through. I plant flowers that will be ready to sell by the middle of May. Winter is a very busy time for me!" Sylvia was quite animated.

Ahhh! Maggie thought. *That's how she's able to bombard me with full-grown vegetables the first week of June.*

"Wonderful!" Maggie lied once again.

She looked at Marla, who beamed at her friend Sylvia. Marla really was the sweetest person.

"The castle was a great idea, Marla, and I think our little ones will really enjoy it." Maggie meant that sincerely.

The bouncy castle was inflated on the flattest part of the beach. It was very successful until Carrie and Carl Moffet and Molly and Penny

Porter all bounced around together. As they all tumbled down, Carrie's fairy wand went into Molly's ear and ruptured her eardrum. The sobbing Molly crawled from the castle, blood coming from her ear. Fortunately, Ellen-the-nurse was on hand and loaded Molly and pregnant Lynn into her car for a quick trip to the emergency room.

Maggie's entire Sunday school class was also present at the picnic, minus Cate. Maggie was thrilled when she overheard the rest of the class talking about their Bible characters for Youth Sunday—until she heard Mason and Brock Tuggle.

"Yeah," Brock said, "we're going to be David and Goliath so we can fight in church!"

"I'm David," said Mason calmly. "I'm going to kill Brock. With fake blood and everything. It's going to be so cool."

Maggie piped in. "No, you're not. Pick other characters, or I'll pick them for you. We aren't doing murder this year." She walked away before they could start whining.

It was when the grill was heating up that an unfortunate discovery occurred: no one had remembered to bring the hot dogs from the church refrigerator.

Harold smiled at Maggie. "No worries, Maggie. Tom Wiggins and I will head back into town and rescue lunch." Harold felt chivalrous as he turned the gleam of his smile full-force on Maggie. "Tom and I will save the day! Consider us your princes in shining armor."

Maggie didn't want to.

"Is there anything else you need, Maggie?" Lately, he was forgetting the "Pastor" part.

"No, I think everything else is here," Maggie said casually. "Thanks to both of you for rescuing the hot dogs and saving the picnic."

She looked at Tom to avoid Harold's teeth. Marla's husband was just as kind as Marla. Harold and Tom were back within a half hour.

Max's one picnic table was set with paper plates and plastic utensils. Several card tables had been set up with folding chairs from church. Blankets were laid out on the beach for those who had backs strong enough to eat on the ground. Salads came out of coolers, and Mrs.

Popkin's cookies and cupcakes were set out on pink trays. Maggie found Carrie and Carl poking their fingers into the frosting on the cupcakes and licking them off before plunging them into the next cupcake. She hauled them over to their mother, who was chatting with Charlotte Tuggle. Cassandra took no notice of her children until Maggie interrupted the conversation.

"Cassandra, your little darlings were having some fun in the frosting," Maggie said, smiling at Carrie and Carl.

"Oh, well now," Cassandra said, "that's not so bad, is it?"

Maggie didn't know quite how to respond to that. "Most people like cupcakes without little finger holes in them." Maggie was still smiling but felt at a loss. Cassandra didn't really think this was proper behavior, did she? Maggie knew not to tangle with mothers over their children, but she had thought Cassandra had a little more sense.

She left the children with their mother, where they stayed for all of five seconds before heading back to the bouncy castle, sans wand. At least Carrie had learned something.

Bill Baxter, the wordless builder, grilled the hot dogs, and Maggie noticed Sylvia stuck close by, pretending to be helpful. Bill was so painfully shy that Maggie couldn't imagine him ever asking Sylvia out for dinner or even an ice cream cone. *I wonder if she ever made him that vegetable soufflé she had threatened . . . um . . . mentioned?*

Mrs. Abernathy was in her usual flowered dress and practical shoes, sitting under a tree, looking sour. Vacation Bible School had fallen by the wayside. Now children were not learning the important biblical tenets to keep them on the straight and narrow path.

"Hi, Mrs. Abernathy," Maggie said with slight trepidation, "isn't this a beautiful day for our picnic?"

"It's a beautiful day. It has nothing to do with our picnic. God does not design the weather for random human get-togethers." Mrs. Abernathy sniffed and stared at a tree.

"Well, it's a happy celestial accident then," Maggie said, taking a deep breath of the lake and the sun-drenched marsh grasses. Maggie loved the smell of the lake. "How's Caroline?"

"I wouldn't know. She is a cat. She doesn't speak," Mrs. Abernathy clipped. "But more importantly, I heard those Tuggle boys talking of murder and blood in church. I won't have it! We'll have a council meeting over this."

"Don't you just love the smell of the lake, Mrs. Abernathy? I can't get enough of it. Of course, Lake Michigan was in my backyard growing up. We were there all the time. And about what you heard, you don't need to worry about murder and blood in church. It's not going to happen. They're just being boys. Mrs. Abernathy," Maggie couldn't believe what she was about to ask, but she couldn't stop her mouth on time, "do you have any children?"

Silence.

"I do not." Mrs. Abernathy narrowed her eyes. "Please spend your time controlling the young people of this church. If you were doing a decent job of this, we wouldn't have them planning murder at church." Mrs. Abernathy stood unsteadily in the sand and stalked away.

Maggie sighed. *One step forward, twelve steps back.*

Irena showed up to the picnic for an hour, unintentionally looking like the picnic clown. Her makeup was even harsher in the bright daylight. She didn't have a stack of music, but she was wearing her five-inch heels, which kept sinking into the sand. Irena happily grazed around the card tables where there was more of the picnic food. Maggie noticed she had helped herself to three cookies and a cupcake as an appetizer. Maggie pondered how such a tiny person like Irena could put away food like a football player. It was a mystery.

"Isn't this fun, Irena?" Maggie smiled.

"Ov cooorse. Dis foood ees goood. Not Romanian, but steel goood." Irena was working on a plate of pasta salad, potato salad, baked beans, and two hot dogs covered in onions.

As Maggie helped herself to salads and a bright-pink cupcake, she felt a light touch on her elbow. It was Jack. He must have just arrived since he hadn't been there earlier in the day for the punctured ear incident.

"Pastor Maggie?" Jack looked down at her.

She really wished he would just call her Maggie.

"Dr. Elliot?" she said in a faux serious voice.

He laughed.

Oh, good grief! She could listen to him laugh all day.

"Okay, I get it. Maggie?"

"Yes, Jack?"

"It looks like the picnic is a great success. I saw Molly Porter earlier at the hospital," Jack said.

"She's going to be all right, isn't she?" Maggie asked. "It was a scare when we saw the blood coming out of her ear. Ellen was right on it. You would have been proud of your cousin."

"Molly will be fine. It's too bad she had to miss most of the day. But I wanted to let you know that Mrs. Landry is coming to the end. She has stayed positive and kept her sense of humor, but I would be surprised if she lasted through the weekend." Jack reported this with care and without emotion.

Mrs. Landry was the woman who called Maggie the "Angel of Death." Maggie hadn't known her long but was impressed by her cheerful attitude about The Great Beyond.

"Should I get over to the hospital right now?" Maggie asked, already trying to remember what she did with her purse earlier in the day.

"Her family is there now. It's up to you, but I would think after the picnic would be fine. I'll be heading back there too."

Maggie smiled. "After the picnic, then."

They would be there together.

As the sun went down, everyone gathered around Max's bonfire and made s'mores. Fresh air, swimming in the lake, and picnic food had supplied a memorable day for all. Also adding to the memory was Carrie's wand and Molly's poor little ear.

Maggie overheard Marla saying to Sylvia, "You know Carrie and Carl, they have the run of everything. Especially that little Carrie. She's sweet, but a little naughty. It seems Cassandra has no control over them."

Marla sadly shook her head. Sylvia mirrored the action.

After the picnic, Maggie followed Jack to the hospital to see Mrs. Landry. They entered her room and found at least twenty people crammed into the tiny space. Mrs. Landry was still awake, and when she saw Maggie, she smiled.

"Well, Pastor Maggie," Mrs. Landry said weakly, "how do you like my family? Most of them are quite spectacular. There are only a few stinkers in the bunch." She laughed and then began to cough. Jack quietly made his way to her and used his stethoscope to listen to her heart and lungs. When she stopped coughing, she continued, "Now they are all wondering if they are the stinkers or not." She smiled and took a deep breath without Jack having to ask her to.

Maggie smiled and introduced herself to the family. She couldn't help thinking how blessed Mrs. Landry was to be able to die with so many loved ones gathered around her. Some were crying, some kept their eyes glued on the remarkable and obviously loved woman. The love and grief in the tiny room were palpable.

Maggie caught her breath and sought Jack's eyes. He was already looking at her. Mrs. Landry didn't miss a thing.

"Well, now, what do I see here?"

Jack and Maggie both looked at the old woman. She chuckled.

"Come here, Pastor Maggie," she said softly.

Maggie bent closer so the old woman could whisper in her ear. Maggie's eyes widened at what she heard, and she tried to swallow a giggle, which didn't work. Jack looked at her quizzically.

Then Maggie invited the family to take hands as they moved into a lumpy and awkward circle around their mother and grandmother. Maggie prayed straight from her heart with both humor and thanksgiving. After the prayer, she sat gently on the side of Mrs. Landry's bed and kissed the wrinkled cheek that was proffered to her.

"Remember what I said." Mrs. Landry smiled. "Now, I'm tired. Please go away. All of you. You may come back in the morning."

She closed her eyes as the family, Jack, and Maggie filed out of the cramped room. Jack and Maggie visited with the family for a while longer and then headed for the parking lot.

"It's a late Saturday night for someone who has to preach tomorrow," Jack said.

"Yes, it is. I don't have any pie at home, or I'd invite you over for some. That's the way our last 'double duty' mission ended."

"I have heard Mrs. Abernathy has a kitten," Jack said.

"Yes, yes, she does. Caroline." Maggie was embarrassed. First, for the pie invitation, and second, for his kitten discovery. *He must think I'm an idiot.*

"I'm sorry you don't have any pie. I would love a piece," he said, smiling down at her. "And I think a kitten for lonely Mrs. Abernathy is a perfect cure for what ails her."

Maggie breathed in a cool breath of relief. He didn't think she was an idiot!

"I have some chocolate toffee cookies in the freezer. How does that sound?" she asked.

"Perfect." He began moving toward his car. "I'll follow you." Then he turned and called to her. "Hey, what did Mrs. Landry whisper in your ear?"

Maggie smiled. "I might tell you. One day."

She got in her car and started the engine.

Mrs. Landry never reopened her eyes. She died ten minutes after her family left her room, just as she had meant to. The nurse said Mrs. Landry looked as though she was having the sweetest dream by the smile on her face.

September continued with the last beautiful days of summer. Maggie officiated two more funerals: Mrs. Landry's and Mr. Thompson's. Mr. Thompson, the man who was so afraid to die, yet wanted death's release from his years of depression, died one day after Mrs. Landry.

As expected, the funerals were completely different in every way. In her first four months of ministry, Maggie had buried four people. She fervently hoped that trend would stop. Death was a gift everyone would receive one day. Maggie hoped the next recipients were in other churches for a while.

16

Maggie worked feverishly on her first animal blessing service. It was scheduled for the first Sunday in October at two o'clock in the afternoon. It sounded like there would be several pets to be blessed. She wondered if Mrs. Abernathy would bring Caroline.

Maggie remembered how Mrs. Abernathy had fought against the animal blessing service at the August council meeting. It would be interesting to see how she felt about it now. Maggie had visited Mrs. Abernathy once a week since Caroline's advent. Mrs. Abernathy always welcomed Maggie stiffly but had a pot of tea ready.

One day, Maggie had shown up a little early and found Mrs. Abernathy in the garden with Caroline close by.

"Mrs. Abernathy, how fun to have Caroline help you with your garden." Maggie laughed.

Mrs. Abernathy stood and wiped the soil from her hands.

"Yes, she is very interested in bugs." She almost sounded friendly.

"I've wanted to ask you for a long time why it is you only grow zinnias in your garden. They're very pretty," Maggie lied, "but it seems you could grow everything with your green thumb."

"I have appreciated zinnias since I was a little girl," Mrs. Abernathy said simply. "I learned how to grow them from a beloved . . . friend, and they became my favorite flower."

Silence.

Maggie didn't know exactly where to go next, so she turned her attention to Caroline, who was chasing a flying beetle.

"It's fun to see the kittens grow. Caroline and Cheerio look so much alike. I've heard that Ellen Bright went over to Cassandra's and adopted the little brother of our kittens. Now they each have a home."

"I'm sure Cassandra will find another litter somewhere and place that same sign in her front yard," Mrs. Abernathy said crossly, but she gave herself away when she picked up Caroline, gave her a gentle pat, and tucked her into her arm. "Shall we have tea?"

On October fifth, at two o'clock in the afternoon, Caroline was blessed. Mrs. Abernathy had purchased a cat carrier and brought her small feline to Loving the Lord with her head held high, as if she, and not Maggie, had come up with this brilliant idea of blessing animals.

Ralph, the ferret, was in his own cage. Mason took him out so that Maggie could pet him with a blessing. Marmalade and Cheerio were in their carrier. Ellen brought her kitten with the unimaginative name of Tabby—because he was one. There were several dogs in attendance, and Maggie was surprised by how many cute and well-behaved dogs were part of her parish.

Cassandra, Carrie (bedazzled in a new orange princess tutu), and Carl had brought Dusty, the Siamese cat; Butterball, the fattest cat Maggie had ever seen; and Black and Blue, the two Labradors, on their leashes. There were three parakeets—Shadrack, Meshack, and Abednego—and a cockatiel named Vincent.

Following the forty-five-minute service, a service, where everyone behaved and no one piddled on the floor of the sanctuary, they had a reception with dog treats, cat treats, bird treats, a small piece of liver for Ralph the Ferret, and cookies for the humans. All in all, it was a successful service. Mrs. Abernathy received many compliments about Caroline and beamed in the positive attention.

September and October had Maggie and her Sunday school charges working each week on Bible Alive! Youth Sunday. Since she had been able to talk Mason and Brock out of the David and Goliath scenario at the Sunday school picnic, they began brainstorming anew.

Maggie grabbed Sylvia one Sunday before worship and asked, "Is there any way you could help me with some costumes for Youth Sunday? You're so creative with everything else, I'm just assuming you know how to sew."

"I love to sew. I learned how in the sixth grade and never stopped. What are you thinking of?"

"Well, I can give you a list of the Bible characters. Mainly robes in various shades of white and beige. And then something that might make their character stand out. Like Cate's Queen Esther, you could make her a crown. Maybe out of something from your shop. Do you have wheat stalks in there?"

Sylvia laughed. "No, Pastor Maggie. I don't grow wheat in the greenhouses."

"It would be great if the costumes could be used again at Christmas and Easter. I plan to use these kids more often in worship. They bring fun into the sanctuary. When they're awake."

"I'd love to make the costumes. I'll get started on Queen Esther. Get me the list as soon as you can. This will be something the congregation has never seen before!"

On the Sunday morning when Sylvia brought the costumes to the parsonage, there were actual *oohs* and *ahhs* from the students. Cate had come home from the U to see her Queen Esther costume and was delighted.

Bible Alive! Youth Sunday was planned for the last Sunday of October. The characters had been chosen, and each student had written a monologue, under continual pressure from Maggie. Maggie had asked them to come to the church each afternoon the week before Bible Alive! Surprisingly, they did.

Cate was only able to come on Wednesday afternoon. She did her whole monologue dressed in her costume. She was a regal Queen Esther, and the others watched her with fascination. Cate's willingness to become Queen Esther took some of the nerves and embarrassment out of the rest of the class. Jason Wiggins had chosen to be Zacchaeus.

"Pastor Maggie?" Jason asked, "I think it would be really cool if I did my monologue from the top of a ladder, you know, like, if I was in a tree, like Zacchaeus."

"Of course," Maggie said. "Yes, indeed." She would have said yes to just about anything in order to keep him interested.

She immediately went to the church basement and found a ladder.

Brock, Mason, and Liz Tuggle went to Maggie with their new piece of brilliance.

"Pastor Maggie," Liz said, "we would like to be Moses, Aaron, and Miriam. They were siblings too, you know."

"Why, yes. I believe I've read that story once or twice." Maggie smiled.

"So," Mason said, "can we all be up front together? We don't need to have three separate monologues, do we?"

"Yes, you can absolutely all be 'on stage' together. But yes, you each still have to have your own monologue. Please don't think you'll sneak your way out of this."

Brock, who was Moses, said, "I don't think I should have to write a monologue. After all, Moses was 'slow of speech and slow of tongue.' I'll just stand there." Brock looked at Maggie. She wasn't budging. Brock continued, "I think Mason should be the mouthpiece, you know, as Aaron, the good speaker."

Maggie didn't buy it and told Brock to write.

Addie Wiggins was the most interesting, and Maggie marveled at her creativity.

"I've decided to be the mother of the boy who brought the five loaves and two fishes Jesus used to feed the five thousand."

"I love that!" Maggie said.

"I admit that my mom came up with the idea, but I think it will be really fun to think about someone who isn't mentioned in the Bible but must have existed."

Bible Alive! Youth Sunday finally arrived. The students gathered at the parsonage for Sunday school. They each went over their mono-logue and then donned their costumes. They snuck in the back door of the kitchen at church and took their places behind the secret door. Cate was keeping them calm and excited all at the same time.

Maggie began the service, and Irena attacked the organ like a rabid dog with a piece of meat. Then Jason Wiggins walked from behind the secret door and climbed up his ladder, which Sylvia had decorated with leaves and flowers. He had a "tax collector bag" slung over his shoulder. He looked out at the congregation, and at first Maggie thought he had forgotten his entire monologue. But he hadn't.

"I am Zacchaeus. I am a tax collector. I am rich. I am hated. I am short. But I heard Jesus was in town, and I wanted to see him. That's why I have climbed this sycamore tree."

Jason continued easily and moved off the ladder to tell the congregation about his encounter with Jesus. He ended with, "I was lost, but now I'm found!"

Irena dove right into "Amazing Grace, How Sweet the Sound."

Next came the Tuggle trio. As Moses, Aaron, and Miriam, they looked natural, just like three siblings. They each said their monologues, except for Brock, who forgot three paragraphs in the middle of his. He just shrugged his shoulders and laughed nervously.

Irena bounded into "When Israel Was in Egypt's Land."

Addie did a lovely job as the mother of the fish and loaves boy. She had to make up her entire monologue until it got to the part about Jesus feeding the five thousand.

"And I was there," she said breathlessly, "when my son walked right up to Jesus with our lunch! He handed him our five loaves of bread and two fish. Then, well, then . . . we all watched a miracle." Addie's voice cracked. "Jesus fed thousands of men, women, and children with our small picnic. I'll never forget it as long as I live. And my son was the one who knew it was okay to give our lunch away."

Addie sniffed. Apparently, the role had an effect on her. When she looked up, she saw several eyes glimmering at her.

Irena, more gently this time, played the first notes of "Jesus, Our Divine Companion."

Cate took everyone's breath away when she walked out as Queen Esther. Her monologue was biblical, witty, and regal. She ended her monologue by bowing her crowned head toward the congregation and saying, "In reality, it always takes a queen to make a kingdom. The men tend to just mess things up."

Maggie hadn't heard that last line in the practice. It made her smile.

Irena played "Crown Him with Many Crowns," which sort of went with the monologue, but not really.

No one noticed when Maggie slipped out of the sanctuary during the last hymn. When the organ finished, Maggie walked out from behind the secret door dressed in a cream-colored long robe, belted at the waist, with a matching head wrap. Sylvia had made the costume for her and successfully kept Maggie's secret.

"I am Ruth," Maggie began. She continued with her story and the loss of her husband. She talked about her sister-in-law, Orpah, going back to her own people. But she, Ruth, had decided to stay with her mother-in-law, Naomi. Then Maggie looked out at the congregation and took a deep breath. "'Do not press me to leave you or to turn back from following you! Where you go, I will go; where you lodge, I will lodge; your people shall be my people, and your God my God.'"

She removed her head wrap and looked around her. Then she said to the congregation, "Thank you for being my people."

A flustered Irena, who had no idea about this bit of the service, had to do what she hated most in the world: think fast. She thumbed through her hymnal and then jolted the congregation, as if with electricity, as she began to play "Fight the Good Fight," which was exactly what she intended to do once she got her hands on Pastor Maggie.

Following the hymn, Molly, Penny, Carrie (wearing a pale-green tutu and a sparkly golden crown), and Carl all stood up front and sang "Jesus Loves Me! This I Know." Carrie did an elaborate twirl and curtsy at the end, which had everyone laughing.

Maggie closed the service. "Now let's celebrate our youth in the gathering area with special refreshments for this very special Sunday!"

Marla had ordered a cake from Mrs. Popkin to feed the whole congregation (and perhaps the five thousand). On the top was written "You are all a COG!" in purple icing. No one had any idea what that meant.

Marla rang a little bell and got everyone's attention. Her eyes were still dewy with pride over her children's performances. She said, "This cake is decorated to remind us that we are each a Child Of God—a COG! Please enjoy, and let's give our youth a big round of applause!"

Marla enthusiastically began the applause, and the congregation joined in.

"Pastor Maggie, that was just a beautiful service." Marla grabbed Maggie and shoved a plate of cake into her hands. "To see our youth be so daring, and you. You had us all fooled when you came out as Ruth!" Marla almost sounded hurt at the last part. Why hadn't Maggie let her in on the secret?

"You have two very talented children, Marla. I am impressed with them both. I think we need to have a special meeting to figure out how to use the youth more in our worship services. What do you think?" Maggie knew exactly what she was doing.

"Umm, okay. When would you like to meet?" Marla queried.

"How about tomorrow morning? We will start our brainstorming. Advent is just around the corner."

Maggie smiled as Marla began to wriggle. She looked as if she needed to use the bathroom. Just then, Irena appeared. She took Maggie by the elbow and pushed her into a corner of the gathering area. Irena had recently dyed her hair the color of the inside of a sweet potato. Her red and green (war paint) makeup still frightened Maggie. Would she ever get used to Irena?

"Vat you tink you doo? I not know you doo costume!"

Maggie, caught off guard, was honest enough to realize she certainly should have told Irena.

"Oh, Irena, you are right, and I am so sorry. I should have told you up front so you would have had time to choose a hymn. I am completely in the wrong."

Irena didn't know how to respond. She had been geared up for a fight, but Maggie wasn't fighting.

"I vill overloook dis von time. Neveer again!" Irena turned and took her third piece of cake as she filtered through the congregation.

Maggie sighed. She could see the blue tarpaulin on Hank's desk through the open door and saw both Hank and Doris on trash watch. All was well at Loving the Lord.

Until Harold appeared at Maggie's side. For the last two months, Maggie had successfully avoided alone time with Harold except for the briefest of meetings prior to the larger council meetings. She and Jack, on the other hand, had been spending a little more time together, especially when Mr. Thompson and Mrs. Landry died. Jack was helpful in filling Maggie in when she visited the parishioners he was treating. Neither of them believed they were violating any HIPAA laws by sharing in their professional roles. Maggie enjoyed these conversations. Jack seemed to enjoy them too. Maggie also seemed to regularly have pie available these days. On the other hand, she had no intention of sharing pie with Harold.

"Maggie, what a great service. Those kids were fantastic, and we all know it's because of you. I've never seen any of those kids do anything in church but fall asleep." Harold's smile was overwhelming.

"Thanks, Harold. We all had so much fun, and I give Cate the credit. Those high school students follow her like she's the pied piper. It's unfortunate she's so bright and ambitious and is determined to stay at the U. I'd love to have her back." Maggie chuckled, trying to lessen Harold's obvious attempt at meaningful eye contact.

Maggie looked over his shoulder, hoping to find someone to rescue her. She should have been looking down rather than up. Carrie appeared and grabbed Maggie's hand.

"Pastor Maggie, do you like my crown?" Carrie batted her little eyelashes and smiled coyly.

"Carrie," Maggie knelt to look Carrie straight in the eye, "I love your crown. I wish I had one. But you are the fairy princess, and I am just your humble servant."

"Yes! I am the fairy princess! I am the fairy princess!" Carrie twirled faster and faster until she became dizzy and fell into Maggie's arms. Just then, Molly, Penny, and Carl all came running over. They were laughing at Carrie and had all obviously eaten cake since the remnants were still on mouths and noses. They ran into Maggie, as children do, completely unaware of their velocity. She fell backward, and they piled on top of her like the peewee-est of football players.

Cole and Lynn came over to remove Molly and Penny from the equation. Lynn was six weeks from her due date, but Maggie couldn't imagine her stomach getting any bigger.

Maggie helped Carrie and Carl to their feet. Cassandra was across the room, talking animatedly to Mrs. Abernathy, no doubt about cats. Maggie smiled at Harold as she took the hands of the fairy princess and her brother and walked them over to their mother. Cassandra took no notice, and Carrie and Carl escaped into the sanctuary. Maggie followed—not to collect the children, but to use the secret door and get to her office.

As she walked away, she heard Mrs. Abernathy say, "I have to admit, the children were interesting, if unconventional, in this morning's service. Apparently, they know their Bible stories sufficiently well. Although I don't know that I've read the verse about queens running the kingdom before."

Maggie smiled to herself and kept on walking. She wanted to find Sylvia and thank her for the work on the costumes and for decorating Jason's ladder. She was in luck, sort of. Sylvia was in Maggie's office with potatoes and rutabagas, stacking them on the bookshelf.

"Hi, Sylvia."

Sylvia turned, dropped the potatoes in her hands, and gave Maggie a huge hug.

"Pastor Maggie, what a fun service. The youth were spectacular."

Sylvia retrieved the potatoes from the floor.

"Sylvia, I can't thank you enough for all you did to make this day extra special. I thought the youth would have to come to church in bed sheets, but each one looked like their biblical counterpart. You are so gifted. Jason's ladder actually looked like a flowering tree."

Sylvia smiled at the praise. "It was fun to do. What shall we do next?"

Maggie thought for a second and then said, "A Christmas pageant! What do you think?"

"I can't remember the last time we had a pageant here," Sylvia said. "When shall we meet to begin planning?"

"Can you meet tomorrow morning?" Maggie asked. "Marla is coming in, and we can put all of our heads together. Maybe we can brainstorm about Advent too. We will use our youth and the little ones. They were fantastic today."

Maggie gave Sylvia a quick hug and remembered that she needed to find Charlotte and Fred Tuggle. They were standing in the gathering area, chatting with Tom and Marla.

Maggie interrupted. "I'm guessing proud parents, one and all!"

They looked at her and beamed.

"Pastor Maggie, I have never seen my children so excited to go to church," Charlotte boomed. "This entire week, they could hardly wait to get home from school and come straight to church for your rehearsals."

Neither Charlotte nor Maggie had ever brought up "the ticket incident" again. It was an embarrassment for both women.

"And it wasn't just for the cookies you baked them," Fred chimed in, grinning.

Maggie didn't think she had ever heard his voice before. It was nice.

"I have to thank you all for lending me your children," she said. "I am crazy about them. You should get ready to see them up front more often. They are too talented to leave in the pews."

Maggie's genuine and sincere words filled the parents with pride.

She felt a soft touch on her elbow and knew exactly who it was. He always used this gentle way to get her attention. She turned and looked up into Jack's face.

"Well done," was Jack's simple praise.

"Thanks, Jack. We were all talking about the amazing youth of this church."

Maggie stepped back so Jack could join the circle of happy adults.

There was something in the air that only shows up when youth lead the way, a lovely breeze of the Spirit that blows away the old and musty and ushers in the new and hopeful. Maggie closed her eyes for a second and let it wash over her.

It was another hour before Maggie left the sanctuary for the parsonage. She and Jack had decided to meet that evening at O'Leary's for dinner. *Little thrill!* She and Cate had a chance for a quick chat before Cate had to head back to school. Cate wouldn't be back until Thanksgiving, but they agreed to have coffee or pizza or something over the break.

Once she made it home, Maggie sank down in one of the bean bag chairs in the Sunday school/family room and was immediately joined by Marmalade and Cheerio. She told them all about the youth service, and they blinked approvingly. Two hours later, she awoke from a nap she had no intention of taking when she sat down.

Dinner with Jack was comfortable. They met at O'Leary's and found a table in the back. Maggie was momentarily dismayed when she saw Redford at the bar. He hadn't been to church in weeks and had even missed the last two council meetings. She knew she had to call him to find out why he had been so absent, but she kept putting it off. She turned her attention back to Jack, and the negative feelings disappeared.

"This is fun," she said. "I'm usually squirreled away in the parsonage on Sunday nights with a bowl of popcorn."

"I know. I'm trying to expand your diet," Jack said.

Maggie wasn't the only one who enjoyed staring across the table. Jack thought he had never looked into such lovely eyes. Maggie's goofiness was also a huge attraction. Jack, by nature, was a serious man. Maggie's ability to be impulsive and silly was an invitation for him to play.

He also thought he would like to kiss her.

They ordered their meals and rehashed the youth service. Their conversation easily turned to more personal talk as they continued doing "background checks" on one another.

"So," Maggie began, "what do you eat for breakfast? What's your favorite flavor of ice cream? When you have an afternoon off, what do you do with it? How do you take your coffee?"

Jack looked startled for just a tiny second and then dove in. "I eat Honey Nut Cheerios with a banana and orange juice for breakfast.

However, after a long night at the hospital, there's nothing like a sausage biscuit with egg from McDonald's." He smiled. "Cookies and cream is my favorite ice cream. When I have an afternoon off, I like to fix things around my condo. In the summer, I like to golf. I take my coffee black."

Maggie took in all the new information and found it very acceptable.

"Now for you," Jack continued. "What do you like on your pizza? Who are your three favorite authors? What's your favorite flower? What kind of music do you listen to?"

Maggie took a mouthful of her fried fish, chewed fast, and swallowed. "Okay, I like veggie pizza the most but have been known to eat supreme pizza on occasion. Authors. For theology, Barbara Brown Taylor. For fun, G. M. Malliet. Flowers: carnations. I listen to classical music because that's what my mother raised me on. I love it." She smiled and took another bite of fish.

"First of all, I asked you for three authors, and you only gave me two. And second of all, why carnations?"

"Okay, Charles Dickens, the best author on social justice issues, ever. And second, because carnations last so long—sometimes three weeks! I also love the spicy smell. And in case you want to know, my favorite color is red."

Jack laughed. He was filing each piece of information carefully away in his brain.

"Now," Maggie said, "tell me about your practice. Who do you work with, and why Cherish?"

Jack was a family practice doctor. He did a whole lot of everything for a variety of patients.

"I work with Dr. Charlene Kessler. She and I were in medical school together. The head of our practice is Dr. Allen Douglas. Our nurse practitioner is Sandy Parks. We do a variety of things from OB to pediatrics, youth, adults, and seniors. We are the all-purpose doctors, and we are in short supply. Most medical students go for the specialties these days, but I like knowing my patients. I've only been doing this for three years, but I know I made the right choice. And why Cherish?

I like small towns, there was a need, and I'm close to family. Pretty simple."

Maggie was also doing some brain filing.

Their conversation continued in this light vein as they finished dinner and each ordered dessert. Occasionally, Maggie noticed Redford watching them as he ordered drink after drink. Then she'd focus back on Jack. When they finished eating, Jack walked Maggie around the corner and back to the parsonage.

"Jack, dinner was wonderful. So much better than popcorn."

"Maybe I can lure you out again, then," Jack said, smiling.

Maggie impulsively stood on her tiptoes and gave Jack a quick kiss on his cheek.

"Anytime," she said as she walked through the front door and into the parsonage.

Jack stood on the porch and smiled.

Maggie picked up both cats and swung them around the living room until she landed on the once-white-now-gray couch. They weren't impressed and immediately began to put their fur back in order once she put them down. Maggie relived the evening with Jack and every word of their conversation.

Bradley Cooper was completely off the radar.

Dr. Jack Elliot had stealthily taken his place.

17

"Ed, I need your advice about Redford. He still hasn't come back to church. And I don't want to find out why. I just don't."

Ed balanced the phone on his shoulder as he set aside the stack of Greek tests he was grading. He listened thoughtfully as Maggie continued.

"He's a jerk and a probable thief, but what am I supposed to do as a pastor? How do I care for him? I don't even like him! Am I allowed to say that?"

"Not everyone is likeable," Ed said calmly. "Look, Redford has been humiliated. You are in a small church in a small town. The plus side: it's like one big family. The down side: it's like one big family. It is hard to escape gossip in a small town. I would guess Redford is the subject of the latest gossip mongers, which is an isolated place to be."

Maggie thought about that. She hated the thought of people feeling on "the outside" of anything, but what should she do with someone like Redford? He was the schoolyard bully. The Cherish bully.

"What else is going on?" Ed asked. Maggie would have to sort out the Redford issue over time.

"I'm realizing this is a time of year with many special worship services. I love the creativity of it. I've added the animal blessing and Youth Sunday on my own. I wouldn't change those services, no matter what you say about animals." She laughed. "I also want to do a good job with All Saints' Day, Thanksgiving, and the whole season of Advent. And Christmas Eve. Then Lent and Easter will be just around the corner." Maggie raced through the calendar.

Ed chuckled to himself. He knew Maggie would be fine because of her passion, not to mention her crazy planning skills.

"You are a pastor, Maggie. And quite a tenacious one. The seasons of the church year will become more of a guide for your life and soul than the seasons of nature. Yes, I think it was slightly ridiculous to have an animal blessing service, but you will do another one next year. You saw how much it meant to your congregation, my dear. And that's what you do. You create worship services and worship spaces to bring comfort to your people. So stop worrying, and do what you do so well." Then he raised his voice in exaggeration. "Maggie, *you are a pastor. Believe it!*"

"That wasn't the kind of sympathy I was expecting," Maggie harrumphed.

"You're welcome. Plan your All Saints' Day service and send me a copy. Jo and I both send you our love."

Ed smiled when he hung up. Maggie did too.

November first was All Saints' Day. Maggie did what Ed commanded. She and Irena planned a special service for Saturday evening. Maggie wasn't at all sure people would come out for the service on a Saturday night. Irena was certain they wouldn't.

"Dis peepol don't vant to come to church on de Saturday. Day vant to go out and drink de licker," Irena said, pointing her finger sharply.

Maggie looked at Irena and said without thinking, "Maybe that's what people do in Romania, Irena, but it's not what they do in Cherish. Pick some hymns to remember our loved ones and God's goodness."

Maggie caught herself and was going to apologize, but Irena said, "Vell, yooour probably right. I vill choose de dead hymns."

Members did show up, to Maggie's delight. The service was simple with Scripture readings, all funereal in content, several "dead" hymns, and the church bell tolled after the reading of names of the dearly departed. Maggie had asked the congregation to let her know of any loved one who had died, no matter how long ago. She didn't want to limit the list to only those who had died the previous year. She ended up with sixty-seven names. She read the names, birthdates, and death dates of Rupert Solomon, Wanda Becker, Lillian Landry, and Henry Thompson. Doris solemnly tolled the bell after each name. Then Maggie continued with the rest of the names. She was surprised when she saw the name Caroline Charles submitted by Mrs. Abernathy. Who was that, besides Caroline-the-kitten's namesake? Maggie kept reading, and Doris kept tolling.

The service ended in silence, with Maggie handing a white carnation to each member as they left the sanctuary.

"Vell, done vit de dead for dis year," Irena said practically.

Maggie wasn't surprised by this statement. Irena was becoming familiar.

"Yes, Irena, we are done with the dead for this year. I'm sure we'll rack up some more by next All Saints' Day," Maggie replied as she gathered the remaining flowers and headed to her office.

"As looong as ve're not on de list, eh, Pastooor Maggie?" Irena chuckled to herself and stacked her music.

Maggie thought about Irena's statement for a moment. She wondered who would be on the list next year. She thought about the older members of the congregation she visited each week. She thought of the fears parents must have for their children who were just beginning to drive. She remembered baby Anna Lee in Holland Hospital, who died before living one single day.

Death was an equal opportunity saint maker.

"Hey, Irena!" Maggie called. "You want to come over for a piece of pie?"

"Vat kind?" Irena asked suspiciously.

"Apple cranberry," Maggie said.

"Do you hev any vodka?" Irena asked.

"No vodka, but I have rum and brandy I use for baking," Maggie said.

"Okay. I vill drink vit you."

Irena tottered on her high heels and headed for the door.

The next morning at Loving the Lord, Irena played the organ with her exceptional verve and vigor—her makeup horrifically bright, breasts bulging. Maggie was astounded. The previous evening, Irena had emptied the rum bottle along with eating two pieces of pie. Maggie hadn't known anyone like Irena before but thought she was possibly the single most interesting person she had ever met.

November was getting colder, and Bill Baxter wanted to get the ramp finished and painted before the snow flew. But with Fitch stopping by the church every day to "inspect" the progress, it was slow going for Bill.

One morning, Maggie came back from her run and saw Bill working. It was earlier than usual. She trotted over to the front of the church.

"Hi, Bill. You're here early today."

Bill stood up and ran his fingers through his hair. He looked tired.

"Hi, Pastor Maggie." Bill stared at the ground. "I'm trying to get this done by the end of the week."

"Is Fitch making you crazy?" Maggie clenched her gloved hands into fists.

Bill looked up at this directness and laughed. "Yes, Pastor Maggie, Fitch is making this project almost impossible. Sometimes I wonder if he makes up fake codes. He questions everything from construction to the paint, which I don't think is actually part of his job. The paint, I mean. Actually, he's really just supposed to inspect the site before and after. I'm not doing any plumbing or electrical. But he shows up almost every day. And . . . he's clumsy. He makes more work by tripping over my tools or the lumber."

"You must be frustrated because of what an excellent builder you are. I'd guess you know more about codes than Fitch does." Maggie began to shiver as she cooled down from her run. "What time will he show up this morning?"

"He's comes around eight. I try to get here as soon as there's enough light to see what I'm doing. Sometimes I bring my work light."

"How much time do you need to finish the ramp?"

"Well, I can have the ramp attached to the bell tower door and painted by tomorrow, if I don't have any more interruptions. The last thing I have to do is rebuild the small brick wall under the ramp. That will take about two days.

"So, including today, you need four days?"

"Yep."

Maggie had a thought. She looked at poor, shy Bill. "Count on it, Bill. You will have four days Fitch-free, I promise. Now I've got to go before I freeze to death."

Maggie turned and jogged toward the parsonage.

Bill watched her go, then picked up a piece of railing to attach to the ramp. There was no way Pastor Maggie could keep Fitch Dervish away for four days.

Maggie quickly cleaned up and mechanically ate her oatmeal, banana, and pure maple syrup as she formulated her plan. She loaded her breakfast dishes in the dishwasher, then made three phone calls.

"Hi, this is Pastor Maggie. I was wondering if you could meet at church this morning. Would nine o'clock work? Great. I'll see you then."

It was eight o'clock when Maggie donned hat, coat, and gloves and headed across the lawn. Fitch's truck was parked behind Bill's.

Fitch was bundled up in a puffy black coat, his man-bag slung over his shoulder. He flipped papers on his clipboard and looked at something Bill had attached to the ramp. He pointed a long finger while he shook his head. Bill's fingers went through his red hair in frustration.

"Fitch!" Maggie said too loudly.

Fitch turned. Bill stared.

"Good morning, Pastor Maggie," Fitch said.

"Fitch, I need your help. Is it possible to tear you away from Bill for a bit?"

"Well, I don't know about that. He's attaching the ramp this morning. I'm here to make sure it all goes smoothly and is up to code." Fitch used his professional voice.

"Well, that's too bad. I guess I'll have to figure out something by myself."

Maggie began to walk away.

"Wait, Pastor Maggie, what are you talking about?"

Fitch waddled behind Maggie as she walked toward the parsonage.

"Just a little building project. But I can handle it. I think."

"Well, now, just a minute here, you can't build anything without my okey-dokey. I think you know that. Now why don't you show me what you're thinking about building?" Fitch condescended.

Maggie shot a quick glance at Bill and gave him a wink.

Bill gave her a shy smile back, then quickly got back to work. He knew Fitch would be back.

Maggie led Fitch to her study in the parsonage. She pointed to the floor-to-ceiling window.

"I want to have a deck in the backyard," Maggie said. "I really don't have any place to entertain people in the summer. But how would I put a deck out there with this window in the way? Should I ask the church to take out the window? Or should the deck go on the side of the parsonage? I don't really like that idea, unless there was some way to have a little privacy. I don't know, more trees?" Maggie chattered like a bird. She knew she wasn't making much sense, but she could tell by Fitch's face that he was hooked. It was fortunate for her that Fitch knew nothing about how the church worked. There was no way a window would be removed for a deck to be built.

"Now let me get this straight," Fitch said as he pulled out a pen and found a blank page on his clipboard. "You want a deck to come out of the back of the house."

"Parsonage. Yes."

"And about how big do you want it?"

Maggie had watched her dad and Bryan build a deck on the back of their home in Zeeland. It was twelve feet by twenty feet.

"I'd like it to be twenty-eight feet by forty feet. Then I can have church members over for food or meetings or whatever. And I want some steps, you know, going down from the deck, because I would like the deck to be two tiered . . . and a flagstone path." Maggie took a breath and bit back an urge to laugh.

"Oh, Pastor Maggie, that's much too big for this backyard. Now, why don't we go out there and do a little measuring." Fitch smiled paternally at her. "I guess Bill would be your builder? He's pretty good, but he needs a watchful eye."

Maggie swallowed what she wanted to say and led Fitch to the backyard. Then she pretended to remember something important.

"Oh, Fitch, can you measure? I just need to make a quick phone call. It's a church matter. I'll be right back."

Fitch reached into his man-bag and pulled out his tape measure.

Maggie went in the parsonage and called The Sugarplum Bakery across the street. Then she made her way back to Fitch. She got a quick look at Bill Baxter in front of the church, using his nail gun at a rapid pace.

As she rounded the corner of the parsonage, she saw Fitch bending over to measure. He tripped backward slightly and knocked over the little red wagon under the pine trees. Flowers and black dirt scattered everywhere. Fitch tried to right himself, but his left foot slipped in the dirt and he landed on his ample behind, smashing the marigolds. He didn't seem to know quite what to do. Maggie got to him quickly.

"Fitch, are you okay?"

"Well, um, yes. I think so." He struggled to stand up, but finally did so. He then began to scoop dirt and broken flowers back into the tipped wagon. Dirt slipped through his fingers and fell on his shirt.

"Oh, just leave that. I'll clean it up later. No big deal."

Maggie cringed when she saw the marigold massacre. *Drat!* Although she had to admit to herself that the marigolds had hung on a lot longer than she had expected. The colder weather hadn't dampened their enthusiasm.

Fitch tried to regain a shred of dignity. "As I thought," he said, overdoing his voice of authority, "the measurements you quoted are much too big. You'll have to set your sights a little smaller, Maggie."

All Maggie wanted to do was smack him in the head with a brick.

"Pastor Maggie," she said.

"Of course, of course." Fitch put his tape measure away, smearing more dirt on his pants and his man-bag. "Now, the first thing you need to do is go to city hall and get yourself a building permit." He wiped his brow, leaving a smear of black dirt and a single marigold pedal above his eyebrows. "Since I'm already overseeing the church project, I can just set up camp over here once Bill gets started. I'll have to be the one to sign off on the project, of course."

She walked to the front of the parsonage. Fitch followed and explained each step of the building process to a might-as-well-be-deaf Maggie.

Right on cue, Maggie saw Mrs. Popkin burst out of The Sugarplum, waving her stout arms and shouting, "Mr. Dervish! Hokey tooters. Mr. Dervish!"

Fitch stopped mid-sentence and looked up.

"Mr. Dervish, you come right on over here and warm yourself up with a cinnamon bun fresh out of the oven and nice cup of just-brewed coffee. My goodness, you work so hard for our church. Come here right now!"

Fitch looked a little startled. First, he looked at Maggie, then he turned and looked at Bill, who was adjusting the lower half of the ramp. Fitch was conflicted.

"Fitch," Maggie said, "you can't turn down a fresh cinnamon bun. Mrs. Popkin would feel terrible. Let people appreciate you for all you do for our town, and especially our church." Maggie almost sounded sincere.

After a battle with his conscience, Fitch's stomach won out.

"Well, thank you, Mrs. Popkin. I suppose I can spare a second from overseeing the church building project."

Fitch waddled across the street, flowers and dirt all over the back of his pants. Mrs. Popkin hustled him right into The Sugarplum. She had her marching orders from Pastor Maggie. She would stuff him full of butter, sugar, carbohydrates, and caffeine. Then she would ask him about every single building project he had overseen. That should buy Pastor Maggie a little bit of time to go forward with stage two of her plan. Fitch disappeared into the bakery as the fairy bells on the door cheerfully rang out.

Maggie thought she better get to The Sugarplum later in the morning and help clean up the mess Fitch would be leaving on Mrs. Popkin's floor, chair, table, and everything.

But right then, she ran over to the church.

"Keep working, Bill. He's in Mrs. Popkin's web now." She ran up the steps and into the sanctuary.

Bill grinned at the piece of wood in his hand. Maybe he could get this project done.

Maggie was in her office at nine a.m. when Fred Tuggle, Sylvia Smits, and Max Solomon arrived. Hank ushered them in, along with a folding chair, and they all took seats across from Maggie.

"Hello, friends and fellow conspirators."

The three conspirators smiled.

"We have a Fitch issue."

Fred laughed out loud. "I've had many of those, I can tell you that for free."

"That's why I called you. I need you, and you too, Sylvia, to call Fitch and ask him about your new building projects."

"I don't have a new building project," Fred and Sylvia said at precisely the same time.

"Right. Now you do. At least you are each contemplating a new building project. You will need much advice and help with plans. And Fitch is your man."

"Why?"

"Because, Fred, Bill Baxter is working his fanny off to finish our handicapped accessible ramp. Fitch is putting up one road block after another. It has been months, now. Bill has just about had it."

"Poor Bill," Sylvia said, shaking her head. "He's such a sweet man."

"Yes, he is." Maggie plowed on. "Sylvia and Fred, you each own your own business. And Fred, your gravel pit is far enough out of town to get Fitch out of Bill's way for a while. Bill says he needs three more days after today to finish everything. I want to shorten that. That's where you come in, Max. But first of all, Fred and Sylvia, would you please call Fitch. Sylvia, in about twenty minutes, and Fred, in an hour. Ask him to come out and give you estimates for your new projects."

"What projects?" Sylvia asked, completely confused.

"Well, I think you would like to know what it would take to build another greenhouse on your property behind The Garden Shop. And Fred, you must need some kind of shed or outbuilding at the gravel pit." Maggie grasped at invisible straws.

"I can't afford a new greenhouse," Sylvia said.

"Of course you can't. That's why you're not going to build one." Sylvia shook her head. "I'm confused."

"I get it," said Max. "This is just busy work to keep Fitch away from Bill. Sylvia, you're confused because pastors aren't supposed to do dirty work like this and tell huge lies." He winked at Maggie.

"Exactly. I'm a dirty, rotten liar." Maggie grimaced at the small truth in those words. "Just ask Fitch for his input. Then decide why you can't move forward with the project at this time."

"What about me?" Max asked.

"You are retired. Do you know how to build anything?" Maggie asked.

"Sure. I kept things in decent shape at dad's farm."

"I hoped that was the case. Can you help Bill? Even handing him bricks as he builds the little wall or anything else would be great. And you've got the time. Maybe it could all be done before Fitch even notices."

The four plotters continued their conspiracy. Once everyone knew their piece of the plan, Fred and Sylvia left, while Maggie and Max went out to where Bill was working.

"I've brought reinforcements," Maggie said. "Well, one reinforcement. Max is here to help."

Max and Bill shook hands. Although they sat in church every Sunday, they had never talked before. Maggie gave the quick explanation while she looked across the street at The Sugarplum.

"Fitch will be out any time. He should get a call from Sylvia within twenty minutes and Fred an hour after that. You two make hay while the sun shines. Get to work."

Bill told Max the plans for completing the ramp and small brick wall. A quiet friendship was formed on the steps of Loving the Lord Church.

Ed laughed through the phone line. "So, through lies and deceit the ramp and the wall are finished. Well done, Pastor Maggie."

"Yes. Fitch was kept busy with false projects just long enough. Of course, Sylvia and Fred had to tell him that it was getting too close to winter to begin the projects now. Maybe in the spring. But that won't ever happen. Should I feel guilty about all this?"

"I find your creative ways of problem solving . . . entertaining."

"I'm really going to try to stop lying. I guess God wouldn't be quite as entertained as you are."

"I wouldn't say that. But thank you for brightening my day with this story. I can't wait to tell Jo. It will be fun to see the ramp the next time we're in Cherish. You are taking care of your flock, Maggie. Keep up that good and sneaky work."

"Yes, sir."

"By the way," Ed said quickly, "what do you know about Fitch? Is he a member of the church?"

"No, not here." Maggie thought for a second. "I actually don't know anything about him except for his reputation of being the most annoying building inspector ever known. And clumsy. I admit, I haven't tried to get to know him. I've only tried to avoid him and help my parishioners do the same." She felt embarrassed.

"I just wondered. Have a good week, Maggie."

Thanksgiving was fast approaching, and the Thanksgiving service at Loving the Lord was planned for the evening before Thanksgiving Day. Maggie and Irena brainstormed the service over a plate of Mrs. Popkin's pumpkin spice cookies—vodka for Irena, and tea for Maggie.

"I think we need more music than words for this service," Maggie said, shoving a pumpkin cookie in her mouth. "If people are actually going to take time to come here the night before Thanksgiving, when they have a million other things to do, the service needs to be short and full of Thanksgiving hymns."

Maggie had learned that music stuck with people much longer, and in a more meaningful way, than any spoken word. A familiar hymn would pop into people's minds throughout the week. A sermon was forgotten during the car ride home from church, if not before.

"Ov course," Irena said, taking a swig of vodka. "Not to voorry. Ve vill sing de night avay."

Irena already had a list of ten hymns. She planned to play them one right after the other.

Maggie had asked the parishioners to send her lists of things they were thankful for throughout the month of November. She was learning that people liked to be involved in these types of services. It was personal. At Maggie's request, Irena acquiesced and reduced her ten hymns to five, with one special anthem for the choir.

The evening of the service, in lieu of a sermon, Maggie read the lists of thanksgivings without attaching names. On one list, there was a single word: Caroline. When Maggie read this during the service, she smiled at Mrs. Abernathy, who gave a smileless nod back. Everyone in the congregation knew about Caroline.

"Mrs. Abernathy," Maggie said at the door, "someday I want to know how Caroline got her name. Will you tell me?"

"Perhaps," Mrs. Abernathy said abruptly. "Happy Thanksgiving, Pastor Maggie."

And then she was gone. Maggie wondered what Mrs. Abernathy was doing for Thanksgiving.

"Irena, what are you doing tomorrow?" Maggie asked as they prepared to leave.

"Vat I alvays do. Prractice, prrractice, prrractice. Advent is dis Sunday, you know it, yes?" Irena said pointing her finger at Maggie in typical Irena fashion.

"Of course, I know it's the first Sunday of Advent. We've been planning for it since October. I meant for Thanksgiving." Maggie wanted to bend Irena's skinny finger backward.

"Vy vould I do anyting? In Romania, we not celebrrate dis day. Rrridiculous."

"Well, I hope you have a nice day anyway. I am thankful for you, Irena. I'm glad we ended up here together."

"Yess, eet ees veerry goot," Irena said and looked Maggie in the eye for a nanosecond.

With happy thanksgivings shared and Irena tottering down the sidewalk toward her apartment, Maggie turned out the lights in the church, locked the doors, and walked across the lawn to the parsonage. She had a two-and-a-half-hour drive ahead of her to Zeeland for Thanksgiving with her parents. She would have one glorious day. She left Marmalade and Cheerio with several bowls of food and water, enough to last them several days instead of just one, and got in her car for the drive. She didn't think of it as going home. Instead, she was leaving home. She was leaving her Cherish. But just for one day.

∞

Mrs. Abernathy woke up on Thanksgiving morning to the purring of Caroline. After she made the bed and dressed, she went downstairs, with Caroline right behind. The kitty had her regular breakfast of cat chow, while Mrs. Abernathy carefully measured out her half cup of bran flakes and poured her small glass of orange juice. After reading her devotions for the morning, she and Caroline sat on the living room sofa and stared out the window. It was beginning to snow.

Irena awoke while it was still dark. She dressed in her typical miniskirt, fishnet stockings, low-cut blouse, and high heels. She ate her breakfast of French bread spread thickly with lemon curd and strong black coffee. She then carefully applied her makeup, although no one would be in the church that day. No Hank. No Doris. No Pastor Maggie. Irena would go and practice alone. When she stepped outside her apartment, the snow was coming down in large, fluffy flakes. Not stopping to put on her boots, Irena wobbled down Middle Street toward church on very high heels. She would have to turn the furnace up when she arrived at the sanctuary. It was cold.

Thanksgiving Day at the Elzinga household was different. Maggie woke up thinking of Irena and Mrs. Abernathy and Jack. Then her mind began to wander down the list of her other parishioners. Were they with family? Were they up early putting turkeys in the oven? Were they happy?

Maggie grabbed her phone. She dialed and let it ring. No answer. When the voicemail kicked in, Maggie left a message.

She dialed another number. Three rings and then, "Hello?" Mrs. Abernathy said.

"Happy Thanksgiving, Mrs. Abernathy! This is Pastor Maggie." Maggie smiled through the phone.

"Happy Thanksgiving to you," Mrs. Abernathy said, taken aback. She hadn't expected to speak to anyone today.

"I hope you and Caroline will have a nice day, and I wanted to tell you I am thankful to know you." Maggie purposely did not ask if Mrs. Abernathy had any plans. She could guess the answer. "Anyway, I just wanted to say hi. I'll see you on Saturday for the greening of the church."

"Yes, well, thank you for your call. Please give your family my greetings," Mrs. Abernathy said uncertainly. "I'll see you on Saturday."

They said their goodbyes.

Mrs. Abernathy gave Caroline a pat. Then she did something very un-Mrs.-Abernathy-like. She put on her coat and hat, got in her car, and drove to a grocery store in Ann Arbor. Nothing was open in Cherish. She bought a small fresh turkey, canned pumpkin, a bag of potatoes, and one of stuffing. She bought green beans and some cranberries. When she got home, she began to cook. She had once been a good cook. Caroline Charles had taught her, but she hadn't a reason to do much cooking these days. Caroline the cat purred and meowed and begged for tastes of these smells she had never smelled before. She was treated to the turkey's gizzard.

Mrs. Abernathy and Caroline ate Thanksgiving dinner together. It was delicious. Then Mrs. Abernathy had another ridiculous thought. What was getting into her? She knew the people of her congregation well, being one of the long-term members. She thought of their families and possible celebration plans. Thanksgiving was meant for families and friends.

If you had a family or friends.

She could think of only one other person who would be spending today alone.

Without Bryan at home, Maggie and her parents tried to carry on as usual. A roasting turkey perfumed the house. Maggie baked a pumpkin pie and whipped up a raspberry cheesecake.

"That is a lot of dessert, Maggie," Mimi said, although she was secretly happy.

"I know. You and dad will have to eat pie and cheesecake for breakfast the next few days."

They ate their feast for three, chatting about work, Cherish, and the cats. They Skyped with Bryan later in the day and found he was having a perfectly wonderful time in his new home of San Francisco. He and some of his work-mates were going out to a trendy, environmentally friendly downtown restaurant for their Thanksgiving dinner of rooftop grown vegetables. He didn't even sound kind of sad about not being in Zeeland. And he was wearing shorts! What was Thanksgiving coming to?

Maggie's parents told her they were planning on driving to Cherish for the Christmas Eve service. Bryan would be home for several days at Christmas, so he would come too.

"Perfect! You can spend the night in the parsonage with me, and we can have Christmas together in the morning."

Maggie was excited over this news. Christmas in Cherish. Then she realized how much she missed Cherish for Thanksgiving. Next year would be different.

"We'll come if the weather is good, Maggie," Mimi said practically. "If there is a blizzard or an ice storm, we will stay here."

"I wouldn't want you on the road in those conditions. We will just expect a cold, dry, sunny day on Christmas Eve," Maggie said brightly.

Even though it was snowing heavily and Maggie wanted to get back to Cherish, she had one more stop to make.

Finally, with containers of leftovers, Maggie said goodbye to her parents and headed over to Ed and Jo's for her third piece of Thanksgiving pie. She was going to need her run tomorrow morning.

∞

Irena spent six hours on her organ bench practicing for Advent, some for Christmas, and playing some of the music her mother had taught her as a child. The church was filled with Irena's musical emotion. The somber minor chords of Advent hymns like "O Come! O Come! Emmanuel." The joy of Christmas Carols, "Angels We Have Heard on High!" The familiar and dramatic beauty of the "Waves of the Danube." She exhausted her hymnal and her own personal repertoire. She was with her mother again. Her mother came to her in the music.

Finally, she stacked up her music, turned the thermostat down in the sanctuary, and carefully made her way down the snowy street. Her high-heeled feet were completely covered in snow by the time she reached her apartment. Then she saw the covered box, also with a layer of snow on its lid. Once Irena got inside, she set her music down, took off her frozen shoes, and hauled the box onto her small kitchen table. She opened it and pulled out a note.

> Dear Irena,
>
> I wish you a Happy Thanksgiving. Please enjoy this traditional Thanksgiving meal. I do not know how to cook Romanian foods.
>
> Verna Abernathy

Then Irena saw her phone light blinking. She hit the red button and heard Pastor Maggie's voice.

"Hi, Irena! I know Thanksgiving isn't celebrated in Romania, but I wanted to tell you again how thankful I am for you. I hope you have a nice day. Oh, this is Pastor Maggie, by the way. Bye."

"Crazy Pastoor Maggie," Irena muttered, but she had half a smile on her face.

Irena then turned her attention to the box. She took each container out of the box and looked inside. She sniffed. She was hungry. She put the different foods on a large plate to heat. Then Irena ate her very first

Thanksgiving dinner. She poured a little vodka, of course, to go with the spicy pumpkin pie.

"I'm sorry this has to be such a short visit." Maggie apologized as Ed took her coat and scarf. "We have quite a service planned for the first Sunday of Advent, so I only have today on the west side."

"Come on in, Maggie," he said. "We'll enjoy the time we have."

Which they did. Maggie had kept Ed (and through Ed, Jo) more up to date with the church happenings than she did her parents. Ed's advice was mandatory in her mind. When she felt as if she were losing her equilibrium with people or events, Ed was her compass, drawing on so many years of experience blended with his loving compassion. Jo had wisdom and insights from her own experience with Ed in the ministry and now in seminary life.

"Tell us what you have planned for Advent," Jo said as she brought in the pie.

Ed followed her with the coffee pot and poured two cups. Jo and Maggie drank theirs black, but Ed needed heavy doses of sugar and cream with only a splash of coffee on top.

"Well, I'm so excited!" Maggie began. Her excitement animated her. "We are doing a traditional advent wreath, but this year I suggested using 'untraditional' families to light the advent candles each week. When I looked back at old bulletins, I saw that it's always been families of four: two parents and two children. That doesn't make sense anymore since families are created in so many different ways. For the first Sunday, we do have a traditional family—Cole and Lynn Porter with Penny and Molly. Lynn is expecting her baby in two weeks, but she said she'd be happy to bring her big belly up front this Sunday. Everyone will be thinking of Mary, of course." Maggie took a bite of her pie. *Mmm* . . . apples, cinnamon, and nutmeg filled her mouth. "Jo, you are my pie idol," Maggie said with her mouth full. Her mother would have shuddered.

"For the second Sunday," Maggie continued in-between bites, "we have asked Max Solomon. He lives alone but has become such a part of our church family."

"He helped the ramp and wall get built," Ed reminded Jo, who smiled at the memory of The Great Ramp Scheme.

"The third Sunday will be Ellen Bright and Dr. Jack Elliot. They are cousins. And the fourth Sunday will be Cassandra with Carrie and Carl. I'm expecting something adorable."

"Creative, inclusive, and welcoming." These were Ed's words of blessing on the plan.

"But that's not the best part!" Maggie wriggled in her chair. "I have the youth ready to do dramatic readings of the Old Testament lessons each week. I'll see Cate tomorrow, and she'll do the first reading this Sunday. The other youth would follow her off a mountain, so that's how I got them to say yes to this whole thing. They have been practicing every week in Sunday school. I can't believe the energy Cate brings into a room. I think she would do great in seminary."

As usual, Maggie was taking another flight of fancy with someone else's life. Ed let her go. He knew her well enough to let her dream and then watch her adjust the dream if necessary.

"We'll take her," he said.

"I'll do my best to get her there." She looked at her watch and thought of the long drive back home. "I think it's time for me to take my leave," she said as she scraped the last bit of pie from her plate.

"Has it been good to be home today?" Ed asked, watching Maggie's response.

"It's been . . . good and hard. I know there are some people in Cherish who are alone today. I wonder how they are," Maggie said quietly.

"Cherish feels like home?" Ed asked knowingly.

"Cherish *is* home." She threw her arms around both of them. "Thank you for the pie and conversation. You know how thankful I am for you two."

Jo said, "And we for you, Maggie. You are fun to listen to and fun to watch. I wonder what 2015 will bring you and your lovely Cherish community. I believe it will be a happy year for you all."

"I do too," Maggie said as she pulled on her coat.

She hadn't told them about Jack. She wanted to see how things progressed. All she knew was that he wandered around in her brain regularly and had made his way into her heart. It might be a very good year indeed.

PART 2

To Love

18

The Friday morning after Thanksgiving, Maggie woke up and pulled on her sweats, hat, and mittens. It had snowed the previous day and the entire way back from Ed and Jo's. She woke to what looked like fluffy white icing over the roofs across the street and on the ground below. She gave the kitties their breakfast and headed out for a run.

When she returned, she showered and dressed and walked over to The Sugarplum to meet Cate. Today there would be no oatmeal for breakfast, just a huge, gooey cinnamon bun from Mrs. Popkin's pastry case. Cate was waiting when Maggie arrived. Maggie noticed Cate was chewing on her fingernail as she stared into the case. Maggie had guessed correctly, it was a nervous habit. She remembered how regal Queen Esther looked, unless someone had glanced at her unqueenly hands. Maggie gave Cate a hug, and they each chose their breakfast.

"I'll have a cranberry bran bar," Cate said to Mrs. Popkin. Although that seemed like a healthy choice, Cate knew the bran bars were loaded with butter and sugar and slathered with icing.

"Hokey tooters, Cate!" Mrs. Popkin bellowed. "Don't you want a couple of maple donuts? Those are your favorites."

Mrs. Popkin took it upon herself to place two freshly iced maple donuts on Cate's plate along with the cranberry bar.

"Mrs. Popkin, I can't eat all this for breakfast. You have no idea how much I ate yesterday for Thanksgiving. I started first thing in the morning and grazed all day long. I think I gained my whole freshman fifteen in one day."

Cate said this as she took the plate from Mrs. Popkin and immediately bit into one of the donuts. Cate was a good nine inches taller than Mrs. Popkin and thin as a stick insect. No one would ever take her seriously about how much she ate. She was beautiful with long, thin legs, shoulder-length golden hair, and long-lashed blue eyes. But Maggie thought it was her smile that would make the male students at the U catch their breaths.

"Pastor Maggie, what can I get for you?"

"The largest cinnamon bun you have, please."

Mrs. Popkin carefully removed a cinnamon bun the size of a salad plate, which she set in the middle of a dinner plate. She handed it over the counter, took Maggie's money, and made change.

"You girls enjoy!"

Cate and Maggie took a small table in the corner and settled themselves with their plates of potential heart disease.

"Okay, Cate," Maggie began, "tell me everything about this first semester." Maggie leaned forward to hear Cate's stories.

"This has been a crazy semester. I had heard this first semester was the one profs used to 'weed out the weakest links,' and I can see why," Cate mumbled with her mouth full of cranberry bar. "I have never worked so hard in school before. All those AP classes I took at Cherish High didn't quite prepare me for the U." She took another huge bite.

"But I did join this cool club that focuses on shared living," she said. "You would love it, Pastor Maggie! We find ways to live in a shared economy by controlling waste and being mindful of what we use and how to use it more efficiently. No lie, I have learned so much from this group. I sound intelligent when I describe the club, right? This spring we are having an awareness week of how to use our 'stuff' more wisely. People waste everything from paper towels to cars. We will have places to buy used items and places where we can get things fixed for cheap. We are also learning a lot about how people in developing countries are so much better at the 'less is more' concept." She chomped down on her second donut. Cate was full of exclamation points and university lingo. She was also adept at talking with her mouth full of baked goods.

Maggie was impressed with Cate's new world awareness.

They finished their breakfast, quickly talked through Cate's reading for Sunday, and walked out of The Sugarplum onto snowy Middle Street. Maggie gave Cate a hug and headed back to the parsonage. She wanted to memorize more of her sermon and then get ready for that night. Jack was picking her up at six thirty for dinner. Maggie would be lying if she didn't admit that this date had been on her mind all week. For the first time ever, Maggie wondered what to wear.

Thanks to her mother, Maggie had new and stylish winter clothes. Mimi's biggest fear was Maggie standing in the pulpit looking like a wannabe bag lady. Maggie looked in her closet and chose black wool pants, black leather ankle boots, and a beautiful periwinkle blue blouse that did something amazing to her eyes. Mimi had taken the opportunity during Thanksgiving dinner to give Maggie this simple rule of thumb: "If Princess Kate wouldn't wear it, neither should you." She then handed Maggie several magazines with Princess Kate fashion photos for Maggie's edification and education.

By the time the Westminster chimes rang at six thirty, Maggie would have made her mother proud. She also made Jack catch his breath.

"Maggie, you look beautiful. Let me guess, your mother took you shopping."

Maggie's smile dimmed. *Am I really that bad of a dresser?* "No, Jack, she didn't. She bought these things without my knowledge or assistance and gave them to me yesterday after Thanksgiving dinner." Maggie lifted her chin and turned toward the door.

"Your mother has great taste," Jack said, ignoring Maggie's chin, "especially in daughters."

"Yes. I hear she ordered me from Amazon.com. Poor mom. She ordered the sophisticated version and ended up with me." She smiled now and thought how close to the truth that was.

Jack laughed and thought he had never seen such blue eyes.

He helped her into her (new) winter-white wool coat, and they set off on foot to the Cherish Café. Contrary to the casual name, the Cherish Café was the only high-end restaurant around for miles. It was directly across the street from O'Leary's on Main Street. Maggie had never been to the Café before and was enchanted.

"I've wanted to come here," she said with a slight gasp as they walked in. The café was lit completely by candlelight, and the tables were covered in white linen tablecloths with white linen napkins folded into swans. Tasteful twinkle lights were wound around large indoor trees, and Christmas music played softly in the background. "I've heard people talk about this and also the Rosebud Theater."

"The Rosebud is one of the best community theaters in Michigan," Jack said proudly. "But calling it 'community theater' is a misnomer. Most of the actors are professionals and have even starred on Broadway. I've seen a few shows there. Do you like theater?"

"I love it. I was in plays all through high school and college."

Jack tucked that little piece of information away for future date nights. He intended there to be many evenings with this woman.

They were seated at a cozy table, slightly hidden by one of the indoor trees. The hostess took their coats and gave them menus to look over.

Jack's manners were impeccable, and Maggie wondered if he learned them from his mother or in medical school. Staring at him in the candlelight gave her a little flutter, and she had to remind herself that she wasn't sixteen. Jack asked her preference, then ordered wine. They sipped their wine and began the easy conversation they were getting used to.

"So, you didn't get to go home at all yesterday?" Maggie asked after Jack explained that he had been at the hospital delivering a baby.

"No. I had Thanksgiving dinner in the hospital cafeteria with Ellen," he said. "Did you have a good time with your parents?"

"Yes. It was different without Bryan. I guess I've been spoiled having twenty-five years of the same Thanksgiving dinner with the same people. The four of us have never been separated before. But it seems that's the way it is for most families these days. I found myself missing Cherish yesterday. Certain people occupied my thoughts. Then, when I saw Bryan was having a grand old time without us, I just wanted to come home." Maggie laughed.

Jack reached across the table and linked his index finger through Maggie's. He said, "I would like to meet your family, I mean really meet them, not just in the gathering area at church. And I would like you to meet mine. My family would love you."

Maggie smiled and felt a rush of fizzy emotion. Maybe it was just the wine, but she doubted it. *He wants me to meet his family.* Their fingers remained hooked together.

They ordered their dinners. Jack ordered the apple and squash stuffed chicken breast, while Maggie ordered the ginger salmon. The mix of holiday spirit, good wine, delicious food, and comfortable conversation led the evening down a winsome, lingering path. They shared lemon cream cake for dessert, which made a scrumptious ending to a scrumptious evening.

Jack walked Maggie back to the parsonage and up the front steps. He wasn't going to let her get away with a kiss on the cheek again. He looked at her and said, "I'm going to kiss you now."

And he did.

And it was perfect.

Nora! Dinner with Jack ended with a kiss.
I kissed him back, but feeling a little wobbly now.

It's about time.

Feeling happily romanced.

See my previous text.

∞

The first sparks of love tend to fly at all times of night and day. Even the most mundane tasks, such as cleaning cat boxes, can take on the most romantic overtones. Maggie went through Saturday only half concentrating on anything she did. What she really did was relive the previous night in microscopic detail, over and over and over again. She mixed up a pumpkin chiffon pie but almost forgot to add the sweetened condensed milk. She looked over her sermon notes, but all she could think about was how handsome Jack looked in his gray suit with the cranberry tie and his penetrating brown eyes. She looked through the bulletin to have a good grasp of the extra Advent pieces of the next day's worship service, but all she could think about was how good Jack smelled when he put his arms around her. She thought she would clean the parsonage, but she cleaned the same table in the living room three times because she was thinking about the feel of Jack's finger entwined with hers, his laugh, and his chiseled jaw.

She was a happy mess.

She finally walked over to Loving the Lord and met Doris, Mrs. Abernathy, Hank and Pamela, Sylvia, Bill, and Marla and Tom. They began the "greening" of the church. Doris had laid out all the Christmas decorations with precision on the front pews. With strict oversight, Doris and Mrs. Abernathy barked commands for where the decorations went. Christmas music was playing from an iHome set in the corner of the sanctuary.

"No, Hank!" Doris snapped. "The nativity set does not go on the communion table!"

"Why not?" Hank asked. "It looks good here."

"Tell me, Hank," Doris said, dripping with condescension, "where will the bread and grape juice go for communion tomorrow?"

This obviously hadn't occurred to Hank, even though he had typed the bulletin with the full communion liturgy inside.

The nativity set was placed on the altar table by Doris and Marla. Wreaths were hung with purple ribbons on every inside and outside door by Tom and Bill. Mrs. Abernathy followed them to each door to oversee the hanging, which was precisely what she wanted to do to them when they didn't use the tape measure to get the wreaths perfectly centered. The Advent wreath and candles were set up in front of the pulpit by Sylvia, who seemed to be unable to take her eyes off Bill. There was a beautiful nativity banner of purple satin cloth and white silk scarves. It depicted Mary holding infant Jesus. Pamela and Hank hung it above the altar. There was a small Christmas tree in the gathering area to be used to collect scarves, mittens, and hats. These items would be donated by the congregation then brought to the local mission, Grace in Action. Maggie and Marla set up the tree and put a few pairs of mittens around the top as a reminder. The last thing was a huge Christmas tree in the corner of the sanctuary, decorated with white and gold Chrismons and small, white twinkle lights. Everyone helped with this while singing along with the Christmas carols playing in the background.

Maggie stood at the back of the sanctuary and took in the beauty of the decorations. She felt only gratitude at being part of this loving congregation and their lovely traditions. Now these were her traditions. Maggie looked around and found Mrs. Abernathy.

"Hi, Mrs. Abernathy. How was your Thanksgiving?" Maggie asked. She was ready for a curt answer.

"It was very nice. One of the nicest I can remember. I appreciated your phone call. Thank you. Did you enjoy your family time?" Mrs. Abernathy sounded pleasantly human.

"I did. But it was good to get home. I have an invitation for you," Maggie said.

"What might that be?" Mrs. Abernathy cocked her head to one side.

"You are invited to Thanksgiving dinner at the parsonage one year from now. Can you bring a salad?" Maggie grinned.

"One year from now? Well, Lord willing, I will be there. With a salad. May I make a suggestion?" Mrs. Abernathy asked.

"Of course."

"Perhaps Irena could also be on your year-from-now guest list."

"What? Irena?"

"Yes. Irena." Mrs. Abernathy thought about the previous morning when she went out to get her paper and found a bottle of vodka with a large purple bow wrapped around it on her front door step. No card, but no question of whom it was from.

"Absolutely!" Maggie said with confused enthusiasm. What was happening to her church?

The greening committee ended their evening by eating turkey soup, made by Doris, and butternut squash muffins, made by Pamela, Hank's wife, in the dining room of the parsonage.

"Pastor Maggie, where are your cats?" Mrs. Abernathy asked tartly.

"Let me check. Lately, they have been curling up in the bean bag chairs in the Sunday school room." Which was exactly where they were.

Maggie brought them into the dining room and handed Cheerio to Mrs. Abernathy.

Everyone tried not to stare, but it was hard. Mrs. Abernathy took Cheerio in her arms and looked at her little face.

"Well, now, you look a lot like your sister, don't you?"

No one in the room recognized her voice. Could it be? Was Mrs. Abernathy talking baby talk?

Maggie laughed out loud.

"Mrs. Abernathy, aren't they the cutest kittens? I enjoy watching Cheerio grow. She and Caroline must do a lot of the same things, like finally being able to jump on the bed."

"I must say, I was relieved when Caroline could finally jump down after she clawed her way up the couch." Mrs. Abernathy stared at Cheerio, who purred happily with the attention.

Everyone in the room was dumbfounded. Except for Maggie and Mrs. Abernathy, who were both quite fluent in the language of cat.

Maggie brought out the pumpkin chiffon pie, to the delight of the group. The evening ended with excitement for the next morning when the congregation would see the Christmas decorations around the church. It had been a very satisfying day.

At three thirty-seven a.m., Maggie's phone rang. She had been dreaming of hanging maple donuts on a huge Christmas tree that was so tall it had broken through the sanctuary roof. Cate was sitting on top of it and calling, "Climb up here, Pastor Maggie. It's so beautiful!" as she ate an entire tray of cranberry bars. Maggie sat up and reached for the phone.

"Hello, this is Pastor Maggie." She tried to sound awake, but her voice was an octave lower than usual.

"Pastor Maggie?" Cole Porter said. "I'm not even going to apologize about the time. I wanted you to know we are at the hospital."

Maggie was wide awake now. "Cole! Has someone made an appearance?"

"Pastor Maggie, would you come over and meet the newest Porter?" Cole's voice quivered just slightly.

"I'll be right there," Maggie said breathlessly as she pushed back the covers and accidentally rolled the cats onto the floor.

She hung up the phone and grabbed her jeans and a sweatshirt. She brushed her teeth and threw her long hair into a ponytail. *But it's too early for Lynn to have her baby. They have to light the advent candle this morning.*

She arrived at Heal Thyself and followed the signs to the maternity ward. At the nurses' station, she asked for Lynn Porter's room. When she knocked on the door, she heard a muffled, "Come in."

Maggie walked through the door and saw Cole sitting on the bed next to Lynn, who was holding a little bundle wrapped in blue. Both Cole and Lynn looked up at her and smiled. Maggie felt the tears spring to her eyes and made her way to the bed.

"Meet Samuel Cole Porter," said Lynn, whose eyes responded in kind to the tears in Maggie's.

Maggie pulled a metal chair close to the bed and looked at the tiny face. He was exquisite.

"Hi, Samuel," Maggie whispered. "It's so nice to meet you." She looked at Lynn. "So everything is fine? You both are well?"

Lynn smiled. "We are. Sammy decided he wanted to get here a little early, but he's just fine. Would you like to hold him?"

"Yes, I would."

She carefully took the bundle Lynn offered her and settled him in the crook of her arm, where he fit perfectly, as babies do. She sat back in the chair and took in every detail of his little face. Just holding him calmed her breathing and chased away previous anxieties of his early arrival. He had shown up right on time. Maggie had held lots of babies before, but never one who had arrived only ninety minutes ago.

"He's perfect," she said, her eyes glued to his face. "Molly and Penny will be so surprised, won't they? What sweet big sisters they will be."

"I'm heading home in a couple of hours to be there when they wake up," Cole said. "Sylvia is at our house now. She came right over when I called her at midnight."

Maggie thought there couldn't be a more caring church than Loving the Lord. She felt Sammy grasp her finger. She leaned over and kissed his little hand. He snuffled.

They all looked up when they heard the door open and saw Jack and Ellen enter the room. Both were on official duty—Jack as the one who brought Sammy into the world and Ellen as Lynn's nurse.

Jack saw Maggie holding the baby. She beamed a smile at him. He felt something he had never felt before, something mushy in the heart region. He had to drag his eyes to Lynn and Cole.

"And how are the parents doing?" he asked in his breezy manner.

Cole reached out both hands and shook Jack's.

"Jack, we can't thank you enough. Everything went so fast. Samuel caught us off guard, but not you."

"He was ready to meet the world," Ellen chimed in. "And what a gorgeous boy he is." She began to check Lynn's vital signs.

Maggie carefully stood up. "I think I'd like to thank God a minute, and then I'll leave so you can keep marveling at this little miracle." She said a prayer full of exclamation points, then gave Lynn a kiss and Cole a hug. "We won't expect you to light the Advent candle today." Maggie laughed as she carefully gave Sammy back to his mother.

"That might be a little tricky." Lynn smiled. "How about next year? You can have all five of us."

"I'll plan on it."

Jack walked out with her and stopped her in the hallway.

"It's good to see you." Some of his heart mush seemed to be affecting his brain.

"You too, Jack. What a wonderful night to welcome that darling boy into the world. I'm jealous of your job on a night like this." Maggie was never short on mush.

"I'll be in the pews in a few hours to listen to you do your job. And then I would like to know when we can have dinner again. I've written down a list of questions I expect you to answer," Jack said with mock seriousness.

"I'll have answers for you. And I have my own list of questions, so be prepared." She looked up and down the hallway, and seeing no one, she tiptoed up and gave him a quick kiss on the cheek. "I'll see you in a bit!"

She walked toward the exit.

Jack watched her until she turned the corner and was gone.

19

Unable to go back to sleep after meeting Samuel, Maggie turned on her Keurig, brewed a cup, and sipped coffee as she contemplated the miracle of life. The images of Lynn's tired but beautiful face, Cole's ear-to-ear grin, Sammy's tiny fingernails, and Jack's assuredness played in her mind. She knew not every room on the maternity ward was so peaceful or had such a sense of security. But tonight had been a step out of harsh reality. There was a baby boy in the world who was completely loved. He would want for nothing. He would not feel neglect or harm. Maggie prayed a prayer for all new babies. *May each one be wanted and loved.*

When dawn arrived, she pulled on her sweats and other warm clothes and headed out for a chilly run. She ran past the Porter's house and saw Cole's car in the driveway. What a fun morning he would have with Penny and Molly. When she got to the cemetery, the trees were standing naked and stark, which made everything seem a little eerie. She was happy to turn onto Freer Road and run past houses that came alive with lights here and there. Cassandra's house was aglow, and Maggie knew that Carrie and Carl were up and busy. She continued down Freer to the dirt road and ran steadily as she got lost in thoughts of her first Advent sermon.

When she returned to the parsonage, she slurped down another cup of coffee and cleaned up for church. After her oatmeal and banana,

Maggie crossed the street to The Sugarplum to buy the donuts for Sunday school.

"Hokey tooters, Pastor Maggie, I have them all ready for you!" boomed Mrs. Popkin.

"I think I need you to add a couple of cranberry bars. Cate is coming this morning, and I know my Sunday school class will rise up in protest if asked to share a crumb of their donuts."

Maggie smiled and waved at the regular crowd (minus Sylvia, who was catching up on sleep) who sat at the corner table pretending to have adult Sunday school. Marla scooted over and gave Maggie's arm a squeeze.

"I just came for some coffee. I'm going over to church for the little ones," Marla said as she buttoned up her coat.

"You may be down by two," Maggie said with a smile. "Lynn had her baby early this morning. I think Cole is spending the morning with Penny and Molly to tell them all about their little brother, Samuel." Maggie watched Marla's face light up.

"A boy!" Marla exclaimed.

Mrs. Popkin overheard this and immediately began to bustle around the pastry case, filling up a box with a variety of sweet and savory treats.

"Bill!" she hollered. "Would you be a honey bun and bring this box down to the Porter's?"

Bill Baxter stood up and came over to the case.

"I'd be happy to."

His smile was shy. Maggie wondered if he would ever have enough courage to ask Sylvia out on a real date. Now that Maggie had experienced the most romantic evening of her life, she wanted everyone else to follow suit.

"Hey, Bill," Maggie said as she followed him to the door, holding her own white bakery box. "Sylvia stayed with the girls last night while Cole brought Lynn to Heal Thyself. I bet she would like a little company today. What do you think?"

Bill looked at the floor.

"Good grief!" Maggie dragged him out onto the sidewalk. "Bill, I'm going to give you the advice you so desperately seek. Ask Sylvia on a date. I assure you she will say yes." Maggie waited until he finally looked her in the eye. Then she smiled. "Dates are fun. You get to sit at a pretty table with someone you like and eat good food. Why not give it a try?"

Bill smiled back. "Yes, Pastor Maggie. I had no idea you were so bossy."

"Only when it comes to affairs of the heart."

She patted him on the arm and walked across the street, feeling very satisfied with herself.

Bill remembered how Maggie had orchestrated the completion of the ramp and small wall in front of the church. Her bossiness was complete on many levels. But should he really ask Sylvia out on a date? He walked slowly to the Porter household, wondering how to ask the enchanting Sylvia out for dinner. Bill was at a loss.

Mason, Brock, Liz, Jason, and Addie were all waiting in the parsonage. They looked as if they had just seen daylight for the first time in their lives. Maggie set down the bakery box and opened it to try and bring her students back to life. She could hear noises in the kitchen. Cate bounded into the Sunday school room.

"Pastor Maggie!" Cate threw her arms around Maggie's shoulders and said, "I'm so glad to be back! I'm a little nervous about my reading, but it should be okay. Right?!"

Maggie marveled at Cate's ability to use such huge amounts of enthusiasm so early in the morning.

"You will be fantastic. There are some cranberry bars in the box along with the donuts. Help yourself."

The youth would be part of the Christmas pageant the Sunday before Christmas. Maggie, Sylvia, and Marla had worked together to write the Christmas story from the perspective of the innkeeper and his wife. Mason and Addie were the two main characters. Jason and Liz were Mary and Joseph. Brock and Cate were the last couple to get a room in the inn right before Mary and Joseph arrived in Bethlehem.

Marla had worked with Penny, Molly, Carrie, and Carl, who were all sheep.

Maggie and Irena had gone round and round about the choir of five doing Handel's *Messiah*. Finally, Maggie won out. The choir would sing Christmas carols in-between the scenes of the pageant.

Following donuts and Sunday school, which was as lively as it ever had been, everyone trooped over to church. Maggie's first Advent service went well, except for when the lighter didn't work to light the first candle in the wreath. Maggie had chosen to do the reading and light the candle herself instead of putting someone on the spot at the last minute. When she went to light the candle, the long lighter just clicked over and over again. Finally, Redford, who was in church for the first time in weeks, sauntered down the aisle, pulled a cigarette lighter from his pocket, and lit the first candle.

"Easy does it, Madge," he said.

He reeked of cigarette smoke. His sneer was only for Maggie to see. She could hardly believe his nerve. Maggie controlled her face.

"Thank you, Redford," she clipped and then turned to the congregation and finished the reading for the day.

In the pew, Jack watched Redford. What game was he up to?

Cate did a beautiful job with the Old Testament lesson, reading dramatically in all the right places. But the best moment of the service was when Maggie announced the arrival of the newest member of the congregation.

"I want to make a very special announcement," Maggie said, almost bouncing. "A brand-new member has joined our congregation today." People began looking around for someone new in the pews. "He's asleep in his mother's arms at the hospital right now, but you will meet Samuel Cole Porter very soon."

Everyone burst into applause. It was a lovely way to end the service. Marla stood up and raised her hand.

"Yes, Marla," Maggie said.

"I have made a sign-up poster to bring meals to the Porters," she said, her eyes shining with emotion. "Please take a moment to sign up during coffee hour."

After the service, Maggie could hear people *ooh* and *ahh* over the decorations as they talked excitedly about Sammy. Hank and Doris were on trash patrol. All was well at Loving the Lord. Maggie took a moment to bask in this perfect moment.

Then she felt a familiar gentle touch on her elbow. *Jack.*

Except it was Harold. Maggie was shaken from her perfect moment of happiness. She did not like Harold touching her elbow the same way Jack did.

"Great service, Pastor Maggie!" Harold enthused, his teeth on full display. "Listen, I'm going to dive right in here. I would like to take you out for dinner. Are you free tonight or any night this week?"

Maggie had not expected that. In her nonconfrontational mind, she had hoped Harold would fade away and not keep trying to ask her out. She had known, or at least strongly suspected, that this was his ultimate plot, but she had skillfully avoided him the last several weeks. The problem was, Harold was a nice guy. He was successful, handsome, and a vital member of Loving the Lord. She just didn't want to date him. She couldn't say anything about Jack because she didn't know what to say about Jack. It was no one's business. All these thoughts ripped through her brain as she tried to figure out what to say, standing in the middle of the gathering area, surrounded by everyone. What a ridiculous place for Harold to make his request! Although, if Jack had asked her the same question, it would have been completely romantic.

"Harold, let's step into my office," she said and moved through the crowd. Her mind raced.

When they got to her office, Harold looked down at her expectantly. Sometimes she really hated being so short.

"Harold, I'm not going to say all the lame things people say when they don't want to date someone. The bottom line is, I'm not interested. I do want to keep working well with you here at church. Do you think we can do that, even if I don't have dinner with you?"

Harold's teeth faltered but then rebounded. "Pastor Maggie, thank you for your directness. I appreciate being spared the clichés. Of course we can continue to work together. I apologize if I have made you feel uncomfortable."

He was a gentleman. Maggie felt her hands begin to shake and clasped them behind her back. Her relief was immense, but she experienced the after-nerves of disappointing someone she appreciated.

"No, Harold, you haven't made me feel uncomfortable," Maggie white-lied to be polite.

"I'll stop by later this week to run through the council agenda."

"Great. Thanks, Harold, I really mean it." She smiled.

They turned and rejoined the humming crowd in the gathering area. Harold stayed for a few minutes, but when Maggie looked up from giving Carrie and Carl a hug, she saw Harold walking out of the sanctuary doors. His bruised ego would take a little time to heal.

When Maggie first arrived in Cherish, she'd brought communion to the shut-in members of the congregation on the first Sunday afternoon of each month, except for October when she had the animal blessing. She made other weekly visits just for little chats with her oldest members. By December 7th, the second Sunday of Advent, the ritual of sharing communion had become comfortable. When she first started in July, she had been awkward and too wordy. She learned that communion was extremely intimate and had deep meaning for those saints who had spent their lives in the church.

To be honest, Maggie had some older members she enjoyed visiting more than others. Her favorite was Howard Baker. Howard wasn't technically a shut-in—he regularly made it to church on Sundays—but in November he'd had a full knee replacement and was out of commission for a while. Howard had one of those cheery attitudes of gratitude. He was also a big flirt. When he found out Maggie was a runner, he told her about all the marathons he ran when he was younger.

"If I were thirty years younger, Pastor Maggie, I'd put on my running shoes and chase after you!"

Maggie enjoyed their visits and always brought a little something from The Sugarplum for Howard's sweet tooth. Since she met him on the search committee, Maggie had a huge spot in her heart for Howard. It was mutual. They both hoped he would be able to come back to church for Christmas Eve.

Maggie also went to the Friendly Elder Care regularly to visit Katharine Smits, Sylvia's mother. Katharine looked as if every bone in her body was bent the wrong direction. Her arthritis and osteoporosis had crippled her. But it was obvious Sylvia had inherited the sweet generous heart of her mother. Maggie was crazy about Katharine and enjoyed hearing her stories about growing up in a large Victorian home just outside Cherish. She was a master gardener in her younger years. It seemed that Katharine was also annoyingly generous with vegetables when she was in her prime.

"Katharine, what made you want to own a garden shop?"

"Well, now, I was raised on a farm with my three brothers. I figured out early on that, while they got to do chores outside, I was always stuck indoors learning how to do 'women's work.' I hated being cooped up in the house." Katharine chuckled. "I drove my mother crazy. So, when I grew up, I asked for part of the farm. It was a section closest to town, and I did that on purpose." She sounded proud of herself. "I grew flowers and vegetables and even fruit trees. First, I sold them at a stand in town. But when I had saved enough money, I built a small store of my own. The Garden Shop. I was married after that and had my beautiful Sylvia. I never made her stay indoors. I'm glad to say, she's not much of a housekeeper, which makes me prouder than punch. But she can grow anything with a little bit of dirt and a smile."

Maggie felt the tiniest of lumps in her throat. Katharine had chased her passion, even when it wasn't proper to do so. And she gave Sylvia permission to do the same thing. Maggie loved meeting strong women. Katharine's room was a favorite place to visit.

Marvin Green was a different story. He was definitely the most difficult person on Maggie's visitation list at the Friendly Elder Care. Marvin was sarcastic, rude to nurses and volunteers, and regularly told Maggie that women should not be pastors because it went against the Bible. She often wanted to bang him over the head with his lunch tray.

The first time she brought him communion, he refused to take it because she wasn't a man. She never brought it again.

On one particularly difficult afternoon in September, after he insulted her dress, her hair, and her voice, she looked at him and said, "What is your problem, Marvin? You are such a crank! You are like a human vat of poison, and you leak out on everyone who comes near you. But you are not going to chase me away. I'm going to keep showing up here in this dress, with this hair, using this voice. Why are you so miserable?"

Marvin looked at her, astonished. His sandpaper personality usually worked perfectly well to keep people away. He counted on it.

"Get out of my room," he growled.

"Okay, I'll leave. But I'll be back next week, and the week after that, and the week after that." Maggie sounded churlish but didn't care. This old man was not going to get the best of her.

From that day on, each time she visited, Marvin refused to talk. He sat absolutely still in a stony silence. Maggie seated herself comfortably and began a thirty-minute monologue. She talked about all the happenings at Loving the Lord. She described her Sunday school class, the animal blessing service, Youth Sunday, and all the other services throughout the fall. Marvin never looked at her or said one word.

Maggie also visited several parishioners who were on the Alzheimer's wing of the Friendly Elder Care. These visits were the hardest for Maggie. She watched as memories faded and lights slowly dimmed in the eyes of these sweet people. Maggie held the nurses on the Alzheimer wing in the highest esteem. They were so compassionate and knew how to treat each patient with particular care. Every time she saw a nurse she quietly said, "You are an angel."

When she spent some time taking stock of her days, Maggie was thankful for the work she was called to do. From baby Sammy Porter to seasoned Howard Baker, and everyone in-between, she walked on the sacred ground of life, sharing so much with those who invited her in.

Maggie was in her office the Monday after the third Sunday of Advent, sipping Lady Grey tea out of her yellow happy face mug. Hank was banging around in his office, and she could hear Doris vacuuming somewhere. She was thinking about that coming Sunday's sermon and the Lessons and Carols service for Christmas Eve. Jack was also wandering around in her brain. Again.

They had gone to Ann Arbor for dinner the night before. Jack had chosen a swanky Italian place where they ate warm Italian bread and delicate pasta dripping in Alfredo sauce mixed with chicken and peas while they continued with their happy interrogations of one another.

"If you won a million dollars, what would you do with it?" Maggie asked Jack as she sipped the delicious white wine he had ordered.

"How do you come up with questions like that?"

"I just do. Now answer please."

"Uh, well, I would probably make sure my family had what they needed. And, uh, put the rest in a retirement account," Jack said hesitantly. "Why, what would you do?"

"Well, I would make a large donation to the seminary in Holland to help future students who don't have enough money. Then I would start a fund for the church so there would always be enough money to repair the roof or the heating system or whatever. I would send some to local cat protection societies. Oh, oh, oh! I might buy a little farm outside of town. I would like some chickens. Maybe I would take all the high school students to Disneyland. I've always wanted to go there. Umm, I think I would figure out a way to keep Grace in Action and their foodbank completely stocked with good food forever. I don't know, stuff like that." She put a forkful of creamy pasta in her mouth.

Jack was feeling dizzy. Not from the wine but from trying to follow her brain's flight path. He started laughing.

"You are the funniest, scariest, kindest woman I have ever known."

Maggie smiled. "My brother says I'm only funny when I'm not trying. I'm going to let him know over Christmas that I have been described as funny by a very intelligent, although lacking in imagination, friend of mine."

"Lacking in imagination?"

"Yes, definitely. But don't worry, we'll work on it."

"I have another question for you, o funny one. What did Mrs. Landry say to you when she was dying?"

Maggie looked up at him, and he saw . . . embarrassment?

"I can't tell you tonight," she said with a little cough. "I will tell you one day, I think, but not tonight. And don't think you can wheedle it out of me with some fancy Italian dessert."

Jack dropped the question for now and said he wouldn't do any wheedling, but they had to have dessert. They shared a plate of tiramisu and cups of rich Italian coffee.

Maggie looked Jack in the eyes and asked quietly, "Why aren't you married?"

Jack coughed into his napkin and then laughed. "You are very direct. I like it. I'm not married because I honestly haven't had time. I dated in college, I even got serious once with a girl in my class, but being pre-med kept my nose to the grindstone. We tried to make it work, but I think she saw the writing on the wall. Medical school would be a lot more time-consuming than college. She dumped me. I just didn't get to play very much. Organic chemistry was my regular Friday night date." He looked thoughtful. "I actually don't think I've ever played a lot. Until I met you, and you asked me what I would do with a million dollars. In medical school, there wasn't any time to date, at least not for me. Plus, I have been waiting for just the right goofball, I mean woman."

"I'll take that as a compliment, of course," Maggie said with a slurp of her coffee. "I didn't date a lot in seminary. I was very busy preparing to save the world. Also, a lot of weirdos go to seminary, I'm not going to lie to you. I'll tell you more about it another time. Mainly, a lot of people with issues they have never dealt with go to seminary to be able to tell others how to deal with their issues. I've heard about it in other helping professions, like social workers, etcetera, but I don't know about you doctor types."

"We're all a mess," Jack said with his adorable smile.

Maggie wanted to climb across the table right into his lap.

"Well, I think this has been very enlightening," Maggie said, not embarrassed to drag her fork across the tiramisu plate to get the last remnants. "I guess we're sort of starting from scratch, which is how I like to bake. Then I know each ingredient going into the pie plate. No surprises. So you don't have any random children hiding under bushes or in closets or anything?"

"Not to my knowledge." Jack wanted to grab her and drag her across the table into his lap.

The evening ended with some more of those kisses they both dreamt about when they were apart.

20

It was the fourth Sunday of Advent, and Maggie was working with the youth in the sanctuary. They were having one more quick practice of the Christmas pageant. Bill Baxter had built the set for an inn in the front of the sanctuary—without telling Fitch—and the youth were standing around in the same costumes they wore for Youth Sunday. Mason, Brock, and Jason were horsing around in the back of the sanctuary until Maggie went over and flicked them each on the arm.

"Knock it off! Now get down front, ready to practice." She sounded like her mother.

She knew from having a little brother, and watching him with his friends, that high school boys appreciated affection of the rough-and-tumble sort, rather than lots of hugs. She took every opportunity to lightly punch and push her male youth members. They secretly loved this abuse from Pastor Maggie.

The girls, on the other hand, were affectionate, chatty, and dramatic. Maggie completely understood this. Having Cate around kept Liz and Addie in awe of what it would be like to go to the University. "Just like Cate!" their faces squealed.

Rehearsal went well once Marla brought in the little sheep and everything got started. Carrie was in fine form and very excited because she was not only a sheep but also an Advent candle wreath lighter with her mother and Carl. She had a new purple crown and tutu for the special day.

When the day finally came, the service was delightful. Church congregations seem to be in agreement on one thing: there is nothing more adorable than watching children acting out the Christmas story. The high school students did their parts well and with a little comedy. Addie griped at Mason for trying to find one more corner in the inn for the couple expecting a baby.

"No way!" she said with her hands on her hips. "There is no more room in the inn! I don't care if she is having a baby."

"But what are they supposed to do?" Mason asked. "Sleep in the barn?"

"Why not?" said Addie then sat down on an upturned bucket. "I'm not cleaning up after one more couple around here."

Cate's voice shrieked from behind the secret door, indicating the last room in the inn. "You call this an inn? This place is filthy!"

The whole congregation laughed, except for Mrs. Abernathy, who thought this was all tiptoeing over the line into blasphemy.

When the pageant concluded, it was time for the Advent wreath. Carrie and Carl—still in their sheep costumes—came forward with Cassandra. Carrie had her crown perched precariously on her head. Cassandra began the reading, Carrie recited the prayer, and Carl said, "Amen." Cassandra lit the fourth Advent candle. The other three had been lit before the service began. Carrie began her trademark twirl and curtsy, but several of the cotton balls on her sheep costume got too close to the flames. Before anyone realized it, her head was on fire!

The congregation couldn't believe what they were seeing. Cassandra stared at Carrie's head but couldn't seem to move. There were several gasps. Maggie heard a few people scream. Members moved in their pews, trying to get up front to help.

Suddenly, Bernie Bumble, in his officer's uniform, jumped up from the pew and shouted: "STOP! DROP! AND ROLL!"

He ran toward Carrie and pushed her to the ground, grabbed the communion table cloth, and slapped it on her head. Mason, who was sitting up front, grabbed the altar flowers, pulled them out of the vase, and poured the water on Carrie and Officer Bumble.

By then, Cassandra had come back to life and rushed to her daughter. Maggie followed close behind, as did Jack.

Carrie was crying. No, Carrie was *shrieking*. The sound made Maggie's blood turn cold. She thought she might throw up. Bernie removed the table cloth.

Everyone was gathering around, but Jack got there first. He picked Carrie up carefully and looked at the back of her head. The fire had not only burned through her costume but had also burned her skin from the nape of her neck to the top of her head and part of her ear.

"She needs to go to the hospital," Jack said gravely. "We've got to get her there immediately."

Carrie's shrieks turned into sobs. Cassandra and Jack carefully bundled Carrie into Jack's car and drove over to Heal Thyself. Marla took Carl, making many reassuring noises, and guided him back to the nursery, inviting Molly and Penny to join them. She also grabbed a plate of Christmas cookies from the gathering area.

Maggie publicly thanked Bernie for his quick thinking as she rolled up the communion table cloth and shoved it under the pulpit. She nodded to Irena to begin the last hymn, "O, Little Town of Bethlehem."

Coffee hour was subdued, to say the least. What should have been a lovely ending to the Advent season was tainted by the smell of burned hair and flesh as people tried to eat their "Happy Birthday, Jesus!" cupcakes and Christmas sprinkled sugar cookies. The congregation drifted away quickly. Marla brought the children out from the nursery. Cole thanked Marla then took Molly and Penny home to Lynn and Sammy.

Marla said to Maggie, "I'll take Carl home with us. He can stay as long as needed. Addie will be thrilled. Carl, we're having spaghetti for lunch today. Do you like spaghetti?"

Carl looked up at her with his huge, solemn eyes. "Yes, Missus Wiggins, I do. Whewe's Cawhey and my mama?"

"Dr. Elliot is taking good care of Carrie right now. He will help her owie get all better. Your mama is there too. She will come and get you soon, I'm sure."

Carl reached for Marla's hand as Addie and Jason walked over. Addie looked at Carl and said, "Do you like the movie *Frozen*?"

"Yes, I do," Carl said like a perfect little gentleman.

"Good! Me too." Addie laughed. "I think we will have to watch it at my house, okay?"

Carl smiled. "Yes, okay."

They all left the dreadful-smelling church and moved on to a less dramatic afternoon.

Maggie headed over to Heal Thyself to find out about Carrie. She could still smell the burnt flesh. *What if Carrie is seriously injured? What if she has brain damage or horrible scars for the rest of her life?* Maggie took a deep breath that turned into a sob. *What if Carrie dies?*

She was furious with herself for having the candles so close to where the children stood up front. She began to wonder if the church would be liable for the horrible accident. *I can't bury a child. I can't bury a child. I can't bury a child.* Maggie's fear mounted.

By the time she arrived at the hospital, it was all she could do to not run down the hallways searching for Carrie. *Please, God, please let Carrie be all right.* Maggie had never before felt so panicked and out of control. *Please, God, please!* Maggie gasped another sob and then stopped herself when she saw Cassandra in the hall outside of an examining room.

"Cassandra, how is Carrie?" Maggie asked breathlessly.

Cassandra looked at Maggie with sheer terror. "Pastor Maggie, I can't watch. They've had to cut away more hair, and her little scalp is so burned. Dr. Elliot gave her a sedative to calm her down and ease the pain. She's in so much pain." Cassandra looked at the ground and shook her head, as if to get Carrie's screams out of her ears.

Just then, Jack came out of the room. He looked at Cassandra.

"Carrie will be okay," he said carefully. "She has serious second-degree burns on her scalp, but her sheep costume protected her more than we thought."

Cassandra took a deep breath. Then she burst into tears. The stress and the fear she had been holding in for the past hour unleashed itself. Both Jack and Maggie put their arms around her and helped her to a chair.

"Carrie needs to stay here for at least a couple of days. We can make sure there is no infection and keep her pain under control," Jack said. "I'll try to have her home for Christmas, but I can't promise."

Cassandra nodded as she blew her nose into a napkin. "I have no idea how I'm going to deal with all of this." Cassandra cried and looked toward Maggie.

"But you will," said Maggie. "You are a mother. You will handle this for Carrie. And we are all here to help." She continued, "Just so you know, Carl went home with Marla. They'll watch him until you're able to leave the hospital. I can call Marla for you to let her know you'll be by later."

"I don't know what we'd do without this church," Cassandra sobbed.

Maggie handed her a wad of clean tissues. She had learned to always have handfuls of Kleenex in her purse. She spent time with people who often cried over one thing or another, and she used plenty herself.

On the Tuesday before Christmas, Maggie visited Carrie at Heal Thyself. The little girl was doing better since the candle incident. She was carefully watched by the medical staff for any signs of infection, and she was on strong painkillers, but her smile was bright when Maggie walked into the room. Jack told Maggie that nurses and doctors alike were besotted by the little girl. Maggie completely understood.

It looked as if Carrie would be able to return home the following morning, Christmas Eve. Maggie had brought her a pink sprinkle donut from The Sugarplum, and Carrie gobbled it down.

"Thank you, Pastor Maggie," Carrie said with her mouth full. "Don't worry, I will still be in the Christmas pageant next year."

"Thank you, Carrie. We couldn't do it without you," Maggie said, kissing Carrie's cheek. She loved this little girl.

∞

Back at church, Maggie did the last preparations for Christmas Eve. She was excited because Bryan would be with her parents the next day in Cherish, and then he would stay at the parsonage for the five days following. She couldn't wait to talk and talk and talk. She also thought she might introduce Bryan to Jack.

She went into the sanctuary, where Irena was playing the organ loudly. At least she was playing Christmas carols. Maggie had a box of votive candles and began setting them on the window ledges and around the communion table. She also set out a box of small pillar candles, each with a thin cardboard protector. These were for the members of the congregation at the end of the service. Maggie was sure, after Carrie's accident, everyone would be especially careful with the candles. Wouldn't they? As if Irena could read her mind, she stopped playing the organ and turned to Maggie.

"Ees stuuuupid, dis candles. Vy use dem? Vy not flashlight?"

Maggie regarded Irena's orange hair, sparkly green eye shadow, red lips, and dangling Christmas tree earrings.

"Don't forget our staff Christmas lunch today, Irena. Twelve noon at the Cherish Café. It should be delicious."

Maggie walked back to her office. *Flashlights?*

The staff lunch was a festive time. Maggie discovered this was the only time of the year they splurged and ate at the Cherish Café as a staff. Hank, Doris, Marla, Irena, and Maggie sat at a table by the window. Everyone enjoyed hot apple cider, except for Irena, who drank several hot toddies. They took time after lunch and before dessert to do a small gift exchange. Hank gave each of the women chocolates.

"Pamela said I couldn't go wrong with chocolates." He grinned.

Doris had baked everyone a loaf of date nut bread and wrapped each in pink Saran wrap. "This is my grandma's secret recipe. No, I won't share it."

Marla gave everyone an amaryllis plant. "To remember, 'A shoot shall come out from the stump of Jesse.'" Marla had just taught that passage from Isaiah 11 to the children in Sunday school.

Irena gave everyone a bottle of Peppermint Schnapps with a red ribbon and a bell tied around the neck of the bottles. "Christmas cheerrs to you," she slurred slightly.

Maggie had made a collage of pictures. She had used her camera phone to take the pictures while the others weren't looking, doing their different jobs around the church. There was a picture of Hank snapping his blue tarpaulin. There was Irena sitting at the organ, her huge stack of music at her side. Maggie got a shot of Doris looking into planters for trash. And she had a picture of Marla doing a children's sermon with the little ones sitting around her. Maggie had added a goofy picture of herself shoving a cookie into her mouth at coffee time. Bryan had taken it last summer and texted it to her. She had put the collages into wooden frames.

"I am so grateful to all of you. Don't we have fun?"

Everyone was delighted and laughed at the goofiness of themselves. They finished their desserts and coffees and headed back to church. Irena was a little happier than the rest.

Christmas Eve finally arrived. Maggie was thrilled to see her parents' car pulling into the parsonage driveway with Bryan in the backseat. She was shocked to see Ed and Jo's car following right behind.

"We couldn't miss your first Christmas Eve service, Maggie," Jo said when they were all inside. She gave Maggie a big squeeze.

Ed and Jo would be heading back to Holland after the Christmas Eve service to spend the next day with their children and grandchildren.

"I'm so glad you're all here. Mom, Dad, and Bryan, all the rooms are clean upstairs, so pick one and settle in. I have some snacks and coffee."

Maggie began to scurry, pulling down cups and saucers. She set the dining room table, began making coffees from the Keurig, and put the snacks into bowls and on plates. Then she quickly ran up to her room and found the dark-gray dress with burgundy piping around the wrists and neckline. She snapped the burgundy belt around her waist and took a look in the mirror. Her mother really had exceptional taste.

Ed walked around the downstairs of the parsonage into Maggie's study and looked out at the beautiful evergreen trees covered in snow. The sun was setting in the west, and the shadows were long across the backyard. Marmalade and Cheerio were curled together on one of her wingback chairs. They regarded him for two seconds and promptly went back to sleep. He looked at her desk with its books and papers and something that looked like a sheep's head made of cotton balls. He picked it up and saw the back of it had been burned. A large hole was left right in the middle. One of her desk drawers was partly opened, and he saw some familiar handwriting. His own. He opened the drawer and saw that the entire drawer was filled with his letters to Maggie. It looked like she had saved every one. Ed was touched.

Coffee and snacks were enjoyed hastily by all. Maggie told them about Carrie catching on fire by the Advent candles. She was hopeful Carrie might be in church tonight but knew the pain was still rough for the little girl. Everyone reacted as they should have, in sad horror. Maggie talked about the hospital and how the congregation had come together to care for Carrie, her mother, and brother by bringing meals and toys.

Maggie was the first to leave the table.

"You go get ready for the service. I'll take care of the dishes," Mimi said.

"Thanks, Mom."

Maggie grabbed her coat and walked across the snow to the sanctuary doors. Irena was at the organ playing "Infant Holy, Infant Lowly" on the organ chimes. Maggie immediately felt a lump in her throat. Until she looked at Irena and saw that she was wearing a fire-engine-red, spangled, low-cut top that highlighted her pink lace bra and pushed-up bosom. She was also wearing a green headband in her hair with a piece of mistletoe dangling in front of her forehead. But that wasn't the worst. Irena had dyed her hair a cheerful black for Christmas.

"Wow, Irena, your hair is really black," Maggie said, gasping slightly. Irena looked like Morticia Addams with face paint.

"Yes," Irena said still playing. "I deed eet. Eet ees verry festeeve."

Maggie easily swallowed her lump then smiled and waved at Irena as she walked toward the offices. Hank was there, looking appropriate in khaki slacks, a red-and-burgundy checked shirt, and an evergreen wool vest.

"Hi, Hank."

Maggie was happy to see him. If Hank was in the church, all was well. He was carrying the box of bulletins to take to the table at the entrance of the sanctuary. He and Pamela were ushers for the evening, and Maggie knew that every single person who came through the doors would have a bulletin and a candle before they sat down in the pew.

"Pastor Maggie, this is a great night. There's nothing like Christmas Eve. Even with all the trials and travails of the world, when we all sing 'Silent Night' together, along with millions around the world, we can truly say 'Merry Christmas.'" Hank took a deep breath.

Maggie stared. She had never heard him speak so philosophically.

"You're right, Hank. This truly is a night of hope. I think we're ready."

Maggie was full of anticipation. She had never led a Christmas Eve service before, but the thoughts of what happened that night so long ago made her tremble a little bit. Her life's work now was telling the story. Forever. She had been asked to do this through a whisper in a faraway land, on the hills of Bethlehem. *Tell the story.* She had said yes, and tonight she would be back on those hills, sharing the story of a baby's birth, astounded shepherds, singing angels, and two exhausted parents holding the miracle of all miracles.

When the congregation arrived, the sanctuary was aglow in candlelight, and Irena was actually playing softly on the organ. Maggie was thrilled when she saw Howard Baker slowly make his way into the sanctuary with a cane. He had gotten his wish of being in church for Christmas Eve following his knee replacement. When he saw Maggie, he gave her a flirtatious wink and a saucy wave. The Christmas tree was shining with lights reflecting off the Chrismons. The smaller tree in the gathering area was loaded down with hats, mittens, and scarves. Those would be delivered to the local shelter the day after Christmas.

The service began. The readings were traditional and beloved, beginning with creation and working through God's good works in the Old Testament and then into the New Testament. The carols were sung by all. But when Maggie began reading from the second chapter of Luke, a hush fell over the congregation.

"'Joseph also went from the town of Nazareth in Galilee to Judea, to the city of David called Bethlehem, because he was descended from the house and family of David. He went to be registered with Mary, to whom he was engaged and who was expecting a child. While they were there, the time came for her to deliver her child. And she gave birth to her firstborn son and wrapped him in bands of cloth, and laid him in a manger, because there was no place for them in the inn.'"

As Maggie read this, the secret door to the sanctuary opened. Cole and Lynn Porter slowly walked out. Lynn was holding Samuel, wrapped in a pale-blue blanket. They were dressed in their regular clothes. There was no need for costumes. The image was beautiful. Cole pulled a small chair out onto the altar. Lynn sat with Samuel, who was fast asleep. Cole then stood behind the chair, looking at his new son. They stayed there for the remainder of the service.

When the congregation prepared to sing "Silent Night" at the very end of the service, Marla led Penny, Molly, Carrie, and Carl down the aisle and onto the altar to sit around Lynn and her baby boy. There were other children who were visiting with relatives. Marla invited each one to join them. Carrie had a large white bandage wrapped around her head, but she was wearing a red-and-green tutu covered in little blinking lights. And her smile was even brighter.

No one was able to sing to the end of "Silent Night." It ended in silence with the notes of the organ fading away and the lights of the candles gently glowing.

After the congregation blew out their small candles, Maggie read by the light of the Christmas tree from the Gospel of John.

"'In the beginning was the Word, and the Word was with God, and the Word was God . . . What has come into being in him was life, and the life was the life of all people. The light shines in the darkness, and the darkness did not overcome it . . . And the Word became flesh and lived among us, and we have seen his glory, the glory as of a father's only son, full of grace and truth.'"

Irena, in a moment of clarity, quietly played "Away in a Manger" on the organ as the congregation made their way to the gathering area to find their coats. Maggie hugged Cole and Lynn.

"Thank you so much," Maggie said, her eyes glowing. "Thank you for making it all so real for us."

Cole and Lynn smiled back. Neither of them seemed able to speak as they marveled at their son.

Maggie gave all the children little squeezes and whispered thank yous in their ears. Then she made her way through the secret door, through the offices, and into the gathering area to wish the rest of her parishioners "Merry Christmas!"

She felt an arm around her shoulder and turned her face to see Ed. His eyes were shining.

"I've never been to a Christmas Eve service like this," he sniffed quietly. "Pastor Maggie, thank you for bringing us all, but especially me, to the manger tonight."

"I had a pretty amazing story to work with, didn't I? I can't take much credit for Jesus being born." She looked into his eyes, but his compliment overwhelmed her.

"You truly brought us there."

She kissed his cheek and then felt a little tug on her dress.

Maggie looked down at Carrie and knelt to look her in the eye.

"Merry Christmas, Carrie, darling. Are you excited for Santa tonight?"

Carrie giggled. "I'm staying up all night. I want to see his sleigh land on our house!"

Carl shyly stepped over once he heard the magic "Santa" word. "Pasto Maggie, I'm staying up too. Santa is bwinging us pwesents!" Maggie had never seen Carl quite so animated.

Children are the best people to watch at Christmastime, no doubt about it. "Well, I would like to know all about it, please. Will you tell me how many reindeer he has and what his voice sounds like? Are you leaving him a snack?"

Carrie and Carl burst in together. "Oh, yes, yes!"

Carrie added details. "Pretzels and a Diet Coke for Santa. And carrots and dog biscuits for the reindeer." They looked quite pleased with this menu for their midnight guests.

"That sounds delicious!" Maggie said. "Santa will love being in your house tonight."

"Now, Carrie," Maggie asked seriously, "how is your head feeling? Does it still hurt you?"

Carrie matched Maggie's seriousness. "Yes, Pastor Maggie. My head does still hurt, and it's hard to sleep. I have to put my head on a blow-up pillow, but that hurts too. That's why I will be able to see Santa. I can't sleep." Maggie looked up and saw Cassandra listening to the conversation.

"Remember, Carrie?" Cassandra said. "Dr. Elliot gave you that yummy strawberry medicine to help you sleep."

Carrie slowly shook her head. She looked like an old farmer, unhappy with the weather forecast.

"No, Mommy. It doesn't make me sleep at all."

Cassandra winked at Maggie and gave a little nod. Maggie didn't need to worry. Carrie would sleep tonight.

Once everyone had buttoned coats, pulled on mittens, and headed out the door, Maggie began to turn off the lights in the church. Jack helped. Her family and Ed and Jo were back in the parsonage getting ready for a more substantial Christmas Eve repast. When Jack and Maggie reached the sanctuary, only the Christmas tree was lit. Jack took Maggie's hand and led her to the altar steps. They sat quietly together in the twinkle lights, breathing in the smells of the sanctuary—furniture polish, the pine of the Advent wreath, and the mustiness that made their church smell like their church.

Jack pulled a small jewelry box out of his pocket and put it in Maggie's hand.

"Merry Christmas, Maggie."

Maggie looked at the small box in her hand. "I have something for you too," she said. "It's in my office. Just a second. Don't go anywhere."

She walked quickly through the secret door and into her office. She grabbed a package out of her bottom drawer and hurried back to the sanctuary. Unfortunately, no one had moved the chair Lynn had sat on with baby Samuel. Maggie plowed right into it in the dim lighting, tripped, and flew off the altar steps onto the sanctuary floor. The package for Jack went flying.

Jack was up from the steps immediately and helped her sit up on the floor. She was spectacularly embarrassed. He made sure she hadn't broken anything. Her right elbow was sore, but intact.

"I think you will have an attractive bruise on your elbow in the morning," Jack said. "But otherwise, you seem to be okay."

"Except for my ego," Maggie mumbled. *Oh well.* That's who she was—an impetuous, badly dressed, clumsy person. "I hope you realize what you're getting into with me," she said, smiling. There was nothing she could do about the embarrassment but wait for it to dissipate.

"As long as you keep tripping, I can keep catching you. I'll have to be a little faster, but I'll work on it."

Embarrassment completely dissipated.

They moved back to the steps, and Maggie opened her small box. Inside, resting on silver velvet, was a perfectly delicate gold cross. The detail highlighted the femininity with the slightly rounded corners of the cross.

"Oh, Jack, what a beautiful cross. It's so feminine. Help me put it on, please."

Jack hooked the cross under her hair and then looked at the result. It rested between her collar bones and glittered in the tree lights.

"Jack, thank you for such a thoughtful gift. You will see me wearing it from now on."

"It's a reminder to us, and to everyone who sees it, of who you are. You are our pastor. It's just that I get to kiss our pastor." He then did so.

Maggie was pretty sure this was the best Christmas in the history of the world. She almost forgot about her package for him.

"Here, this is for you."

Jack carefully unwrapped the slim package. He was delighted to see two volumes by Sherwin B. Nuland: *The Soul of Medicine: Tales from the Bedside* and *The Uncertain Art: Thoughts on a Life in Medicine*. Maggie could see that Jack was pleased.

"He is a brilliant author," Jack said. "These are the kind of books I could sit up and read all night. Thank you so much, Maggie." Of course, that netted another kiss.

"We should probably get to the parsonage. Now you get to be scrutinized by my family."

They cleaned up their wrapping paper, locked the sanctuary doors, and walked through the snow to the parsonage. But before they made it across the lawn, Maggie gave Jack a slight push. Then she grabbed his arm and pulled him down in the snow.

"It's Christmas Eve! We have to make snow angels!"

She fell backward and began moving her legs and arms into an angel. Jack sat on his bum, watching her in semi-shock.

"What are you doing?" he said feeling the cold seeping through his clothes.

"Jack, you grew up on a farm in Michigan. Don't tell me you never made snow angels."

Her arms and legs flailed away. The snow soaked her tights and got in her shoes.

What could he do? He lay back in the snow, balanced his new books on his stomach, and made the very first snow angel in his life. And he laughed out loud as he did so.

21

Maggie had invited Jack to join her family after the Christmas Eve service for some pigs in blankets and pea soup. He was learning the ways of the Dutch. When Maggie and Jack came through the front door, shaking off the snow from their coats, Mimi, Dirk, Bryan, Ed, and Jo were chatting in the living room, sipping warm spiced cranberry punch. They all looked up at Jack and Maggie and smiled like people who knew more than they were supposed to know. Maggie stared at them.

"You look like a litter of Cheshire cats. Jack, I would like to introduce you officially to my family. My father, Dirk. My mother, Mimi. And my brother, Bryan. These are two of my dearest friends, Ed and Jo James. And this is Dr. Jack Elliot, everyone. Feel free to *ooh* and *aah*."

The smiles turned into laughter, and Dirk, Bryan, and Ed all stood to shake Jack's hand. If Jack was nervous, there was no evidence. He sat down comfortably next to Mimi on the once-white-now-gray couch. Maggie went into the kitchen, followed by Jo, to get the food ready.

Jack and Mimi chatted about small-town doctor life. Mimi reminisced on her own childhood in Zeeland when house calls from the local doctor were de rigueur. Jack said that living in a small town made it easier to do house calls, and house calls were often easier on the patient. Maggie listened as she brought punch in for Jack and herself. It seemed that Jack had been part of the family for years.

Once the oak dining room table was set, they brought the food in and called to everyone else.

"Everyone may sit down," Maggie said happily. "I hope you're hungry."

She prayed over the meal, and everyone enjoyed the feast. Maggie had made a special peppermint white chocolate pie for dessert that brought many accolades.

"Did you make up this recipe?" Bryan asked, diving into his piece.

"Yes, I did. I had to throw the first one away. Too much peppermint. But I liked the taste of this one."

She put pies together the same way she put sermons together (and now a possible relationship): add ingredients, give it a try, then readjust when necessary. Sometimes, throw the whole thing out and start over from scratch (maybe a pie, certainly not Jack).

Ed and Jo left the parsonage after the late supper. Their children would be driving to Holland from Chicago and Kansas City to celebrate Christmas. Once they had left, Jack also said his goodbyes. He was heading to his parents' home in Blissfield. His siblings, all except for his oldest sister, Anne, would be home tonight. Anne would come at noon tomorrow with her husband, Peter, and their children, Gretchen and Garrett. Mimi would have liked to do more reconnaissance on the topic of Jack's family but restrained herself.

Maggie walked Jack to the door. They had already decided they would spend New Year's Eve together. Just the two of them.

"I like your family," Jack said as he moved in for a kiss. "Your mother is formidable, but I think I can win her over. Eventually." He kissed Maggie again.

"My mother loved you," Maggie said simply. "I was watching her face. You made it laugh. That's quite a feat. She doesn't waste laughter on just anyone."

"Your father is fascinating," Jack continued. "His work as an architect is something I want to talk about more with him. He doesn't let people know how brilliant he is. Does he play golf?"

"Not in Michigan in December," Maggie said, giving Jack's neck a little snuffle. He smelled so good. "But in warmer months, yes, he golfs. He's actually very good, so I've heard." Inhale. One last lingering kiss. "Parting is such sweet sorrow!" Maggie said dramatically with the back of her hand against her forehead.

"I'll see you the day after tomorrow when we bring the mittens and scarves to the shelter, you nut," Jack said as he kissed the top of her head.

Then Jack was gone into the winter night.

But their snow angels sparkled in the moonlight. Side by side.

Christmas in the parsonage was truly festive. With Marmalade and Cheerio chasing balls of used wrapping paper and Christmas carols blasting from Maggie's iHome, the Elzinga family enjoyed sipping coffee, eating sticky buns, and sharing gifts. They had never emphasized gift giving at Christmas. Mimi would ask the children to think of places where there were people in need. At Thanksgiving, Dirk, Mimi, Maggie, and Bryan would each bring their idea for where money could be used to help others. The week before Christmas, Dirk would write out the checks, and they would all go to the post office together and mail their envelopes. Christmas morning was meant for small gifts for one another, often handmade.

This year it had been easy to choose one charity that all four of them wanted to give to: Africa Hope. Bryan had shared the many projects Africa Hope supported in several African countries. Dirk had chosen a health clinic in Tanzania. Mimi chose a primary school in Uganda. Bryan chose a sustainable agriculture project in Kenya. And Maggie chose an orphanage in Ghana. Because Bryan worked for the Africa Hope organization, he was able to give the rest of the family regular updates for each project. It was a whole new world, and they enjoyed sharing in Bryan's work.

"Christmas dinner will be ready by four o'clock," Maggie said. "Can you make it with only snacks for the time being?" She was mainly asking Bryan, who seemed to be able to eat for an entire football team.

"What kind of snacks?" he asked as he dragged a string around for Cheerio to chase.

"Kale muffins and quinoa sticks," Maggie said, enjoying Bryan's change of face. "Just kidding. The regular: smoked Gouda and salmon, crackers, hummus and veggies, nuts and cookies. There's some leftover soup and a few pigs in blankets too. Can you survive?"

"Does Jack eat that weird stuff?" Bryan asked.

Mimi's ears perked up.

"There is nothing weird in the foods I just mentioned," Maggie said, banging around in the kitchen. "And yes, Jack eats all of it. He has a very adult palate, unlike yourself. You're going to have to learn to eat more than cereal and bagels if you have a chance to go back to some country in Africa someday."

"Thank you, Maggie," Bryan said as he stood and took a bow. "Mom, Dad, Sister Margaret, I have an announcement to make. Drumroll, please!"

Maggie came out of the kitchen with flour on her nose.

Bryan made his own drumroll noise that sounded like a cat purring. "I will make my next trip to Africa this year, as a staff member of Africa Hope. I will actually visit all the sites where we sent our Christmas money. Ta-da!"

Mimi's brain did a quick U-turn. Having hoped to hear a little more information about Jack and Maggie's relationship, she now had this new information hurled at her. Her children were going to drive her insane one of these days, she was sure.

Dirk spoke up. "Bryan, that's great. When are you going and for how long?"

Maggie often thought her father should smoke a pipe. He had the face, and the affect, to have a pipe constantly sticking out of his mouth.

"Well," Bryan looked a little less cavalier. "I leave on Maggie's birthday, actually. And I'll be gone for three months." He almost whispered the last part.

"January twenty-eighth?" Mimi was assimilating information like an NSA computer. "You are leaving in just over a month, and we are hearing about it today? Christmas day? And for three months?"

"I haven't known all that long myself," Bryan said seriously. "I'll be heading off with the CEO of the organization, Joy Nelson. She wants me to see the projects because I'm the program manager. I didn't think it would be this soon. But I've applied for the visas that I need for each country, and I'm getting things ready. Actually, I'm really excited."

Being an extraordinary mother, Mimi set aside her own motherly worries and gave Bryan a huge hug.

"We are so proud of you. Now, tell us all the details."

Bryan did. He dissected his trip by each week he would be gone.

"I'll be able to call or text you when there is a signal or electricity. I'll also send pictures of each site and the people who live there. It's going to be so cool." Bryan had such a great smile. *Too bad his face fur covers up half of it,* Maggie thought.

"I'll spend the most time in Ghana at the orphanage, Maggie. I'll be able to tell you exactly what your Christmas money is doing there."

Maggie thought how this year had been so different. Changes in both her and Bryan's lives had sent them into two different worlds. As children, they had shared every experience together. They could fight like cats and dogs. They could read each other's thoughts. What brand-new stories would they be sharing next Christmas day? Would they even be together?

Dirk and Mimi enjoyed the rest of the afternoon hearing Bryan's plans and eating Maggie's delicious Christmas dinner. When the sun began to go down, they wrapped themselves in their coats, hugged and kissed their children, and began the journey back to Zeeland. The car ride wasn't silent. Their children's lives required much discussion.

Bryan was going to stay with Maggie in the parsonage for four more glorious days. Maggie would drive him back on the twenty-ninth. Until then, there would be very many words between the two of them.

Maggie wanted to immerse herself in Bryan's work. She had always known everything happening in his life. It was strange to have to learn new things she had no knowledge of, and now he would be leaving in just over a month.

"I have one important question for you," Maggie said gravely.

"What?" Bryan couldn't imagine what had her so serious.

"Are you going to shave that junk off your face before you leave? You look like a bum."

Bryan gave her a dirty look. "Stop asking me that. I'm not going to shave. I think it looks great, and the girls like it too."

"I bet they don't," Maggie said simply. "Just think about it. It's going to be so hot in Africa. Whew! Hot! Don't you want your neck and face to be as cool as possible? Plus, it would give our longsuffering mother a moment of happiness if she could kiss your smooth cheek before you go off to the wilds of the world. Just think about it."

"You're such a pain in the butt," Bryan said, petting Marmalade.

"So, seriously, are you nervous at all about your trip?" Maggie asked. "This is much longer than your trip to Uganda."

"Not really. I'm learning about the cultures of the places I'll be staying. I'm learning about the paperwork it takes to enter each country, and I'm learning a lot about different medications and vaccinations. The best thing is, I will be able to see each of these projects in action. I talk to the people on the ground every week on the phone or Skype, but I want to see the people and projects with my own eyes."

"Will you go *every* year?" Maggie asked.

"At least once a year. We hope to set up more projects in different countries. I'll oversee those. One of the best things in all this is I have begun a master's degree. I get credit for the work I'm doing, and I attend intensive courses a few times a year at the University of San Francisco. Of course, I have to write papers, and in the end, a huge thesis." He grimaced. "But I'm excited to keep learning."

"Does mom know?" Maggie asked excitedly. "She would go crazy nuts to know you are getting a master's degree!"

"Of course. I told her first thing when I got home. I thought it would soften the news of me leaving on your birthday," Bryan said conspiratorially.

Maggie laughed. There was nothing like the bond between siblings when trying to manipulate parents. The bond was stronger than iron between Maggie and Bryan.

Maggie had a lightning bolt of a thought. "Hey, Bry, what if you discover some of these projects need things we could send them? What if the church could raise money or gather clothes or gardening seeds or something?"

Bryan looked skeptical. "We are trying not to interfere with the communities sustaining themselves and strengthening their own economies. But . . . they all need money to start new projects. Let me talk to Joy. Maybe it would be a fun way to connect two cities far away from each other."

Maggie suddenly had new and extraordinary dreams drifting and floating in her brain. There had to be a way to help without interfering. When she looked at the clock, she saw it was two a.m. Way past bedtime. Marmalade and Cheerio were both curled up in Bryan's lap.

"Can I sleep with them tonight?" he asked.

"You'll have to let them decide, but you can give it a try."

Before Maggie went up to bed, she saw that her study light was on. She went in to turn it off and saw a package on her desk. Removing the paper, she held a book in her hands: *Learning to Walk in the Dark* by Barbara Brown Taylor. She had almost bought the book herself just a week earlier but had decided to wait. Inside was an inscription.

Christmas 2014

My dear Pastor Maggie,

You are a light in the darkness that other people encounter from time to time. You are also the comfort of darkness when the light is too bright. May this beautiful book be a guide for you, if you ever need it, or one to share with the people you hold so dear. Your life shines a light on God. You can't do more than that as a pastor. I'm so proud of you.

All my love,
Ed

Maggie brought the book upstairs and placed it on her nightstand. Ed's thoughtfulness rushed through her heart and made her eyes drippy. What a lovely Christmas.

The morning after Christmas, Maggie was up early, totally bleary-eyed, but it was time for her run. The time seemed to fly by as she thought of Bryan's news and also how delicious Jack smelled the night before. She relived all of Christmas day and thought of her plans for that morning and night.

Jack was picking her up at ten a.m. to box up the knitted items on the mitten tree. They would drag Bryan along to deliver the knitted treasures to Grace in Action. Jack said he would come back to the parsonage for dinner after seeing a few patients in the afternoon. *But tonight, ah yes, tonight.* Maggie had invited Cate to come over to the parsonage for dinner with Maggie, Jack, and Bryan.

Jack arrived at ten on the dot. Maggie had just dragged Bryan out of bed, shoved a cup of coffee in his hand, and thrown his coat over his shoulders.

"C'mon, Bry, you lazy bum!"

Bryan rolled his eyes and decided Maggie would go headfirst in a snow bank as soon as he was awake.

"Hey, Bryan," Jack said laughing, "you have quite the taskmistress here."

"It's been this way my whole entire life," Bryan said, taking a gulp of coffee. "It's pretty rough. But since I can pick her up with one hand, it's easier to get revenge when needed."

"Move it!" Maggie barked. "We don't have all day. How in the world are you going to function for three months in Africa?"

"You sound like Mom," Bryan said.

"Thank you. Now move it!"

Once they dropped off the hats and mittens, Jack left for the hospital. Maggie and Bryan headed to The Sugarplum for a nice, unhealthy breakfast. They also chose a chocolate torte to serve for dessert that evening.

"If I lived in Cherish, I'd eat here every day," Bryan said, cramming a chocolate donut in his mouth while grabbing an egg and bacon bagel off the plate.

"You would have to run twenty-five miles a day," Maggie said, biting into a blueberry scone.

At six p.m., the Westminster chimes rang, and both Jack and Cate were standing at the front door. Bryan ushered them inside and took their coats, as instructed by Maggie ahead of time. Maggie and Bryan had spent the afternoon looking at maps of African countries, talking about life in Cherish, baking homemade bread, and making spaghetti sauce. Now it was time to share their Italian feast with Cate and Jack.

While chatting with Bryan, Cate was thrilled, and not a little surprised, to see Jack kiss Maggie on the cheek. Jack and Maggie hadn't made their relationship public knowledge, but there seemed to be a mutual understanding that they would. Cate was too well-bred to say anything, but she gave Maggie a smile and a raise of her eyebrows. Both were returned in kind.

The four of them sat in the parsonage dining room. The table was so large, they huddled at one end. Maggie lit candles on the table and turned off the brighter overhead light. Dinner began. Maggie started off the conversation by mentioning Bryan's upcoming trip. As he described the places he would be visiting and the projects that were underway, Cate became more and more interested. The more interested she became, the more she gnawed on her fingernail. Maggie wanted to slap her hand.

"How does each community decide what they need most?" Cate asked as she twirled spaghetti on her fork.

"It's really the project that comes first. Take the orphanage, for example. One of our staff people met the pastor, who was taking in unwanted and abandoned children. But there wasn't enough room for the children. He didn't have enough food, medicine, or clothing. We partnered with the pastor to build an orphanage. We sent volunteers, raised money, and hired local workers to build. The volunteers helped get the other needs taken care of. That's a pretty simplistic explanation. A lot more went into it than that, but now the orphanage feeds local children who don't have enough to eat, and we're looking to build a school that would serve the whole community. They're beginning to sustain themselves with a farm and fish ponds." Bryan stopped. He looked embarrassed. "I'm talking too much," he said and shoved a piece of bread into his mouth.

"Oh, no, no, no," Maggie and Cate said in unison.

"Tell us about the medical clinic," Jack said. He had colleagues who had gone on medical mission trips. The idea interested him.

Bryan explained the steps it took to begin with a simple clinic that dispensed oral medicines. Once this small clinic was in place, it can be expanded to a clinic that performs simple procedures, such as setting broken bones and caring for open wounds. Next, it expands to a larger clinic for surgeries and obstetrical care.

"It takes lots of local people to build the clinics and lots of volunteers to raise money and get the needed supplies."

"How do people volunteer to go to these different places and help?" Cate asked. She completely forgot about her dinner and was eating her finger instead.

As Bryan explained the process of volunteering, Maggie watched Cate watch Bryan. Maggie saw Cate slowly take a large step out of her Ann Arbor world and set her heart into a much larger one. Bryan must have felt it too because his manner relaxed again, and he spoke directly to Cate. Jack and Maggie were quickly relegated to being bystanders.

After dessert, Bryan asked Cate if she would like to go for a walk and check out the neighborhood Christmas lights and decorations. It took a nanosecond for Cate to reply and grab her coat, mittens, and hat. They were out the door and into the frosty night.

Jack grabbed Maggie around the waist as she loaded the dishwasher and kissed the back of her head.

"I think I saw a little romance simmering at the table tonight," he said.

She turned and laughed. "I believe there were two romances simmering at the table."

That earned her a proper kiss.

"I couldn't have planned that better myself," she said. "I knew Cate had a crush on Bryan. But he spoke her language tonight, and he didn't even know it. They both have incredible servant hearts."

"I'll make a wager that one Cate Carlson will find herself somewhere in Africa volunteering at an orphanage or clinic or farm, sooner rather than later. And . . . I think she will be with one Bryan Elzinga." Jack sounded smug, in a good way.

"Maybe one Dr. Elliot will volunteer at a clinic," Maggie said.

"Only if one Reverend Elzinga is with him," Jack replied.

That earned him several kisses.

22

The next morning, Maggie wrapped herself in her coat, hat, scarf, and mittens and headed down Main Street. She was on her way to The Page Turner Book Shop, on the hunt for a baby name book. Sammy Porter's baptism was scheduled for January 4th. Maggie's creative juices were running wild. She wanted to make her first baptism special, especially for Cole and Lynn. Maggie thought tying the meaning of Sammy's name into the service would make it personal.

She left Bryan asleep in the parsonage after his late night with Cate. When he and Cate had come home from their walk, they sat up in the parsonage family room/Sunday school room until after midnight, talking nonstop. Jack had left at ten. He knew he would have a full day in the office the next day. Maggie went to bed with the kitties shortly after that. She hoped Bryan and Cate would figure out how to see each other again before he had to go back to Zeeland.

But now she was on a mission to The Page Turner. The first time she had gone to the book shop, she was surprised to see Jennifer Becker behind the counter and her sister, Beth, arranging Christmas books in a display window. Maggie had no idea Jennifer and Beth owned the store. It never came up when their mother died. Maggie was now a regular patron.

Beth was there alone that morning.

"Good morning, Beth."

"Good morning, Pastor Maggie. You're out and about early today."

"I have my brother at the parsonage for a few days. While he sleeps, I can get some errands done. I need a baby name book. Do you have any?" Maggie asked, looking around. She loved book stores.

Beth looked at Maggie quizzically. "A baby name book?"

"It's for Sammy Porter's baptism," Maggie said, smiling. "That's all."

Beth immediately found *The Very Best Baby Name Book in the Whole Wide World*. It had over thirty thousand names, as well as meanings, origins, and nicknames.

"That should just about cover every baptism I will ever do in my entire ministry," Maggie said, thumbing through the book. "Did you and Jennifer have a nice Christmas?"

"It was quiet, but okay," Beth said as she rang up the purchase.

"It was your first Christmas without your mother. I'm sorry. This year is hard with all the 'firsts' you have to go through."

"We knew it would be different. So we spent a day baking mother's recipes for Christmas cookies and brought them to our neighbors and to the Friendly Elder Care. It helped to see the happy faces of the folks there." Beth smiled sweetly.

"What a great idea," Maggie said, thinking this would be a great idea for the church to do next Christmas. She had to write it down when she got home or she'd forget.

Maggie returned to the parsonage with her book.

Bryan was still asleep, so Maggie began to memorize her sermon for Sunday. She wondered how many people would show up to church the Sunday after Christmas. After another hour of sermon prep, she looked up to see Bryan in the doorway.

"Hey, Megs," he said with a sleepy smile.

"Hey, yourself! I've been waiting for you to get up so you can tell me everything about last night."

"What if it's none of your business?"

She walked over and grabbed him playfully by the ear and said, "You will tell me everything or I will call Cate. I know she'll tell me."

"Coffee," he said.

Over coffee and oatmeal, Bryan told her about his evening with Cate. They'd walked up and down the streets of Cherish to see the Christmas lights and Nativity sets on front lawns. They talked about the U, Cate's work with her shared living club, and of course, all things Africa.

"The university has a semester abroad program to Ghana, did you know that?" Bryan asked.

Maggie did not.

"Cate was thinking of going to South America, but she may be changing her mind." Bryan waggled his oatmeal spoon and grinned.

Maggie listened for a bit longer and then cut to the chase. "Did you kiss her?"

"No! I really just met her. Talking during coffee time at church once or twice doesn't count. Plus, I don't know, she's almost four years younger than I am."

"So? She's more mature than you are, and even though I have been thinking she should go to seminary, maybe she should go to Africa too." Maggie winked.

"Well, you can ask her yourself because I invited her over here again tonight. You can make us dinner, wench."

Bryan poured more maple syrup on his oatmeal.

This new development had Maggie crackling with excitement. She thought she would spend every minute with Bryan before she had to take him back to Zeeland, but she was happy to abdicate if he and Cate wanted to spend more time together. It was going so much better than she had hoped.

"Why don't you take her out to eat? You're a working man. The Cherish Café is really nice." Maggie was almost ready to tell him what to order.

"I think I'll take it a little slower than that. Have you already picked out her wedding dress?" Bryan knew his sister, oh, so well.

"We'll order a pizza tonight. I'll stay out of the way. Although I might eavesdrop."

Maggie laughed and wished she could see Jack that night, but she knew he was on call and would probably stay home or at the hospital for most of the night. "I'm glad you two like each other, whether it turns into something else or not."

The weekend went quickly. Bryan and Cate spent each evening together and even sat in the same pew at church Sunday morning. By noon on Monday, Bryan was packed and ready for the drive back to Zeeland. Cate came to the parsonage to say goodbye. Maggie pretended to feed the cats while she unabashedly eavesdropped.

"I'd like to see you again before I leave for Africa," Bryan said.

"I would like that too," Cate said quietly. "Maybe we can meet here, even though it's a much longer drive for you."

"We'll do it," Bryan said. "That means we don't have to say goodbye now."

Bryan gave Cate one of his massive bear hugs.

Maggie smiled.

As they drove back to Zeeland, Maggie and Bryan tried to figure out the best way for him to see Cate. They decided Bryan would drive back out to Cherish on Friday before he had to fly to San Francisco on Saturday.

When they arrived in Zeeland, Mimi had prepared dinner, and they enjoyed being a family of four again. When Bryan told his parents that he needed to borrow a car on Friday to head back to Cherish, Mimi's eyebrows raised slightly.

"Haven't you had enough of your sister?" Mimi asked.

"He wants to see Cate Carlson," Maggie said plainly.

"Yep," Brian agreed.

"He might even shave that junk off his face and get a haircut," Maggie said.

"Really?" Mimi couldn't contain her voice.

"No," Bryan said, "I'm not." Then, "Does it really look that bad?"

"Yes!" Mimi and Maggie said together.

"Dad?" Bryan looked pleadingly.

"You look your age. As soon as you want to look mature, I would shave and get a haircut." Dirk made a precise hit to Bryan's ego.

"Well," Mimi said, "it looks like Cherish has cast some sort of spell on both of you. Or at least two people in Cherish have." She quickly changed the subject from Bryan's hair and actually sounded pleased about the Cherish "spell."

"It's just like a fairy tale," Maggie said. *Oh, I miss Jack.* "True love and all that."

"I don't know about true love," Bryan said. "I think Cate is great, though. And smart."

"Don't forget beautiful," Maggie said. She wondered what Jack was doing right that second.

"I won't forget," Bryan said.

"I remember when I first saw your mother," Dirk interjected.

"Was she the most beautiful girl in the room?" Maggie asked in a fake sing-song voice.

"Maybe. I don't remember that. I just remember how scary she was. She was pointing out to the English teacher that she, the teacher, had written a run-on sentence on the chalkboard. I was warily smitten. That was the sixth grade." Dirk smiled at his wife.

"I'm sure that poor girl was right out of college and barely knew a piece of chalk from a pencil," Mimi said unsympathetically about the long-ago teacher.

Jack and Maggie's New Year's Eve began with dinner at the Cherish Café. Maggie already thought of the café as "their restaurant." They were relaxed, comfortable, and had an easy affection for one another. After dinner, they went to the local movie theater to see *Into the Woods.* It had just been released on Christmas day and was one of Maggie's favorite musicals. She was excited to see the movie and all the hopes of happily-ever-afters, even if the story took a dark turn or two. She was also excited to feel Jack's arm around her as they watched it.

Once they were back in the parsonage waiting for midnight to show up, Jack pulled her closer on the once-white-now-gray loveseat and said, "Maggie, I am so glad for 2014 because I met you. Now I can't wait for 2015 because we will begin it together."

"I have never been so happy," Maggie said simply. "I think 2015 will be a wonderful year."

New Year's Day had passed quietly. Maggie did laundry and worked on her sermon and Samuel's baptism service. She was excited to see Bryan the next afternoon when he came back to Cherish. She had asked him if he and Cate would like to have dinner at the parsonage. She would invite Jack too. Bryan had expected that all along.

When Bryan arrived, Cate and Maggie were waiting for him. Both of their mouths dropped open. Bryan had shaved and gotten a haircut while in Zeeland. He looked completely different. Cate began to bite at the skin on the side of her finger as she stared at Bryan. Maggie couldn't stand it.

"Cate, you must stop biting your nails. You have such beautiful hands, except your fingers look as if they have been through a meat grinder. If Bryan can shave, you can leave your poor fingers alone." Maggie felt like a nagging mother. She kind of liked it.

Cate looked embarrassed and then rebounded. "I've chewed my nails since I was little. But maybe that should be my 2015 resolution. Stop biting."

"As soon as you do, we'll go get a manicure together," Maggie said, although the thought of a manicure made her sigh. It was a waste of money and lasted less than an hour on her busy hands.

Cate grinned, clearly excited by the idea.

"Bryan, you look like a man." That was the highest compliment Maggie could give her baby brother.

"Thanks, wench. Your insults were too much for me, I guess." Bryan spoke to Maggie but looked at Cate, who appeared to be on the verge of drooling.

"Let's go into the kitchen," Maggie said, secretly delighted at the progress.

Maggie had baked a homemade chicken pot pie, one of Bryan's favorites, and a pan of triple chunk brownies. Jack was there within the hour.

"Bryan, are you ready to get back to the West Coast?" Jack asked. Bryan had impressed Jack with his maturity and his vision. Jack hadn't mentioned the shave and haircut but suspected a certain sister had worn Bryan down.

"I am ready. There is a lot to do before I leave for Africa, and I need to be in San Francisco to do it. But this has been such a good trip home." He glanced at Cate.

"You're welcome," Maggie said.

"What?" Bryan asked.

"I arranged magical moments for you and the lovely Cate. That made your trip home very special. So, you're welcome."

Cate laughed out loud.

"Oh, thank you, Sister Margaret, for planning my life and introducing me to the lovely Lady Cate." Bryan made a little bow.

"I'm hungry," said Jack.

The entire evening was one of quick repartee and lots of teasing. Maggie was silently thankful she could spend that last night with her brother. Her mother had certainly made a sacrifice to "allow" him to be in Cherish and not in Zeeland. Two hours went by too fast. Bryan had to make the two-and-a-half-hour drive back to his parents.

He wrapped his arms around Maggie and gave her a big bear hug. "I love you, Megs."

"I love you," Maggie said. "We'll talk when you get back out West."

Jack and Bryan shook hands. Then Bryan leaned forward and gave Jack a hug.

"My sister is crazy about you. I've never seen her like this. You're cool, man."

"Just so you know, I'm crazy about her too. Man."

Jack and Maggie watched Cate walk Bryan to his car. They watched them talk for a few minutes then turned away. They didn't see Bryan give Cate her own bear hug or their first kiss.

Samuel Cole Porter was baptized on January 4, 2015. Maggie had revolved the entire service around the baptism. She shared the meaning of his name and gave him special verses to go with his name. She held him and said, "Samuel, your name means 'asked of God' or 'heard God.' It is a strong name. And God knows your name. God will call you by name all the days of your life. I have chosen these verses for you, little one, verses I hope you will learn one day and always keep in your heart.

"Isaiah 40: 28-31 'Have you not known? Have you not heard? The Lord is the everlasting God, the creator of the ends of the earth. He does not faint or grow weary; his understanding is unsearchable. He gives power to the faint, and strengthens the powerless. Even youths will faint and be weary, and the young will fall exhausted; but those who wait for the Lord shall renew their strength, they shall mount up with wings like eagles, they shall run and not be weary, they shall walk and not faint.'

"Samuel Cole, for you Jesus Christ came into the world. For you he died, and for you he conquered death. All this he did for you, little one, though you know nothing of it yet. We love because God first loved us."

As she sprinkled warm water on him, he snuffled and then began to cry. Penny and Molly had been standing very close to their brother, and when he cried, they both tiptoed up and kissed him. Maggie wiped his face with a soft cloth, then walked with him in her arms as she asked the congregation to promise to love him, to support his parents as they raised him, and to change his diapers if they had nursery duty. Everyone laughed. Then they became very quiet as Maggie walked him up and down the aisles of the church, introducing the newest member of Loving the Lord. Penny and Molly followed Maggie as she traversed the sanctuary. They weren't going to let their brother get too far away. Cole and Lynn stood up front, watching the whole procession. Tissues began flying out of purses as the congregation regarded the littlest Porter.

That was the day Maggie realized baptisms would be her favorite holy service to officiate in the church. She felt the joy of the parents and the weight of being the pastor. She had a part and a responsibility to help raise Samuel to know he was loved by God in every way.

All Jack could see was Maggie smiling down at Sammy as she unknowingly began to sway gently with the baby in her arms.

January was cold, and Maggie felt the usual glumness that descends after the holidays. Sammy's baptism helped the holiday feeling last a little longer, but now it was just plain-old January. Her birthday was coming up, but that was bittersweet. She knew Bryan would be flying from San Francisco to Africa that day. And it was cloudy outside. Again. She couldn't remember when the sun had shone last.

She put on her coat and walked over to church. Hank was copying the bulletin, and Doris was wiping down the pews with Murphy's Oil Soap. Irena pounded away on the organ. All those things were Maggie's normal existence. She wasn't startled when Doris flourished her can of Raid to kill a wayward insect. Irena's makeup and hair, now the color of cooked beets, never made Maggie look twice anymore. Hank and his blue tarpaulin were the expected sights when she entered the office. Loving the Lord Community Church was home. Better than that, it was comfortable. She knew every nook and cranny of the church. She wasn't asking as many questions anymore, and she actually had some answers when other people asked.

She went in the church kitchen and made herself a cup of Lady Grey tea. She would take some time that morning to think about the season of Lent. She was hoping to do midweek Lenten services, beginning with Ash Wednesday in the middle of February. She and Irena would plan a very special Holy Week and a celebrative Easter service. Even in the midst of her self-pity over the end of the holidays and the grayness of January, Maggie was excited for her first Easter service at Loving the Lord. It would be a morning like no other, and no matter how loud Irena played the organ, it would actually work. Maybe they should have a sunrise service *and* a regular service. Maggie walked dreamily into her office as she thought about those things.

The days passed, and Maggie's birthday was only three days away. Jack had asked her out for dinner. He hoped she wasn't going to Zeeland for her birthday.

"I am absolutely free on the day I turn twenty-seven," she said nonchalantly.

"I'll pick you up at six o'clock, then."

Early on her birthday morning, Maggie went out for her run and contemplated what being twenty-seven meant. It didn't feel any different from twenty-six. She wondered what the new year would bring. She thought that every year on her birthday. There were twelve months stretching ahead of her, blank days, but by next year she would be able to look back and marvel at what all those days gave to her. One year ago, she had never even heard of Loving the Lord Community Church. She had never heard of Cherish. Now this was her happy life, living out her calling to ministry.

Jack was a completely unexpected gift, but she fell more in love with him every day.

One year ago, she never would have thought her little brother would have a job with an NGO and that he would leave on her next birthday for a three-month trip to Africa. She and Bryan planned to Skype at two p.m. Maggie's time, before he left for the airport. Her head was spinning with thoughts as she made her oatmeal and gave Marmalade and Cheerio their breakfast twice without noticing.

Her goodbye with Bryan that afternoon was short and sweet. She could see his excitement and knew he didn't want to see her cry. So she didn't. He had already Skyped with their parents, and he was going to do the same with Cate after talking with Maggie.

"I'll either call you or try to find internet and Skype whenever I can," he said. Maggie knew he had said the same thing to their parents and guessed Cate would get the same promise.

"I love you, Bry. Be safe, have fun, and keep a journal so you won't forget any stories," Maggie said, choking up. "And don't forget to take your anti-malaria pills. Remember what a baby you are when you get sick."

"I won't forget. I love you, Megs, and I'll talk to you soon. Have a super happy birthday with your doctor tonight."

He was laughing when they disconnected.

Maggie allowed herself one short wallow in self-pity and then got over it. Marmalade came and crawled into her lap. He promptly fell asleep. Maggie petted his furry little body and, without realizing it, nodded off herself. She was startled awake by the Westminster chimes and groggily answered the door.

A beautiful woman, Maggie thought she was absolutely exquisite, held a large bouquet of red carnations and baby's breath. She greeted Maggie with a smile.

"Umm . . . Maggie Elzinga?"

"Yes," Maggie replied.

The flower lady looked like a fashion model. Maggie had never seen her before.

"These are . . . umm . . . for you. And happy birthday."

The woman turned gracefully and was gone.

Maggie wondered if she was in a dream. She finally opened the card attached to the flowers.

Dear Maggie,

Happy birthday! I can't wait to celebrate YOU tonight.

With all my love,
Jack

Maggie put the flowers in the living room and went upstairs to dress. She put on a soft-gray wool dress (thanks to her mom), black pumps, and a deep-turquoise scarf tied jauntily around her neck. She took extra time with her hair and makeup. When the Westminster chimes rang, she opened the door and saw Jack.

"You look beautiful," Jack said, kissing her. "Happy birthday."

He noticed the bouquet of flowers displayed on the coffee table in the living room.

"Thank you for the flowers," she said. "It was such a fun surprise. There is nothing like having flowers delivered to your front door. Especially knowing they're from someone you . . . care about." Maggie stumbled over the last bit.

"Or from someone you love," Jack said smoothly. "I would guess it's even nicer when the flowers come from someone who loves you. If that's the case, then this is your lucky birthday. I know for a fact that the man who sent you these flowers does love you." He pulled her closer. "I love you, Maggie."

This is just like the most romantic movie ever made in the history of eternity.

"I love you too, Jack. I really do."

They shared a lovely birthday kiss to prove the point.

He helped her into her coat, and they stepped out onto the porch. Maggie looked over at the church and could see a light shining from the back bathroom window.

"Oh, bother," she said.

Jack followed her gaze.

"Let's turn it out when we get back. Maybe it's Irena or Doris." Jack wanted to go.

"I better turn it out or I'll forget later," Maggie said.

She walked down the sidewalk and pulled her keys from her purse. Jack followed behind. She unlocked the doors, and they stepped into the dark sanctuary. Maggie remembered their private Christmas together under the tree. She reached around for the lights and flipped them on. The sanctuary still smelled of Murphy's Oil Soap. Maggie loved the smell of the sanctuary and the beauty of the wooden pews. She and Jack walked to the back of the church, and she turned out the bathroom light.

Then Maggie heard something. What was it? It sounded like the organ playing. It startled her until she recognized "Happy Birthday to You!" She and Jack walked into the gathering area and back into the sanctuary, and Maggie gasped as she took in the sight. The pews were filling up with her congregation, who were coming from the dining room in the basement where they had been hiding. Irena was at the organ wearing a pink party hat and a Lone Ranger mask. She was playing as if it were the last song she would ever play.

Jack took Maggie's hand and said, "Surprise, Pastor Maggie."

Maggie was surprised. She actually had never been so surprised in her twenty-seven years of life. She looked around, and her mouth kept dropping open. Everyone from the congregation—including the youth group, Cate, and the little children—all filed in. She saw Sylvia and Bill. Mrs. Abernathy, the Tuggles, the Wiggins, Hank, Doris and their spouses were there. But as Maggie watched the crowd enter, she was the most thrilled to see her mom and dad, Ed and Jo, and Nora and Dan.

Maggie was led to the front of the church, and her surprise birthday party began. Marla put a gold cardboard crown on Maggie's head, while Sylvia placed a sash around Maggie that said "It's my birthday. Let's eat cake!" Ellen stood up as the mistress of ceremonies. Several people got up and shared stories about Maggie. Some were funny, some were embarrassing, but when Ed got up, there was silence as he began to speak.

"I could tell you how proud I am of Pastor Maggie, but that's obvious. I have many stories of her in the classroom that would make you laugh. She is a goofball. But you already know that. Jo and I have watched her for years now, and we have enjoyed her intellect, her thoughtfulness, and her crazy sense of humor. We have questioned her fashion choices more than once. We have no idea how she can love cats so much. But the most remarkable thing we have seen is what has happened here in Cherish. It's a beautiful love story. It's a story about a church who needed a pastor and a pastor who needed a church. Rarely does a match occur like the one in this place. You are a remarkable congregation, a dream congregation. And Pastor Maggie is blessed to have you. You know for yourselves how blessed you are to have her. So, on this special night, we celebrate a birthday. We also celebrate a relationship between congregation and pastor. May this be a love story that continues for years to come. Jo and I will be watching. God bless you all."

Everyone applauded.

Maggie was overwhelmed by words she was certain she didn't deserve. She looked at Ed and saw him take a quick swipe at his eyes. Jo whispered something in his ear, and they both smiled.

Ellen returned to the microphone and cleared her throat. "Thank you, Dr. James. Your words are kind and true. Now, Mrs. Popkin has prepared sandwiches and a huge birthday cake for the celebration, if everyone would please make their way back to the dining room. It's time to feast!"

But before anyone could move, there was a crash as the sanctuary doors flew open and hit the wall. Redford Johnson stumbled into the sanctuary and grabbed the back of a pew to steady himself. The congregation stared in shocked silence.

"So! Itsh the little lady's birthday!" Redford yelled condescendingly. He let out a long belch and then laughed at himself. "Well, happy birthday to you, Madge!"

He grabbed the pew again as he began to tip. Those sitting in the back could smell the alcohol on his breath along with a wreath of cigarette smoke.

Redford continued, "I bet you think you're somethin', don'cha, Margaret Elzinga? You think you've got this whole town wrapped around your finger?" He flourished his arms and leaned into Jennifer Becker's shoulder. Jennifer tried to move away, but Redford had a tight grip on her. He leaned in close. "Where you goin'? I think I'll sit here with you and enjoy the party."

His breath made Jennifer want to vomit.

"I'm here to see the birthday girl! I might just be visiting her in the parsonage later and give her a real present! Ha!" Redford let out a disgusting laugh.

Jack got up from the front pew and stood in the center aisle, then he headed toward Redford. He wanted to protect Maggie from this cruelty. He was torn between staying near Maggie and wanting to drag Redford out into the street to shut his mouth with a fist. Then Jack saw Charlotte.

Charlotte Tuggle stood up and quickly walked to the back of the sanctuary. Bernie was right behind her. Jack stopped and watched with the rest of the congregation. Charlotte was a good six inches taller than Redford, and she made good use of her height. She grabbed his arms and twisted them both behind his back. Then she pushed him face first onto the floor.

"Redford Johnson, I'm arresting you for disturbing the peace, public drunkenness, and for attempted lewd conduct!" She knew that last one wasn't a real offense, but it sounded good.

Bernie helped Charlotte get Redford to his feet and march him out the doors. As they were leaving Redford yelled, "Happy birthday! You're the most useless person who ever came to this town!"

The words stung. The party atmosphere had completely dissipated. Maggie realized that the most humiliating part was that Ed had heard it all. She looked at her lap and bit her lip to fight the tears of anger and humiliation.

Ellen spoke, her voice was strong and steady. "That was terrible, truly terrible. We are all shocked by such disgusting behavior. Pastor Maggie, whatever you are feeling right now, please know this party was planned because we love you and we want to celebrate your birthday with you. One person does not get to ruin the fun of this special night." Ellen spoke with conviction, and people began nodding their heads. "I want to remind everyone of what Dr. James said because he's right. We were a church searching for a pastor, and God brought us you, Pastor Maggie." Ellen looked out at the rest of the congregation. "It's only been seven months since she arrived, but I know we all feel the same. What did we ever do without her?"

She turned toward Maggie. "Pastor Maggie, thank you for teaching us so much about how to care for each other. Thank you for opening your heart so completely. We have come to celebrate you tonight. We have planned this surprise for weeks, and we have a few more surprises for you."

Then, from out of nowhere, Carrie's small voice could be heard: "We should eat cake. Cake will make your tummy feel better, Pastor Maggie. That bad man will never have cake because he is mean. And he smells bad."

That did it. Ellen thought she should have had Carrie emcee the entire evening.

"Let's eat cake!" Ellen said.

Jack's fists had stopped shaking, and he took Maggie's hand and walked her to the dining room.

Everyone noticed. No one said anything, but everyone secretly stared.

After the party, it would be a completely different matter when the phones of Cherish would burn up the lines. People would be talking about Redford's drunken display and Dr. Elliot holding Pastor Maggie's hand.

But for the moment, the party continued with food and small presents and more funny stories about Maggie until little ones needed to get home to bed and the people from Zeeland and Holland had to make the long drive home. Maggie was able to spend time with Nora and Dan, who each told hilarious stories to her congregation of Maggie from seminary. Dan and Nora had driven over on their own, but her parents, and Ed and Jo, came in her father's car. She was glad Ed didn't have to drive back.

Maggie watched her parents throughout the night. They seemed to be fine as they chatted with the people of the church. But Maggie knew they were thinking of Bryan, just as she was, high up in the air, flying far away from them to his brand-new world.

As Maggie said goodbye to the Zeeland/Holland contingent, she felt her mother's hand on her shoulder.

"Tonight was lovely. You were celebrated well, as you deserved to be. Redford is a man with problems. You will see versions of him throughout your ministry, but remember all the other voices of those who appreciate you. Those are the voices that matter tonight."

She gave Maggie a hug, and Maggie wondered for the millionth time, *How does she do that? How does she always know what I'm feeling and how to make me feel better?*

Ed gave Maggie a hug and asked if he could speak to her for a moment.

In Maggie's office, Ed said gravely, "Redford is a sick man, Maggie. It's hard when we're in ministry, and we believe redemption for all is as easy as giving a hug. Some people don't want redemption. They enjoy hate and retribution. For one person to be forgiven by another, he or she must want it, must find a way to ask for it, at least hint at it. Redford wants to share his pain with everyone he meets. You don't have to accept it. It will fill you with doubt, anger, and pain. It is God's work to figure out the varied complications of redemption. You can't fix Redford. You must remember who you are, Pastor Maggie, and believe it. Continue to use your beautiful heart and your bright mind as a blessing to this church."

"That's probably the best mini-theology lesson I've ever had. And I needed it tonight." She smiled and threw her arms around his neck.

"I'll call you in a few days, Maggie," Ed said when she finally freed his neck. "We'll work through some of the ways to handle the 'Redfords' of the world, but especially this one."

Maggie walked Ed, Jo, and her parents to their car. With more "Happy Birthdays" in the air and hugs and kisses for all, Maggie felt the night was actually redeemed.

Jack walked Maggie back to the parsonage.

"Were you surprised?" he asked her.

"I was shocked. In more ways than one. It was a great night. My mom was right, there were many wonderful voices tonight. They drowned out the bad one. And Ed gave me the greatest gift. A practical gold nugget of wisdom. And you never gave anything away! You are a very good liar." Maggie smiled.

"Only when it's for a good cause, then, yes, I can lie with the best of them." He slipped his arms around her shoulders and said, "You were well birthday-ed tonight, and that makes me happy. I'm sorry for Redford's behavior. He's a fool. But enough of that, I have something I need to get out of my car. I'll meet you inside."

"Okay," Maggie said, thinking she couldn't handle anymore kindness.

Jack came in a few minutes later with a large, bulky package. They sat in the living room with two curious cats in attendance. Maggie tore the paper from the package and couldn't believe what she was looking at. It was a painting of Loving the Lord. It had the perspective from an angle down one block and across the street. There was the small sign that was on the west lawn of the church. It had Maggie's name as pastor and a sermon title underneath.

"Who . . . where . . . how did you get this?" Maggie stumbled. The emotion of the night decided to show up at that moment.

"There is an artist in town. Her name is Arly Spink. The week before Christmas, I asked her how fast she could paint our church. She had it finished this past Sunday, which is when I picked it up. Do you like it?"

It was an unintelligent question. Maggie's eyes and nose were running as she threw her arms around him.

"I love it. You have given me a picture of home."

"Happy birthday, Maggie. My Maggie."

The next morning, the Westminster chimes rang at the parsonage. When Maggie opened the door, she was surprised to see Redford standing on the porch. She had to remind herself it was daylight and she had nothing to fear, but she wished she wasn't so small at times like this. She was going to speak, but Redford began first.

"About last night," he blurted.

Maggie noticed there was no use of her name or title.

He continued, "I had a couple of drinks and . . ."

Or several, Maggie thought.

"And . . . I saw the lights on at church and stopped on by."

Stumbled on in, more like it.

"I just wanted you to know I didn't mean anything by it." He turned to leave.

"I accept your apology," Maggie said clearly.

"What?" He looked confused.

"It's a poor apology, but I accept it."

"I don't owe you an apology for anything." Redford's temper made an appearance. "You think you deserve an apology when I didn't do anything wrong?"

Maggie felt a warning flag go up. It might be daytime, but that didn't mean she was safe from someone like Redford. His threat from the night before flashed through her mind. She did her best to keep her voice calm and professional.

"Redford, I don't want to talk about this anymore. Please don't come back to the parsonage unless there is a council meeting. If you need to speak with me, make an appointment at the church office." Maggie took a breath. "But thank you for the affirmation."

"What are you talking about?" Redford sneered.

"You have made it clear you don't want forgiveness. It's good for me to know. Goodbye."

Maggie closed the parsonage door and locked the deadbolt. Her hands were shaking, and she felt a drip of sweat running down her back. She went to the back door and locked it as well. It was a silly thing to do. All the council members, including Redford, had keys to the parsonage.

When she went back to the front door, she looked out of the fisheye. Redford was standing and looking back at her. He was smiling and smoking a cigarette. Slowly he turned, dropped his cigarette on the porch, and walked down the steps.

23

On Friday the 13th, the day before Valentine's Day, Maggie couldn't sit still as she thought of the special date she and Jack would have the next night. She could hardly concentrate on her sermon memorization. The following Wednesday was Ash Wednesday, the beginning of the Lenten season. Her first Lent. She and Irena had made plans for the midweek services throughout the season. Maggie was mostly pleased with the services, but Irena had insisted on playing Barber's "Adagio for Strings" at each one. Maggie wanted it played only at the Good Friday service. It was over ten minutes long. But Irena won out. Maggie told her she could play it at the end of the service and that people would be invited to leave quietly.

She couldn't be bothered about Irena now. Jack had been very secretive about their Valentine's date, and she was aflutter. It really was too bad she hadn't dated more in college and grad school. She was going through all the first thrills of love and acting like she was sixteen. Her mother would just roll her eyes and say something practical like, "Maggie, act your age. You are too old to be this flaky and unfocused."

But Mimi wasn't there, and Maggie decided to let her romantic fantasies run wild. The past three months with Jack had been fresh, exciting, and insightful. Although she had watched Nora and Dan fall in love during seminary, she had always been on the outside. She was happy for her friends and celebrated each new step in their relationship.

But she was the audience. She received reports from those involved in the "real deal." Now she knew what the real deal was. She walked around in it all day long. She dreamt about it at night. She had more patience with parishioners. She was always smiling.

If she thought she was doing any kind of a decent job keeping it all under wraps, she would have been shocked to discover that everyone around her was as captive an audience of her love affair with Jack as she had been with Dan and Nora. The handholding incident at her birthday party had given it all away. Now she and Jack were being watched and reported on regularly among the congregation.

As she continued halfheartedly with her tasks of the day, such as cramming her sermon into her brain, she realized that the "in box" in her head was full. Her brain couldn't hold another word. She finally decided to choose what to wear on her first Valentine's Day with Jack. Her mother had bought her three new outfits for her birthday. Maggie chose a navy-blue dress with pink and cream stripes. The matching pink cardigan and small navy boots would finish the outfit perfectly. She had an appointment to get her hair done in the morning, a highlight and style. It was a first.

Gratefully, Maggie's bumbling day finally came to an end. Externally, it had been very quiet. Internally, it had been a riot of the soul. She crawled into bed after writing out the card she had purchased for Jack. It was romantic, and she thought he would like it.

She put her G. M. Malliet book down since it had hit her in the face twice already. She was readjusting the cats when her phone rang. She and the cats jumped. It was eleven p.m.

"Maggie," her mother said quickly.

"Mom?"

"Maggie, please listen. I think you need to get to Holland. I've had a phone call from the Care Committee chairwoman. Ed James is very ill. He's had a stroke. He's had a massive stroke. Jo is at the hospital. Maggie, I think you should hurry." Mimi's voice cracked.

Maggie stopped breathing. Then she could feel her head begin to spin. She wanted to hang up the phone and make her mother's cracking voice go away.

"Mom, I'll come right now. Should I go straight to the hospital?"

"Yes. We will meet you there. Be careful driving, Maggie. Pay attention."

Mimi hung up the phone.

Maggie's movements and thoughts were not in sync. She refused to process her mother's words. If she did, she would fall apart. She pulled out her duffel and threw in random clothes. Then she picked up her phone and dialed Ellen.

When Ellen answered groggily, Maggie said, "Ellen, it's Maggie. I'm sorry to call you so late. I have to drive to Holland tonight. I don't know how long I will be gone. Ed James has had a stroke." Maggie sounded like a news reporter, but her breathing was all wrong. She felt her lip tremble when she said Ed's name. "Can you check in on the cats for me?"

"Do you need someone to ride along with you," Ellen asked immediately.

"I think I will be okay. I just can't deal with the cats."

Maggie sounded like the cat issue was the most pressing issue of the night, but Ellen understood. Focusing on something completely inconsequential shifted the true crisis.

"Maggie, I will be right over. I will just stay at the parsonage until you come back. I'll bring Tabby, and we will handle everything here. Just get on the road."

"Thanks, Ellen." Maggie's throat tightened. She didn't think she would be able to breathe. She felt fear, like a tidal wave, growing stronger and stronger.

"Does Jack know?" Ellen asked.

That did it. "No . . . he . . ." Maggie let out a sob. "I . . . uh . . . have a hair . . . appointment . . . in the morning." The sobs made her gasp.

"Maggie, it's okay. I will call Jack and the hair salon. Hold yourself together and get on the road. You can do this."

They hung up. Maggie grabbed her duffel and her coat and was out the door.

She never was able to clearly remember that drive from Cherish to Holland on Friday, February 13th. She saw nothing as she drove. Her mother had to be wrong.

Maybe Ed had a stroke, but people heal from strokes so quickly these days. There are special drugs. At the most, he might need some rehabilitation. Ed will heal. He will be a great patient and do whatever his physical therapist tells him to do. And Ed would not want to miss being at the seminary. No one will be able to fill in for his classes. If anyone has reasons to live, Ed does. Too many people depend on him. Jo will see him through. *Ed will not dare . . . he will not . . .*

Maggie drove over the speed limit, not that she noticed. Her thoughts whirled from her birthday party, the last time she saw Ed and Jo, to this terrible night. Her mother's words on the phone echoed in her brain: ". . . you should hurry."

Will Ellen know where to find the cat food? What if she forgets to call the hair salon? No, Ellen will remember. Ellen is going to handle things.

Then Maggie thought of Jack. She wanted Jack to be with her. The tears began to flow. Jack would know exactly what was wrong. He would walk into Ed's room and see things and know things that others wouldn't know. He would talk to Ed's doctors and understand what they were saying. He would tell Maggie that it would all be okay. Jack would make it okay. Jack would hold her and make Ed better. Maggie reached for her Kleenex box (something her mother taught her to always have in the car), grabbed a handful, and blew her nose. She pulled into the hospital parking lot at one thirty a.m.

Maggie rushed into the main entrance of the Holland hospital and went straight to the information desk. There was no need. Her parents were sitting in the visitor section, watching for her arrival. They surrounded her immediately.

"Tell me," Maggie whispered.

Mimi's voice was soft. "He had the stroke around nine thirty p.m. tonight. Jo called the ambulance right away. The damage is great. Maggie, the damage is too great. We'll take you to Jo and Ed now."

Maggie's dad kissed her and kept his arm around her shaking shoulders. Mimi led the way to the Critical Care Unit like a gentle general.

When they reached the CCU, Jo came out to the nurses' station. Her eyes were swollen and blotchy. When she saw Maggie, fresh tears overflowed. Maggie threw her arms around her, and the two women shook with grief. Dirk and Mimi kept up their guard and moved in closely.

When Jo finally led Maggie into Ed's room, Maggie saw he was on a ventilator to keep him breathing. He was wired up to machines, which surrounded him on both sides of the bed. His eyes were closed, and his skin looked grayish. She realized that he would never open his eyes again. She would never see Ed's kind, blue eyes again.

"I'm waiting for John and Elizabeth to get here," Jo said resignedly.

John and Elizabeth were Ed and Jo's children. Each was married with children of their own. John and his family lived in Chicago. Elizabeth and her family were coming from Kansas City.

"The doctor has said we can keep his heart pumping until they get here."

Maggie thought about how she would never hear Ed's voice again.

"Jo," Maggie said, "what are you thinking right now? What do you need?"

"I think I want my children here. I think I want this night to disappear so Ed and I can wake up and step into tomorrow the way we always do. I think I want to hear him tell me he loves me before I fall asleep tonight." She paused and tried to control a sob. "I think there won't be a day worth living without him at the breakfast table, in the garden pulling weeds, or on our evening walks. That's what I think."

Jo's raw pain scraped up and down Maggie's soul like sandpaper. In that moment, she had no idea how Jo would go on without Ed. *How do you live with half a heart and not bleed out?*

Maggie sat with Jo in silence for the next hour and a half. The beeping of the machines marked time as Ed was forced to breathe so his heart could keep beating. Both Maggie and Jo knew this was not living. Maggie thought to herself, *This is how death will sneak in. Machines create false life. Death is waiting for the machines to be unplugged and then will take the one we love, the one who should have so much more life.*

Jo got up every once in a while to wipe Ed's brow or whisper loving words into his ear. She held his hand. She rubbed his feet. Maggie watched helplessly.

She watched Jo's heart break, piece by piece.

Maggie suddenly felt intrusive. She looked around at the room and felt more strongly than ever that she didn't have a legitimate place by this hospital bed. This was for Jo and her family.

This is a sacred place. Jo is his wife. He has children and grandchildren. Who am I? Just one of hundreds of students who have learned at his feet, who have valued his wisdom, and who learned how to pastor by his presence in our lives. Maggie had never felt so out of place yet so desperate to stay right where she was.

Shortly after three a.m., John and his family arrived. They had driven straight from Chicago and looked more frightened than tired. Maggie stood quickly, shook John's hand, and gave Jo a hug.

"I'm so sorry, John. I'll let you be together now."

Maggie was heading to the door when Jo spoke.

"Maggie, stay here. I'd like to talk to John in the hallway first."

Jo followed John and his wife out of the room.

Maggie knew Jo was giving her the chance to say goodbye.

Maggie went to the side of Ed's bed and got down on her knees. She carefully held his hand with the IV needle in it. Her eyes quickly filled with tears, her throat clenched, and her head throbbed. She had one chance to tell Ed what he had meant to her. Past tense. She took a deep breath and tried to pull her thoughts together.

"Ed, I have to tell you goodbye. Not . . . um . . . goodbye until we meet for lunch again. Not goodbye until you and Jo come back to church in Cherish." *Oh, Ed, you will never be in Cherish again.* "I have to tell you the last goodbye. But please let me begin my goodbye with a thank you." *There aren't enough words to thank you.* "Thank you for listening to my . . . my . . . ramblings over the past four and a half years. Thank you for taking me seriously . . ." *You are the only one who ever took me seriously.* ". . . when I was acting immature, over-confident, childish, and emotional." *I can't tell you goodbye.* "Thank you for your wisdom and patience. Thank you for calling me 'Pastor' for the first time." *You gave me my identity.* "Thank you for your unconditional love." She took a deep breath and closed her eyes as she placed her head on the side of the bed.

"Now, for the hard part. I don't know what to do now." Maggie's voice became a high whisper as she wiped her eyes on his blanket. "I'm not prepared for this . . . I just can't . . . I . . ."

Maggie tried to stifle her sobs with the blanket. She felt the emotion of the night take control, and she knew she had to pull herself together before Jo came back in. She took several deep breaths, and she used a wad of tissues to wipe her eyes and nose. Then she rose from her knees. Maggie leaned forward and put her young cheek on Ed's old one.

"We will all take care of Jo. Don't worry. I love you. Goodbye, Ed."

When Jo and John came back in the room, Maggie tried hard to smile. She gave Jo a hug that was almost impossible to release. Finally, Maggie left Ed's room and let her parents take her home. They said they would get her car in the morning.

At seven thirty a.m., Ed was taken off life support. His son and daughter had both had a chance to see him first. Jo sent them away to care for their children and get some sleep at her house. She wanted to be alone with Ed at the end. Ed kept breathing. For a while. When the nurses came in an hour later, they had to gently unclasp Jo's hand from Ed's dead one. They called John, who came to take his mother home.

Maggie woke at noon on Valentine's Day. She was disoriented, and it took her a few minutes to recognize her old bedroom. Once she did, the memory of the hospital hit her like a train. Ed was gone. She knew he must be. Silently, tears flowed onto her pillow. How many mornings would be like this? How many mornings would arrive with the deep sadness and loss of last night to shock her senses? Would she ever wake up happy again?

She went into the kitchen and found her parents at the table, drinking coffee.

"Is Ed gone?" she asked, hoping for a miracle.

"Yes," Mimi said. "He died around eight thirty a.m. John called to let us know. Jo is home with her children and grandchildren now. You also had a call from Ellen in Cherish. I told her about Ed."

She made Maggie a cup of coffee as Maggie sat at the computer on Mimi's kitchen desk. She had two emails from Cherish. The first one said:

Pastor Maggie,

We are so sorry to hear about Dr. James. Do not worry about church on Sunday. We will take care of it. God bless you.

Ellen

P.S. The cats are fine.

She opened the second message:

Maggie,

I know you're hurting, and I am so sorry. I am also sorry that you have lost such an important person in your life. I am here for you.

You know I love you,
Jack

That made Maggie cry. She grabbed some Kleenex and slurped her coffee, spilling it down her robe. Her dad came up behind her and put his hands on her shoulders. That just caused more tears. *Why is it, when a tragedy occurs, the kindness of others can be so painful?*

Maggie looked up at her dad and asked, "Do you think I can call Jo? What is the right thing to do? Ed was my friend, but he was her husband and John and Elizabeth's father. I don't know where my grief belongs."

Just then, the phone rang. Mimi reached to answer it.

"Hello? Yes, hello, Nora. Maggie is right here." Mimi handed the phone to Maggie.

"Maggie?" Nora's voice was choked with emotion.

"Hi, Nora."

"May I come over?"

"Please."

They hung up, and Maggie got up to get dressed.

"Maggie," her dad said. "You're grief matters. Your sensitivity to Jo and her children is appropriate. But your grief is appropriate too."

Maggie nodded and walked out of the room.

When Nora arrived, the two young pastors sat in Maggie's room together and cried. Maggie cried for herself, and Nora cried for her best friend. Nora had not had the same kind of relationship with Ed that Maggie had, but she had taken every class he taught at the seminary and counted him as one of her favorite professors. She understood immediately Maggie's conflicted feelings about the loss she was feeling over Ed's death. Even though Maggie felt almost like another daughter to Ed, she wasn't. She was on the outside. The two girls talked and grieved into the early evening until Mimi knocked on the door.

"Come in," Maggie said.

"I don't know if this will be helpful or not," Mimi began, "but I think there is something very practical you can do for Jo and her family."

Maggie and Nora both perked up. "Doing" something was exactly what they needed, but they had no idea what.

Mimi continued, "Food. Not casseroles. I've never understood why people bring casseroles to grieving people. But after a death, family members are up at all hours of the night and day. They need easy-to-prepare food. You can buy things from the deli, like meats, cheeses, breads, salads, cookies, potato chips, and the like. Then they will be able to make a meal or a snack quickly. It will be easy to feed the grandchildren as well. It's just a thought."

Mimi closed the door. The girls both felt the same relief to have a plan. They bundled themselves into their coats and headed to the grocery store.

Forty-five minutes later, they were on Jo's doorstep. Both Maggie and Nora each held two stuffed bags of deli foods. Maggie rang the doorbell with her little finger. Elizabeth opened the door, looking exhausted and worn.

Maggie said, "Hi, Elizabeth. I don't know if you remember me, but I'm Maggie Elzinga, and this is Nora Drew. We were students of your dad's." Maggie spoke slowly and carefully, holding in her emotion the way an actress releases hers. "We just wanted to drop off some food for you and your family. We hope it makes these days a little easier."

Maggie stopped then as she saw Jo come up behind Elizabeth. Maggie hardly recognized her. Jo looked as gray as Ed had looked when Maggie saw him the night before.

Elizabeth said, "I do remember you, Maggie, and I have heard so many stories about you too. You meant a great deal to my dad."

Jo came to the door as Elizabeth spoke.

"Hello, Maggie and Nora," Jo said with the politeness she used when greeting guests for a fundraiser at the seminary.

Maggie could tell she was on autopilot. Maggie couldn't take any more.

"Jo, we just wanted to quickly drop these things off for you and your family. We won't stay. We're just . . . so . . . sorry."

Jo took the bags from Maggie but didn't seem to know what to do once her hands were full. She reached for Nora's bags, but Elizabeth intervened.

"I'll get these, Mom," she said. "Would you like to come in?"

"No, but thank you," Nora said, sensing Maggie was about to fall apart again. "We hope this helps in some small way."

Jo set down her bags and stepped through the door. She took Maggie's hands and said, "Maggie, you know he loved you so much. He was so proud of you. Don't forget that."

Maggie nodded mutely.

"The funeral is Tuesday morning at eleven a.m."

Nora slipped her arm through Maggie's as Jo released her hands.

"We'll be there, Mrs. James. We'll go now."

The four women stared at each other until Elizabeth helped her mother into the house and retrieved the grocery bags. Nora led Maggie to the car and drove her home.

On Sunday morning, most of the congregation at Loving the Lord had already heard about Dr. James's sudden death over the weekend. The church was full, with everyone waiting to see what would happen. It was the first Sunday in the history of the church that a pastor wasn't in the pulpit. It was the first Sunday since last June that pastor Maggie wasn't there.

Ellen had gone through Maggie's parsonage office and found a book by Frederick Buechner with short devotional writings. She called Harold, who met her at church on Saturday, and they chose three passages for Harold to read the next morning. As the chairperson of the council, he would lead the service. They would use the bulletin as printed but would insert the readings in place of the sermon.

Irena—dressed in a low-cut black blouse, tight black skirt, black fishnet stockings, and black high heels—began playing "Just a Closer Walk with Thee," which didn't help alleviate the tension everyone felt. When she finally finished, Harold quickly stood up before Irena could have another go at the organ.

"Welcome, everyone," Harold said. "Our service this morning will be a little different. As most of you know, Pastor Maggie is in Zeeland after the sudden death of her dear friend, Ed James. We have all had the opportunity to meet Dr. James and his wife during their several visits to Cherish. I know we all grieve with Pastor Maggie and Dr. James's family at this time of loss and sadness. As of now, we believe the Ash Wednesday service will still be held this Wednesday, with Pastor Maggie leading us in that service. If there is a change, we will let you know by email. Now, let us stand and sing our first hymn."

Harold had a confidence and a strength of presence that gave comfort to the congregation. The service proceeded with Irena's dirges and Harold's spoken word. Coffee time was subdued as the parishioners talked over the sad happenings of the weekend ad nauseam, rehashing it and examining every angle. The problem was, they needed their pastor to help them work through the grief. But it was their pastor's grief. Everyone felt Maggie's absence that morning.

Maggie's Sunday morning was spent in dreamless sleep. When she awoke, the memories of the last two days hit her again. It made her not want to go to sleep because waking up was so horrendous. She groggily made her way to the kitchen, where Dirk and Mimi sat in quiet conversation. They ceased talking when Maggie came in. It began to dawn on Maggie that they were treating her in a way she had never experienced before. They watched her carefully, as if she might disintegrate in front of their eyes. She had no idea of the depth of their worry for her. They knew their daughter had never experienced a grief like this before, and they ached for her.

"Morning," Maggie said.

"Good morning, Maggie," Mimi said. "Coffee?"

"Thanks. I'll get it," Maggie said, going through the motions of operating the Keurig machine.

"What do you need for today?" her mom asked.

"I'm going to see Nora and Dan this afternoon. We decided to make some more wedding plans. I need to send a couple of emails this morning. I'll let the church know I will be back after the funeral on Tuesday. I can't stay home forever." Maggie sounded cavalier.

"I'm sure the church would understand if you needed more time," Dirk said quietly.

"I need to get back. I think that's exactly what Ed would tell me to do."

Maggie sat at the computer and felt the sharp pain in saying Ed's name out loud.

She sent a generic email to all the members of the council, letting them know she would be back on Tuesday night. Then she wrote briefly to Jack, thanking him for his email of yesterday. It was time to soldier on.

On Tuesday morning, Maggie put on one of her mother's black suits. She had not packed her black lace funeral dress because she had no intention of attending Ed's funeral when she'd received her mother's call Friday night.

Maggie, Dirk, and Mimi entered the church where Nora and Dan waited in the narthex. The five of them went silently into the sanctuary. Maggie wished she was anywhere but in a church. Slowly, the entire sanctuary filled. The seminary had cancelled all classes for the day. Students and professors filed in to fill rows of pews. After the prelude, Ed's coffin was wheeled down the center aisle. Jo, her children, and grandchildren followed behind. Maggie felt like the entire congregation inhaled the depth of their grief as one.

The service perfectly honored Ed. The entire choir had prepared two anthems and sang through their tears. The pastor remembered Ed with poignant, funny, and vivid stories of his work at the seminary, his love of his students, and especially his love of his family. The congregation sang several of Ed's favorite hymns. As his coffin was wheeled out at the end of the service, everyone watched Jo walk beside it with her hand resting on top. She walked him all the way to the hearse. Only the family went to the graveside. Maggie and the rest of the congregation waited for them at church for the typical luncheon.

Maggie felt as if she were in and out of consciousness as the morning progressed. She spoke with many of her other professors and students she had known before graduation. She was polite and acted interested but didn't hear one word that anybody said. People talked, reminisced, cried, and laughed. Maggie felt as if she were watching a movie. She saw all the characters, but she was not one of them. She waited in line to talk to Jo and finally had the chance to speak, but Jo beat her to it.

"Maggie, this isn't the day for us to talk, but I want to see you when this is all through. Do you understand? I need to see you."

"Yes, Jo, I understand. I'll be back. I promise."

24

Maggie pulled into the driveway of the parsonage the evening of Ed's funeral. The long drive from Zeeland gave her time to decompress. The emotion she had expended during the past four days had left her depleted and wound up at the same time. She was now on brain auto-pilot. She hoped no one would be at the parsonage when she returned, and it appeared no one was. She carried her duffel into the house and was greeted by two little beasts who had no knowledge of death or loss. They just wanted their treats and some affection.

Maggie looked around and noticed the parsonage was immaculate. Ellen must have cleaned it from top to bottom. That thoughtfulness was the kind of thing Maggie was trying to avoid. The pain of being cared for overwhelmed her. She was better at caring for others than being cared for.

When she entered the kitchen she saw a note on the table.

Dear Pastor Maggie,

I hope you are doing okay. Everything went fine with the cats and church, but we have missed you. Please find some food in the fridge and Mrs. Popkin's cup-cakes in the pantry. Marla, Sylvia, and Bill came over, and we gave the parsonage a good scrubbing. We just needed to do something for you. Marmalade and Cheerio oversaw the entire procedure. They weren't too sure about Tabby at first but then settled down. If you need anything, please call. We are all supporting you through this terribly sad time.

Love,
Ellen

Maggie set the note down. She didn't know what to do next. She brought her duffel upstairs and unpacked her clothes. She took her laundry basket to the washing machine and began a load. She went downstairs and looked through her mail, which Ellen had neatly placed on her desk. On top of the pile was a handwritten envelope. She recognized the writing immediately. *Jo.*

Maggie carefully opened the envelope. It was a Valentine card from Ed and Jo. It said simply, "We are wishing you a 'true love' day this Valentine's Day." They had each signed it. Maggie set it upright on the corner of her desk.

She opened the rest of her mail completely free of emotion. Thank God for phone bills and dentist appointment reminder cards. She finally picked up the phone and called Jack. He answered immediately.

"Maggie?" His voice was tense. Maggie had never heard him sound like that before.

"Yes, Jack. I'm back in Cherish, and I wanted you to know." She sounded absolutely calm.

"I'm glad you're back. What do you need?"

Now his voice was tense *and* concerned. Any second he would say something kind and she would have to hang up on him.

"I think I need to go to sleep. I'm tired." Just saying it made her yawn.

"I'm sure you're exhausted. Maggie, I'm so sorry about Ed's death. We all are."

That did it. She couldn't go that direction right now.

"Are you coming to the Ash Wednesday service tomorrow night?" Maggie asked matter-of-factly.

Taken aback, Jack replied, "Of course. But are you up for it? You don't have to do the service. Everyone understands."

"I think the sooner I get back to church life, the better. It is unfortunate Lent begins tomorrow, such a depressing time of the church year. But it is what it is." Maggie sounded offhanded.

"I'll be there tomorrow night. If you want, maybe we could spend a little time together after the service. I want to see you." Jack treaded carefully. He couldn't read Maggie's mood. Was she working very hard to disguise her grief?

"Yes, that sounds fine. Good night, Jack."

Maggie hung up the phone. She went into the kitchen and opened the refrigerator. A casserole. *Yuck.* She would have to teach the people of Cherish the value of a bag of deli food. She took one of the cupcakes out of the pantry and made a cup of Lady Grey tea. Then she brought them both upstairs, followed by Marmalade and Cheerio, who were a little concerned as to why they hadn't received their treats.

Maggie sipped her tea. She tried to read a little G. M. Malliet but kept reading the same page over and over again. She finally turned out the light, but sleep did not join her that night. She watched her bedside clock tick away the hours. She had never been afraid of the dark, even as a child. She and Bryan would set up tents in the backyard on warm summer nights and listen to the sounds of the night. They were always more curious than fearful. That night, she felt afraid. The darkness closed in tightly around her. Is this how Ed felt after his stroke? Was he aware that his body was slowly shutting down? Was he afraid? Did he know she had been there?

Maggie turned on her light. It was three thirty. Her pink cupcake was sitting untouched on the small, white plate. The kitties woke and stretched then fell back into their nightly naps. Maggie pulled on her robe. She went downstairs, turning lights on in every room.

At four a.m., when Mrs. Popkin arrived at The Sugarplum to begin her morning baking, she saw the parsonage ablaze with lights. As she opened the shop and fired up the ovens, she kept glancing out the window. *Poor Pastor Maggie. She's back from the funeral and doesn't know what to do with herself. Hokey tooters! Grief is a nasty thing.* Mrs. Popkin mixed up batters and doughs. All the while, she kept one eye on the parsonage.

Mrs. Popkin remembered when her own husband had died twenty years earlier. Having to deal with other people's grief, which supposedly meant they were caring for her, only made her feel as if she had to take care of them. At the time, the only person she wanted to talk to was her mother. Other people were a burden. They made too much emotional work. She knew better than to walk across the street. The work of having a conversation would be too much for Pastor Maggie. It was too much for anyone in grief.

At five a.m., Mrs. Popkin saw Maggie leave the parsonage in her running clothes. Mrs. Popkin shook her head. *She will try to run from the grief. She'll do anything to escape it, but it's so damn persistent. It will remain her unwelcomed guest until it decides to leave. She won't be able to shift it by sheer will. God bless Pastor Maggie.*

Maggie ran down Middle Street as if she were in a race. The cold air burned her lungs, but she didn't feel the pain. She just needed to run. She would go for her run, clean up, eat her oatmeal, and head to the church. She had to get ready for tonight's service and work on her sermon for the first Sunday of Lent. There would be plenty to do. Where were the ashes for the service tonight? She had to put an ash cross on each parishioner's forehead. What was the phrase she was supposed to say when she did that? She must check in with Irena about the music.

She would look over both bulletins with Hank. She would make sure no one was ill or needed a visit. Maggie's mind continued in this rapid-fire way. Her thoughts hurled themselves at her psyche like hailstones.

When she returned to the parsonage, she showered, dressed, and made her oatmeal. It looked disgusting, but she ate a bite or two anyway. Then she walked over to church and forced herself to plow through the morning.

"Good morning, Hank," Maggie said with a fake smile as she entered the office. "I guess I need to be brought up to speed for the service tonight. Is there a bulletin?"

Hank took his cue from her. He would be cheerful and pretend nothing had happened.

"Yessireebob, Pastor Maggie. I have tonight's bulletin here and also this coming Sunday's. The urn of ashes for tonight is on your desk. Marla took care of that little chore. She burned the palms from last year's Palm Sunday service. That is the tradition, yessireebob, it is."

Hank could have kept on talking, but Maggie took the bulletins from his hand, went into her office, and shut the door. Hank took a deep breath and then broke out in a sweat.

When Irena arrived at the office an hour later, Hank tried to warn her to be careful when she spoke with Pastor Maggie, but Irena barged into Maggie's office, as usual.

"Pastoor Maggie, dis serrrvice tonight, ees rready?" Irena said from behind her music. Her beet-colored hair was pulled back into a severe bun on the top of her head, pulled so tightly her eyes looked almond shaped.

"Irena, the service is ready. Hank has the bulletins in his office," Maggie said. "It is as we planned. There will be music and Bible passages interspersed. At the end, there will be the imposition of the ashes. You will end the service with Barber's 'Adagio.' If you'll excuse me, I have to work on Sunday's sermon."

Irena stared and was, for once, wordless. *Vat is wrong vit Pastoor Maggie? She sounds like one ov dose mechanical thingys from de moovies. A rrobot.*

Maggie walked out to Hank's office briskly.

"I'll be working on Sunday's sermon at home for the rest of the day. I would rather not be disturbed. Thank you, Hank."

She wanted to run. She wanted to run to the parsonage before she saw any more people. As soon as she got through her front door, she locked it. She did absolutely nothing for the rest of the morning.

Just after noon, her phone rang. She saw it was her mother.

"Mom?" Maggie's voice sounded high-pitched and raw.

"Maggie, how are you doing today?" Mimi listened carefully to the silence on the other end of the phone.

"Mom . . . I can't figure this out," Maggie said, not making sense.

"What can't you figure out, Maggie?" Mimi asked quietly.

"What to do next. I can't figure out what to do next. I can't go to church," Maggie rambled.

"Why can't you go to church?" Mimi kept her voice soft.

"It's not a good place. It's a bad place. These people are so needy and annoying. I never should have come here." Maggie sounded petulant.

Mimi quickly decided how best to respond. It was obvious Maggie was in some state of shock.

"Maggie, should you take some time off?"

"I have the Ash Wednesday service tonight. Lent begins now. Who would do the services? I'm stuck here." Now Maggie sounded mechanical.

Mimi couldn't tell if Maggie wanted to stay in Cherish or not, but she became more worried by the minute.

"Yes, Maggie, those are important services, and you are the pastor. I wonder if the council would be willing to give you just a little time to rest after the trauma of Ed's death. What do you think?" Mimi wanted to drive over to Cherish and pack Maggie into the car and bring her home.

"Maybe. I'll ask. I don't know."

Mimi could hear the weariness in Maggie's voice.

"Have you seen Jack?" Mimi knew, if Jack could hear Maggie talking like this, he might be able to do something for her.

"I will see him tonight. I should probably go now. I'll call you later." Maggie sighed.

"Maggie, you need some rest. Please consider asking for a few days off. The church will be fine." Mimi hated feeling so helpless.

"Okay. Bye, Mom."

Maggie switched off her phone. She should work on her sermon for Sunday.

Maggie sat on her bed with Marmalade and Cheerio on her lap until six forty-five p.m. The Ash Wednesday service was set to start at seven. She slowly put on her black lace dress and black pumps. She put on her coat and walked over to church. She had her readings for the night printed out and placed in her bulletin. Then she remembered she had never looked at the specific words she was supposed to say when she imposed the ash crosses. She grabbed her worship book and flipped to the section titled "Ash Wednesday." Then she made her way through the secret door, successfully avoiding all human contact.

The service began with Irena playing music even more depressing than that for a funeral. *This must be what hell sounds like*, Maggie thought. She felt her emotions switch off. She read her passages like a paid actress. Irena played depressingly on. By the time parishioners began to line up at the front of the church for their ash cross, Maggie had completely disconnected. Unable to look her beloved people in their eyes, she focused on their foreheads and made the crosses, one by one.

"From ashes to ashes and dust to dust; remember you are dust, and to dust you shall return."

She repeated the words over and over again. She saw no one, just black ash crosses as she repeated those horrible words.

When Irena finally dove into Barber's "Adagio," people began to silently file out of the sanctuary. Maggie stayed in her pulpit chair on purpose to make sure everyone had left, but Jack was waiting in the back of the sanctuary. Irena played on. Finally, Jack made his way to Maggie. She stood up and stiffened as he hugged her close.

"I don't know how you did that," he whispered in her ear. "Please, let me take you home."

He walked her out of the sanctuary and called to Irena, "Irena, will you please lock up the church?"

She nodded while staring at Maggie.

Maggie hadn't retrieved her coat from her office, but Jack had his arm around her for the short walk to the parsonage. They were quickly inside, and he switched on the Keurig.

"What have you eaten today?" Jack asked.

"I had some oatmeal for breakfast," she replied.

Jack looked in the sink and saw the uneaten oatmeal congealed in the bowl.

"Anything else?" he asked.

"No, I don't think so, not really." Maggie suddenly felt exhausted. She laid her head down on the kitchen table. "I think I'm tired, Jack. I want to sleep."

Jack switched off the Keurig. He helped her upstairs and waited for her to change into her pajamas in the bathroom. Then he tucked her into bed and pulled the covers up under her chin.

"My dad used to tuck me in like that," Maggie said quietly.

Jack kissed her on the forehead, and it struck him that Maggie was the only one tonight who hadn't received a cross. No one had thought to place a black ash cross on her forehead. He kissed her again and then left with hope she would sleep.

But Maggie didn't sleep. She didn't sleep well for the next four nights. She would begin to doze and then be jarred awake by dreams of Ed laughing and shaking his head at her. She had dreams of Jo carrying caskets, one by one, out of the church doors. One recurring dream was of black ashes raining down on her. She couldn't breathe or see because the ashes were so thick. The ashes filled her house, and when she ran outside, they covered the church, the street, and the parsonage. Everywhere she went, the ashes fell harder and harder. When she awoke, she was covered in sweat and gasping for air.

Each morning for the rest of that dreadful week, Maggie walked over to the church office. She dreaded hearing eager and sympathetic parishioners, but it seemed they were avoiding her. Hank worked quietly at his desk, and Doris must have cleaned her office when Maggie wasn't around because she was nowhere to be found. Irena came in and practiced her Lenten dirges then left without entering the office. Marla didn't come in at all. By the time Saturday night came around, Maggie had no sermon prepared for the following morning and was living under a cloud of dread for her first Sunday in Lent.

Jack had called each day, but Maggie made excuses as to why she couldn't see him just yet. He didn't believe her but gave her the space she claimed to need.

On Sunday morning, Maggie made her way to church. She'd had Hank send out an email on Thursday cancelling her Sunday school class. People milled about, as they usually did on Sunday mornings. Maggie smiled politely and shook hands while moving toward her office as quickly as possible. She gathered her bulletin and Bible and went through the secret door into the sanctuary. She put her Bible on the pulpit.

Irena began her dreadfully depressing music while the congregation entered the sanctuary and took their seats. They stared at Maggie expectantly. She stood behind the pulpit and began the morning liturgy. If the parishioners had expected a personal word from Pastor Maggie or acknowledgment of Dr. James's death, they were disappointed. Maggie soldiered on through the service.

Until it was time for the sermon.

Maggie looked out at the many people who had filled her with so much joy and inspiration. She had called them "family," and she called Cherish "home." She didn't believe that anymore.

Maggie took a deep breath and said, "On this first Sunday of Lent, we read the story of Jesus being sent into the wilderness for forty days and forty nights. This occurred immediately after his extraordinary baptism by his cousin, John the Baptist. The public ministry of Jesus had begun. The gathered crowd had heard God's own voice at the baptism, but then Jesus was sent into the desert with no voice but that of the devil. Cruel taunts. Jesus . . . Jesus . . . was in the wilderness . . . and God . . . was . . . God was absent."

Maggie looked around her and panicked.

Jack watched her and was ready to get up when he saw the delirium in her eyes. But she opened her mouth again.

"I'm sorry. I can't do this. I can't stay here anymore. I . . . I'm . . . so sorry."

She couldn't see her way to the secret door through her tears. She took a few steps, then tripped over the flower stand and sent the flowers and water cascading down the altar steps. Maggie's stumble caused her to fall. She didn't move for a moment, then she scrambled, got up quickly, and kept going, trying to find her equilibrium. As she walked down the center aisle of the sanctuary, she leaned on the pews. Then she was out the door and staggered across the snowy lawn. The congregation didn't move. Everyone seemed frozen in their pews. Irena sat stock-still on her organ bench.

Maggie burst into the parsonage and went up the stairs. She pulled her duffel from the closet and haphazardly added clothes. Then she heard someone coming up the stairs two at a time.

It was Jack. He had been on his feet the minute she fell on the altar, but he couldn't get to her quickly enough through the other stunned members in the pew.

"Maggie, what are you doing? You can't go anywhere right now. You have got to lie down." Jack sounded like a doctor, not like a boyfriend.

Maggie spoke rapidly. "Jack, I can't stay here. I can't take care of any more people. I want to go home. This place is choking me to death. How can I stay in a church and take care of people without Ed to rely on? How am I supposed to do anything related to God or God's work without Ed? God doesn't care. God isn't here. God is busy randomly sucking the life out of people. He doesn't have time to care about the living!"

Maggie screamed and slammed her fists against the closet doors. Jack could see the grief, confusion, anger, and exhaustion on her face, and he couldn't stand it. He walked over to her and put his arms around her to keep her from packing anything else. She made a halfhearted attempt to push away but was too weary after her burst of anger. Jack sat them both down on the bed and kept his arms around her. He held her as she sobbed out one more layer of grief.

When her crying subsided, he took off her shoes and tucked her under the covers once more. This time, she fell asleep almost immediately. Jack sat in the chair in the corner of her room to keep watch.

He didn't move for four hours.

25

Across the snowy lawn, the congregation of Loving the Lord sat in stunned silence. Finally, Carrie Moffet said loudly, "Why is Pastor Maggie crying? Is it because she fell down?"

Her simple question seemed to give the congregation an invitation to breathe. They had seen Jack follow Pastor Maggie out of the church, but no one else seemed to be ambulatory. Harold finally got ahold of his senses and strode up to the pulpit.

"It appears Pastor Maggie is struggling following the death of Dr. James. I would like to ask the council to remain after church this morning for a special meeting. For everyone else, please be patient as we make decisions regarding the future." Harold didn't know what else to say.

Mrs. Popkin stood up in the back and cleared her throat.

"Pastor Maggie is more than struggling. I have watched her every day this week, and I say she is in crisis. Everyone who has ever lost a loved one knows a version of what she is feeling. Hokey tooters, folks, I'll say this too. Pastor Maggie has been the best thing that ever happened to this church. She has given her heart and soul to care for each and every one of us. And I would guess we aren't always the easiest bunch of sinners and saints to care for. I don't know what you're going to yap about in your council meeting, but I think it's time to show Pastor Maggie that we have learned a thing or two from her about loving and caring. It's time to love her up!" Mrs. Popkin plunked herself back down in the pew.

Cole Porter stood next. "Thank you, Mrs. Popkin. I agree wholeheartedly. Pastor Maggie has gone through a great loss and a shock. There is no way she can carry on with the day-to-day work here at church for the near future. We wouldn't expect that of anyone else. I would like to go on record saying Pastor Maggie needs to be given bereavement time. However much time she needs."

"Amen!" Max Solomon said loudly.

Both Marla and Sylvia vigorously wiped tears from their eyes. Several others sniffed loudly.

Everyone was surprised when Redford Johnson stood up and moved into the center aisle. Redford had kept a low profile since his disruptive behavior at Maggie's birthday party and his rudeness to her the following day on the parsonage porch (Maggie had told Jack, Ellen, Harold, Charlotte, and Hank about the incident on the porch—the more eyes watching Redford the better). There was talk of changing the locks on the parsonage doors, but it hadn't happened yet. Redford was seen daily at O'Leary's, drinking his lunch. He appeared to be biding his time.

"I don't want to sound like an idiot or anything, but we aren't going to pay her salary, right? I mean, if she's not working, right? As the head of the finance committee, I just want to make sure we aren't throwing our money away. If I don't go to work, I don't get paid. Once she's back—if she actually comes back—we can reinstate her pay." With a toss of his arrogant head, he sat down.

The parishioners, who had been wiping away tears after Mrs. Popkin and Cole spoke so kindly, felt their sadness quickly turn to anger. The general consensus was that Redford was an ass.

Irena bolted off the organ bench and marched to the front of the church. Her face was as red as her hair. She bumped Harold out of the way and pulled the microphone down to reach her mouth. Not that she needed a microphone.

"Meesterr Rredforrd Johnson, you arre an eediot," Irena growled. "But vat do vee expect frrom a barr-shtooler?" Irena-the-vodka-queen calling Redford a bar-stooler was odd, but people nodded in agreement. "Pastooorr Maggie vould neveerr say deese vorrds about no one. Leesten, people!" Irena was on fire. "Eet ees de season ov de Lent. Vee supposed to give up tings. You know, shtop doing tings as sacrifice. But I say, vee shtarrt *doing* tings. Vee do tings foorr Pastoorr Maggie! She's having pain. A sad loss in herr life. Meester Rredforrd, go to your bar-shtool. Yourr hate doesn't verk here no morre." Although Irena looked like an angry doll, she sounded more like an angry politician.

The church erupted in applause. Irena nodded knowingly. Of course she was right. She was always right. She toddled back to the organ on her high heels, waving to the congregation as if she were the queen.

Harold tried to get things back under control. "Thank you, Irena. I think we can agree that right now Pastor Maggie needs our support. The council will meet immediately after we sing our closing hymn. We will send an email through the church office as to our decisions. Irena, the closing hymn please."

Unfortunately, the closing hymn of the morning was "Jesus Walked This Lonesome Valley." Many of the congregation left feeling the totality of the weight of Lent as they had never felt it before.

The members of the council remained in the sanctuary and moved up to the front pews. Harold grabbed Hank, Doris, and Irena after the dismal postlude and invited them to the meeting. Everyone would have to pull together now.

Doris began to clean up the spilled flowers and water on the altar steps. For anyone looking closely, they would have seen her wipe her own eyes with the rag she used to sop up the water. Just remembering Pastor Maggie as she stumbled and fell on the altar brought a new flood of tears. Doris kept cleaning as Harold began the impromptu meeting.

"Charlotte, are you ready to take the minutes?"

"Yes," Charlotte responded seriously. She was already miffed by Redford's comments and had no patience for any more shenanigans.

Harold continued, "As the council of Loving the Lord, we have the responsibility to make decisions for our congregation, and we also oversee the long-term and day-to-day running of the church. I have asked Hank, Irena, and Doris to join this meeting as staff members. Now, as to the decisions we must—"

Mrs. Abernathy stood up. "Thank you, Harold. But we are in a church, not in a courtroom. I would like to make a suggestion. We each have a specific responsibility on this council. We each head a small committee. I recommend we carry out Pastor Maggie's duties under the auspices of our council positions. Tom Wiggins, you are in charge of building and grounds. Until we know how much time Pastor Maggie needs, you will make decisions regarding our building and grounds of the church."

Tom nodded. He already did all the snow removal and set the furnace before church on Sundays and each weekday morning.

Mrs. Abernathy continued, "Marla Wiggins, you are in charge of education. You will make the decisions regarding education for all ages and make sure all classes are running smoothly."

"But Mrs. Abernathy, I can't do that all by myself. Pastor Maggie and I make those decisions together. Plus, she teaches the high school class." Marla sounded more scared than whiny.

"Marla, you are very good at what you do. We have several people in our congregation who are not part of a committee. Tap one of them to take over Maggie's class. Redford, you are in charge of finance. But from the issues of this past summer, Fred and Charlotte will continue to count and deposit the weekly offerings. I also recommend Harold join the committee for the time being. No financial decisions will be made without the four of you in agreement." Mrs. Abernathy sounded like a schoolmarm from 1850. She was brilliant.

Redford turned bright red.

"I am not in need of others to 'help' me do the finances anymore. And there weren't any 'issues' this past summer." He snorted. "I want to return to my point about salary. If she's not working, she's not getting paid!" His rage was palpable.

Mrs. Abernathy thought Hank was going to jump up and pound Redford like a street thug.

"As the clerk, you all know I write the paychecks for our staff," Charlotte interjected. "I make a motion that Pastor Maggie will be paid her regular salary for as long as necessary. Will someone second my motion?"

Harold had completely lost control of the meeting, but he seconded Charlotte's motion.

"All in favor?" Harold asked.

A cacophony of "Ayes!" rang out.

"All opposed?"

"Nay." Redford's petulant voice hung in the air.

"Passed."

Harold turned toward Mrs. Abernathy, but before she could speak, Redford pushed past her in the pew.

"You are all a bunch of morons. That old guy who died wasn't even a relative. Just an old, stuffy, waste-of-space idiot! So now she gets to boo-hoo about that? She's taking us all for a ride. You have no idea what I can do to each one of you! And that pathetic Maggie. I'm going to—"

Hank and Charlotte slammed into Redford at the same time. He hit the floor hard, and Hank sat on his back while Charlotte pulled out her ever-ready handcuffs.

"Redford Johnson, you just threatened each one of us. That means you threatened me, a police officer. That was unwise." Charlotte read Redford his rights. "I think some time in the one and only Cherish jail cell will do you a little bit of good."

She didn't need help from Hank. She hauled Redford to his feet and shoved him down the aisle. He kicked out hard at one of the beautiful wooden pews. A small piece of scrolling at the bottom of the pew broke off with a crack.

Redford turned and spat at the other church members, "You can all go to hell!"

Charlotte shoved his shoulder into the door jam. Perhaps on purpose. Redford yelped.

"Maybe you should stop misbehaving in this sacred place. I seem to be here every time you throw a tantrum, Reddy-boy."

His howls slowly drifted away as Charlotte helped him into the back of the police car. She was thankful she was on duty.

Back in the church, everyone stared at one another. Such ugliness was always a shock for the good people of Loving the Lord. Everyone but Irena. She slapped her hands together hard, as if brushing Redford right out of Cherish.

"Goot rriddance. He ees like de cancer. Time to cut himm out. Dun and dun!"

Mrs. Abernathy cleared her throat. Her hands were shaking ever-so-slightly. Redford's rage and cruelty touched something inside her she hadn't felt in some time. She took a deep breath.

"That was unfortunate," small cough, "but shall we continue with our duties?"

"Thank you, Mrs. Abernathy," Harold said. "Let's continue with our care plan for our church and our pastor."

Mrs. Abernathy nodded. "Ellen Bright, you are the head of the worship committee. Your job may be a little more difficult. I recommend you find pulpit supply for the next four weeks. We may not need them all, but let's be prepared. I think it would be helpful to remove the burden of preaching until Pastor Maggie tells us otherwise." Mrs. Abernathy was back on track.

Ellen smiled gently. "I can try to find clergy, maybe the chaplain at the hospital. But . . . what if some of us took a turn up front? It's the season of Lent. Perhaps we could share how we sacrifice or do special things for others during this time of the church year? We have wonderful Irena, here, who can hold the services together with her music. We could even add an extra hymn or two each week so that no one has to speak for too long." Ellen was coming up with these ideas on the fly. Why couldn't they do their own services for a few weeks? "It would also take care of the financial issue by not having to pay someone to do pulpit supply."

She was met with silence.

"Okay," she continued, "I'll go first. Next Sunday is the second Sunday of Lent. Irena, are you with me?"

"Ov coourrse. Eet vill be brrrillliant. I peek de extrra hymms dis veek and call you."

Irena was on board. This was going to work. Maybe.

"Who else will take a Sunday?" Ellen prodded.

Silence.

"Who will take the third week of Lent? If you don't volunteer, I will help you." Ellen spoke lightly and smiled to beat the band.

"I will," Hank said. "And I can get everyone the Scripture passages for the weeks they are speaking. I have them all in my desk. I am happy to help Pastor Maggie any way I can."

"Thank you, Hank," Ellen said. "Now how about the fourth week of Lent?"

Everyone caught their breath when they heard the next voice. No one was more shocked than Marla.

"I'll do it," Tom Wiggins said.

"But, Tom . . . You don't speak," Marla sputtered.

"Nope, I don't. At least not often. But I can say a word or two about what Lent means to me. I can at least give it a try."

"Tom, I can't wait to hear what you have to say," Ellen said. "Now, how about the last week of Lent?"

"Well, I can't be shown up by my husband, now can I?" Marla said, still somewhat bewildered. "I will say something, but may I have the children sing something too?"

"Of course," Ellen said. "Now let's hope we don't have to plan Holy Week and Easter. Mrs. Abernathy, I think I've completed my responsibilities. Irena, you and I will stay in touch as far as the music goes."

Ellen knew that Maggie often locked horns with Irena and her music selections. Ellen would try to oversee but could imagine Irena's glee at having complete control for possibly the next four weeks.

Mrs. Abernathy gave Ellen a nod of approval. "I am the chair of member caring. I will take it upon myself to visit the shut-ins and make visits to the hospital, if necessary. Hank, I will need a list of shut-ins and their addresses."

"Yessireebob, Mrs. Abernathy! I will get that for you right now."

He left the sanctuary and returned a few minutes later with the Lent Scripture passages and shut-in list.

Mrs. Abernathy continued, "Sylvia, you are in charge of fellowship. Your committee plans the Easter breakfast. Do you feel confident to carry that out?"

"Yes. We have already met, and I will have a sign-up sheet on the bulletin board next Sunday for volunteers. I will also order the Easter lilies."

"Thank you, Sylvia." Mrs. Abernathy looked at Harold. "Anything else, Harold?"

"If anyone has a need or concern, please let me know," Harold said. "We must all be the eyes and ears of this church and congregation. Mrs. Abernathy, thank you for your work here today. You . . . uh . . . surprise me."

He didn't elaborate, and Mrs. Abernathy warmed up inside. She knew people wondered what had happened to her previous personality. They could just keep wondering.

"Well," Doris said a little too harshly to cover her churning emotions, "as I always say, onwards and forwards! You all have a church to run, and I have a church to clean. Out with you!"

When Maggie awoke, she couldn't remember what day it was. She didn't know why she was in bed. Her alarm should have gone off to get her out for her run. As she turned her head, it began to throb. Then she remembered. She curled into a ball to fight the onslaught of pain and rolled her face into her pillow.

Then she felt someone next to her. It scared her out of her immediate pain. She quickly looked up and saw Jack's face. His hand was on her shoulder, and suddenly she remembered. It was Sunday. The first Sunday of Lent. She hadn't written a sermon. She had spoken incoherently to the congregation, tripped over the flowers, and stumbled out of the sanctuary like an old drunk. Humiliation washed over her and mixed painfully into her memory of Ed. Jack had tucked her into bed, and he was still there. She looked at her clock: three p.m.

She wiped her nose with her pillow case and looked up at Jack.

"I'm a mess. Why are you here?"

"Because you are a mess," Jack said, brushing her hair away from her face. "I'm very good at cleaning up messes. If it won't embarrass you too much, I'm going to wipe your nose."

He grabbed a tissue and gently wiped her nose. He took another tissue and dabbed under each eye. The sweetness of Jack's actions made the need for more tissues immediate.

"Have you been here all day?" Maggie asked through her tears.

"Yes. I've been sitting in your chair and have enjoyed several visits from Marmalade and Cheerio. I also began reading your G. M. Malliet's *Wicked Autumn*. I might have to borrow it because I want to know who the murderer is."

"Jack, I think I need to go home. I need to get back to Zeeland. I'm not sure, but I don't think I belong here anymore. I think it was a mistake." She looked plaintively into his eyes.

Jack controlled his face so it wouldn't give away the fear that was creeping into his heart.

"Maggie, you need some good rest. If you want to rest in Zeeland, then you should. But don't make any decisions in the next couple of weeks about life here. Please?"

Maggie nodded her head, but her eyes had already checked out. She slowly sat up and took his hand.

"I need to go home. I will be all right, and I will call you . . . but I need to pack now. I will head home this afternoon."

Jack wanted to stop her. He felt, if he let her go, he might never find her again.

"May I help you?" He sounded stilted.

Maggie got out of bed, and her brain switched into gear. She needed to take as many clothes as possible. She needed the cat carriers from the basement. She would like to take her books out of the study. How much time would it take to do all that? She also wanted to get on the road. Maybe her mother and father would come back with her and help her clean out the parsonage in a few days or so. She would have to figure out how to tell the church she was leaving so they could get on with finding a new pastor. Her mind continued to race in this vein—jumping ahead, then pulling back to the present. Her emotions dictated her decisions. Her powers of reasoning seemingly evaporated.

"It would be great if you could get the cat carriers out of the basement," she said as she got out of bed and found her duffel on the floor.

"I'm sure Ellen would stay and watch the cats for you while you're gone." Jack winced. If the cats stayed, she would have to come back.

"I'll just take them. Ellen is so busy." *Hmm . . . What will my parents think about having two cats move in?*

Jack left the room in search of the carriers. Maggie packed as many clothes as she could manage into her duffel, then grabbed all the books on her nightstand and shoved them in too. She used a smaller bag to pack up her bathroom. Her books in the study would have to wait. Jack helped her pack up her car, putting the yowling cats in their carriers on the backseat.

Maggie was exhilarated. She had so much adrenaline pumping through her, she felt as if she could run all the way home. Then she felt Jack's arms around her. She looked up at his face.

"Maggie, drive safely. And please, please, don't make any big decisions right away." Jack felt completely out of control. That was not a feeling he was used to.

Maggie took a deep breath. "I will try not to make any decisions yet." She sounded insincere, even to herself.

"Maggie, I love you. Do you understand me?" Jack tried to control his voice. He wanted to yell so that maybe she would hear him.

She did hear him, and she did understand. "I love you too, Jack. But I have to get out of Cherish. I have to go home. We'll talk soon."

She gave him a brief kiss and got in her car.

If Maggie would have looked in her rearview mirror before she turned onto Main, she would have seen Jack standing in the middle of the street, watching her go.

At seven p.m., Mimi and Dirk heard their front door open. Then they heard some very loud meows. They went to the front room to see their daughter holding two cat carriers from whence the meows erupted. They couldn't have been more surprised.

"Mom, Dad," Maggie said, "I've come home. And I've brought two friends. I hope it's all right."

Her parents stared, unable to speak. Finally, Dirk took the cat carriers, and Mimi led Maggie to the kitchen table.

"What's happened?" Mimi asked.

But as she looked into her daughter's eyes, she watched her slowly pull inward and disappear.

26

Verna Abernathy awoke on the morning of February 23rd and was a woman with a mission. Caroline was curled up on the pillow next to her and purred as Verna gave her several pets. That was how they began each day. Verna looked out the bedroom window and noticed a fine snow falling. It must have fallen through the night because everything was covered in white.

They made their way downstairs for breakfast. Of course, Caroline always had her breakfast first. Verna put the tea kettle on and poured her bran flakes. After breakfast, she put on her winter coat, hat, and mittens and made her way outside to shovel the snow from her sidewalks and driveway. She had things to do, and snow would not deter her. As she shoveled, she wondered how Pastor Maggie was doing that morning. It hadn't taken long the previous evening for word to race through the congregation that Pastor Maggie had left the parsonage. With her cats. That last fact worried Verna. As long as the cats were there, Maggie would be back. But what now? Verna shoveled feverishly, as if to push the worst possibility out of her mind.

Maggie just had to come back to Cherish.

After finishing her shoveling and getting ready for the day, she once again wrapped herself into her winter clothes, gave Caroline a loving pat on her small head, grabbed her list of shut-ins, and made her way to the Friendly Elder Care building. Her first stop was Katharine Smits, Sylvia's mother.

"Good morning, Mrs. Smits," Verna said somewhat mechanically. "I don't know if you remember me. I'm Verna Abernathy."

"I do remember you, very well indeed. What are you doing here?"

Mrs. Smits looked at Verna with her head cocked like a parrot. Due to her arthritis, her neck was bent downward so she had to look up at everyone. Verna thought it looked terribly painful.

"Why, I'm here to visit you," Verna said matter-of-factly.

"Why?" asked Katharine.

That stumped Verna. "I'm visiting you as a member of our church."

"Where's Pastor Maggie?" Katharine asked, looking out of one bright eye.

"Well, yes. Pastor Maggie has suffered the loss of a dear friend and is taking some bereavement time."

"When will she be back?"

Verna felt as if she were on trial. *Good heavens.* This is not how Verna thought shut-in visits would be.

"We don't know, exactly. She is home with her parents for a time." Did she just tell a lie? What if Maggie wasn't coming back at all? "But, Katharine, tell me how you are."

"I'm an old, crippled woman. But I have a daughter who loves me and a lifetime of happy memories. I can't ask for more. God is good." Katharine smiled a crooked smile.

Verna could not comprehend that kind of attitude. Katharine should be miserable, bitter, and angry. She couldn't even go to the bathroom without help. Verna bumbled stiffly through the visit and left as soon as she possibly could.

Her next visit was with Marvin Green. Nothing could have prepared her for the onslaught of negativity awaiting her.

"Who are you?" Marvin croaked when she entered his room.

Her answer was utilitarian. "I'm Verna Abernathy from Loving the Lord Community Church. I'm here to visit you."

"I don't want no visit. Get out. Where's that little one?" His eyes were narrowed into slits.

"What little one?" Verna wondered if Marvin should be on the Alzheimer's wing. Maybe he wanted a certain short nurse.

"That little one who always comes here to bother me!" he yelled.

"Marvin, stop yelling. Who are you talking about?" Verna wondered how Maggie did this week after week.

"I'm talking about that little one pretending to be a pastor," Marvin said, crossing his arms.

Verna's anger rose swiftly. She felt her hands begin to shake, but her voice stayed even. Her fear of losing Maggie manifested itself in a harsh rebuke.

"You ridiculous man. Are you talking about Pastor Maggie, the minister of Loving the Lord Community Church? Do you know of her education and qualifications for the ministry? She's a lot smarter than you'll ever be."

"I don't care what you say. Women can't be preachers. It goes against the Bible. Women are meant to be quiet in the church. She comes here every week and talks her head off. I don't pay her no nevermind. I just ignore her." He tried to sneer, but it just looked like he had gas. "Where is she, anyway? I should be relieved. That girl bothers me to death."

If only that were true. "She is on bereavement. She has lost a dear friend, so I will be visiting you for the time being." Verna looked at the clock on the wall and wondered how quickly she could end this little nightmare. "Marvin, would you like me to get you a cup of coffee or a cookie from the dining room?" *Anything to get out of this room.*

"No! I don't want nothin' except to be alone."

"Now, you see, that's your problem, Marvin. You make everyone around you so miserable that you are alone. No one wants to be near you."

Mrs. Abernathy had a flash of insight. Marvin lived the way she herself had lived before Maggie arrived. She had pushed everyone away with her brusqueness and flat-out rudeness. And then another thought came to her. Marvin was like her husband had been: cruel.

Without realizing it, she began to shake her head, as if to shake the memory right out of her brain. She stood up.

"Marvin, you are doing a fine job of having a very bad day. I'm sure you will continue to do so. I'll be back next week."

Verna stood and left the room before Marvin had a chance to spew any more hate.

Back at Loving the Lord, Hank fielded phone calls right and left. It seemed the entire congregation wanted to know the details of Pastor Maggie's meltdown. Hank, always the professional, gave away nothing. Between calls, he tried to get a start on the bulletin for Sunday. Ellen Bright would be "speaking," but was he supposed to call it a sermon?

Irena burst through the door as only Irena could. She wobbled on a brand-new pair of six-inch high-heeled boots while she balanced her requisite stack of music.

"Goooood moorrnig, Hunk. Heeerrre I am vit de musik for Sunday. Any vord frromm Pastoorr Maggie?"

"Good morning, Irena," Hank replied. He had never thought he would enjoy Irena's presence in his office, but she was a piece of normal in what had become very abnormal. "I haven't heard from Pastor Maggie, but I have heard from half the congregation already this morning. I hate to sound cynical, yessireebob, I do, but I can't tell if they actually care or if they just want gossip. It's the curse of a small town."

"Tell dem to shut eet. Now, I peek extra hymns to tek moorre time in serrrvice. Should be verry good."

Irena was standing in front of the door when it opened again and almost pushed her right off her boots. She dropped all of her music and grabbed onto the wall for support. Mrs. Popkin entered carrying a large bakery box and didn't see Irena, who was completely smashed against the wall.

"Hokey tooters, good morning, Hank. How goes it this Monday morning?"

"Help!" Irena screamed from behind the door.

Mrs. Popkin jumped and then moved into the office and closed the door. Irena gave Mrs. Popkin one of her best glares, but Mrs. Popkin paid no attention.

"Well, looky there! Irena, what are you doing hiding behind the door?" Mrs. Popkin laughed and kept right on talking. "I know that Pastor Maggie regularly brings a box of donuts over here for you folks, so I thought I would step in while she was away. Enjoy these on the house." She set the box on Hank's desk and then peeled Irena off the wall and gave her a slap on the back. "Where's Doris? She should have some of these too. I'll go take a look-see in the sanctuary. Thanks to all of you for keeping this office running!"

Mrs. Popkin's animated words and happy laughter filled the office, then she went on her search for Doris. Even Irena was speechless, or maybe she was breathless. No matter, she tottered over to the donut box, tore off the lid, and grabbed a donut with each hand.

When Jack had a break in his morning appointments, he went online to find a flower shop in Zeeland. He called and placed an order. His instructions were specific, and the woman on the other end of the phone was delighted to carry them out. Jack went back to his appointments. He was frustrated with himself as he found he was less patient with his patients and more preoccupied as the day progressed. *What is she doing now? How is she processing what's happened the last few days? Is she coming back to Cherish? To me?*

Marla sat at her kitchen table and sipped her third cup of coffee. She had been trying to figure out who could teach Pastor Maggie's Sunday school class. She knew she couldn't with her own two children in the class. They would rebel at having their mother teach. Then she thought of Cate. Even though Cate was at the U, maybe she could help out for a couple of Sundays. The kids loved her. Marla's biggest fear was that the class would fall apart without Maggie. She had been so happy when Addie and Jason said how much they liked Sunday school. Actually, she'd almost fainted when they told her that bit of information. She got to her computer and sent Cate a brief email, asking if she could teach Sunday school for Pastor Maggie for a couple of weeks. An hour later, she had Cate's reply.

Hi, Mrs. Wiggins!

It's so nice to hear from you. My mom told me that Pastor Maggie was having a rough time right now. I was sorry to hear that, and I have been praying for her. About Sunday school, I would love to step in, although I'm nothing like Pastor Maggie. And the best part is, I have winter break beginning this coming Friday. I can for sure teach the next two Sundays, and then we can see what's needed. But I do have a question, what am I supposed to teach? Let me know if there is something specific, or else I'll have to wing it. Oh, and I'll pick up donuts!

Love,
Cate

Marla was thrilled. She would ask Addie and Jason what they were doing in Sunday school and then get back to Cate. As for Marla's Sunday school class of little ones, she knew exactly what she was going to do with them.

∞

Sylvia was working in her garden shop hot house. She had begun her plantings two weeks prior and was now watching her seedlings grow.

Finally, fresh vegetables again. She would be sure to give Pastor Maggie the first harvest. She knew how much Pastor Maggie loved vegetables. Sylvia quickly dashed her dirt-stained hand across her cheek. Every time she thought of Pastor Maggie in church the day before, especially when Maggie fell over the flower stand, she couldn't stop the tears. Pastor Maggie had seemed so lost and almost delirious. Hopefully, being with her mother would help. Mothers knew everything. Sylvia thought of her own mother at the Friendly Elder Care. She made a habit of going to see her each day. Maybe she should do that sooner in the day than usual.

Sylvia returned to the shop and washed her hands. As she buttoned up her coat, the front door opened. It was Bill Baxter.

"Hi, Bill." Sylvia wondered why he was in The Garden Shop. She looked at his bright-red hair sticking out from under his gray cap and smiled. "I was just going to close up for a few minutes and visit my mother."

"Oh, I don't want to interrupt you." Bill mumbled his words, shuffled his feet, and began to turn around.

"No, you're not interrupting me, Bill. Please don't go. Why did you come here on such a snowy day?" Sylvia smiled and tried to restrain herself from grabbing his arm and clinging to it for dear life. Why was he so shy?

"I've been out plowing snow, and I thought I would stop by to see . . . if you . . . uh . . . needed your driveway plowed." His embarrassment was palpable.

"I shoveled it this morning, but thank you for asking." As she wrapped her scarf around her neck, she realized she was tired of whatever this was between herself and Bill. She felt embarrassed for flirting. It wasn't a cute game anymore. "I better go," she said flatly.

"Sylvia, wait." Bill looked as if someone had just stabbed him with a hot poker. He winced and closed his eyes for a moment. "I had a thought about something for Pastor Maggie."

That caught Sylvia off guard. She leaned forward expectantly. "What?"

"Maybe . . ."

There was that anguished face again.

"Bill! What is your thought for Pastor Maggie? Please just tell me."

Bill had never heard her voice that strong before. It seemed to embolden him.

"May I take you to lunch after you visit your mother and tell you my idea?" He actually looked Sylvia in the eyes.

"Yes, you may. I'll be back here in an hour. I'll see you then."

Sylvia walked from behind the counter and out the door. She held it for him so that she could lock up. He quietly walked to his truck.

Redford Johnson sat in O'Leary's Pub, taking the first gulp of his third whiskey. It was lunchtime. His "jail time" had consisted of two hours in the archaic jail cell at the police department. Charlotte took her time to do the paperwork but finally had to let him go.

On this day, Redford felt good. Or maybe he felt drunk. But whatever it was, Redford was certain that Maggie was gone for good. Women were so stupid. How did anyone think Maggie, or any woman, could lead a church? She'd been a disaster since her first day in Cherish. And look at that inept Tuggle woman. Police Chief. Whatever. It was time to get rid of her too. Women needed men to direct them. He'd never met a woman who wasn't weak and brainless. Women were good for a couple of things, but it was a short list. It showed what an idiot Jack Elliot was. Redford decided he would tell Jack to his face, he'd tell Jack what a fool he was. Redford smiled. It was an ugly smile.

Mrs. Abernathy made her way down the hallways of the Friendly Elder Care. Marvin had left a bad taste in her mouth, but really it was the stirring of bad memories she had buried, or thought she had. Memories of a bad man. A bad husband.

George Abernathy first saw Verna when she was seventeen. She was tall and thin, with long honey-colored hair. She wasn't beautiful, but she was good enough, George thought. George was thirty years old and prided himself as being a top writer for the local newspaper. Once he discovered that Verna was being raised by Walter and Caroline Charles, he made sure to get to know Walter. George was a charmer. His blond hair and blue eyes seemed to dazzle the women in town. When he was with the men, he presented himself as a man's man. He was well read, he could talk sports, and he went to church.

Once he decided that Verna would be his wife, he charmed his way right into the Charles's home. He was invited for dinners and picnics. He and Walter went to baseball games. He was respectful to Caroline and to Verna. Verna didn't really pay attention. She was finishing her senior year in high school and had the promise of a scholarship to the university waiting for her. Caroline's consistent love and care for Verna had restored much of the self-esteem stolen from her as a child, which is why she was shocked when she found herself walking down the aisle of church into the arms of George Abernathy.

Leaving the safety of Caroline's home threw Verna into a terrible depression, although at that time no one would have used that word unless it was about a financial crisis. When George returned home from work each evening, there was no dinner. He began to eat out. Although Verna had learned how to clean and be tidy from Caroline, her own home was unkempt. George used her for what he wanted but soon grew tired of her glum demeanor and lack of interest in anything. Verna's hopes and dreams of the university were turned to ashes. The only thing she was able to do was go into her backyard each morning and tend the flowers Caroline had given her for a wedding present.

Once George began seeing other women, Verna was relieved. He stopped coming home regularly and instead went out drinking and looking for women far flashier than she. She lived like this for over three decades. The best day of her life was when the police knocked on her door to say George had been in a fatal car accident. In his drunkenness, he had driven into an electric pole just outside of town. The woman who was with him also died at the scene.

Verna had thought of the details of her doomed marriage over the years. But once he died, she began to slowly throw those memories away. One by one, they went into the fire. No need to relive any of those horrible days.

Somehow, visiting Marvin brought a lot of those ancient memories back. She would relegate them back to the fires of forgetfulness. She had to.

She visited the few shut-ins on the list who were on the Alzheimer's wing. Her frame of mind made those visits even more depressing. She had one more visit to make, and then she would go home. Little, purry Caroline would be waiting.

Howard Baker was as much a friend to Verna as anyone could be. They had known each other for years through the church. Howard greeted her at his front door with his cane and invited her inside. He had his coffee pot on and poured two cups. The hot coffee tasted good and warmed Verna, body and soul. Their conversation was light, revolving around Howard's surgery, his stellar recovery, and the fact that his doctor said he was a perfect patient. Howard never took himself too seriously. He was quick to see the humor in almost anything, and he had the gift of being able to talk with just about anyone. Verna rested comfortably in his chatter.

Bill picked up Sylvia exactly one hour after they had parted. In that hour he had given himself a talking to.

Bill, you can do this. You know Sylvia, and you like her. Plus, she's the prettiest thing you've ever seen. Take her to lunch and tell your great idea for Pastor Maggie. And remember, it was Pastor Maggie who said you had to take Sylvia on a date. That's practically like God.

They went to the Cherish Café, and Sylvia felt extremely underdressed for such a fancy place.

"This is really nice, Bill, but we could have just gone to O'Leary's," Sylvia said practically.

"I . . . uh . . . wanted to take you here."

Oh dear, did I hurt his feelings? "Thank you. Now tell me about your idea for Pastor Maggie." Sylvia smiled.

Bill gained more courage now that he could talk about a project.

"I was thinking about Pastor Maggie's office. It's so dark and dingy. All the brown, fake paneling and brown carpet that's about a hundred years old. Maybe that was good enough for our other pastors, but Pastor Maggie needs something brighter. Plus, it stinks in there."

Neither of them was aware that the stink was rotten vegetables hiding in all the cracks and crevices.

Sylvia took this all in and felt the happiest she had been in the last twenty-four hours.

"Bill, this is a fantastic idea. I mean it. We can paint and recarpet, and what else? What are you thinking?"

"Well, we should probably talk to the council, but then maybe we can get her some new furniture, at least a new desk. The one she has looks like it should be in a medieval castle. But I think we should try to get going on this, if we're going to do it. Who knows when she'll be back?" Bill forgot his embarrassment at being himself and jumped into the conversation wholeheartedly. "But we've got to keep it somewhat of a secret." Bill lowered his voice and looked around the café. "I don't want Fitch Dervish to hear about this. We wouldn't get it done for a year if he started nosing around. I don't think we need a building permit."

"You're right. We can tell the council but swear them to secrecy. We'll work on it at night and maybe after church on Sundays. Fitch will never know."

She decided then and there that everything was going to be okay. Everything single thing.

Mimi had come home for lunch to check on Maggie, who was in her room. Mimi was making tuna fish sandwiches in the kitchen when the doorbell rang. She went to the door and was surprised to see a delivery man on the front porch holding a large flower bouquet.

"Maggie Elzinga?"

"I'll take them. Thank you very much."

She brought the flowers inside. She had never seen such a huge bouquet of red carnations before. She walked back into the kitchen to put the flowers on the kitchen table for Maggie. When she turned around, she saw Marmalade and Cheerio on the counter, helping themselves to the tuna fish.

27

Maggie awakened in her room with the groggy feeling that had accompanied her since Ed died. It reminded her of Eeyore the Donkey from Winnie the Pooh, complete with a dark rain cloud over her head. Everything was gray. Was this how life would continue? Would she be living in gray days from now on? What day was it? She thought it was Saturday. She had been home for almost a week, but the individual days rolled into one long, hideous day for Maggie.

A large orange head smashed into Maggie's, accompanied by a loud purr. Marmalade was elated to see his pet had finally come to life. He could not contain his glee. Cheerio joined in with her requisite squeaks and then put her tail in Maggie's face. Maggie smiled. There was nothing like cat therapy.

Maggie wrapped herself in her robe. When she went downstairs, followed by her two best friends in all the world, she was surprised, as she had been each day, by the flowers. The kitchen was filled with five large vases full of red carnations. Jack had sent a bouquet each morning since Maggie left Cherish. Each bouquet was accompanied by the same message.

My Maggie,

Thinking of you every day.

With all my love,
Your Jack

"Good morning, Maggie," Mimi said from the kitchen table. "How did you sleep?"

"Fine, thank you. It doesn't seem to be difficult to sleep. It's difficult to be awake."

Maggie moved a vase of flowers in order to make herself a cup of coffee.

"We may have to move some of these flowers up to your bedroom," Mimi said practically. "If 'Your Jack' is going to continue with this behavior, we will not be able to use our kitchen. Carnations last so long, it's not like we can throw any out. They all look freshly cut."

"That's why I like them. They last."

Maggie sipped her coffee while Marmalade and Cheerio jumped on the kitchen table, looking for cereal bowls with leftover milk dribbles.

Surprisingly, as fastidious as Mimi was in all corners of her life, cats on tables and countertops didn't bother her. When Dirk was home, he would put the cats back on the floor. As his mother would have said, it was *fease* to have animals on the table, which was the Dutch word for "disgusting." Marmalade and Cheerio didn't hold it against him. They just hopped right back up again.

Mimi looked at Maggie across the table. "What are you thinking today?"

"I want out of this dark cloud. But I don't want sunlight. I can't handle the dark or the light. Does that sound like I'm trying to be profound? Because I'm not."

"It sounds like grief. Grief is a power that cannot be controlled or manipulated. But you already know that. Think about the people you have met in just the last year who have been in the grip of grief." Mimi spoke pragmatically but gently.

Maggie nodded. "There was Kristy at Holland Hospital, grieving the death of her infant daughter, Anna Lee. Max Solomon, in some strange way, grieving when his father, Rupert, died. Jennifer and Beth

Becker when they lost their mother. Mrs. Landry's family. So much of their grief came because of her happy heart and generosity. And now Jo and her children and grandchildren."

"I don't want to sound simplistic or condescending to you, Maggie, but grief is something different for everyone who is captured by it. It can be that dark cloud that you are walking in right now, which is almost comforting compared to the harshness of sunlight. For others, grief is a roaring monster that seems to consume them bit by bit. Those people need a good deal of help just to get out of bed. For some, grief remains a lifelong companion because to dismiss it or grow away from it means betrayal of the lost loved one. And there are so many other permutations and agonies of grief that we don't need to talk about right now. But here's what I think."

Maggie looked up. Whenever her mother said those words, they were words worth listening to.

"You are appropriately grieving a man you admired, learned from, relied on, and loved dearly. Your description of the gray cloud makes sense. Perfect sense. You have cried many tears, awakened to the shock of his death day after day, and you will cry many more tears. I'm sorry for that, Maggie. You will miss Ed for a very long time. You will pick up the phone to call him before you remember he will never answer. Ed mattered in your life. Whenever we allow someone to matter, we risk experiencing the pain that counters the experience of the day-to-day joy of having known them. It doesn't matter if it's a dear friend, a family member, or a true love. The only way to avoid grief is to never let anyone matter to you. And you, Maggie, are incapable of doing that. You let people matter. Goodness, you let cats matter!"

Maggie smiled. It made her face look normal for a second.

The doorbell rang. Mimi got up and went to the door, knowing what was on the other side. She came back in with another bouquet and a stack of mail from the door mail slot.

"'Your Jack' is persistent. I also see many postmarks from Cherish in this stack of mail." Mimi put the newest bouquet on top of the refrigerator and handed Maggie the mail. "You're a great pastor, Maggie, because you allow people to matter. And they know it."

The church was aflutter. It was Saturday morning, and the office was full of people. Pastor Maggie had been gone for almost one week. Since then, Bill and Sylvia had met with some of the council members to pitch the idea of redecorating her office. The initial plans had been "blessed" by the council. Because no one wanted to be confronted by Fitch Dervish during their little project, they swore an oath to never speak of the redecorating outside the walls of Loving the Lord.

Hank, Pamela, Doris, Mrs. Abernathy, Bill, Sylvia, Marla, Tom, Harold, and Cate (who had nothing better to do over her winter break) all crowded into Hank's office. They were dressed in work clothes. Standing in everyone's way, Doris had her trash can, cleansers, dusters, brooms, and rags. Hank had arrived early to cover his own precious desk and the copy machine with his trusty blue tarpaulin.

Stage one was to tear out just about everything from Maggie's original office. Secretly, all the men could hardly wait for this demolition day. They were going to rip things up and tear things apart. Secretly, all the women were dreading this day because they knew the men were going to leave one huge mess, which they gleefully did.

"Okay," said Hank, taking on the four-star general role, "first, we will move all the furniture into the gathering area to be given to the Salvation Army later."

"All the furniture?" asked Marla. Marla abhorred waste. Maybe the disgusting furniture could go somewhere in the church.

"Yes. All the furniture. The council said Pastor Maggie should have all new furniture. Next, we will rip up the carpeting. Following that, the paneling comes off the walls. I tried to pull a piece off already, and it appears to have been put on with cement. So we are really going to have to jack hammer it off!" He sounded way too excited about it.

"Where is all that supposed to go?" Mrs. Abernathy asked, concerned it would be in the way for church in the morning. Her flowered kerchief was wrapped tightly around her head to protect her from dust and destruction.

"We have permission to use Mrs. Popkin's dumpster, which we moved to the side door of the church for the day." Hank enjoyed having answers to every question.

Everyone worked to first remove the smaller items from the office, then the large pieces of furniture, then the difficult work of pulling up unwilling carpet. There were several coffee breaks to discuss "next steps." Mrs. Popkin's donuts and egg sandwiches were a constant form of sustenance, along with pots and pots of coffee.

Irena came in around ten a.m. to practice the organ for the next morning. She had been made aware of the work day and was delighted to have a "captured" audience who had no choice but to listen to her play her Lenten dirges. She also helped herself to half a dozen donuts. Irena refused to believe Pastor Maggie wasn't coming back to Cherish. Pastor Maggie wouldn't dare not return.

After four hours, Irena finally turned off the organ and began stacking her music. No one was sorry to see her totter out of the sanctuary. If they hadn't been having so much fun ripping Pastor Maggie's office apart, they would have felt as if they had been at a four-hour funeral. But even Irena's best efforts couldn't get their spirits down.

Everyone was surprised when Irena came back inside. She wasn't alone.

Fitch Dervish stood right behind her. The joviality of the day came to a crashing halt.

"Well, now. What do we have going on here?" Fitch asked as he walked into the destruction. He stepped over the rolled up carpeting and old blinds from Maggie's windows. A dark bookcase was lying on its side with stacks of books from previous pastors shoved in a corner of Hank's office. "It certainly looks like a building project. The thing is," he began flipping through his ever-present clipboard, "I don't see a request for a building permit in my records."

Everyone stood still and stared. For some insane reason, they all felt like high school kids caught at a party instead of being in school. Finally, Bill Baxter stepped forward.

"Hello, Fitch. You don't have an application for a building permit because we aren't building anything. We're decorating."

"I'm pretty sure I should be the judge of that. I am the building inspector."

They collectively wanted to punch the guy. Mrs. Abernathy thought Bill might just wield a fist.

"Mr. Dervish," Mrs. Abernathy said, "our pastor is gone for a time of bereavement. We just want to freshen up her office before she returns. It hasn't been updated with paint, carpet, and furniture in many years. You can try to roadblock this if you wish, but I assure you we aren't doing anything that's under your jurisdiction."

She wiped the dust from her hands and tightened the scarf around her head.

Fitch was at a loss. He looked confused, then embarrassed.

It was Marla who spoke next. "Mr. Dervish, would you like to help? You would have to go with our plan, but we could certainly use another pair of hands."

Everyone stared at her in disbelief. Bill hung his head in despair. What was Marla thinking?

"Why is Pastor Maggie away? Who died?" Fitch asked.

Mrs. Abernathy spoke again. "She has lost a beloved professor and mentor."

"So, not a family member?"

"Not as such. But I believe he was the person who recognized her gifts as a pastor before anyone else. He held up a mirror for her, and his abiding encouragement is what brought her here. The loss is quite devastating for Pastor Maggie." Mrs. Abernathy stared Fitch in the eye.

Fitch thought for a moment. "I lost my father three months ago. My mother can barely function. I would be happy to help with Pastor Maggie's office."

Bill quickly did the math in his head. Fitch's dad would have died right around the time he was building the ramp and brick wall in front of the church.

"We're all sorry to hear about the loss of your father. Where does your mother live?" Mrs. Abernathy asked kindly.

"In Phoenix. A retirement village. She has some neighbors who check in on her, but the reports aren't too good." Fitch looked at the faces around him and felt his face get hot.

"Let's get this old carpet out to the dumpster," Hank said a little too loudly. "Give us a hand here, Fitch."

Fitch put down his clipboard and man-bag. He hung his coat on the back of Hank's chair and grabbed an end of the rolled carpet.

Irena had taken in this whole scene. She turned to leave and whispered to herself, "Deth ees de stealer of all happiness."

Fitch was a hard worker, but seemed to be as accident-prone as the rumors around town purported.

"Fitch! Watch out for that paint can!"

"Fitch . . . whoa, don't trip over that old carpet."

"Fitch, Fitch, Fitch! Look out for that—" *Thwap!* ". . . door."

"Fitch, are you okay?"

Fitch seemed to be able to trip and fall over any object in his vicinity. The collision with the door left him with a bruise on his temple. He didn't mind. He couldn't remember the last time anyone had been concerned about his well-being. It felt nice.

Removing the furniture and ripping up the carpet had laid bare some disgusting remnants of old and rotted vegetables. There were dried-out potatoes, withered carrots, shriveled onions, and moldy squash. The squished tomatoes were particularly difficult to see. It looked as if a farmer's market had vomited all over Pastor Maggie's empty office.

"Sylvia," Mrs. Abernathy said, looking down her long, thin nose, "I recommend you not bring vegetables to this office again. I declare this a vegetable-free zone. Either grow less or find other victims to share your surplus with."

Sylvia looked stricken, but everyone else mentally bowed down and worshiped Mrs. Abernathy. Sylvia's vegetables were simply out of hand.

Fitch looked at Sylvia and whispered, "I like vegetables, Miss Smits."

Sylvia smiled at him. "That's good to know, Fitch. You can count on fresh vegetables this summer."

"And you know, we can still plan that new greenhouse you wanted to build behind your shop," Fitch continued.

Now it was Sylvia's turn to blush. "Yes. I still don't know about that, Fitch." She felt guilty about the trick she had played on Fitch in the fall. "Maybe there will be a time this year."

Bill watched the exchange in silent dread. He knew he couldn't sit around with his mouth shut anymore. Was Fitch flirting with Sylvia? Was Sylvia blushing?

After the anti-vegetable speech, Mrs. Abernathy looked to Hank for leadership on what to do next. It was the old, dark paneling. Removing the paneling took lots of muscle and the use of crow bars and power sanders. The men were all in little-boy heaven. Cate had proven herself to be freakishly strong, but of course, she was quite a bit younger than the rest of the demo team. She had enjoyed ripping up the carpet and was quite adept with a chisel as she scraped the paneling away from the cement on the walls.

Mrs. Abernathy, Pamela, Sylvia, Marla, and Doris all tried to stay ahead of the destruction by throwing remnants away as quickly as possible, but they finally made another pot of coffee and waited for the demolition work to be complete. Ellen showed up after her shift at the hospital and was thrilled with the mess. She was also slightly shocked to see Fitch Dervish as he carried out several pieces of ugly paneling.

Ellen had plans to clean the parsonage, stock the refrigerator with all of Pastor Maggie's favorites, and throw in a few cat toys to boot. She missed Marmalade and Cheerio almost as much as she missed Maggie.

Sylvia had brought paint samples and carpet swatches. She also had a catalog of office furniture. The council had authorized a sub-committee—mainly Sylvia, Bill, Ellen, Hank, and Doris—to bring recommendations for the new office décor. It wasn't hard to agree on colors for walls and carpet to brighten up the room. Ellen and Sylvia had dog-eared pages in the furniture catalog with more feminine-looking furniture in smaller sizes. Sometimes Pastor Maggie had looked like a child sitting behind the dark old "castle desk" that had been in residence for far too long.

The Salvation Army truck came and hauled the old furniture away at five in the afternoon. Mrs. Popkin's dumpster was returned, with an agreement from the waste company that they would come and empty it first thing Monday morning.

The office was completely bare, and it already looked lighter. The worker bees, mainly the female bees, cleaned up the dusty, dirty mess once they got the men out. The men left to pick up pizza, and when they returned, everyone went down to the church dining room to feast. It was a good day. The hard work had made everyone hungry, but they also felt hopeful for the future. Pastor Maggie would come back to them. She must.

"I sure hope Pastor Maggie will be okay," Fitch said taking a huge bite of pizza.

"We all agree with you, Fitch," Hank said. "It will be good to have her back in Cherish."

Everyone around that table knew what kind of reputation Fitch had around town. That day he had proven some of their thoughts wrong. Maybe he was an annoying building inspector, but he was also a lonely man who had recently lost his father and was worried about his mother. That day he had been surrounded by a kind community of people. It had buoyed his soul. It had also changed some minds about what kind of man he was.

Fitch also thought Sylvia Smits was quite a sweet lady. Maybe he could help her with her new greenhouse after all.

After the quick dinner and cleanup, everyone said good night with lots of see you in the mornings. Sylvia offered to turn out the lights and lock up the church. Bill quietly stayed with her. They walked together into Maggie's empty office and looked around.

"Bill, this was the best idea ever," Sylvia said. "I'm so glad you thought of it and knew exactly what had to be done. The way you explained it to the council seemed to turn a light bulb on in everyone's head." Sylvia laughed.

Bill thought he had never heard anything as beautiful as that laugh. He looked at the ground.

"Thanks. It was a good day. Even Fitch couldn't ruin our fun." He looked to see how she would respond to Fitch's name.

"Nope. He sure couldn't. And I think he actually needed us. He's a lonely man. He sure is clumsy, though." Sylvia laughed, then immediately felt guilty.

Bill exhaled and relaxed a little.

"I think it was a great day, even with Mrs. Abernathy's lecture on my vegetables. Sometimes I wonder how that woman was raised. She can be so harsh."

"Maybe we can come up with another idea for some of your vegetables."

"Really? Like what?" Sylvia never knew quiet Bill Baxter was such a problem solver.

"Let me think about it. We have some time yet, right?" Bill asked.

"Yes. My first harvest of the greenhouse will be sometime in May."

"Then how about I walk you home tonight and we'll think about vegetables a little later?"

Bill took her hand. They finished turning out the lights and locked up the church. Bill held Sylvia's hand all the way back to her house.

She held his hand back.

Maggie brought the stack of mail up to her room. The cards and letters had begun to arrive on Wednesday. She had quite a stack on her desk now. They were all unopened. She wanted to climb back into bed but forced herself to put on her running clothes. She hadn't had a run in over a week. *Maybe I'll just walk. And I can turn around after one block*

if I want. I don't have to go far or fast. She kept on with these internal deals with herself.

She went downstairs and told her mother she would be out for just a bit. Mimi was relieved. Maggie needed to get out of her room.

She ran eight miles. She had lost all track of time until she realized she was four miles from home. She turned and easily ran the four miles back. When she arrived back home, she felt elated and exhausted.

"I was getting a little worried about you. The afternoon is disappearing," Mimi said much more calmly than she felt.

"I ran without thinking until I realized I was four miles away," Maggie said, her face still bright red from the exercise and cold air. "But it felt good." She was huffing and puffing. Marmalade came up to her, gave her a sniff, and turned away. "I might call Jo. What do you think?"

"I think that is a good idea," Mimi said with typical brevity.

Maggie cleaned up, threw her clothes in the washing machine, and made a peanut butter sandwich. After eating, she took a deep breath and picked up the phone.

"Hello?" Jo's voice came through the line.

"Jo, this is Maggie. Is this a good time to call?" Maggie felt her voice weaken.

"Maggie. Oh, Maggie, it is good to hear your voice. Where are you?" Jo sounded like Jo, and that gave Maggie courage.

"I'm in Zeeland. I've been here for about a week now. I want to know how you are doing."

"Zeeland? For the past week? Are you all right, dear?" Jo stepped into her usual caretaker role.

"Jo, I'm calling about you." Maggie kept up the caretaker sparring tournament.

"Maggie, are you busy? I mean right now?"

"No."

"Would you like to come over or meet somewhere?"

"I can be at your house in a few minutes. I would really like that."

"I'll have the tea on."

When Maggie arrived, the tea was on. The table was set with cups, saucers, the creamer, and the sugar bowl.

Jo poured out the tea.

Maggie poured out her heart.

Maggie told Jo what had happened in Cherish on Ash Wednesday and the four horrible days which followed. She told Jo of driving home and basically hiding in her bedroom for a week. She told Jo how guilty she felt for grieving for Ed when Jo had lost her husband, best friend, and life-mate. Maggie's guilt seemed to surmount her grief as she searched for Jo's forgiveness and affirmation. When Maggie looked back on this conversation, she would cringe. It was buoyed by selfishness guised in caring for Jo.

When Jo looked back on this conversation, she would remember a young woman just getting her footing in the world of ministry—a woman who had idolized Jo's husband and loved Jo too. Jo could overlook the bit of selfishness, knowing ministry would blow that out of her soon enough.

"I'm so angry at God. Aren't you, Jo?" Maggie asked. "How are we supposed to say he's any good? He's a dirty thief. He destroys life and then laughs at us when we cry about it. I hate God."

That was the most honest Maggie had been and the harshest. Jo was relieved. She knew Maggie needed to get angry, really angry, to be able to move on. Maggie felt her hands begin to shake and a chill in her shoulders.

"Jo, tell me what to do. Please?" Maggie's tears dripped silently into her tea. "I don't know what to do. I can't work for a God I don't love and who doesn't love me. But I can't abandon people I've made vows to. Why are ordination services so similar to marriage ceremonies?"

Maggie's nose started running. Jo handed her a tissue.

"Maggie, you are what I would call a snarl-ball of conflict. At some point you will untangle, but only you will know when. May I make a suggestion?"

"Of course." Maggie looked at Jo and saw her fatigue.

"There is something I have been doing for a few days now. A good friend of mine suggested it after Ed died. Each night I write a letter from Ed to me. He tells me a variety of things. Whatever comes into my head that I think he'd say, I write it down. I always sign the letters the way he signed every loving note or card he ever gave me. It helps. You might want to try it, Maggie. Write a letter from Ed. What would he tell you to do now? What would he think was best? What would he tell you about Cherish, your parishioners, and even Jack?"

Maggie was startled at Jack's name. "He's sent me a bouquet of red carnations every day this week," Maggie said quietly.

"I wonder what Ed would say about that?" Jo said, not wondering at all.

Maggie could sense it was time to leave. She didn't want to. Being near Jo was like being near Ed, but she stood and cleared the table.

When Jo walked her to the front door, Maggie hugged the older woman for a long time.

"Thanks, Jo. May I call you in a couple of days?"

"Of course. Call or stop by. I love having you here, Maggie."

When Maggie had gone, Jo sat down in her quiet, empty living room. She put her head in her hands and began to weep.

Maggie returned home and gave each of her parents a kiss on the head. Then she went upstairs and sat at her desk. She took a deep breath and pulled out a sheet of stationery and a pen. She stared at the paper, then glanced around the room. Her eyes rested on the book *Learning to Walk in the Dark*. Maggie picked up the book, opened the cover, and reread the inscription from Ed. She sat very still for twenty minutes. Finally, she picked up the pen.

Dear Maggie, . . .

28

The second Sunday of Lent saw a full church in Cherish. Perhaps it was people being nosy, or maybe it was people needing to feel connected to one another because of the uncertainty of their pastor.

Cate had taken Maggie's Sunday school class that morning. All the youth were there, along with the requisite box of donuts. Although every crumb of the donuts was eaten, no one was eating with any enthusiasm. The parsonage felt empty and cold. Marmalade and Cheerio didn't interrupt Sunday school, as was their habit. It was glaringly obvious that Pastor Maggie had disappeared.

"When will Pastor Maggie be back?" Addie asked. She must have known the answer, and she must have felt her mother's concern at home. Marla was a mess.

"We don't know exactly," said Cate. "She is going through a rough time right now, which is why, this morning in Sunday school, we are going to spend our time writing her notes. I will mail them right after church so that she'll have them in a couple of days."

Cate pulled out note cards and pens and passed them around. She thought she might get some complaints, especially from the boys, who hated anything that resembled homework, but they all settled in and wrote their notes.

Dear Pastor Maggie,

I'm sorry you are feeling bad. I hope you feel better soon. Cate is nice, but I miss Marmalade and Cheerio. And you too. Please come back soon. Also, we're gonna have to listen to boring people in church while you are gone. I don't like it much.

Sincerely,
Mason Tuggle

Dear Pastor Maggie,

There is a big surprise waiting here for you when you get back. My mom told Addie and me all about it. It's pretty cool. I bet you can't even guess what it is. I've been busy with baseball training. I have to be at the high school gym every morning at 5:00 a.m.

Jason Wiggins

Dear Pastor Maggie,

It's been cold here. I don't like February. It's a dumb month. We have had a lot of snow. Are you having a lot of snow where you are? Mason and I got in trouble at school this week. I won't tell you why. Boy, was my mom mad!

Brock Tuggle

Dear Pastor Maggie,

Brock and Mason got in trouble at school this week for hiding all the violin bows in orchestra. They have detention every day next week. My mom is so mad! She said, "The police chief's children acting so heinously! Detention is the least of your worries!" I don't know what she's going to do, but it will be good. Sorry you're not here to see it!

Love,
Liz Tuggle

Dear Pastor Maggie,

Mom says you are very sad. I am sorry to hear that. You make all of us so happy, even when you make us dress up in costumes and act out Bible people. I hope your sadness relents (that's a new word I learned in English. It means "to surrender or yield"). I will be so happy to see you back again. We all will.

Lots of love,
Addie Wiggins

Cate got a chuckle from reading all the notes and hoped Maggie would too. She added her own heartfelt note to the stack and slipped them in her backpack to mail after church.

Ellen led the worship service with Irena's depressing Lenten music. The service only lasted forty-five minutes. No one complained.

Secretly, the demolition/decorating crew could hardly wait for everyone to leave after coffee time so they could get back to their project. They all had brought their work clothes and changed quickly after the last coffee pot was washed and put away.

With so much cement on the walls, the group had quite a time sanding it all down to make the surface smooth and ready for paint. Bill had brought his Shop-Vac to suck up what was left of the scraped cement and carpet padding remnants. As they looked around, they were all pleased. They would meet again the next evening.

"I'll bring the paint and trays and brushes," Sylvia said with authority. "Then we must choose the carpet and the furniture. Bill, Tom, and Fitch will lay the carpet themselves. I know we are all grateful to them for this." Sylvia was only looking at Bill as she spoke. "So, we'll meet back here at seven tomorrow night."

Everyone prepared to leave, but Bill pretended to contemplate the walls in Pastor Maggie's office. He would walk Sylvia home again. Unfortunately, Fitch also seemed to be hanging around, waiting for Sylvia.

"Sylvia, do you need a ride home tonight?" Fitch finally said. "I'd be happy to give you a ride in my truck."

Sylvia looked confused for a moment. Then she caught on. "Oh, thanks, Fitch, but I always walk to and from church. I don't live far away."

"I'd be happy to drive you," Fitch persisted.

Bill pretended to organize the tools in his toolbox and listened with frustration.

"I'm fine, Fitch. But thank you. Will you be back tomorrow night?"

"I sure will."

Fitch reluctantly left the church. He would have to think of another way to spend time with Sylvia.

Once the church was locked up, Bill didn't waste a second to take Sylvia's hand in his.

"I've had an idea for your vegetables," he said as they walked together.

"Really? What is it?" Sylvia asked, amazed at his brilliance.

"Soup."

"Soup?"

"Yes. Lots of soup for the shut-ins, the sick, church suppers. Soup freezes great. We'll make soup." Bill smiled shyly.

"We'll make soup!"

Sylvia took her hand back and linked her elbow through his. She felt a thrill. It might have been the thought of soup, but she was sure it was the feel of Bill's arm wrapped around hers. He made her feel safe.

Mrs. Abernathy had been absent from the cement-scraping party at church. It was the first Sunday of the month and the official shut-in visitation day. She had discovered a few more shut-ins that had not made Hank's original list. She made a point of visiting each one. She would have to let Pastor Maggie know of these few that had fallen through the cracks over the years. Several were still in their own homes but could not get out for church or other activities. Mrs. Abernathy felt their loneliness and lengthened her stay with each one. She promised to return in the middle of the week. There was no way Pastor Maggie could keep up with all of these lonely people. Mrs. Abernathy would just have to continue with some visitations herself.

When she got to Marvin's room at the Friendly Elder Care, she figuratively girded her loins for battle. Marvin was sitting in his chair, staring out at the dark sky.

"Good afternoon, Marvin," Mrs. Abernathy said in her most Mrs. Abernathy voice.

He turned and looked at her. "What do you want?" he said trying to sound gruff but actually sounding like a three-year-old child.

"You know why I'm here. Don't be a fool. I'm here to shed Christian love on you," Mrs. Abernathy clipped.

"How many times do I have to tell you and that little one that I don't want visits?" Again, his voice had no oomph to it. Marvin looked like a deflated balloon.

"You will have to tell Pastor Maggie and myself every time we walk into your room. I know you like the visits. You can't fool me, Marvin.

I also know that you hate being trapped in here and trapped in a body that won't do what you tell it to do anymore. You're old, Marvin. But you're not dead. What if we find a way to get you to church one of these days? You could see some of your old friends and see a lot of new people."

Mrs. Abernathy was already hatching a plan to bring many of the shut-ins back to church. It would only take a few willing people with cars.

"Why would I want to do that? See a bunch of people I don't know? No!"

"I'll take that as a yes," Mrs. Abernathy said tartly.

"And when's that little one gonna get back? Why's she gone? Clergy aren't allowed to have vacation, are they? They never did when I was in the church. I want to know where she is!"

Mrs. Abernathy kept control of her emotions. "Of course clergy take vacations. Otherwise they would die taking care of people like you all the time. She will be back when she's back. She is still with her parents in Zeeland."

When leaving Marvin's room, Mrs. Abernathy felt the same relief she had felt the last time.

Her last visit of the day was Howard Baker. He was slowly able to make a few steps without his cane and was proud as a peacock to show this to Verna, who was delighted.

"Howard, you are walking splendidly! Your doctor must be so pleased."

"She is. She thinks I'm brilliant. Her name is Dr. Charlene Kessler. She works with our Dr. Elliot. She reminds me of Pastor Maggie. She's always smiling, and I'm not sure, but I think she has a crush on me. I'm pretty sure Pastor Maggie does too." He laughed. "But when is Pastor Maggie going to be back in Cherish? Not that I want you to stop visiting me, Verna. I have a strong expectation of seeing you at least three or four times a week. What do you say about that?"

Verna smiled. "I wonder, Howard, do you by chance like cats?"

Howard gave her a saucy smile.

Sylvia was sure Bill was far too shy to ever kiss her. That's why she was happily shocked when he gently pushed her up against her front door, held her face in his hands, and gave her a long, slow kiss. It was definitely movie-worthy. It took her a good five minutes after he said good night to get her legs working properly again.

In Zeeland, it was the Friday of Maggie's second week at home. She had spent most of the week trying to find places for the daily bouquets of red carnations, going out for long runs, and writing letters to herself from Ed. They were helping. She still hadn't opened any of the mail from Cherish. The stack was growing each day, but she couldn't bring herself to read familiar and even unfamiliar handwriting from folks wishing her well or telling her of things she wasn't (she thought) interested in reading about Cherish and Loving the Lord.

Maggie had called Jo twice since her last visit. They made plans for Maggie to visit again the following Monday. For tea and sympathy.

That afternoon, however, would be spent with Nora and Dan. Maggie was going to see her seminary friends and hear about their wedding plans. The wedding date was set for Saturday, July 4th. This date was chosen so that family from faraway places would have the third of July to travel to Holland. It also worked well that the Jesus Lives and So Do We! megachurch butted up against Lake Macatawa. There would be a splendid fireworks display over the lake for Dan and Nora's reception, thanks to the city of Holland.

The three friends met at Nora's apartment. Maggie got there before Dan.

"Maggie, how are you doing?" Nora asked.

"I miss Ed. And trying not to feel sorry for myself too much."

"What have you heard from Cherish since you've been home? I bet they are missing you terribly."

"I don't have any idea what's going on in Cherish," Maggie said quietly. "I have a stack of mail I can't seem to open. I receive a bouquet of red carnations every day from Jack. But I don't know what's going on." Actually hearing it said out loud, she was as surprised as Nora.

Dan arrived with sandwiches and drinks. The conversation quickly changed to the wedding. The afternoon flew past with all the details of bridesmaid dresses, flowers, tuxedos, cake, and the photographer. Then they talked about what really mattered: the ceremony. Nora and Dan had put a lot of work into a parents' blessing and choosing the verses Maggie would read and preach from. They had chosen special music (which would be sung by Nora's cousin) and two congregational hymns. They wanted to use traditional vows instead of writing their own. And they'd found three wedding blessings—one Gaelic, one Native American, and one from the *Book of Common Prayer*. They hadn't decided yet which one they would use. Maggie suggested using all three, with different readers from the congregation. Dan and Nora liked that idea.

Maggie took detailed notes on everything. All in all, since never having a class in seminary on how to do a wedding, Maggie ended the afternoon feeling quite prepared.

"How long are you going to stay in Zeeland?" Dan asked as Nora searched Maggie's eyes.

"I'm not sure. It hurts to think about it."

"Maggie," Nora said impatiently, "living hurts. Whether you like it or not, God's fingerprints are all over you. You can't do *anything* but be in the church!" Nora sounded more upset than encouraging. "Do you think Ed died because God randomly kills for fun? You know better. If Ed heard you talk this way, he . . . he . . . oh, Maggie." Nora took her friend's hands. "Maggie, he would be heartbroken."

"I know that," Maggie said. "Jo suggested I write letters from Ed to myself. I have been doing that. It hurts, but it helps. Last night I wrote a letter to him. That helped too. I know I can't leave the church. I just haven't figured out how to stay."

Dan put his arm around Maggie's shoulders. "Maybe opening that stack of mail from Cherish would be a start."

He smiled, and Nora moved in for a group hug.

Maggie made a quick stop at the store before heading home. When she arrived, Mimi and Dirk were sitting in the kitchen. Mimi was doing her daily crossword puzzle, and Dirk was looking at some architectural plans that could have been for the hull of a ship, a children's playground, or a space station. Maggie knew her dad was brilliant, she just had no idea how he did his work.

"How are Dan and Nora?" Mimi asked without looking up.

"Oh, perfect and madly in love, blah, blah, blah," Maggie said, smiling.

She began to unpack her grocery bag. Mimi did look up then. Flour, butter, caramel, cream cheese, vanilla, apples. That was the moment Mimi knew Maggie would be okay.

Maggie was baking a pie.

With the caramel apple pie cooling on the kitchen counter, Maggie went upstairs and put the stack of Cherish mail on her bed. One by one, she opened the letters. She didn't try to control her emotions. Some of the letters made her laugh. She could hear Irena's accent when she read that letter.

Pastooor Maggie,

What you tink you doing? We cannot have more pulpeet shlop. You come beck now and we work it out, okay? Remember, everry budy has to die. It is what it is.

Irena Dulca

All the notes from the youth made her smile. She could just see Mason and Brock hiding all the violin bows in orchestra. Cate was so sweet to force them all to write. She opened envelope after envelope. One was a complete surprise.

Little one,

I hear you're gone. Are you gone for good? Although you are very annoying, that old biddy who is coming up here to visit me is much worse. Now she's saying I have to come back to church. I won't do it! Do you understand me? And why do you have a male secretary? I called for your address, and some man said he ran the office. What in the hell is going on at that church anyway?

Marvin Green

Maggie laughed until she was crying with hysterics. Letter after letter worked their way into her grieving heart. Especially the one she saved for last.

My Maggie,

How are you? I ask you that insane question because I actually want to know. I want to know how you are physically (are you sleeping and eating?). I want to know how you are emotionally (I want to wipe away your tears). I want to know how you are spiritually (I worry your soul has taken a pretty big hit). It is hard to be here without you. But I hope you are finding comfort in Zeeland with your parents and also with Jo.

Maggie, this may sound like undue pressure, but I

want to be clear: I'm not actually willing to live without you. I didn't know that I had been waiting for you to be in my life, but that is the case. So, however it happens, I will be with you, My Maggie. You are the woman I want to give red carnations to for the rest of my life.

I love you.
Your Jack

Maggie took out a piece of stationery and a pen. She stopped, took a deep breath, and started to write. She was quietly crying, but she didn't have that awful pain in her stomach.

Dear Maggie,

It's time to go back. When you are ready, go back to Cherish.
Cherish is where your heart belongs.
You will continue to love well there.
Not just Jack, but every member of your beautiful congregation.
And just a reminder, God gave them to you—for you to love and to cherish.

Ed

Maggie put the letter with the rest of the letters from Ed. Then she crawled into bed, and for the first time in days, she didn't cry herself to sleep.

∞

The third Sunday of Lent was cold and gray. That's how everyone felt as they entered the church. Hank was on board to "speak" for the morning, and Irena was already bellowing away on the organ. At least Hank had some good news for the congregation. When they were all seated, he stood behind the pulpit and announced, "Friends, Pastor Maggie is coming back!"

That wasn't exactly how he had wanted to make the announcement, but he just blurted it out like a child on Christmas morning opening a most-beloved present.

"She has spoken with our council chairperson, Harold Brinkmeyer, and myself." He grinned. "She plans to return within the next few days. She is thankful for all the cards and apparently some flowers she has received while at her home in Zeeland. We can thank God for this good news!"

Jack thought quietly to himself, *She called me too, Hank. She called me first.* He smiled.

The congregation erupted in applause. Sylvia and Bill looked at each other. They had to get the new office finished. They would have to get the furniture delivered earlier than planned. Bill and Tom had just finished the carpet the night before. Sylvia had stayed with them. She handed them tools she didn't recognize and stared at Bill while he worked.

The office was a work of art. The walls had been painted what was called "lemon cream," which was a lovely soft yellow. The carpeting was another pastel: "seafoam green." The pale yellow and green looked fresh and spring-like. The new furniture was a delicate Victorian style, with rounded corners and pretty scrolls around the edges of the desk, work table, and bookshelves, all painted a pale cream. Sylvia could hardly wait to see the entire office put together.

There was be something else Pastor Maggie would have to "put together" when she got back to Cherish.

The night before, smelling like new carpet, Bill had waited for Tom and Fitch to leave. Fitch had slowly realized Sylvia wasn't interested in a romance with him, but then again, no woman ever had been.

Once they were gone, Bill had stood on the brand-new carpet, then fallen to one knee. He pulled together every ounce of courage he possessed and took a small box out of his pocket.

"I know we haven't dated very long. But I know for sure how much I love you. And I know I want to make vegetable soup with you for the rest of my life. Sylvia, will you marry me?"

Sylvia fell to her knees too. Her eyes were filled with happy tears. Bill was asking her to marry him. Right in Pastor Maggie's new office! It was so romantic.

"Yes, Bill! I will marry you. And I will make soup with you for as long as we both shall live."

29

Maggie made another visit to Jo, bringing the latest bouquet of carnations, which was supposed to be the last, along with some peanut butter cookies. Ed had told her once they were Jo's favorites. The two women had cookies and tea while Maggie told Jo of her plans.

"I feel like I need to tiptoe back to Cherish in a way," Maggie said. "I think you know what I mean when I say I can't handle too much kindness."

Jo nodded, taking another cookie. "People are so kind, generous, and thoughtful. Sometimes I want someone to be rude to me at the grocery store or anywhere. Then I wouldn't feel like a piece of china anymore. It will be good for you to get back."

"I'll be in Cherish for the end of Lent, but it sounds as if they have everything covered. I'll need to deal with Holy Week." Maggie didn't want to think about that just yet.

"Ed loved Holy Week," Jo said. "He never tired of the one week in the church year that takes all of humankind straight to the grave and then out of it again. He loved the truth and the mystery of it."

Maggie smiled. "Jo, I'm sorry for last week. I didn't know where I fit. Your grief is something I can't begin to understand. You and Ed loved each other so much. You were a strange and unordinary couple because of your love. I don't know if I will ever see anything like it again. I'm really sorry for my selfishness and maybe even my intrusion. If you would like me to do something rude to you now to make you feel better, I'll happily do so."

Jo smiled and then became serious. "Maggie, will you visit me? I want to see you when you're in town. I even want to be selfish and take you away from your family and drink tea with you."

"I promise."

Maggie stayed a long time that afternoon. Then she said goodbye to Jo, who sat alone with her shredded heart. Jo's work now was to figure out her new life without her husband.

The week before Pastor Maggie's return was one of crazed busyness at Loving the Lord. Sylvia, who was not wearing the pretty sapphire ring Bill had given her yet, wanted Pastor Maggie's office to be perfect. Both Sylvia and Bill wanted Pastor Maggie to be home before they shared their good news.

Ellen was at the parsonage to clean and stock the pantry. She got everything in order, especially turning up the thermostat so Maggie could walk into a warm home. She noticed it had been turned down to fifty-five degrees by someone. Ellen thought she knew who, and she wondered when the locks would be changed on the parsonage doors.

Happy Hank was preparing all the bulletins through Easter so that Pastor Maggie could see everything ahead of time. Doris was cleaning the church with military zeal. Irena had been seen smiling. Mrs. Popkin was preparing an extra-large batch of hot cross buns for coffee time on Sunday. Marla had worked with the children for the coming Sunday's service and was thrilled to be able to welcome Pastor Maggie back to the fold via the children.

Jack could barely concentrate all week. He and Maggie talked on the phone every day now. He stopped the flower deliveries, at her request, but there would certainly be flowers waiting when she arrived at the parsonage. He just wanted to hold her and smell her hair.

Maggie was doing both physical and mental preparations. She did her laundry. She helped her mother clean the house. She bought a notebook and began writing daily entries of things she wanted Ed to know and things she thought he would want her to know. She saw Nora and Dan for coffee and, without realizing it, relieved both of them. She was moving forward.

In Cherish one afternoon, Mrs. Abernathy was petting Caroline. There was a fire burning in the fireplace and tea brewing. It was one of those cold, windy, March days that were meant for staying inside. Caroline was now a luxurious cat with long calico fur and large green eyes. Mrs. Abernathy was certain that not even Cheerio could compare to Caroline's beauty. But what Mrs. Abernathy really thought about was Pastor Maggie coming home.

What a relief it would be to have her back in the parsonage and back in the pulpit. When Mrs. Abernathy thought back to the first Sunday evening in June, when the search committee had welcomed their new pastor into the parsonage with a pizza supper, it seemed like centuries ago. Mrs. Abernathy had been silently against calling the young woman from Zeeland to their church, but the other search committee members were gung-ho for Pastor Margaret Elzinga.

It had been nine and a half months since that pizza supper. Nine and half months of new experiences and so much excitement in the church. Maggie had brought different ideas, and Mrs. Abernathy fought them off tooth and nail. Now she would happily follow Maggie through raging waters and roaring fires. Visiting the shut-ins had given her another insight into her pastor's life. Why was it that people thought pastors sat around reading Augustine and Aquinas all day long?

In the midst of her memories and musings, the front doorbell rang out. Caroline jumped, mainly because she rarely heard a noise in her large, silent home. Mrs. Abernathy went to the door and was astonished to see Howard Baker standing there without a cane. She looked and saw his car parked in her driveway. So much for being a shut-in.

"Howard Baker, what on earth are you doing out on a day like this? You don't even have your cane. What's the matter with you? Come inside at once before you slip and fall and need more knee surgery."

She grabbed his arm and led him inside. Howard grinned all the way. He obediently handed over his coat and hat and then let himself be directed to a chair near the fireplace. The plan was working perfectly. He took the proffered cup of tea and a slice of date nut bread.

"Now, tell me what you are doing here," Mrs. Abernathy insisted.

"Well," Howard said with a bit of a smirk, "I thought it was time to meet your cat." He was enjoying this immensely.

"My . . . cat?" Mrs. Abernathy was flabbergasted. "You came out in this weather, without your cane?"

"You already mentioned that," Howard said, helping himself to more date nut bread.

"To see my cat?"

"I figured I would need her approval."

"Caroline's approval? For what?"

Howard looked Verna in the eye and smiled a naughty smile.

"To ask you on a date, my dear Verna. May I take you to dinner?"

On Monday, March 16th, Dirk helped Maggie pack up her Dodge Caliber. Last to go in were the two cat carriers with their disgruntled inmates. The howls and protests began immediately.

"I don't envy your drive with all that noise," Mimi said grimly.

"I'll put the classical music station on. Maybe the music will calm them. Isn't that what you teach in your psychology classes?"

"That's for babies. Not beasts."

"I'll let you know if it works. Thanks for everything, Mom and Dad. You gave me quite a gift these three weeks. You knew what I needed to do from the start, but you let me figure it out for myself. Always the way I seem to learn anything. So, you'll come to Cherish for Easter?" She sounded slightly plaintive.

"Of course," Dirk said. "You don't think we would miss your first Easter sermon, plus something delicious to eat afterward, do you?"

Dirk hugged his girl tightly. Both he and Mimi hoped Maggie was ready to go back, but only time would tell.

"We will be there, Maggie. And that's less than three weeks away." Mimi knew that Maggie did well when there was a practical time frame. It worked. "Right! Three weeks. I love you both!"

She hugged and kissed them.

Then she headed east.

As she got closer to Cherish, her nerves began their first fluttery flight. Part of what she felt was embarrassment. It was as if she had gone AWOL from her ministry. So immature. But then, all the cards and letters from her parishioners reminded her they understood. They cared. Mrs. Abernathy had written something so beautiful Maggie could have sworn it was forged by someone else. She would take it slow. She would make her way back into church life carefully. She would apologize. She would be thankful.

It was noon when she drove down Main Street. When she got to Middle Street, she turned right. Everything looked quiet. She pulled into the parsonage driveway, turned off the engine, and took a very deep breath. Unfortunately, her car companions did not afford her the luxury of more than one breath. She opened the door, grabbed the cat carriers, and walked up to the front door.

"Pastor Maggie! Pastor Maggie!"

Maggie turned to look across the street. Mrs. Popkin, wrapped in her large white apron, was waving from The Sugarplum's open door. Maggie set down the carriers and waved back.

"Hi, Mrs. Popkin!"

"I'm glad you're back, Pastor Maggie! We all are!" She blew Maggie a kiss then went back inside the shop.

Maggie brought the cats through the front door and unloaded the rest of her car quickly. Fortunately, she hadn't brought too many possessions to her parents' house. What a relief she hadn't packed up all her books. What had she been thinking?

The parsonage was spotless and smelled wonderful. The heater was turned up to seventy-eight degrees. Maggie turned it down to seventy-two. Marmalade and Cheerio let their noses take the lead as they sniffed familiar smells and reexplored their home. There was a doubly large bouquet of red carnations on the dining room table. Maggie buried her face in their spiciness and breathed deeply.

In the kitchen, there were two large bunches of bananas along with a bakery box of Mrs. Popkin's treats on the counter. Maggie peeked inside. The sweet smells of cinnamon, vanilla, fried donuts, and cranberry bars wafted out. She broke off a corner of a cranberry bar and put it in her mouth. *Mmmm.* The refrigerator was full of fresh fruit, milk, yogurt, and other perishables. The pantry had five cylinders of oatmeal, two large jugs of maple syrup, and several bags of popcorn. Maggie laughed. Her habits were well known. Then she saw a note on the table.

Hi, Pastor Maggie!

Welcome home. We are all so happy you are back. Please find food in the refrigerator to get you through the week. Marla said she is all set for church on Sunday, so just settle in. I can't wait to share a bowl of popcorn with you soon!

Love,
Ellen

Maggie walked through the parsonage and seemed to gain strength as she walked from room to room. Her cell phone rang. She pulled it from her pocket and smiled when she saw who the caller was.

"Jack?" Her voice was smiling.

"My Maggie?"

"Oh, Jack! It's so good to hear your voice. I want to see your face."

"Do you have dinner plans?" Jack teased.

"Yes. You're taking me on a date, and I'm going to apologize for being a lousy girlfriend."

"I am taking you on a date. But if you apologize, I'll have to bring you home immediately." He used his fierce doctor voice, the one he used with uncooperative patients. Then his voice changed. "But really, how are you feeling about being back?"

"It feels good to be back. I feel totally loved by this congregation. I don't think there's another congregation like this in the entire world."

"You are loved. But remember, you taught us how to do that. Don't forget it. I'll see you at six o'clock."

After they hung up, Maggie made a cup of Lady Grey tea and slowly unpacked her clothes. Marmalade and Cheerio were already curled up on her bed. Apparently, they were over the trauma of the car ride.

At four o'clock, the Westminster chimes rang. Maggie went to the front door and was happy to see Sylvia standing there.

"Sylvia, I've missed you." Maggie was surprised at the level of emotion she was feeling. Her head felt dizzy, and she blinked to keep the tears at bay.

Sylvia didn't blink. Her eyes filled like a fountain. "Pastor Maggie, we have been waiting for you. Are you feeling all right?"

Maggie ushered Sylvia inside and gave her a big hug.

"I am, Sylvia. It's good to be back, and it's good to see your face."

"I've come to invite you next door, if you're up to it, that is."

"To church?" Maggie asked.

"Yes. To church."

"Well, sure. Let me get my coat." Maggie wondered what Sylvia was up to and happily remembered it was still too early for vegetables.

The two women walked into the sanctuary, and Maggie closed her eyes for a moment. The smell overwhelmed her. The old wooden pews rubbed with Murphy's Oil Soap. The musty but newly vacuumed carpet. The smell of ancient books on the shelves in the gathering area.

This sanctuary held the smells of holy, sacred happiness. But there was something new in the aromas of her church.

Sylvia led Maggie into Hank's office. No Hank. The door to her office was closed.

Sylvia said, "Open it."

Maggie opened the door to her office, but she couldn't believe what was on the other side. A pale-green lamp was lit on a lovely cream-colored desk. All the furniture matched this warm creamy color. The walls were the most delicate yellow, and the carpet below her feet was the same shade of green as the lamp on her desk.

She stopped in the doorway and gave a slight gasp. Her eyes took in every detail.

"I think I've walked right into a daffodil," Maggie said quietly. "Sylvia, this is beautiful. How did you do this?"

Sylvia turned Maggie around. Standing in Hank's office were Hank, Pamela, Doris, Tom, Marla, Mrs. Abernathy, Bill, Harold, Cate, and Fitch Dervish. No one seemed to know what to do. Everyone watched Maggie and tried to take their cues from her. Maggie tried to absorb the enormity of what these incredible people had done for her—because they had done it for *her*. This was not just any pastor's office. This office was lovingly created for Maggie alone.

She moved into the circle of tentative faces and reached out her arms. One at a time she embraced each friend, looking them straight in the eye and saying simply, "Thank you."

"Pastor Maggie," Fitch said hoarsely, "I'm glad you're back. I missed you."

Maggie's reentry into Loving the Lord and life in Cherish went gently along. Soon she removed the few rags of guilt and embarrassment she had carried around. She'd left Cherish grieving for Ed, but she returned because it was the only place she could truly heal. She never forgot it, that first look at her new office, which she knew wasn't the real gift. The gift had been the hands and hearts that created it.

Maggie and Jack were spending part of each day together. It might be grabbing a quick lunch or dinner at the parsonage. Friday nights were becoming regular date nights. The whole church knew, and it was one of the favorite pieces of gossip whenever two or three were gathered.

Maggie also prepared for Easter. She and Irena took Hank's bulletins and marked them up over several lunches where Irena had a vodka or two each time. They planned the Maundy Thursday service, the Good Friday service, and the glorious Easter Sunday service. Hank didn't mind retyping all the changes.

"Let's drape the altar in black cloths during the Good Friday service," Maggie said, making notes. "Then, at the beginning of the Easter Sunday service, the black cloths will be replaced with shimmering white satin."

Irena's eyes shimmered with glitter and vodka. The creative stuff was growing on her.

Maggie looked forward to the dramatic and moving transformation of darkness into light—death into new life.

Maggie wrote in her notebook each day. Sometimes she wrote to Ed, sometimes she wrote from him. She found herself working in her church office more and more. She wanted to be close to Hank and Doris. She loved feeling like she was sitting in a spring flower, and she wanted to see people when they came through the office doors.

On the Saturday before Easter, Maggie was grateful that both the Maundy Thursday and Good Friday services had gone well. Both were more than sufficiently depressing. Irena's organ music was worse than funereal—*It would have hurt Satan's ears*, Maggie thought—but strangely appropriate for the reading of the Last Supper and the horror of the Crucifixion.

Hank was in the office, doing last-minute preparations for the Easter service. He checked and double-checked the bulletins and inserts.

"Pastor Maggie," Hank said, popping his head into her office, "here is the final copy of the Easter bulletin."

"Thanks, Hank." Maggie smiled and kept from laughing with some difficulty. "But I have five now." Then she did laugh. Hank hadn't realized he had placed a copy on her desk each day that week. "Hank, I don't know what I would do without you. Thank you for holding everything together while I was gone. This church would crumble without you."

She meant it.

Hank smiled under the praise. "No, you've got that wrong, Pastor Maggie. We would crumble without you." He was just as sincere. "Now, can you help me with my tarpaulin, please? Doris is useless today. Listening to that vacuum cleaner is about driving me insane."

Doris cleaned and recleaned the entire church. It was Easter, after all. Maggie helped Hank with his blue tarp and then made her way into the sanctuary. She could smell the Easter lilies before she walked in. She set about counting the lilies and moving them from where the florist had seemingly dumped them. She heard a noise and turned to find Bill and Sylvia standing at the back of the sanctuary.

"Hi, you two. Happy almost-Easter!" Maggie felt the joy of Easter in little waves.

"Hi, Pastor Maggie!" Sylvia said a little too loudly. "We've come to ask you a favor."

"Of course." Maggie moved one more lily then stood up and waited.

Pause.

Sylvia poked Bill with her elbow.

Pause.

"Uh . . . Pastor Maggie . . ." Bill began, "we would like you to . . . well . . . would you have time to . . . uh . . . marry us? Today?"

Maggie sat right down on a magnificent lily and completely crushed it. Sylvia ran to help her.

"I'm sorry. We didn't mean to shock you. Let me help you up."

The back of Maggie's white gauze skirt was covered in black dirt and golden lily dander. She'd put the skirt on that morning because she hadn't expected to see anyone.

"Marry you?" Maggie sputtered. "Marry the two of you? Good grief, have you even been on a date?" She looked at Bill, but then something caught her eye. A lovely sapphire on Sylvia's left hand. "Oh, I guess maybe you have."

Maggie went into her office to search for her Worship Services book. What was going on here? She didn't know how to do a wedding. *Drat the seminary!* Systematic Theology wasn't going to help her out of this one. She found her book and quickly turned to the Service of Holy Matrimony. Then she remembered Ed telling her once the only things needed to make a marriage legal, besides having a license (*Do Bill and Sylvia have a license?*) was the exchange of vows and the officiant declaring the couple married. Maggie took a deep breath. She could do this.

Bill and Sylvia, along with a disgruntled Doris, were cleaning up the lily mess when Maggie came back into the sanctuary, dragging Hank behind her.

"First of all, do you two have a license?" Maggie asked, sounding wise and learned, as if she had done five hundred weddings in the past year.

Bill pulled the license from his pocket. Maggie looked at it and saw she, as clergy, was responsible to fill out the license. In triplicate. It was also her responsibility to mail it back to the courthouse.

"Doris, Hank, I need to ask you to be witnesses to this wedding ceremony. Are you willing?" Maggie asked, feeling her nervous hands shake.

Doris's face completely changed. She stood up from the flower mess and immediately gave Sylvia a huge hug.

"God bless you, my dear!"

Hank followed suit, giving Sylvia a hug and Bill a manly Hank handshake. Maggie's head was spinning.

Just then, the sanctuary doors opened again. It was Irena. She was coming in to practice for Easter. Irena couldn't see the scene at the altar due to her ridiculous stack of music, but Maggie could see that Irena had made another visit to her kitchen sink. Her hair looked like an egg yolk.

"Irena!" Maggie shouted. "Do you have any wedding music in that stack?"

Irena didn't look shocked at all. "Ov coouurrsse I do." She set her music down on the organ bench, lifted a third of it, and set it aside. She picked up several sheets. "Heerre ve go."

Maggie was getting ready to put everyone in place (whatever that would look like) and then give Irena a cue to play something weddingish, when for the third time in fifteen minutes the sanctuary doors opened.

Verna Abernathy and Howard Baker walked in. Verna wore a cream-colored suit while Howard wore a dapper three-piece pin-striped suit. Verna held a bouquet of zinnias.

"Pastor Maggie, we were wondering . . ."

30

Maggie could hardly believe her eyes. She almost sat down on another lily but caught herself just in time.

Howard spoke. "Pastor Maggie, this lovely woman and I have been carrying on a wonderfully torrid love affair, and I would like to make an honest woman out of her."

Verna hit him over the head with her flowers. But not too hard. It might damage the zinnias.

"He is a vicious liar. I don't know why I agreed to marry him," Verna said as she gave him a smile.

"What has happened around here?" Maggie asked, exasperated. "I was only gone three weeks, and you have all run amuck."

"Only four of them, Pastor Maggie," said Hank. "The rest of us have carried on predictably and with valor."

Doris nodded in solemn agreement.

Verna and Howard walked down the aisle to the front of church. Howard looked at Bill and Sylvia, then Pastor Maggie.

"It looks like brilliant minds reason alike. Pastor Maggie, Verna and I would like to be married. We would like to be married in this church. By you. Today. I believe we are old enough to make this decision and have made it. Although Bill and Sylvia are quite a bit younger, my guess is they have come to the same conclusion. And what could be better,

Pastor Maggie, than waking up on Easter morning next to the one you love?" Howard waggled his eyebrows up and down.

Maggie wanted to stab out her eyes at the image of Howard and Mrs. Abernathy waking up next to each other.

"Is this how you all feel?" Maggie looked at each one.

All four heads bobbled. Mrs. Abernathy added a proper, "Yes, indeed."

Maggie was at a loss. Nothing could have prepared her for this day. *How many times have I thought that in the last ten months?* She looked at the four lovebirds, and then she began to laugh. It felt so good to laugh. And really, what was the problem? These two sweet couples, who had been carrying on behind her back, wanted to make it legal. She was the one who had ordered Bill to take Sylvia on a date, for heaven's sake.

She pulled herself together and said, "I would be honored to marry you. So, let's talk about logistics. I've never done a wedding before, but I do know what needs to be done to make you all legal."

Doris leaped on to the altar and began pulling the black cloths off cross and pulpit.

"Doris, what are you doing?" Maggie hissed.

"Well, good heavens, Pastor Maggie, I'm removing these death cloths. I will replace them after these nuptials."

Doris was superstitious enough to know there should never be black at a wedding. She began rolling up the cloths and then took them into Hank's office to get them completely out of the sanctuary.

Hank asked the couples, "Is this a double wedding, then? Are you all standing here in the lilies together?"

The two couples looked at each other.

"It's fine with us," Sylvia said.

"It will make a great memory," Howard said sincerely.

"Then please face me and link arms with your . . . fiancé," Maggie said. "Hank and Doris, please stand on either side of me."

Hank, with a goofy smile on his face, and Doris, with a kerchief on her head and a smudge of dust on her cheek, took their places.

"Hey!!! I play now? Hey!! Pastoorrrr Magggie? Time for de museek?" Irena was yelling from the organ bench.

Maggie had a thought. "Just a minute, Irena. I have to do one thing first. I guess you could play something. Softly. Excuse me for just one moment," Maggie said to her brides and grooms.

She walked toward her office, and Irena began playing Purcell's "Trumpet Voluntary" very loudly.

Maggie pulled her dictionary off the bookshelf. Quickly she turned to the Cs and then jotted a definition onto an index card. She also made a quick phone call to The Sugarplum Bakery. Then she hurried back to the sanctuary. She waved her arms like a cheerleader to get Irena's attention.

"Thank you! Stop now!"

Irena stopped and settled in to watch the little marital comedy, her yellow head almost glowing over the organ bench.

Maggie began.

"We have gathered here to witness the marriage, the marriages, between this man, these men, and these women." Maggie gave a little cough and smiled at each couple. Her stomach was doing flip-flops. "Marriage is a holy estate and not to be entered into lightly or unadvisedly, but reverently . . ." Maggie continued with her reading until she got to the vows.

"I'm going to ask you to make vows to each other. Sylvia and Bill, Mrs. Abernath, uh, Verna and Howard, will you please face one another and take hands?"

Bill and Sylvia turned and held hands. Bill had no problem making complete eye contact with his bride. Howard turned to Verna and gently held her life-worn hands. And the couples made their vows.

Maggie heard the four different voices as each made their promises.

"Repeat after me: I, Bill, take you, Sylvia, to be my wife."

Bill repeated it steadily.

Then: "I, Sylvia, take you, Bill, to be my husband."

"To have and to hold."

"To have and to hold," said Howard.

"For better, for worse."

"For better, for worse," Verna said. She had tears in her eyes.

"For richer, for poorer."

"For richer, for poorer," Bill said.

"In sickness and in health."

"In sickness and in health," Howard said more quietly.

"To love and to cherish."

"To love and to cherish." Sylvia smiled.

"As long as we both shall live."

"As long as we both shall live," four voices sounded one at a time.

"To this covenant I pledge myself truly, with all my heart."

Each one pledged their troth. Fourteen eyes were filled with tears by this point.

All but Irena's. She just wanted to get on with her Easter music.

"Do you happen to have rings?" Maggie asked. They all shook their heads no.

"We'll have to take care of that after the honeymoon," Howard and his eyebrows said.

Maggie hurriedly continued after wiping her nose with a tissue from Doris.

"I didn't have time to really prepare a wedding sermon." She smiled. "But I would like to read you this. It is from the dictionary but beautiful just the same. It is the definition of the word *cherish*. 'Cherish: To hold dear, to value highly, to take good care of, to treat tenderly, to nurture, to hold in the mind, to cling to, to esteem, to treasure.'"

Maggie sniffed. "May God bless you, and may you cherish one another well, each and every day of your married lives. I now pronounce you husbands and wives, in the name of the Father, the Son, and the Holy Spirit. You may kiss your spouse!"

Irena immediately bombarded them with Handel's "Hallelujah Chorus." She had obviously moved on to Easter.

The couples seemed to enjoy their lengthy kisses.

Hank blew his nose loudly.

When Mrs. Popkin arrived a few minutes later, she joined the happy tear-fest. She had brought one of her delicious white chocolate raspberry tortes as a makeshift wedding cake. The brides and grooms were surprised. No one had thought about a cake. Elopements might be efficient, but there was something to be said for a little planning and organization. Maggie hoped there wouldn't be any more elopements. At least for the rest of the day.

Mr. and Mrs. Howard and Verna Baker hugged Maggie as they thanked her. Howard slipped a hundred-dollar bill into her hand, which she slipped back into his suit pocket when he wasn't looking. She would have to get used to calling Mrs. Abernathy "Mrs. Baker." Maggie thought she liked Baker much better. She hoped Mrs. Abernathy did too.

Mr. and Mrs. Bill and Sylvia Baxter also thanked Maggie and said they would be in church the following morning for Easter breakfast and church before leaving for a brief honeymoon to the Upper Peninsula. Bill had a cabin there. He had forgotten to tell Sylvia that it had no running water or electricity. Surprise!

After the arduous process of filling out the marriage licenses in triplicate, Maggie hugged the new couples one more time, thanked Mrs. Popkin, Hank, Doris, and Irena, and then made sure the church was ready for Easter morning.

Irena was finally left to practice for the next day.

Nora, I'm sorry to tell you this, but your and Dan's wedding will not be my first.

Whaat????????

Nope. I officiated, not one, but TWO elopements this very day at Loving the Lord. 'Tis true, I am not telling a lie!

I'm calling you right now and I want to hear the whole story. I think I might pee my pants, I'm laughing so hard!

The two best friends talked for over an hour about the elopements. Maggie could hardly believe the story she was telling.

"I've actually learned a thing or two. I might be a little better prepared for your wedding now."

They both laughed.

"Maggie," Nora said, "you sound good. You sound *so* good!"

"All I know," Maggie responded, "is that I'm where I'm supposed to be. And days like today remind me that there is nothing I would rather be doing than being a pastor. I'm so glad I'm back."

"We all are, Maggie."

After she and Nora said good night, Maggie pulled out her notebook.

Dear Ed,

You will never believe what happened today . . .

31

Maggie woke up to a whisper. She couldn't quite hear it in that state between sleep and wakefulness. She was also being happily mauled by Marmalade.

Maggie's first Easter Sunday was cold with the threat of snow in the forecast. She was up at four thirty and left for her run by four forty-five. When she got to the cemetery, she stopped and walked in the dark around the graves. *Was this how Mary felt when she went to the tomb? It was dark, and she was sad. She was sure Jesus was dead. What an emotional and life-changing shock awaited her. Hi, Ed. What is Easter like in heaven?*

The whisper was clearer now. The words the same. *The story must be told.*

Maggie ran. Although she left in the blackness of night, she returned to the parsonage with the shimmer of a sunrise.

She put on a lovely pale-yellow lace dress. Princess Kate wore one just like it. She double-checked her shoes and ate her oatmeal and banana with pure maple syrup. Easter dinner would be roast chicken, spring potatoes, fresh peas (the first offering from Sylvia), and a bunny cake. Maggie had everything ready to go. Jack would join the feast with her parents.

When Maggie got to church at eight a.m., the Easter breakfast was in full swing. Sylvia had quickly changed from blushing bride to Sergeant of the Kitchen. She and her fellowship committee members were in charge of this yearly celebration. Maggie thought maybe Sylvia would have passed off the duties due to her nuptials, but no, Sylvia flipped pancakes and barked out orders to beat the band. Maggie laughed. She felt an arm around her waist and looked up into Jack's amazingly handsome face. She noticed he had an apron on.

"I'm in charge of scrambling eggs," he said with a grin. "Happy Easter, Maggie."

"Happy Easter, Jack. You never told me of your egg-scrambling talents. Now I'm absolutely smitten." Maggie was learning to smile all the way to her eyes again.

Even with the whole church watching, Jack bent down and gave Maggie more than an Easter kiss. This was followed by wolf whistles and applause from the happy parishioners. Pastor Maggie was back! It was Easter Sunday! Dr. Jack and Pastor Maggie seemed to be some kind of couple or something! Have more eggs!

Jack went back to his job as Maggie walked around the breakfast tables sharing "Happy Easter" greetings. Then she went up to the sanctuary. She saw Marla and the children in front of the Easter lilies, which emitted a glorious aroma that filled the church (the lilies, not the children).

Maggie, Marla, and Irena (with a little persuasion) had decided Penny, Molly, Carrie, and Carl would begin the service by singing the first verse of "Jesus Christ is Risen Today." The choir and congregation would join in on the second and remaining verses. As the children sang, the black cloths would be removed from the pulpit and cross and replaced with white. Maggie was excited for this visual transformation.

Maggie moved to the front of the sanctuary, knelt down, and grabbed the children to her. Penny and Molly wore matching pink dresses with pink bows in their hair. Carl wore a sailor suit and looked unbelievably adorable. Carrie was wearing a tutu of pink, yellow, pale green, and lavender. She wore one of her lovely tiaras balanced on her head. Her hair had grown out to cover her burn. Maggie kissed them all.

"I have something for you in my office," she said conspiratorially, "if Mrs. Wiggins can part with you briefly." She looked up at Marla, who could still hardly believe her beloved Pastor Maggie was back at Loving the Lord.

"Of course. Our little singers know every word, and they are ready to sing us into Easter. Aren't you?" Marla smiled with a small quiver on her lip.

"Yes! Yes! We know all the words! 'Jesus Christ is risen todaaaayyy, Aaaaaalleeeeia!'" Their small voices rose up, not quite all together, but with much enthusiasm.

"What's in yo office, Pasto Maggie?" Carl asked once he could get a word in.

Maggie took the children into her office and gave them each something her seminary professors would have failed her for. She had four small Easter baskets filled with traditional Easter candies and homemade heart-shaped cookies. The children were enchanted and became bubbly and bouncy at the sight of their treats.

"These are for you, my darlings!" she said taking in their faces and squeals. "Happy Easter! This is such a happy day, and it's all about Jesus being alive and busy and with his friends again. He's alive for us too." She didn't know what else to say. Children were so concrete in their thinking, there was no way to explain the miracle of Easter. Most adults she knew couldn't sort it all out.

Maggie had it beaten into her psyche at seminary to never, never, never mix the sacred with the secular. But after thinking about it in the last week, after watching these little ones bring the palm branches into the sanctuary on Palm Sunday, she came to a new conclusion.

Children could never understand the mystery of Easter. Adults couldn't either. Ever. It was a mystery that no human could fully comprehend. But Maggie knew, as a pastor, she was supposed to find ways to make it a little more understandable. She figured that, if the spiritual leader of the church could tell the story of Easter *and* give a gift that delighted the children, they might be able to get a tiny glimpse of a God who gives good gifts and loves them no matter what. Maggie wanted more than anything to make the secular a little more sacred.

"Thank you, Pastor Maggie! Can we eat them all now?" Penny asked the most important of questions.

"Well, maybe you could hold them for now. We wouldn't want to get any chocolate on your beautiful Easter clothes." *And we probably don't need to have you all on a sugar high.* "But how about you carry them with you while you sing for church?"

They reluctantly agreed. Maggie saw Penny sneak a jelly bean on her way out of the office.

Her first Easter sermon began the way all of her sermons did—in silence, with Maggie looking intently at her congregation. Jack sat with her parents. The children had sung beautifully and now sat with their families and their Easter baskets. The two newly married couples sat, grinning and holding hands. Maggie had introduced them with their new names after the first hymn. The entire church was elated. Maggie was surprised to see Marvin Green sitting in his wheelchair next to Verna and Howard. *How in the world did that happen?* She was also surprised to see Redford. It was the first time she had seen him since arriving back in Cherish. No one had told her about his trip to the Cherish jail or how he wanted to withhold her salary. There was no need.

Perhaps the most surprising face of all was Fitch Dervish. He sat next to Max Solomon and the Becker sisters in the last pew.

As Maggie looked around, her sermon came easily. She talked about how Ed loved this week, when all humanity made the journey to the grave and came out of it again on Easter morning. She talked about different kinds of deaths: losing a loved one, losing one's health, losing a job, losing a friend. She talked about change and new life: the new marriages from yesterday, living with physical limitations (*Marvin!*), supporting one another through all of life's experiences. And remembering, above all, no matter what, there was a God who decided to give the world a miracle. Eternal life. She said much more, of course. And at the end of the service, Irena played the "Halleluiah Chorus" like it had never been played before.

Everyone felt joyful, comforted, and hopeful.

Dirk and Mimi were relieved to see their daughter leading her church so beautifully and, Mimi thought, professionally.

Maggie greeted her parishioners and guests in the gathering area. She was pleased to see several new faces. Jack's partner, Charlene Kessler, her husband, Ethan, and their children were there. There was another couple, maybe her parents' age, milling around the coffee and cookies. She thought about what it would be like to lead a new members class. Maggie heard a slight cough behind her and turned to face Fitch Dervish. His glasses were turning dark due to the bright light coming through the central rose stained-glass window.

"Happy Easter, Fitch. It's nice to see you here for worship today." Maggie smiled. Even Fitch's oddness couldn't diminish her spirit that morning.

"Happy Easter to you too, Pastor Maggie. I was wondering if you might have a moment before you head next door."

"Sure."

Maggie looked at her mother and pointed toward her office. Mimi nodded once. She would take care of things at the parsonage until Maggie got there.

"Let's go into my office," she said to Fitch.

Once seated in the cream-colored visitor chairs, Maggie waited for Fitch to speak. It took him a moment. If he wasn't talking about building codes, it seemed words eluded him.

"Well, Pastor Maggie, I just wanted you to know that I'm leaving."

"Leaving what? Your building inspector job?" Maggie could only hope.

"No. Well, yes. I mean, I'm leaving Cherish. So yes, I guess I'm leaving my job too. I have to go to my mother. She lives in Phoenix."

"Phoenix? For how long?"

"I'm not exactly sure. You see, my dad died last November, and my mother hasn't been doing very well since. I would like to bring her back here to Cherish, but I don't know if she'll come home. So I'm closing up my house and heading south to figure it out." Fitch looked forlorn.

"Well, first of all, I'm sorry about your dad." Maggie did the math, the way Bill had done earlier, and realized the timing of the death: during the building of the handicapped ramp and her games to get him away from Bill. She felt a sharp stab of guilt. "I'm also sorry your mother is suffering. Does she have a house here in Cherish to come home to?"

"I live in the house. It's the house I was born in. When they moved to Phoenix, I had an apartment in town, but I moved into the house right after they left. They didn't want to sell it at the time. So I would literally be bringing her home."

"How long will you be gone, do you think?"

"I'm not sure. If I had to, I could probably stay for several weeks to a few months. I'm leaving May first. I sure would like to get her back here before Thanksgiving. She's a stubborn old girl, my mom is."

"Fitch, I hope you find your mother willing to come back. What about your job?"

"Oh, don't you worry, Pastor Maggie. If there are any building needs around here there will be another inspector assigned. But I'm pretty sure I can have my job back when I return. They say," Fitch looked slightly embarrassed, "I'm the most diligent inspector Cherish has ever had."

"I'm sure they do." Maggie smiled. *Diligent was one word that could be used.* "I'll pray for you and your mother, Fitch. Let us know when you're back in town."

Maggie stood up, but Fitch remained seated.

"I also wanted to say, when you were gone last month, everyone missed you. Including me. I got to know the people here when we redid this office. It's a great bunch of folks in this church. I want to bring my mother here. She's not a church-going woman, but I think she might like it here." He finally stood.

"Thank you, Fitch. That means a lot to me. The people here are truly a 'great bunch of folks.' Have a safe trip, and we'll see you when you get back."

Maggie shook his hand. As she did so, Fitch stepped backward, tripped on the leg of his chair, and fell on top of Maggie's desk. His elbow knocked over a vase of flowers from Sylvia, which sent water and pedals flowing over books and papers. Fitch regained his bearings and looked for something to sop up the water. Maggie grabbed handfuls of tissues from a box on her bookshelf and tried to stem the flow. Ink smeared on papers, and Maggie knew the books would have water damage. Rumpled, crinkled pages would crackle under her fingers once they dried out. *Drat!*

"I'm so sorry," Fitch said. "I sure made a mess."

"No problem. I'll just dry these out and all will be well." Maggie just wanted Fitch out of her office and on a plane to Phoenix.

They went back to the gathering area, where a few stragglers were still visiting. Fitch smiled sheepishly at Maggie and headed out the sanctuary doors. Maggie chatted with Sylvia, Bill, and Marla as the rest of the congregation put on their jackets and left for homes and Easter dinners.

Easter dinner in the parsonage with her parents and Jack felt like a familiar old habit. *What will Easter dinner be like next year?* After plenty of conversation about the service and the two elopements, the topic turned to Bryan's return from Ghana in three weeks.

"I can't believe three months have gone by so fast," Maggie said happily. "And I can't believe he's coming here first. I wonder how much facial hair he'll have? I'm sure he didn't shave the entire three months, even though he left here with a smooth face."

"It won't matter," Mimi said, completely out of character. "But I wonder who he'll be when we see him. When you came home from Israel, we needed to be reintroduced to you. Bryan will be new too. It's fascinating."

Mimi drifted into her own psychological wonderland. She was proud that her children could grow and be formed by other experiences and in different parts of the world. She hoped they would never think Zeeland or Cherish were "normal." She hoped they would discover so many other normals in the world and add those to their lives.

Bryan would fly into Detroit for two weeks of decompression and vacation in Michigan before heading back to San Francisco. Maggie would pick him up and keep him for the first week. She knew her parents would be in Cherish as much as possible that week. Then they would bring Bryan to Zeeland for the remainder of the time. Maggie couldn't wait to see her brother.

She picked up Bryan on the morning of Wednesday, April 29th. He finally peeled her arms off after several minutes of a sisterly stranglehold. Maggie tried to calculate how to keep him from going back to San Francisco. He just couldn't leave so soon.

"You look great!" she said. She could see how brown he was from three months of sunshine. "You've lost some weight, though. I better fatten you up before you see Mom."

"I liked the food when I first got there, but by the end, I couldn't stand one more bowl of rice." Bryan laughed. He sounded like a man. When did that happen? Her mother had been right, as usual. Maggie was meeting a new Bryan. She *really* liked him.

"I want to hear every story of every day you were there," Maggie demanded as they drove back to Cherish.

Bryan dove right in. It became obvious something had changed in him. Story after story of resourceful people working hard to care for the children and elderly in their own villages filled Maggie's imagination. Health clinics, schools in the countryside, orphanages, outdoor markets, and pharmacies were woven into the stories of heroic individuals. It was obvious what had changed in Bryan: he had left his heart in Ghana. Maggie knew he would have to go back to find it again. She wasn't sure if he would ever be able to bring it back.

"But Megs," Bryan interrupted her thoughts, "here's the thing. You asked me before I left if I knew of any way the church could help out. I think I know a way."

Maggie's ears perked up.

Bryan continued, "My boss, Joy, and I will have to put some programs together and possibly send groups of volunteers to Ghana and the other countries. Maybe a group from your church would be willing to go. We need supplies for everything and money to purchase things there locally. We are trying to build up the local village economy. We need baby clothes and baby food. Those can be harder to find. What do you think?"

Bryan was more excited than Maggie had ever seen him. He was on fire, and it was contagious.

"Bry, we have time this week to put a preliminary plan together. You help me with the specifics, I will bring it to the council and then to the congregation. Oh, oh, oh! And this Sunday, I want you to speak in church. You have to tell these stories!"

Maggie spun off into her happy, frantic, impulsive world. Loving the Lord Community Church would be part of this. They would live larger and more fully than ever before. They would literally see the wider world, something beyond what they already knew. There were a lot of unknown, scary, and thrilling things that had to be done in the world. Cherish was not the end-all of ministry. It was just the beginning.

Epilogue

Bryan's visit was too short, but every minute was used productively. A plan was slowly being put together for how Loving the Lord could participate in the work of Africa Hope. The excitement was palpable. Cate was sitting in the front pew when Bryan spoke to the church. She couldn't take her eyes off him. Bryan spoke brilliantly about the need for a new orphanage and school in Bawjiase, Ghana. His fire caught on. Maggie was curious about who might sign on to go as a volunteer for two weeks. Marla already had sign-up sheets for baby supplies and monetary donations, but it was the list of possible volunteers that Maggie kept her eye on.

The month of May brought flowers. Maggie and Jack spent a day planting at the parsonage. It reminded Maggie of the first time she'd seen the parsonage, when she pulled in as the new pastor. June first would be her one-year anniversary. She could hardly believe everything her first year of ministry had encompassed.

But before that anniversary could be marked, there was another celebration. Jack's birthday was May twenty-fifth. Maggie snooped around and found a stethoscope, an old ether bottle, a blood pressure cuff, and a scalpel from the 1800s at an antique shop. She had them framed in a glass and cedar box. She made him a special birthday dinner at the parsonage. The table was candlelit, with flowers, church china, and two magnificent and curious cats. The preparations were going great until the Westminster chimes rang.

It was Sylvia and Bill. They were just stopping by with some vegetables from the hot house.

"We wanted you to have some of the first harvest," Sylvia chortled with glee. "Wait until you see these tomatoes!"

"Oh, thank you," Maggie semi-lied. She did love tomatoes, but she knew she would be eating hundreds of them before the end of summer. "I'm just getting dinner ready for Jack's birthday."

"How fun." Sylvia winked, while Bill smiled shyly.

"Well, would you like to stay?" Maggie asked. She had wanted it to be a private dinner, but it might be fun to have more people to celebrate Jack.

"Don't you just want it to be the two of you?" Sylvia asked.

"Let's make it a party," Maggie said as she got more dishes down from the cupboards. "Do you like chicken and dumplings?"

Sylvia made a salad with many tomatoes sliced on top. Bill took the dishes and reset the table.

The Westminster chimes rang.

It was Cate.

Bill set another plate.

The dinner was delicious and lively. Jack was celebrated well, and he couldn't take his eyes off Maggie all evening.

When the others left after cake and ice cream, Maggie brought Jack his wrapped package.

"This was a very interesting night," Jack said. "Do you often have drop-in dinner guests?" He seemed more curious than anything else.

"Sometimes being a pastor, or being near one, means there's a whole big family who joins in with dinners, quiet evenings, and Saturday mornings. Especially when the pastor lives next door to the church. Just so you know." She smiled.

He answered the smile with a kiss.

Jack couldn't have been more surprised when he opened Maggie's gift.

"How did you find all these pieces?" he asked looking at the antiques. "They're so rare. They couldn't have been easy to find at all. Just like you, Maggie."

"Are you calling me an antique?"

"No. A treasure. But this isn't really what I wanted for my birthday."

Maggie was shocked out of their little love-fest by this. "What?"

"There's something else I would like for my birthday," Jack said, looking unbelievably handsome in the candlelight.

"What, Jack?"

"Will you please, finally, tell me what Mrs. Landry said to you before she died?" Jack pleaded.

Maggie looked into his brown eyes and burst out laughing.

"Yes, Jack, I will." Then her laughing eyes softened as she looked at him. She remembered how surprised she had been when Mrs. Landry whispered in her ear. Would Jack be surprised? She entwined her index finger through his and said, "Mrs. Landry said, 'On the day you marry Dr. Elliot, I'll be dancing in heaven.'"

June first was a Monday. Maggie grabbed her mail from the parsonage mailbox. It was mostly junk mail, an electric bill, and one handwritten envelope. Those were so rare these days, it was almost like a little present. She didn't recognize the names or the return address. When she opened the letter, a picture dropped to the ground.

Dear Pastor Maggie,

It took us awhile to track you down! But after doing some investigative work, we think we have found you. We don't know if you will remember us, but we will never forget you. It's been over a year now since you visited us in the hospital. It was the worst day of our lives. We had just lost our precious little girl, Anna Lee.

I met you first (this is Kristy). You sat and cried with me. You didn't say stupid things, and we heard plenty of those. You let me be mad at God. And I had to be, for a while. You comforted both of us when we had to leave the hospital—and leave Anna Lee.

So, we wanted you to know that someone new has joined us.

A small gentleman arrived on Easter Sunday.

We would like to introduce you to Matthew Lee Brown.

Our joy is complete.

Thank you for your love and care on the worst day.

Please celebrate with us during these blissful, joy-filled days.

Love,
Mike and Kristy Brown

Maggie picked up the picture of baby Matthew. He was beautiful, of course. Tears fell down her cheeks as she walked up the path to the front porch of the parsonage, thinking of Mike and Kristy and their little precious gift.

She felt the wind in her hair.

She heard the whisper.

She looked up to the blue sky and whispered back, "I hear you. I'll keep telling the story. I promise."

Then she went inside.

She had more story to tell.

And another Sunday was just around the corner.

- The End -

But wait . . . there's more!

Bonus pages!

Don't miss the rest of Pastor Maggie's story!

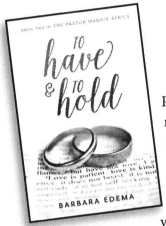

To Have and To Hold
Book Two

Welcome back, Pastor Maggie!

Pastor Maggie of Loving the Lord Community Church has settled into her new position and finally gained the trust and respect of her congregation, but they will all be tested when the church comes under attack through a series of malicious break-ins and vandalism. Maggie tries to hold everyone together and determine if the threat is from an outsider or someone actually sitting in the pews of her church each Sunday. Can she keep her beautiful church safe? Will she still be able to accomplish the planned mission trip to Ghana if the money from a fundraiser is stolen?

While Maggie desperately waits for a whisper from God, she also fears that a major event will be ruined by the well-meaning, very loving members of the church. How will she maintain her own blossoming romance with tall, dark, and scrumptious Dr. Jack Elliot and support the daily needs of her congregation through life-and-death matters when it all feels one step away from collapsing?

Will they catch the villain before he ruins everything?

Get your ebook or print copy today at
www.Pen-L.com/ToHaveAndToHold.html

FOR RICHER, FOR POORER
BOOK THREE

What's Pastor Maggie up to now?

Life at Loving the Lord Community Church in Cherish, Michigan, isn't always easy. Learning how to adjust to a new marriage while caring for her many parishioners keeps Pastor Maggie on her toes. And things get more complicated as she prepares a group of church folks for the coming holidays—AND a two-week mission trip to Ghana, Africa.

While in Ghana, the expectations of good-hearted people clash with the real needs of the villagers. Maggie's frustration boils over and her plans begin to crumble. All her beliefs about rich and poor, success and failure, poverty and wealth, opened hearts and closed minds get turned upside down. The lessons learned in Bawjiase are life changing for all.

As her spiritual beliefs are threatened, Maggie knows her ministry will be transformed once she returns from her time in Ghana. But will she be the richer or the poorer for it?

DISCUSSION QUESTIONS FOR

To Love and To Cherish

1. In a small church, the pastor has many different roles. Were you surprised at the many ways Maggie is expected to care for all ages and all issues? What was the most surprising role for you?

2. There are a number of power struggles in play at Loving the Lord Community Church. What are some of them? How does Maggie's being a young, single woman affect the situation(s)?

3. Maggie's first funeral begins with a flower fight, progresses to Maggie crashing into the casket, and ends with the son of the dead man being quite touched spiritually by the service. How are these kinds of contrasts used throughout the book to entertain and to give insight into community life?

4. Maggie gives a sermon about all of the community members being in the same boat together. Should Redford be included in that boat too?

5. What was your response to Irena Dalca, the organist? What transitions did you observe in her character?

6. There are a number of creative gifts given in the novel. For example, Maggie gives a kitten to Mrs. Abernathy, and Jack gives Maggie a painting of the church. Name some more gifts, including gifts of food, and describe the importance of gift giving in the novel and in community life. How can a unique and personal gift affect the receiver?

7. Marmalade and Cheerio are prominent members in the parsonage. How are these two characters used by the author to release or add tension?

8. Which characters surprised you the most as the story progressed? Which character would you like to have lunch with and why?

9. Does Maggie's response to Ed's death (leaving her job and being angry at God) seem extreme or realistic?

10. When Maggie loses Ed, how does the community bring healing to her?

11. How might Maggie's leadership be affected by not having Ed as a support?

12. Maggie's journey to ministry began with a whisper. Have you ever heard God's whisper, in one way or another, and taken a new turn in your own life?

Recipes

Maggie's Single Crust Pie Crust

Add directly into pie plate and mix with fork:
    1½ cups flour
    1½ teaspoons sugar
    ½ teaspoon salt

In a cup mix with fork:
    ½ cup canola oil
    2 tablespoons milk

Add to flour mixture in pie plate and mix together with fork. Press mixture around bottom and side of pie plate. If crust needs to be baked before being filled (cream pie, etc.), bake at 400°F for 10 minutes.

Maggie's Chocolate Coconut Cream Pie

One baked pie crust (above)

In medium saucepan mix:
    ¾ cup sugar

½ cup flour
¼ teaspoon salt

Slowly whisk in:
3 cups half-and-half

Cook over medium heat, stirring constantly with a rubber spatula. When thick and bubbly, lower heat and continue to cook for about 2 minutes. Remove from heat. Add 1 cup of hot filling to 3 beaten egg yolks, whisking as filling goes in (to keep eggs from scrambling). Then whisk in the rest of the filling. Cook over medium-low heat to a gentle bubbly boil, stirring constantly.

Remove from heat and add:
3 tablespoons butter
2 teaspoons vanilla
½ cup semi-sweet chocolate chips
1 cup sweetened flaked coconut

Mix well, pour into glass bowl, and cover with plastic wrap. Let cool at room temperature for 2 hours. Put filling in refrigerator for 8 hours or overnight. Pour filling into baked pie crust.

Whip with mixer until stiff peaks form:
2 cups heavy whipping cream
1 teaspoon vanilla
½ teaspoon coconut extract
¼ cup powdered sugar

Cover pie with whipped cream mixture, 2 tablespoons toasted coconut, and chocolate curls. Refrigerate until ready to serve.

Maggie's Caramel Apple Pie

1 pie crust, unbaked (above)

In large bowl, put 6 cups very thinly sliced apples.

In small bowl, mix with fork:
- ⅓ cup flour
- ¼ cup brown sugar
- ¼ teaspoon salt
- 2 teaspoons cinnamon
- ½ teaspoon ginger
- ¼ teaspoon cloves

Cover apple slices with above mixture and toss to coat.

In mixer bowl, beat together:
- 4 oz. softened cream cheese
- 1 teaspoon vanilla
- 17 oz. good quality jarred caramel sauce

Pour caramel mixture over apples and mix through. Pour apples into pie crust.

In small bowl, mix with fork:
- ½ cup flour
- ½ cup oatmeal
- ½ cup brown sugar
- ¼ teaspoon salt
- 1 teaspoon cinnamon
- 4 tablespoons melted butter

Sprinkle crumb mixture on top of apples.
Bake pie at 375°F for 50–55 minutes until filling is bubbly.

Maggie's Toffee Chocolate Chip Cookies

In mixer beat together:
    1 cup butter
    ½ cup butter-flavored Crisco
    1 cup white sugar
    1½ cups brown sugar
    3 eggs
    2 teaspoons vanilla

Add into butter mixture and beat until blended:
    3¾ cups flour
    2 teaspoons baking soda
    1 teaspoon salt

Then stir in with spoon:
    8 oz. toffee chips
    12 oz. milk chocolate chips
    12 oz. semi-sweet chocolate chips

Drop dough into 2 inch balls on ungreased baking sheets. Bake at 375°F for 12 minutes.

Acknowledgments

In 2017: I have the joy of rereleasing this book with fun changes and a good scrub of previous mistakes.

Thank you, Duke and Kimberly Pennell and Pen-L Publishing. You have given me a great gift! Thank you, also, for believing in The Pastor Maggie Series.

Susan Matheson and Meg Welch Dendler, you both do excellent work. Thank you for editing this book.

The Rosebud Theater is based on The Purple Rose Theater in Chelsea, Michigan.

Grace in Action is based on the real organization Faith in Action in Chelsea, Michigan.

The Cherish Café is based on the Common Grill in Chelsea, Michigan.

All biblical references come from the New Revised Standard Version.

Someone once said that no one reads the Acknowledgments page in a book. I always do. It gives me a peek into the author's heart. Here is a peek into mine.

I am thankful for the whispers—and from whom they come.

In March 2014, I sat down with a stranger in the hope she would help me figure out a way to publish some prewritten works. She asked what else I had thought of writing. I said, "I'm toying around with a novel about a young woman pastor in her first church—you know, all the funny things that happen." The stranger looked me in the eye and said, "That's it! Write that!"

I sat down and began writing. Four months later, I had the first draft of this book. The stranger is now my dear friend and literary midwife. Her name is Susan Matheson of Matheson Editing. We haven't known each other long, but I feel as if she has been a friend throughout my life. Susan, I can't thank you enough. But I'll keep trying.

My cousin, Dr. Judy Balswick, gave me Susan Matheson's name. That was providential! Thank you, Judy.

Dr. Charlene Kushler raised the green flag and said, "Of course you can do this!"

Many pairs of eyes read the first draft of the book. Some asked me if they could read it (thank you!), and some had the book thrust upon them (sorry!).

My sweet mother, Dr. Mimi Elzinga Keller, was and is a constant, pragmatic cheerleader. She is also a stickler for grammar. Thank you, Mom! I love you. The character of Bryan is my gift to you.

Marsha Rinke, organist extraordinaire, also read the book with an eagle eye for story progression, grammar, and sentence structure. Marsha has the gift of encouragement, and she constantly shared that with me, along with her amazing love and friendship. I am so glad you are nothing like Irena. Your friendship is priceless.

The First Congregational Church of Chelsea, Michigan (where it all began!), thank you for making our ministry together one incredible experience after another. And thank you for loving my children.

My Uncle Craig Hubbell gave me the most specific feedback of anyone, regarding the subtlety of storyline and characters, cats, and tea. You made me cry. In a good way.

Others who read and encouraged from beginning to end were my aunties: Judy Ann Elzinga, Vicki Hubbell, Diane Brower, Holly Fann, Gail VanDyke, and Kim Palma. Hokey tooters! Also my cousin Kay Fountain, daughter-in-law Alli Edema, Judy Teater, Priscilla Flintoft,

Char Gray, Ann Sneller, Ericka Foreman, Lynn Samuelson, Kathi Cary, Ericka Foreman, Ethan Ellenberg, and Howard Baker (who graciously gave me use of his name).

Anne Duinkerken was the last pair of eyes to read the manuscript before it went to the publisher. My friend for over twenty years, I thank you for a million reasons from the bottom of my heart.

Thank you to author G. M. Malliet! What would Maggie, or I, do without you?

Silent inspiration came from my father, the Reverend Dr. Keith Hubbell, and my brother, Todd Hubbell. I miss you both every day.

My children and stepchildren spur me on and make me laugh a lot. I love you, Elise, Lauren, Alana, Wesley, Becky, Todd, and Alli.

Grandchildren are the light of life. I love you, Mason, Addie, Samuel, and Matthew.

Doug, thank you for supporting this little endeavor from the beginning. Thank you for writing our romance every day with your words, your humor, your encouragement, and your abiding love.

About Barbara Edema

The Rev. Dr. Barbara Edema has been a pastor for twenty-three years. That sounds astonishingly boring. However, she is a great deal of fun with a colorful vocabulary used regularly out of the pulpit. Barb has spent decades with people during holy and unholy times. She has been at her best and her worst in the lives of the people she has cared for. Now she's writing about a fictional church based on her days serving delightful and frustrating parishioners as experienced through the life of the main character, Pastor Maggie—a young, impetuous, emotional, clumsy, and not to mention a crazy cat lady, who steps into ministry full of Greek and Hebrew but not much life experience. She learns quickly.

Barb lives in DeWitt, Michigan, with her husband, Dr. Douglas Edema. She is the mother of Elise, Lauren, Alana, and Wesley. Like Maggie, Barb is an avid feline female. Hence, she has collected an assortment of rescue kitties. Barb enjoys date nights with her husband, watching her children do great things in the world, a glass of good red wine, and making up stories about the fun and fulfilling life in the church.

Enjoy visiting Cherish, Michigan, and Loving the Lord Community Church. Pastor Maggie will delight you!

VISIT BARB AT:
www.Barbara-Edema.com
Blog: www.BarbaraEdema.blogspot.com
Facebook: The Pastor Maggie Series
Twitter: @BarbaraEdema1

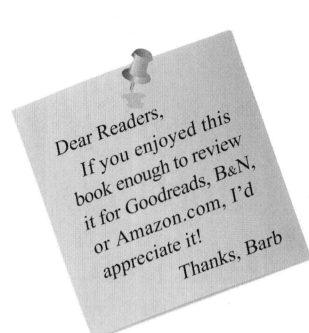

Dear Readers,
If you enjoyed this book enough to review it for Goodreads, B&N, or Amazon.com, I'd appreciate it!
Thanks, Barb

Find more great reads at
Pen-L.com

Made in the USA
Columbia, SC
29 September 2018